ON UNHALLOWED GROUND

ZOMBIE FALLOUT
BOOK TWENTY-FOUR

MARK TUFO

DEVIL DOG PRESS

SWANVILLE, MAINE

DEDICATION

This book is dedicated to you dear reader, I cannot thank you enough for the support and kind words you have given me through the years. I hope you enjoy this book! And remember if you are ever in a situation where you have to make an important decision; ask yourself What Would Talbot Do? And then do the exact opposite.

MIKE JOURNAL ENTRY 1

"THE FOREST SUCKS," I grumbled softly not wanting my traveling companions to hear me as I stifled the words. Although with all the vegetation slapping off our faces it was hard to hear anything else, much less my bitching. Rose, Kirby, Ferdinand, Bando, and I had been in a truck. An actual fuel-powered truck, motoring down the highway, not under leg power. It had been so long since I'd had a machine do all the heavy lifting, the brief ride had been wonderful. The back of that truck was about as comfortable as bouncing along on burlap sandbags, and yet it had still been wonderful. We were attacked. The engine block or something equally as important had been struck by the crazed psychotic Feroz, a Brazilian lieutenant, who was convinced we were all Antichrists who had not only wiped out numerous compatriots of hers, but had captured, kidnapped, and converted her sister Catalina and her lover Major DeLeon into demons. This she partially solved by having DeLeon subsequently executed as he attempted to return to her. That was the level of crazy we were dealing with.

"In hindsight, sir, we should have maybe killed those soldiers we let go," Rose said as I called for a water break. We were in a tiny clearing, the vegetation so dense around us that I couldn't pick a way to go that wouldn't entail suffering numerous thorny scrapes. We'd just survived a brief one-sided gun battle with six Brazilians that had been attempting to flank us. We'd halved their numbers when a hulking greaver showed up. One of the opposing soldiers had offered up a truce, and in my infinite wisdom, I had let the three go. The problem with that was they were now alive to tell Feroz exactly where her rogue gringos had gone. She wouldn't be able to catch the caravan traveling ahead of us, so it didn't take any abundance of smarts to figure out who she was going to take her wrath out on.

Ferdinand had met his end, as we feared. His first mistake had been wearing a red shirt to start the day, the second had been to take off into the woods, offering the greaver the thrill of the chase. His mistakes had given us an opportunity to leave, of course we would have never sacrificed someone in that manner, but when given a chance, you don't brush it away foolishly. He was just a kid, nineteen, twenty at the most. I would avenge him if we could, but we weren't going to go out of our way to seek out the monster. Avoidance was our best chance of survival, and we could better honor him that way. Perhaps pour a shot onto the ground in homage, should we be lucky enough to find something worth toasting a life with. Was debating what was worse, a giant greaver or Feroz. It was a toss-up; I suppose I could make that determination in hindsight after one of them killed me.

The sounds of nature had returned, which was a good thing. It was nice to know there weren't any predators nearby. Of course, as armed humans, we were most definitely predators, but we weren't hunting, we were running away. The goal was to get out of this friggen' jungle. Figured we'd go deeper in then angle-meander our way back toward the direction the caravan had gone. I didn't want to be overly obvious about where we were going. Feroz would figure we would try to get back to the roadway and our rides, I just had to hope she didn't have the personnel to cover too much of the forest. Then it hit me: she wasn't going to chase us into the jungle, she knew a greaver was in here with us, so why would she risk her people? Her best bet would be to have people stationed along the roadway, wait until we came out, and then let the games begin. By now BT would have set up a search and rescue effort; if I could set up some comms, I would tell him to wait until we came out.

"Let's keep moving," I said, heading toward the brush.

"I've got this, Capitan," Bando said as he led the way.

Rose followed, then myself, and Kirby was bringing up the rear.

"Bando, start bringing us back toward the road at a slight angle. I want to come out around two miles further than where we broke down."

He nodded. I was decent in the woods, I had an okay internal compass. It wasn't spot on, but it would generally get me close enough to where we were going that I could wing it from there. Bando, on the other hand, was damn near laser guided. It was nice having a GPS—Global Positioning Soldier. For an hour there wasn't more than some birdsong and our breathing, along with some grunts caused by slapping branches and groans as boots got sucked into mud. I was having flashbacks of the Darien Gap, and I wasn't appreciating it. At one hour and one minute came some heavy chuffing followed by the splintering of trees. No one needed my hand gestures to know to get down. The greaver was on the move and near, which meant it had finished off Ferdinand, the poor bastard. Took a little over an hour to eat some hundred and sixty pounds. If it hadn't been a person I would have thought it impressive. In this case, it was repulsive.

We couldn't take the thing on, not with the weapons we were carrying, and Rose not having explosives on her was like Tommy not having Pop-Tarts. And speaking of the vampire, we had no idea where he was. If anyone could survive on their own it was him, but I was still concerned for his wellbeing and the protection he afforded the rest of the group by being around. Once I got everyone else to safety we would launch a rescue. Even to me that sounded insincere; if all went according to plan, by the time we got everyone tucked away safe and sound, we'd be some twenty-five hundred miles away. Heading back to South America would not be on the top of my list. I don't know what that said about me. Something had fundamentally shifted within Tommy; he'd been pulling away for months, hardly socializing with anyone, going on more and more solo jaunts. I could feel his inhumanity close to the surface on many occasions, and much as I hated the feeling, I worried about the threat he could pose to everyone around him. It was possible he was concerned about that as well, and that was why he distanced himself. I would not willingly bring him back into our midst if he were a danger...we had enough of those already.

The greaver wasn't moving a whole bunch, it was staying close. It had likely picked up a scent or a noise and was waiting for its prey to make a go at escaping. I could only hope we weren't the prey—a fool's hope. I watched the trees sway as the animal brushed up against them, it would move away then it would abruptly change direction and head back, as if it was performing a grid pattern search and I shuddered to think of it devising a logical, systematic way to hunt.

The day was sweltering. Sweat had soaked my uniform and was falling, nope, cascading from my head. At this pace of moisture loss, I was about a half hour from a killer headache brought on by dehydration. We'd been so close to escape I was having a hard time reconciling this new truth we existed in. And to make the day even better, it seemed like the greaver attracted biting flies, not for its impenetrable hide, but for the soft, captive victims it kept locked in place for fear of initiating its chase response. I swear I could feel anemia setting in from the blood loss.

The beast knew something was out here, that was evident from its persistence. We had to move. Staying where we were was not going to work, it would be on us soon enough. When it was at its furthest point I motioned for us to move forward. We were given a few precious seconds where the noise it made as it turned to come back masked our own. Up ahead we could see the lines it was trampling. It stood to reason that if we could make it to ground that it had already traversed, we would be safe, as it was unlikely it would go back. That was a lot of assumptions about a creature that had just come into existence not all that long ago, wasn't like David Attenborough had the chance to narrate its story and tell us exactly what motivates it. We were close to perceived safety—and also in direct line of extreme danger. The thing was less than thirty feet away, and where we had stopped meant an imminent encounter. Felt like a background character in the *Jurassic Park* film franchise about to get run down and eaten by a megalodon. And unlike that lucky bastard, there would be no director to say "Cut!" and then get some free eats at a hospitality cart.

I was motioning with my hand for the trio to go. I fell in line immediately behind them. Just ten feet now...the only thing saving our lives was the jungle density. I generally hated that about it, but right then it was A-okay. Rose made it past the last trampled line, Kirby went to ground on the flattened earth, Bando and I were on the strip in between, meaning we would be mere feet from where the greaver walked past.

A paw thundered down less than six inches from my face. Under the wiry fur, I could see the vestiges of what had once been a human hand, bastardized and repurposed into the anomaly it was now. The fingers had shortened considerably, thick black callouses had formed on the palm to mimic pads, and the thumb had been separated from the rest of its cohorts and affixed high up on the forearm-slash-leg in mockery of a dew claw. I was afraid to exhale, believing that it would feel the sensation of my breath rippling through its fur.

It wasn't moving, and I didn't move. I didn't dare to. I had to figure it was turning its head from side to side, looking for a meal, and if it looked down it would have been granted its request. My head was starting to pound as I continued to hold my breath in. Not sure how many times I'd willed the thing to move away; my Jedi mind trick game was off, or the greaver was resistant. It happens. There was a snorting and then it dipped its head toward the ground on the far side. I was now three feet away and face-to-face with it.

I was wound up so tightly I was surprised my muscles weren't cramping, maybe they were locked in one solid cramp. It had the scent of something in its nose, hard to imagine it wasn't us. Its head turned slightly, its pupils narrowed then grew wide in surprise. Not often that your food is directly underfoot. It recovered quickly. I had rolled away and barely had the chance to mutter *fuck* before its foot stomped the ground where my head had been. I did get to witness the nightmare of watching those finger toes curl up and grab a mound of earth instead of my head. Bando and Rose were popping rounds into the broad side it was presenting to us. Kirby had pulled me to my feet just as the greaver whipped its head and the snout struck me in the stomach like a bat. I was sent sprawling. There was a moment of hesitation as it decided on which of us was the easier target. I lucked out and somehow won the next meal lottery.

I was doing my best to get my legs under me, was having little luck, rolling was my best bet, and I did it for another four full revolutions. The greaver caught its shoulder on the trunk of the tree I had pulled up alongside of and hit with enough force that branches were cascading down on the both of us. All its momentum had been halted and I was able to scurry around to the opposite side of the massive trunk. As a wee lad

I'd never been a fan of the children's song, Here We Go Round the Mulberry Bush, and now that I was the weasel running for my life, I liked it even less. Although, round and round the Patagonia Cypress Tree doesn't have the same ring. We did two solid loops around what had to be a thirty-foot circumference, it was far enough I was able to briefly consider building a house inside it. Kirby had joined in with Rose and Bando trying to put the thing down, it was like shooting at one ugly carousel horse each time it came around at breakneck speed. I wasn't even sure if the 5.56 rounds were penetrating its hide though it hardly seemed possible that could be the case. Yes, as far as military rounds went it was on the small side, but it was an extremely speedy bullet which should have more than made up for its lack of bulk.

When I didn't immediately fall into the greaver's mouth it began to head butt the massive tree. I thought it somewhat comical that the thing thought it could possibly damage a tree some hundred and fifty feet tall. That was until it chased me around again and I could see where car hood-sized chunks of bark over four inches thick had been pummeled free. In an abstract way, I felt bad for the ancient tree that it was suffering because I'd decided to use it as a shield. If I got out of here, I would plant another in its honor and sacrifice. When the greaver paused I had a feeling I knew where this was going.

"Run!" I yelled.

Sure enough, the beast spun and was heading toward my squad, who were already ahead of my assessment. I didn't feel bad about that; they had a better view, unobstructed by tons of prehistoric vegetation, and they were the ones annoying the creature. The thing presented its back to me, but I wasn't overly comfortable shooting at it as my three squad members were on the other side. It flinched and skipped a step when the first shot struck it dead in the ass. Most don't know this, as Hollywood makes it appear like a funny quip, but getting shot in the ass is one of the most painful places to get hit and is extremely dangerous, at least on a person. Greavers are what they are, but they still started as humans, as hard as that was to imagine. And as such they still had some of the same soft spots as we did. The posterior seemed to be one of them. I was able to put another one almost in the same spot, fucker turned so fast—and I was so unprepared for it I'd not moved—and it sprang for me. I turned and was coiling my muscles, knowing full well it wasn't going to be in time. It was likely I'd be able to avoid its mouth, but I was going to take a hit from its body. If it was hard enough, the next sensation I would feel after my body struck the ground would be canines tearing into my flesh.

Sometimes events happen in life that travel so far out of the realm of possibilities that they seem like fictionalized accounts of reality. This was one of those. The greaver's shoulder struck mine—launched is a good word as I was lifted off my feet, hurtling backward through time and space, and landing somewhere in the fifteen-foot range, away. It was heading toward me before my back even touched down. It was unlikely I'd be able to catch my breath before the end, and I did not like the idea of traveling into the afterlife gasping. A yell came from above me, something was in the tree, I couldn't tell what or who it was, all I could see was the glint of sunshine off a highly polished surface. On first guess, I may have gone with a wrathful angel sent down from on high by Maker to get me free from my latest problem. When it was all said and done, I don't think my initial thoughts were too far from the truth.

That gleaming sword of vengeance was driven with the full momentum of Yoki's weight and strength as she landed gracefully onto the back of the beast and buried the blade halfway through the neck of that rotten creature. It wasn't dead but it was most definitely on its last legs; it collapsed to the ground like the bones in its hindquarters had liquefied. She yanked that sword free, jumped off and gave another sharp cry before again bringing that slice of deathly steel down. She struck the same spot, slicing through nearly three-quarters, neatly severing muscle, arteries, flesh and bone, and whatever else had the misfortune of being in the way. The greaver's head hung by skin and canted to the side.

"*Daijobudesuka?*" she asked. The fierceness in her eyes relaxed as she wiped her blade down and placed it in its scabbard before extending a hand to me.

"Sure," I answered, taking her offering.

"Yoki!" Bando yelled, running up and hugging the woman, lifting her off the ground and spinning her around. I got the feeling she wasn't thrilled with the display of affection. Although she did tolerate it, and by the end of the last turn she even wore a smile. Her entire group had endeared themselves to ours, even with and despite the language difference. Many of the people in our group had begun to learn Japanese, while Yoki's group had worked on some English. We weren't going to be having philosophical debates any time soon, but we'd been working toward gaining a level of understanding before they left...though "we" might be a conceit.

There's some shit I hate writing down, I mean, who wants to leave written proof that they're on the asshole spectrum? I was trying—I was genuinely *trying*—to pick up some Portuguese. I had a few words and of course, I could swear with the best of them, but any communication beyond the basics and it was clear to anyone listening I'd not been paying attention. It was even worse when it came to my Japanese. I was so egocentrically North American that there was a deep-rooted part of me that expected everyone else to speak English. Yup, that is just as douchey as it sounds. Now anyone who stumbles across this journal is going to know that.

"Where is everyone else?" I asked her. Yup, I spoke slowly, too, like the aforementioned asshole. Like she was the dimwitted one and my slow speech would enable her to understand. I was working toward being a stereotypical idiot, maybe I should sit in a corner and wear one of those pointy cartoon dunce caps, maybe eat a box of crayons and jump a line of trucks on a snowmobile. I forcibly pulled on the train of my thoughts, attempting to get them back under control. The close encounter with the greaver had me straying as far from my present moment as could be attained.

"Stay…back," she managed, though I'm not convinced she was sure about the meaning she was trying to convey. Then her and Bando spoke, sounded like a blend of Japanese and Portuguese, which it was, but not. I couldn't have been any more lost. Whatever this hybrid language was, it was working. They were both nodding.

"She says that most of the crew decided to stay in the country, that they were going to work on securing a vessel and heading back home. Five have come with Yoki to make a new home with the crazy American," Bando said.

"Isn't that supposed to be plural?"

"No, she was specifically talking about you." He smiled.

"Ah, great. So my feats of insanity have gone international. Good to know."

A couple of minutes later the rest of Yoki's group came into view. Lots of hugs and handshakes. I was genuinely happy to see them all; I'd spent more than a few nights enjoying their company. Strange, because we'd usually said less than a handful of words to each other, on any given meeting, but that was typical of guys, even if we spoke the same language. Kenji had been the one to produce a bottle of sake the night before they headed out. By the end of the bottle, we were singing what I took to be traditional Japanese cantina songs. Pretty sure I told him I loved him a half dozen times that night. He would just smile and nod. Akio was the oldest and the most serious one of the group. I had a feeling he was prior military, though he wouldn't confirm my suspicion. Daku was the youngest, roughly the same age as Justin, he was Akio's son. Good kid near as I could tell. Quick to smile, first to work, last to leave. Haruto and Isamu were cousins, and they fought more than a dysfunctional married couple who had just had a baby and moved in with in-laws to try and make their relationship work. I'm not sure why I had so much fun pushing their buttons before stepping back to watch.

The Gallagher brothers of Oasis fame would have been embarrassed by how often and the intensity with which those two fought. Fists would fly from a sidelong glance. Couple of other things I took note of, they never struck each other in the face, and holy fuck the poor bastard that tried to step in— their volatile tempers would immediately spin onto the interloper who would have to go from peace maker to defender in a heartbeat.

Yoki and Bando caught me up to speed. They'd been in the vicinity of the refinery three days ago. They'd seen the zombies and the Brazilians and were working on a plan on how to help when over half of the Brazilian Army had headed out. Now I knew how they'd set up the ambush. Yoki had seen us take off in the trucks, and the Brazilian army left behind had been on the verge of attacking but were then beset upon by the zombies in the area. That was Avalyn's handiwork, had to be. I'd been wondering how we'd made it out. Feroz's ambush had been planned so that there would not be a full-scale war on the steps of her target acquisition. This way she could ensure that not only did she secure the refinery without damage, but got the bonus of being able to kill us.

Haruto and Isamu had wanted to head into the refinery, and it took some convincing from Yoki that the place was going to be destroyed. At this point in the retelling, she had pulled her sword out and laid it against Isamu's neck. He was laughing like a loon; apparently getting threatened to have your head lopped off was the funniest fucking thing ever. You can see why I was a fan.

"They followed," Bando ended.

"Okay, wait. Not that I'm complaining," I said as I took a

gander over at the dead greaver. "We're at least twenty miles from the refinery, and even if you ran, you're here way too fast."

Yoki nodded after Bando and her talked. She made the infamous villain theme of Miss Gulch riding her bike in *The Wizard of Oz*, I'd spell it out but I'm not sure I could capture what your imagination has already done. A good narrator might give it a try...da, da, da da, da dah; da, da, da da, da dah...

"You rode bikes to get here?" At a good clip, the timing made sense. "Were you planning on riding all the way to Colorado?" I asked.

"They were hoping to catch up when we rested for the night," Bando said.

"Fuck me," I whispered. Odds were we would have gone a minimum of three hundred miles today had we not had issues. At a decent pace, I figured the average bike rider could do ten miles an hour. They would have never caught up. And once we hit Colorado, I had an idea where I wanted to go, but who knows what may have changed along the way, or if that final destination was even viable? Then what? That was a mighty big state to canvas around on a bike, especially in the mountains. For some reason, I had to be thankful we'd been attacked. I was going to have a hard time reconciling that, especially since we'd lost Ferdinand.

"Yoki says we should get going, the zombies are following."

"Fantastic," I muttered. It seemed we were going to have another group tailing us.

By the time it started to rain, we'd been in the jungle for more than three hours. The precipitation was barely noticeable as I was already soaked to the bone. Between the moisture in the air and the sweat escaping from every available pore on my body, I was surprised I was able to breathe. If anything, the downpour was welcome as it kept the biting insects to a minimum. It was slow going as we worked our circuitous way back to the highway. When we could at last make out the tiniest sliver of asphalt, I motioned for Kirby to scout it out. The kid was good at his job. He'd had enough practice, and the one thing about a forward scout was you were either quiet or you were dead, there was no middle ground. We had hunkered down and were watching him. The closer to the roadway he got, the slower and lower he became. He'd seen something, and by his actions, there was little need to question whether it was friend or foe. Once he'd seen all he needed to, he backed up, somehow even slower. I'd watched documentaries on sloths, they would have lapped him in a race.

"Right there," he whispered when he got back. "Twelve feet to my left. I saw ten, there might be more. Top and a few others are about three hundred yards down the road. They're behind cover, but I don't think they know about the approaching enemy."

"Shiiitttt," I hissed the word out, sounded like a leaking tire on a ten-speed. "Yoki, how many soldiers do you believe came to ambush us?"

"Jackie Robinson," came her reply after Bando translated the question.

"What?"

"Forty-two," Rose said. "What? That was his number," she added when I kept looking at her. I was trying to figure out what the hell was going on. I shook my head, we'd go over it later if we could.

"Forty-two," I repeated. There was no reason to think that all of them weren't nearby, maybe even close to where BT and the others were. If BT wasn't aware, they'd be ripe for a slaughter. "We have no choice," I said as I moved toward the roadway. I didn't even pretend like I had any idea what we were going to do. My sole concern was making sure those people waiting and looking for us weren't hurt. Not sure why I ever doubted any of them, they were far from helpless. (Turns out BT, my brother, and Stenzel were playing the part of bait, but I didn't learn that until later; I'd not had an advance play-bill copy to know what was going to happen.)

It was a dangerous game without a doubt, and I was still contemplating our best move when the whoosh of a rocket and an explosion hit not more than twenty yards from where I stood. Safe to say Stenzel had scoped out the enemy, just waiting for them to get into rocket range. I motioned for everyone to fall back, then we headed up the highway just as small-arms fire erupted. Two more rocket attacks later and the rifle fire slowed. When you were outgunned and exposed, your best bet was to withdraw. The Brazilians were going to regroup, and probably grab a few rockets themselves.

We'd covered maybe a third of the distance in the jungle when Kirby tapped me on the shoulder for him to scout ahead. I was under the impression we were out of the woods, so to speak, our current locale notwithstanding. Hadn't gone another twenty feet when he dropped down onto a knee and raised a fist in the air for us to halt, which we did. He then motioned for us to get down as he had.

I had to think the words *fuck me*, couldn't even mouth them, the enemy was that close. Once I looked around, I saw at least five soldiers within fifteen feet of us. There were more, just couldn't see them. They all had their backs to us. If not for the sporadic firefight and the torrential downpour, there would have been no way we could have gotten this close unde-tected. Wasn't a fan of shooting anyone in the back, but what was the alternative? Tell them we were there and then have a good old-fashioned showdown? All's fair in love and war. I didn't necessarily believe in the love part of that equation, but war, yeah, war was waged for keeps. You kept your life or you didn't. Many had survived a broken heart, but few survived a bullet to the heart. I raised my weapon, those with me followed suit. I paused to look for Feroz, if I could remove her, this might all end, but I didn't see their fearless commander. One of the soldiers must have sensed something; he was just turning his head when Kirby put one right through his neck. Our surprise volley struck hard. We killed four instantly, wounded at least three before they were able to muster any type of defense.

More and more of the bastards joined the fray, had to be twenty of them if not more. It was like they were spawning here and we had stepped right into the thick of it. Not sure what BT and the others were going to do, and I couldn't rely on them to do anything. The Brazilians outnumbered us, and position-wise, if BT engaged we were now in danger of friendly fire.

"Move!" I motioned for us to head further into the woods before we could get flanked and again pinned down. We had a very small window—they didn't know our numbers and the effects of the surprise attack hadn't quite worn off—where we could potentially slip away. Bullets were zipping by, but with every foot we moved, we put more protective vegetation in front of us. They kept shooting, but by this point, we basically had a green wall between us and them. It would take a laser-guided adjustable flight bullet to find us now.

I would have killed for a headset right then. I would have told BT to get the hell out of there, and we'd hightail it another mile down the road to meet up.

"At least they know we're alive now," Rose said.

I grunted in agreement. "Both sides do."

The rain picked up in intensity as did the wind, and for the first time that day I was beginning to feel cold. Rose hadn't said anything, but while I stopped to let everyone pass by I noticed her lips were purple and she had her jaw clenched tight to keep her teeth from chattering. Everyone looked like waterlogged rats; we needed shelter. We were all in danger of hypothermia, some sooner than others but all, eventually. No one knew this area. We didn't have a map, a drone, or the ability to see satellite imagery. We could pass within twenty feet of a structure and not know it was there. I wanted to cut back up and over to the road to see if we could get into a vehicle, crank the heat, and leave this accursed land behind. I don't feel like that was asking too much.

Had to figure the enemy had spread out and was following us. I don't know how they could track us in this shit, but I couldn't say for sure that they couldn't; it was more their home field than ours. The wily Feroz would likely not follow us but instead make their way up the highway, guessing we would want to reunite with our people. This was such bullshit. We couldn't go back the way we came, couldn't go further north and then across. We had two choices: we went deeper into the woods to fuck knows where, or we headed south until I was confident we were past all the damn soldiers, crossed the road, and *then* made our way north again, right past the bastards. Feroz may or may not account for that possibility; the real question was, what would BT account for? I didn't want him sending anyone in here looking for us, especially if we weren't going to be here.

The full effects of hypothermia could take about half an hour to set in. Rose's clock was ticking the loudest, though we'd all punched our timecards. I put the odds of us backtracking, crossing over, heading back up, and reuniting with our group before her shift was done at an extremely low number. Somehow it was still statistically higher than us meandering through the woods and finding a home with firewood and dry socks. I would throat-punch a nursery schoolteacher for some dry socks. He or she probably had it coming, calling for naptime just as the good part in the Little Dinosaur movie was coming up. Or possibly snack time. I was so busy thinking up justifications for why I wanted to hurt a made-up munchkin educator I hardly noticed the change around me. I blame that on the rain, which was falling damn near sideways, making me keep my head down and my chin tucked.

It was my stumbling as I went from jungle terrain to hard-packed dirt that caught my attention. When I raised my head and wiped my face, I figured for sure I was in the midst of a hallucination. Not fifty yards ahead was a wooden structure, like a *big* wooden structure. It had to be five thousand square feet with large picture windows ringing the bottommost level. Atrocious to defend, but I think the Monteverde Cloud Forest Reservation Visitor Center had not been built with the intention of keeping tourists safe from cannibals and vicious armed enemies.

"Going in?" Rose asked. She had her arms wrapped around herself in a desperate bid to keep what little internal heat she had left from escaping. She didn't wait for my answer; her legs knew she was in trouble, and the only hope for survival resided within those walls. We were all moving a little quicker when hard-packed dirt became bricks; I think I saw Kirby skip as he pulled ahead. The place appeared deserted, branches, leaves, animal droppings were prevalent. There had been no grounds upkeep here. Kirby made sure to shoulder his way in front of Yoki's group, who had been in the lead. He opened the door and raised his rifle. I was happy he didn't have to break in; from this side the place was intact, and it was preferable not to smash any windows. The noise would be muffled in the storm; it was letting the howling wind in I wanted to avoid.

I waited until everyone was in before entering myself, taking one last look at the jungle to see if anyone was following. Inside, there were a variety of colorful tables and even more colorful chairs all around; it was a cafeteria of some sort. My stomach grumbled at the thought of food. Not sure what would be in here that was still edible, but I wasn't above eating some expired hot soup. As long as the can wasn't bulging, I was under the assumption it was still okay. Kirby was going from area to area clearing it for threats. I tapped Rose on the shoulder, she was now making Morse code signals with her mouth, her lips a shade of blue Revlon would have killed for. I pointed to a gift shop where a stack of folded shirts waited for a keen tourist who never made it. She lurched forward, I grabbed her before her frozen knees could completely betray her. Bando grabbed her other side, and we headed over, Yoki and her compatriots next to us. She had her sword out and ready.

"Do you have her?" I asked Bando.

"Si," he replied.

"Yoki, can you help her get some dry clothes on?"

She nodded.

"Bando, stand guard here. I'm going to help Kirby clear the top floor."

"Yes, sir."

Kirby and I headed up the wide staircase, he went to the right, I went to the left. The entire floor was devoted to a lounge and bar. There were couches as colorful as the tables and chairs below, but what caught my attention—besides the display of liquor—was a fireplace, which had to be close to ten feet across. Wasn't sure why it was needed in a tropical climate. That was exactly the thought I had as I looked down at my cold, red hands. I was barely able to move. I got it at that point; don't ever let anyone tell you I'm not thick sometimes.

"Gas!" Kirby said enthusiastically as he went over to it. He pressed a few buttons, we waited, nothing happened for going on fifteen seconds, then came the stink of propane followed by a muffled *whoomp* that sounded a bit like our makeshift flame throwers, and then there was a flame. Small at first, then Kirby ratcheted the gas flow up. There was no way to know how many gallons of fuel were in the tank, but no sense in conserving it; we needed to warm up now.

"Let's go get some warm clothes."

2

MIKE JOURNAL ENTRY 2

TEN MINUTES later we looked like we worked for the Costa Rican tourist board. I had on a dark blue hoodie and purple sweatpants emblazoned with the National Forest logo. Had some hats, a few village-made blankets, even flip-flops. The only thing lacking were socks, and for that I was sad. We got Rose up to the lounge and parked next to the fire. She was lethargic and mumbling incoherently, or maybe it was coherent, but I couldn't hear her. Either way, I was pretty worried. She was in the worst shape out of the group, although we were all feeling the effects of the weather. Once we had the dry clothes on and we'd soaked up a bit of heat, it was time to take care of some other necessities. The first was keeping a lookout for anyone who followed. It was more likely than not that they had some rain gear, but I knew all about military issue rain gear, and it was by no stretch of the imagination the high-end stuff. They were going to be as wet and miserable as we had been.

Would Feroz call them back to seek shelter? Did they have a place to seek shelter? Maybe if we truly lucked out, they would all succumb to the elements. A boy can dream. The Catholic in me was appalled that I'd be hoping for the deaths of others, but, well, fuck 'em. Hard to feel pity for people who are pursuing relentlessly just to do you in. Got Kirby and Bando on guard duty. Rose and two of Yoki's people were going to need some recuperative time; I got her, Kenji, and Daku squared away on some couches near the fire.

"Are you going to be all right, Kenji?" I asked.

He nodded. His smile said yes, his eyes displayed otherwise. And even if I couldn't understand Japanese, I could hear the slur in his words. He needed medical attention we didn't have access to.

"You'll be fine." It was more of a hopeful statement than anything rooted in knowledge. "Haruto, watch his breathing." I pointed to my chest and exaggerated taking in breaths. Yoki translated. When the trio looked as comfortable as we were going to be able to make them, the rest of us went to check out what the restaurant had to offer in the way of food. We'd already made a dent in what the souvenir shop had, but there were only so many candy bars and stale chips you could eat before you craved something with more substantial nutrition.

I wasn't holding out much hope when we entered the kitchen. The smells of rot and mold had diminished, but it was still there, an underlying current of food spoiled long ago. I was close to heading out when Yoki ventured further in, pushing open a wide aluminum door. I had mistakenly assumed it was a walk-in fridge, and I wanted nothing to do with seeing or smelling years-old meat. Didn't know what the hell Akio was doing at first as he grabbed an armload of pots and pans, but I caught on quickly when I saw him head outside and quickly place them out in the lot to collect rainwater.

"*Pantori!*" Yoki said excitedly, waving me on.

That sounded suspiciously like she'd said *pantry*. Either I was getting better at understanding her, or English and Japanese had synched up on this one word, like "sushi." Had I been on my own I may have gone the overly dramatic route of dropping to my knees and clasping my head between my hands while thanking Maker for answering my prayers. Still thought about doing it as I looked at can after can of food. Soups of all varieties, vegetables, fruits, beans, tuna, chicken, more food than we could eat in a month, maybe two. I was afraid I was going to begin drooling. Yoki exited then came back with a can opener. I was drifting her way, right up until she drove the tiny blade of the opener into that can and a brown mud-like substance that looked and smelled very similar to diarrhea burst out and sprayed the ceiling. We exited fairly quickly. She immediately headed back to the souvenir shop to switch out the infected garments. Yeah, "infected" was a good way to describe that soiling. Akio had the foresight to prop the door open and let some of the worst of the stench waft out.

I had never been a huge beef stew fan, but it was safe to say after what I had just witnessed, I would be crossing that off of the list of acceptable foods forevermore.

"Now what?" I asked him. "This is like being a horny eighteen-year-old and heading to a strip club for the first time. So many great-looking women you can't touch. Staring is great for a minute, then it becomes increasingly frustrating. Know what I mean?"

He nodded.

"Are you going to take one for the team and start opening more of those?" I pointed at the wall of potential food or pressurized shit bombs. My eyes were watering from the stink. My stomach was still full steam ahead, but my brain and nose were securely anchored.

Akio shook his head in negation.

"Do you understand me?"

He shook his head.

"So then..." I pointed to the can opener Yoki had dropped on the floor.

Akio turned so his ass was facing me, he bent over and

gave himself a loud slap on it. Got a feeling that was his answer to my query. Right then Yoki came back, donning new sweats, she smiled at Akio. She went back into the kitchen and returned with an industrial-sized roll of plastic wrap.

"This is absolute horseshit," I said, my hands were above my head as I spun around like a ballerina, Yoki and Akio were helping wrap me up to protect me from armed botulism bombs. I'd surfed the internet enough to know that there were some among us that considered this a fetish and a turn-on; I was not counted among them and was starting to feel a little claustrophobic in my clingy plasticware. "If that beef stew exploded, isn't that enough proof that none of these are good?" I asked, hoping to get out of what I now considered hands-on latrine duty. Like I'd been ordered into the shit vats to scrub them out, and the shit vats were cocked and loaded.

Yoki was speaking so fast she could have been speaking English and I wouldn't have been able to decipher it. Easy enough to figure out, though, she kept pointing to the wall then her stomach. When I was done being wrapped like a trailer trash mummy, I went over to the wall. Yoki and Akio both took a step back.

"Nice, real nice." I held that can away from my body like it was a present from Rose and she couldn't remember if it was disarmed or not. I plunged that small blade in, there was a slight hiss of air then the effervescent smell of pineapple. Wasn't exactly what I was looking for, but it was proof that at least some of this food might still be good. Might have to do with the acidic contents, but beggars and choosing and all that. Finished opening it and bent the lid away from the can. I held it out for Yoki to take a sniff. For a second I thought she might do that strange ass-smacking display, which I would later learn was a rude Japanese gesture. As far as rude gestures, that was far down the list I had compiled from the lengthy litany I had received through the years.

She stepped up. The tentative look on her face was a clear

indication she was still suffering the effects of the beef stew incident. Akio tapped her shoulder, they had a brief discussion. She looked immensely relieved. He placed his nose on the lip of the can, pineapple juice coated his nostrils. Didn't matter how hungry I was, pineapple was off the table now. I think he may have blown some bubbles in the liquid from his nose, couldn't tell from sight, I'd stopped looking.

"Yoi!" he said as he stepped back nodding, first pointing to the can, then his mouth.

I figured he was telling me it was good to go. Right then it was a tie between whether I would eat the remnants of the beef stew that was in a covered trash can or the nose apple—I mean *pine*apple. I shook my head, he kept pointing, I kept shaking my head. It got to the point I was afraid I was going to give myself a concussion from sloshing my brain around inside my skull. Akio grabbed two pineapple rings. I walked the can out of the pantry and placed it on the counter.

"Everything all right, sir?" Kirby asked as he was walking by on his guard route.

"This is for protection," I told him referring to the plastic wrap.

"Are you getting mailed somewhere, sir?" he asked with complete sincerity.

I stiff legged my way back into the pantry, Akio was happily munching his old fruit. I thought about waiting a couple of hours to see if he came down with a crippling case of the runs. We'd be in sorry shape if the enemy came and all of us were bolting for the restrooms, debating on which end we should have face the receptacle. I've been in firefights before feeling far from optimal; most times it was self-induced, like a hangover, but there'd been a couple of times I was battling a bad cold or possibly the flu and we'd been attacked. As a man, it is a well-documented fact that when we get sick it is the worst thing that could ever happen to any living being, and all I'd wanted to do was lay in bed and moan at the unfairness of it all. Instead, I'd been fighting for the right to live and also keep the price of crude oil down. Each bullet fired would send a percussive wave straight into my sinuses, making the already unbearable pressure that much more acute. It felt like my teeth were going to pop out like bursting popcorn. Where was I with this tangent...? Right, right, I'd never been in a battle with the stomach flu. There are lots of ways to leave this world, I didn't want it to be with my pants down and wet offal leaking from my body like a river of mud. I'd be all embarrassed as my spirit drifted over my dead self before heading off into the great unknown. And what if that last image of me was uploaded to the heavenly cloud? All the ethereal beings would make fun of me; I'd become a disgusting meme. It would be horrible.

I had enough nerves in reserve to open twenty cans, then the shakes got to be too much. I figured the odds were looking worse and worse and that I was one can away from another beefy stew blow out. Out of the twenty cans, five were straight out bad; they didn't explode, but there was no mistaking the smell of rot, and even if they didn't stink, there was a thick layer of fuzzy mold I was certain none of us would want to chew through. After the second stinky can, I had the bright idea to place a bunch of the food on a wheeled cart, and dispose of it. The smell had been lingering in the pantry, tainting everything I opened. I headed outside and stayed under an overhang to do the deed. I figured if I did get a gooey coating, I could step out into the hurricane-force winds and rain and get cleaned up quickly enough.

Six cans just didn't smell right. I couldn't say whether they were truly bad, but they felt off. Akio and Yoki agreed. That left us with nine cans of supposedly good food to eat. I gave Akio a good look over; it had been a bit since he'd eaten the pineapple, his pallor still looked good, he wasn't gassy, holding his stomach, or burping profusely.

"You good?" I asked.

He nodded.

"Do you understand me?" I felt like he might.

He again nodded. But his eyes were focused on one of the cans we had on the edible pile. It was chicken. I had to admit it looked appetizing to me as well, but still, salmonella is a hell of a thing. There was only the one chicken, two cans of string beans, two more of baked beans, and the other four assorted fruits. I was not a fan of beans in any form, which meant dinner was going to be a sliver of chicken and a fair amount of fruit, which meant I was going to have the runs tonight, regardless if the food was bad or not.

"Great, just fucking great," I mumbled.

Yoki had resumed opening duties, wearing an enormous apron she found that looked more like a gag gift for an overweight chef than a usable garment. After her fourth straight can of bad food, she wisely decided to take a break. Rose was doing much better, but she still looked more like a burrito than a human the way she was wrapped up in a half dozen blankets. Any closer to the fire and she was going to get a tan. I was hesitant about giving her some of the food only because she was in a weakened state, and I didn't want her having to fight through any illness she might get from eating. I knew it wasn't enough time to truly tell, but after an hour Akio still looked fine. I had relieved Kirby and Bando and was walking around on guard duty when Akio went back outside and grabbed some of the collected water and poured it into a few pots to cook with. He made sure we each got a tall glass of water, which was greatly appreciated. Hard to remember how thirsty you are, especially when you're soaking wet. The battle and the traveling here had wicked us all. He placed a tall pot on the stove and boiled some noodles.

I found myself lingering around the kitchen. If my C.O. caught me I was going to be in some hot water. See what I did there? I was so hungry the thought of plain noodles was mouthwatering, though it left me slightly depressed. Couldn't have been any more wrong if I tried. Akio whipped up an incredible facsimile of Pad Thai. After that first bite, I wasn't sure how I was going to tell Tracy I needed a divorce so I could marry the man. She'd understand. Never seen two, family-sized bags of egg noodles disappear quite so quickly. Rose even got in on it.

"I'm sorry, sir," she said when I took her empty bowl.

"For not leaving any noodles for the rest of us?" I asked.

"This." She was pointing to her blankets.

"Rose, there's nothing to apologize for. We were all dangerously close to becoming casualties. Doesn't help that none of us has much body fat to speak of, and this rain is barely a few degrees above sleet. Relax, get warm."

"Um, sir..."

"Yeah?"

"Is there any left?" She was looking at the bowl in my hand.

"I'll check or see if Akio can whip up some more."

She smiled, then her eyelids dragged down, the heat and food forcing her to rest and regain her strength. Kirby and Bando were out.

I was about to wake them up when one of the other Japanese sailors, Haruto, stood and shook his head. He tapped his cousin progressively harder until he awoke. Haruto had to talk swiftly before Isamu sprang up and began to toss punches. These two were worse than baking soda and vinegar. If that sounds familiar but you're not quite sure what I'm referencing, it's what causes classroom volcanoes, the easy B+ for science fair students everywhere.

Isamu calmed down immediately as his cousin explained what was going on, but, well, it was in Japanese, so I had no idea what the hell Haruto was saying. He made a walking around gesture with his fingers touching his chest and landed a hearty smack to his cousin's chest that almost set them off. It was Yoki's stern gaze that kept them from devolving into a bar fight. I wasn't sure if I trusted them to patrol the area, they'd be too busy trying to kill each other to worry about an outside force. The other side would only need to sit and wait for the opportune moment.

"Professional. Good job," Yoki assured me. My concern must have been on full display for her to try and put me at ease.

She pointed at the couch for me to sit, which I did. I think I was molecularly bonding with the cushion because soon I was pulled into the sleeping position then finally into sleep itself. Wasn't sure how long I slept. When I awoke it wasn't with a start or a noise, I think it had more to do with my hyper-vigilant mind clicking on. If a threat wasn't present presently, it eventually would be, meaning that it needed to be ever prepared. Thus, wakefulness was more prudent than rest. My mind was always trying to convince my exhausted limbs that I would be able to make up for all the lost rest when I was dead. The fire had been turned low; it was comfortable in the room, plus we didn't want to announce that we were in here by any outside observer being able to see the glow.

I looked at those nearest me. Rose was sitting up, staring intently into the fire. Kirby was on the floor near her. He was asleep, as was Bando, Kenji, Akio, and Daku. Out of the corner of my eye, I saw Haruto walking from window to window. There wasn't any way he was going to be able to see anything; it was still pouring, which only made the moonless night that much darker. Although if a force was moving through this, they would need to have flashlights. Rose turned toward me as I sat up, breaking the fusion between myself and the couch. I swung my feet onto the floor, not thrilled I still had my flip-flops on. I rubbed my face.

"How are you doing?" I asked.

"Better, thank you. Angry I was a burden, but better."

"Never a burden, Rose, a duty. We're a team bordering on

family, there wasn't anything we did for you that you wouldn't do for any of us."

She turned to look into the fire. Maybe it was a tear that made her eyes glisten, or it was just the firelight reflecting. I stood, rubbed her shoulder for a second, and was heading over to Haruto. I'd not nearly got enough sleep, but I knew my body and mind well enough to know I wasn't going to get any more this fine evening.

"See anything?" I asked coming up alongside him.

He said what sounded like "Ee-yah." He shook his head as he spoke, so I was going to say that meant no. But then I was left wondering how much English did they understand? For all I truly knew, he could have thought I was asking if there were any Pop-Tarts down in the kitchen. I went downstairs, found it humorous that Isamu was damn near in the same spot as his frenemy cousin. I asked him the same question; he wasn't quite as definitive.

"*Soko ni kaibutsu ga iru.*"

His voice so grave I might not have comprehended the words, but I understood the tone. Seemed he thought something was out there, and it wasn't good. I mean, no shit it wasn't good, not like a traveling band of food trucks making rounds, because I mean how awesome would that be? For whatever reason, maybe Isamu's mood, but it just felt more ominous down here. I was doing my best not to panic, but now I was getting the feeling that something was peering in, and with the entire lower half circled by windows it was unlikely we would spot them unless it or they wanted to be spotted.

The hair on the back of my neck stood up just as I felt the greasy sensation of something prying at the edges of my mind. Isamu felt something too, he slapped at the back of his neck. I turned. I caught a blur in a window on the far side. Hard to say exactly what I saw and what my mind extrapolated. I had the feeling I was pulling imagery from a half dozen horror flicks I'd watched. Obviously, the entity was dressed all in black, extremely tall, slender, and was wearing what looked like a high-crowned, domed hat with a narrow brim, a Capotain, which was what the Pilgrims had once considered high fashion. Why I knew the name of it was beyond me; Talbots were famous for their vast knowledge of arcane and frivolous trivia, which made us great at Trivial Pursuit, but other than that no one wanted or needed the random meaningless information. The scary Thin Man zombie came immediately to mind, but whatever it was, was gone so fast I couldn't even be sure I saw it. That was until I saw Isamu's face, he was looking in the same spot I had.

"Did you see that?"

He nodded as he spoke, "*Are mita.*"

One person seeing something in the dead of the night has the potential to be an illusion brought on by nerves and sleep deprivation. Two seeing the same something is all the proof needed. I pointed to the stairs. If something was coming in, we were not going to be on the main floor. I was right behind him when he paused; I looked up to see Yoki standing at the top of the stairs, her sword by her side. She spoke quickly to Isamu, who continued up.

She stepped to the side as he moved past her. "Zombie," she said.

I had a hard time telling from her inflection if it was a question or not.

"Maybe," was all I could say.

She nodded. Isamu had gone over to the couches and was quietly waking people up. Not sure if I would have done that just yet, but I wasn't opposed to everyone being awake and ready, should something come in. Because if something wanted in, there was zero we could do to stop them. If there had to be something out there, I was leaning toward the hope it was zombies. The Brazilians could pop a few RPGs through the windows and we'd burn. Downpour or not we would end

29

up like hotdogs on a forgotten grill. Maybe if Reggie hadn't got so fucked up on Busch Light and passed out in the neighbor's hedges we would have been cooked to perfection, but no, instead we were hard, blackened husks of our former glory.

"You have problems, Talbot," I whispered. Thought about answering myself in affirmation, but Rose was watching. I quickly checked my rifle over. Horrible cover-up, but it was all I had. I held my hand out when she went to stand.

"Sit for now, nothing's going on."

"I've had a lot of liquids, sir."

"Ah." I left it at that.

Yoki walked her halfway to the restroom. Kirby was now sitting where his on-again girlfriend had just been, busy tying his boots. I could see the water pressing out from the sides as he stood.

It was going to be days until our footwear was completely dry, even if they were close to the fire.

"Shit," I said resignedly as I grabbed my boots which were also still soaked, but now they were warm and swampy, just the way I and my fungus liked them. But if we had to make a hasty exit, running through the jungle in vacation beachwear was going to be treacherous. "Boots everyone." There were groans all around.

Haruto came over, he and Yoki had a quick but intense exchange.

"Any idea what they're talking about?" I asked Bando.

"Too...rapido."

"Too fast," Kirby translated.

I nodded, I left it alone, he was just trying to help. We all turned when we heard a thump downstairs, sounded like a bird had flown into one of the windows. Would have been great if that was what it was.

"Want me to go check, sir?" Kirby asked.

I shook my head. "No, we can hope nothing is out there,

or if there is something out there, that it has no reason to come in."

Without prompting, Yoki turned off the fireplace. We were plunged into darkness. Wasn't sure if we'd ever gain some night vision in this ink, but at least we weren't a beacon. I slowly fumbled my way over to where my pile of drying clothes were, patted my hands around until I found my flashlight. I turned it on, the red lens-covered light didn't illuminate much, but it was worlds better than not having it. Rose and Bando did the same.

"Left mine in the truck," Kirby said.

Another thump.

"Make sure your weapons are ready to go hot," I said as I clicked off my safety. The stairwell was wider than a traditional staircase, but it was a chokepoint that we needed to hold.

"Where's she going to stand?" Rose asked, nodding toward Yoki. The woman was a badass with the blade, and I didn't want to be anywhere near the thing when she was slicing and dicing. There wasn't enough room where we were setting up shop for all of us to be at the head of the stairs, and we couldn't place her down at the first landing—it's never a good idea to be downrange during a battle. Kenji was still on the couch; he was in no shape to do much except hold his seat in place. If we had to run…we couldn't run. He'd need to be carried, and running through a dark jungle wasn't a good way for continued survival.

I was looking around for a secondary place to regroup should we lose this spot; the only place we could retreat was the bathroom.

"Is there a window in the head?" I asked.

"High up, but big enough we could egress if we needed to, sir," Rose said. "It's a good thing Top isn't with us, not a chance he'd get through it."

There weren't many times ever that I would wish BT

wasn't with us and I didn't wish it now. Maybe if we had to use the window I would be grateful.

"Bando, can you see if any of the Japanese are carrying rope in their packs?"

Yoki answered with a no. Dropping twenty feet to the ground was never a good start to an escape. She came over to me and had her hand out pointing at my flashlight, which I handed over. She was looking at the various rugs. A few of them were of the braided wool variety.

"Genius," I said as she cut the end of one and unraveled it. Wasn't sure if that would hold our weight, until she cut a few others and then began weaving them together. It was thick and would make getting a good grip difficult, especially once it got wet, but a fast descent on a slick rope that might lead to some burned hands still beat the hell out of a broken ankle or worse.

Yoki, with help from the cousins, had a long enough rope ready within twenty minutes, and we hadn't heard anything in that time. She'd no sooner stood up and stretched her back than there came the largest thump yet.

"What are the chances someone locked the doors down there?" I asked.

"All set, sir," Kirby said.

"Thank you," I told him, angry at myself for the oversight. If the zombies came in they came in, but I'd be damned if I left the welcome mat out.

Kenji had fallen back into a fitful sleep, and he was mumbling incoherently. Akio went over to check on him.

"He...*netsu*," Akio said.

"Fever?" Bando asked.

Akio nodded. "Yes, fever. *Takai.*" He pushed his right hand into the air. I took that to mean it was a high-grade one. There was zero chance Kenji was going to be able to climb down a rope, and lowering him down would be slow, leaving those already on the ground exposed as they covered him.

We'd need at least three up top to support his weight and give him a somewhat controlled descent. The night was shaping up to be a doozy. Add to that the window might not even be viable. If the zombies surrounded the building we'd be delivering food to them like a drive-thru.

"Why aren't they coming in?" Kirby asked anyone willing to answer.

"In a rush?" I asked.

"I hate suspense, makes my stomach feel like crap. Taking action burns that feeling away."

"Damn, Kirby, if that doesn't hit the nail on the head," I told him. I'd never been a fan of the suspense genre for that fact alone.

"Sure wish I had some party favors," Rose said.

I wasn't sure how I felt about that. Of course, they would be very helpful if this became a combat situation, it was just that I tended to end up as collateral damage.

"Are they screwing with us, or do they not know we're here?" Bando asked Kirby.

Kirby shrugged.

"The food." I was thinking out loud. "Either it attracted something, or it's masking our scent." That didn't take into account the presence of the Thin Man zombie, although it was dark on the first floor, and as far as I knew, normal-ish zombies did not have heightened eyesight. Had we led them here and then confounded them into inaction with the piles of spoiled food outside? Plausible. Two more thuds then nothing. No one got much rest and it was difficult to tell if the sun was going to make an appearance or not in the darkened gloom of a stormy morning. The rain had intensified; somehow the Pacific Ocean had been uplifted into the clouds above us and was now draining back to Earth. At some point, this building was going to be floating down a newly made white water river. That would be fun.

I was looking out the window from where I'd been lying,

looking at the vast jungle canopy, zoning out for the most part, hoping that my family and the rest were okay and how they were doing, riding this storm out. Isamu sat up and stretched, and I reached out and swatted his leg before he could stand. Intuition, maybe instinct, maybe a bit of both compelled me to motion him to sit back down. I mostly rolled off the couch, staying low as I made my way to the windows, to the side that was over the front doors, where we had discarded the rotten food. I can't say I knew with any certainty what I would see, but I had an inkling. Yoki had been sitting on the topmost stair, she turned to watch me.

I moved slowly, pulling a Wilson of *Home Improvement* maneuver, with only the crown of my head and my eyes above the lip of the sill. "Zombies," I muttered. Figured today must be a Monday, a perfect start to the work week. The commute was going to be a bitch. There was more rustling behind me. Isamu was looking at me as I made a downward motion with my arm. He understood immediately and began to tell or direct those waking up as I made my way back. For the next half hour, we all at some point low crawled our way to the restroom. Gonna let you in on a little secret: when your bladder is full, crouched is not a comfortable position to be in, plus it's slow going, which doesn't help. After that basic function was taken care of, the next in line was thirst and hunger. We'd eaten decently the night before so we weren't starving, that didn't mean we wanted to go without, though. The issue was that the food was downstairs, and there was no way we could make our way down there without being observed. Being hungry was a small price to pay to avoid a conflict.

I'd recommended everyone take their boots off and let their feet dry out and hopefully their boots as well. We sat on the ground for the remainder of the morning. There was some small talk, but for the most part, it felt safer to stay quiet. Not heard, not seen meant we got to stay inside where it was relatively warm and very dry, and I liked dry. The rain eased up sometime later that afternoon. We'd still not moved around a bunch. Kirby kept looking longingly toward the stairs, his stomach grumbling like only a young Marine's could. Wasn't long after that almost everyone's attention was on those stairs. It was worse knowing there was food, and we just couldn't have any.

"Do you think Top is looking for us?" Kirby asked.

"He's looking for us, maybe not you," Bando said. Kirby popped him in the arm.

I felt bad. If the big man was out in this crap looking for us, he was going to give me hell when he found out we were riding the storm out in style while he was doing an impression of a wet rag—or beach towel, given his size. For one of the few times since the apocalypse began, I was looking forward to the night. I figured with the darkness it afforded, we'd be able to sneak down into the pantry and grab some food. There was roughly a thirty-three percent chance what we opened was bad, but two out of three it was good, those were decent odds. The problem was we couldn't dispose of the nasty ones outside, and if it was rigged to blow, there was no way to clean up. One of the bathrooms was going to have to take one for the team. The way I saw it, it couldn't be any worse than what BT had been doing to my bathroom daily back in the refinery.

The idea that this was a Monday held fast when late afternoon the rain finally ceased, and the sky cleared. The clouds had hightailed it out of there quickly, and because it was Monday, a nearly full moon sat on the horizon just waiting to illuminate the entire hemisphere like a night game.

"Do the windows look tinted at all?" I asked. If they were, it might be almost impossible to see anything inside once it was nighttime, as long as we didn't have any lights on.

"Most shops tend to have some sun film on to keep the temperatures inside down," Bando said. "At least in Brazil."

We were going to have to chance it. There was no telling when the zombies would get sick of waiting. The elements and the lack of creature comforts meant nothing to them. Rain, snow, hail, freezing temperatures or blazing sunshine, they'd stand tall through it all. I wasn't the least bit thrilled I made a rhyming poem about zombies. As the sun set, the moon rose, and there was not as big a discernible change in lighting as I would have hoped.

"Will they be able to see us if they're pressed up against the glass?" Kirby asked.

I was slipping. I just assumed the bastards were all at the tree line, and as long as we didn't use flashlights, we should be damn near invisible. But if they had their faces pressed up against the glass, that could get dicey. It might come down to merely sensing movement, and then we'd be in exactly the situation I was hoping to avoid.

"Go." Yoki pointed to her chest then the stairs.

Thought about saying no, but she wasn't in my chain of command, and I don't think she would have listened anyway; she would have feigned a translation error. Kenji wasn't doing great, and it seemed she was going with the old adage to feed a fever. We could have all easily gone another day without too much discomfort. Oh, don't get me wrong, it would still have sucked, but we were used to it. In the good old days when your fridge was mere steps away or a store or restaurant was a short drive, missing a meal was cause for consternation; most people wouldn't stand for it. Now a couple of days was more the norm than not. I'd once had to have a medical issue addressed and was told to fast for twenty-four hours. I'd not realized just how difficult that was going to be. Now I could do that standing on my head—although I wouldn't; I don't like the sensation.

I didn't know if what Kenji had was life-threatening, but he had a thick glaze of sweat on his face and his complexion was pasty. We could be screwed if he got delirious and began yelling in his sleep or maybe began to cough uncontrollably, either could give us away. I wondered, and not for the first time, if what ailed him might be from a mosquito bite, dengue fever topped my list. Wasn't like this godforsaken place wasn't rife with the vile little blood suckers. I was trying to tap into my personal WebMD knowledge base regarding the illness but I was coming up short. All I knew was it was semi-serious with a chance of becoming deadly. No idea if medical intervention was needed or if there even was a treatment. That was about as good as the weather forecaster saying there's a chance of precipitation or not or it could be a tornado. Thanks, asshole. If he did have an insect-borne disease, chicken soup wasn't going to do much, and I thought about giving Yoki my expert prognosis, but she was already three stairs down, crawling headfirst.

She was moving slowly, scanning the windows on the first floor. I wanted to get over toward her, see what she was seeing, and maybe ask some questions. I felt a short flush when I realized how bad of an idea that was. She slithered down another step and scanned again. The light was for shit, but I'd bet the farm that she stiffened as if she'd seen something. How she kept that pose I don't know—she had one foot a step above the other and was supporting her weight on her arms and was as still as pinned insect. A slug would have hazed her for being slow. It took over twenty minutes until she pulled her trailing foot over the edge and out of sight. At this pace, she'd have to wait out the daylight in the pantry.

A random thump jump scared the shit out of me. And was that what the zombies were trying to do? Prompt a quick furtive movement that they could see? None of this made sense. Those windows weren't stopping anything; if they thought there was food in here why wouldn't they come in and get it? Or at least look around and if they came up empty be on their way to more fertile grounds. Why camp out? Maybe this was one of those irrational instances where logic didn't apply, couldn't apply. Sure, the zombies had done some things I couldn't explain, but this didn't seem to fit. When food was involved, they were fairly easy to predict. Of course, it was hard to complain about not being attacked, being thankful would have been a better way to while away my time, but as a military person, I was always going to look for the worst-case scenario in the rose bed.

The longer Yoki was gone, the more my stomach began to protest its emptiness. The sliver of a promise that we were going to eat was making me hungry. Sort of like when your wife sent a text while you were at work about some special "us time." That would quickly become all you could think of as you finished your workday, not paying attention while Leonard in accounting discussed the annual projections. Then came the commute home and every craptastic driver behind the wheel conspired to extend your time on the road. Then that night, the kids needing umpteen glasses of water before they'd go off to bed. Then the subsequent trips to the bathroom soon followed by the dog's need to go out. Again. Needless to say, by the time it came down to the deed, I could have hammered nails. I shook my head and laughed internally, that particular day was a lot of build-up for an anticlimactic ending. Wait, I mean there were climaxes, just the whole thing happened exceedingly fast, a learned behavior parents of young children were quite practiced at. Fucking tangents. All I wanted was a damn piece of beef jerky and maybe some more alone time with my wife.

There were two more thumps from different sides of the building. Still no sign of Yoki or of a break-in. Sitting in the dark being quiet was as boring as it sounds. Most of the people had decided that sleeping was a better alternative than focusing on their hunger. I could hear their rhythmic breathing as the lucky bastards slept. I made my way slowly to the top of the staircase, just to do something. Looking out the windows, I was surprised at the amount of light coming in. Downstairs, not so much, but it wasn't the impenetrable darkness I would have hoped for. I could see a couple of windows from the top, but I wanted to see more. Instead of going down front facing, I did the sideways thing, the stairs wide enough to accommodate that stealthy mode of travel. Was on the third step when I noticed the first zombie. Sure enough, it had its face and hands pressed up against the glass because of the light to its back. Tough to say exactly, but I got the feeling its nose was mashed to the side as it peered in intently. It still made no sense.

Fucker almost got me. I'd been looking around for any sign of Yoki when the zombie I'd spotted kicked at the floor-to-ceiling window. I had to catch the banister to keep myself from rolling down the staircase like some comedy routine the Three Stooges would have pulled. After moving quickly to save my dumb ass, my gaze immediately went to the zombie. Its head had turned slightly; it felt like the thing was peering directly at me. I was in an awkward position, my right arm pinned under my body, my left arm extended with a death grip on the railing, part of my body suspended in the air. I felt like Wile E. when he runs off a cliff and it takes him a second to realize he's defying gravity before plummeting to a resounding poof. I watched the zombie's foot rear back again, and the kick came much harder this time—I could see the reflected moonlight vibrating on the surface. Then its attention turned away. I blew out my breath and fixed my awkward pose, my shoulder throbbed in relief.

Out of my peripheral vision, I was positive I'd seen movement, but when I went to look directly at it, I couldn't see anything. Strange how we have evolved to have better side vision than straight-on. Probably a direct result of damn near every other predator being bigger, stronger, and faster than we were. Then when our minds developed enough to overcome and triumph over our many shortcomings, we still had to be wary of that other apex asshole, ourselves. I was slowly turning my head from side to side, trying to pick up something. It had to be Yoki, but I could not get a fix on her. Is it closing in on racism to say she was a ninja? Or was that more of a stereotype? And is it bad if it's a positive statement? I mean, I wouldn't feel bad if BT said I could pull off wearing shorts in the winter type of thing. That's a white thing, right? All the other races seem to have their shit together in that regard. Winter: Cold. Wear appropriate clothing. Seems we missed the memo. Or shit, maybe it's just me.

Another resounding thud, but this was not caused by the one I could see or not. For the hundred and fiftieth time, I was trying to figure out what in the flying fuck was going on. Then it dawned, like the sun after a hurricane. Avalyn. It had to be her holding sway, keeping them from entering. Then for the briefest of moments I was thrilled, because if she was controlling them, that meant she had a good idea of where they were, and by default where we were, which meant at any second a truck was going to pull up and extract us from this sticky situation and feed us. And then, because you know you can't have good in the world without having the accompanying bad, I remembered that Avalyn wasn't the only zombie whisperer.

"Payne," I whispered to the wind, lending credence to the thought. This seemed more up her alley, like a cat playing with a mouse before tearing its head off and leaving the skull and spine on the kitchen counter for its human cohabitator to find in the morning before their first cup of coffee. Tell me that isn't a message worthy of coming from a mob boss? There was still a third explanation, that there weren't enough zombies out there to make a successful attack, which meant for the moment they were merely guarding the pen, waiting for some reinforcements before making a go at us. Two of those explanations indicated we needed to get the hell out as soon as the sun came up. But shit, if this was Avalyn's handiwork, it made sense that we would already be in the back of a truck enjoying a fantastic bagged meal. Of course, I'd be avoiding beef stew until the end of time; now I just needed to make the opportunity to avoid that meal a reality by staying alive. (That seemed clear enough, right? Not sure why I needed to clarify the staying alive part, that was just understood, right? Implied? Assumed?)

I somehow went slower up the stairs than I had going down. I waited at the top with my chin resting on the threshold. I could just make Yoki out at the bottom, looking like some scene in a horror flick as she slowly flowed over the stairs in her approach. Two more thumps as she came up. I grabbed the bag from her outstretched arm then backed up so she would have plenty of room. She was covered in sweat, not sure what brutal yoga poses she'd been forced to hold for an interminable time, but it must have been hell. She was exhausted. I asked if she needed any help, but that was like asking an exterior house painter if they needed any help while they were at the hose cleaning off their last roller and brush. Rose had emptied the contents of the bag; how in the hell Yoki had dragged twelve cans up the stairs without making a noise was beyond my scope of understanding. It was a foregone conclusion that had I been carrying them, the bag would have broken on the top step and all the cans would have rolled down the stairs, exploding upon impact for the grand finale.

The plan was to open them in one of the bathrooms. We couldn't flush the toilets for obvious reasons, so if any of these cans were bad, we were effectively eliminating a bathroom from use forever. Small price to pay, as the one we were going to use was already getting a wee bit stanky. Then came the next hurdle. I realize I have enough problems, but I have to think I share this issue with a good many others. The idea of opening up food cans in a bathroom that smelled only slightly better than an overflowing septic tank did not resonate well with me. Looking at the input while smelling the output, yeah, like I said, that was going to be an issue. Good thing there's delegation.

I was initially going to send Bando in as he was the lowest ranking, and Kirby reluctantly volunteered to help, not wanting his friend to have to deal with it alone. That was until Haruto wrestled the bag away. Isamu followed him. It looked like opening what could potentially be horrendous food bombs was a badge of honor to prove courage under the face of fire. I suppose it was, but there were better ways to earn merit badges. Three cans were opened before Haruto came out with some green beans. Isamu was next with what I thought or hoped was creamed corn, that or some yellow mold that had turned the contents to mush. Haruto came out the next time with some boiled chicken. They were alternating, playing a form of Russian Roulette with the food. I had to think the repercussions even more long-lasting, because when you were dead you didn't give a shit anymore, but the trauma of a rotten can would linger with you for the rest of your life.

It was on Isamu's next turn that things went bad. The hiss of fetid air being released as the can was opened was something we all could hear through the door. Haruto exited from that bathroom like he'd been shot out. Hard to tell in the dim light, but he looked pale. Isamu had taken the bullet and was retching violently, I caught a glimpse of his hands clamped over his mouth as he did his utmost to be as quiet as he could, before the door shut completely. I felt so incredibly bad for the man; he was caught in a vicious loop, couldn't come out, as his coughing, gagging, and retching noises were far too loud, which meant he couldn't escape the malignant stench he was entrenched in that was causing the distress. I was going to miss him. Now came the hard part: I needed to volunteer someone to grab the remaining cans.

"You're up," I told Rose.

"Does this have to do with the time I almost blew you up?" she asked.

"Which time?" Kirby chimed in.

She flipped him off, pulled her shirt and hoodie over her nose, and as she was getting ready to go in, the rest of us backed up. She went in quickly and closed the door to make sure not too much sound escaped. She was back out in under five seconds.

"Now what?" she asked placing the bag down.

"Did you open them?" I asked.

"You were serious, sir? Don't we have enough food here?"

I'd hate to think I was seeking retribution for all the times she nearly killed me. I was hungry though.

"Do you hear that?" Bando asked.

It was unmistakable, a truck engine. Help had arrived. Now we had to make sure our rescuers didn't need rescuing. I headed to the window; I could make out a bit of headlights as they came down the winding roadway. I couldn't see any zombies, they'd either melted back into the woods or were even now moving toward the new sound.

"Rose, get Isamu." I was heading for the stairs down, we were all in, it was time to go. I looked over to see Kirby shoveling some of the canned food into his face.

"Ri'm rungry!" he mumbled.

Yoki directed Haruto and Daku to go help Kenji then we raced down the stairs. I would have beat her, but she jumped over the railing six steps from the bottom. The original zombie I'd seen was still at his post, though his back was toward us. I did a quick turn, registered another seven spaced somewhat evenly around the windows. Yoki threw the turn bolt and was out the door before we could talk strategy, although I guess this was more of a shoot—or swing, in her case—and see what happens scenario, than anything overly finessed.

What happened next was a testament to her skill. The zombie had his back pressed against the window, the blade's edge caught the moonlight as it whizzed through the air. Not sure how she threaded the needle, couldn't have been more than an inch of space between the zombie's neck and the plate glass, yet that head dropped to the ground, neatly severed from the rest of the body, and there wasn't a scratch on the glass. I got a quick glimpse of that classic cut away visual fairly commonplace in horror movies, the zombie's body stood erect for a second or two, and I could clearly see all the muscles, spine, arteries, veins, skin, and fascia before its legs got the message that they'd no longer be getting any messages and collapsed. The blade had cut so swiftly that the wound hadn't even bled yet. I was going to resume my sword lessons the same day we got to safety. Got the added horror of zombie eyeshine staring up at me as headlights swept into the parking lot.

3

MIKE JOURNAL ENTRY 3

"ANYONE LOOKING FOR A RIDE?" someone bellowed from the truck bed. I'd expected it to be BT's booming voice, but when the last helicopter was heading out of Saigon you weren't so focused on the crew chief.

The moment the truck swung into the lot, the zombies that had been looking into the welcome center began to converge on the vehicle. Six wasn't that big a deal in the grand scheme of things, still potentially deadly though. Yoki was moving to intercept the nearest one. I turned to shoot one coming from the other side. Wasn't sure where I'd hit it, only that it went down. Rose was next out, followed by Isamu and Akio. I couldn't see who was driving the truck, but they were coming in fast. Thought by the shape and size of the shadowed figure it might be Justin, which, had I known he was driving, I would have suggested everyone head back upstairs and into safety until he placed it in park. Justin could do a lot of things great, and maybe driving would eventually be on the list, but I still held trauma from when I was teaching him. That fear quickly becomes a lifetime's caution.

I was hanging by the doors, waiting for everyone to come out. A supported Kenji was framed in the doorway, and it was

45

good to see him up and about, not hale of health by any stretch, but not on death's door either. Then I heard the shots. Kenji rocked back, a plume of blood appearing on his chest. Another volley of shots, and Rose fell with a yell.

I don't know if I said it or thought it, but I was wondering what the fuck was going on. *The truck?* The truck was shooting at us? Why would they be shooting at us? I was confused as fuck, but say what you will about me, and what most people say isn't great, but when faced with an unfamiliar danger, I know when to get away from it and when to respond in kind. I wasn't going to question the madness until we were safely away. Kenji had slid from Akio's arms and fallen face-first onto the walkway. Yoki was pushing her people back in, and Rose had dropped to one leg, swearing like a drunken sailor. There was no time for a controlled withdrawal. I slid my forearm under her left arm and dragged her away. A hail of bullets chewed up the ground where we had been.

"Up!" Up!" I shouted. The glass was going to do little to stop the bullets or the two-ton machine. Kirby dropped his can of food when he saw an injured Rose. "Cover our retreat! The truck is hostile!" I shouted at him to knock him into the action. The change was immediate from concern to anger. Marines are awesome like that. He got into position on those stairs as we passed him and dropped half a mag through the plate glass and most likely into the truck. Couldn't see much from my angle, but I could hear the ping of bullets on metal. When we hit the landing, I yelled for him to follow. The front of the building became an eruption of glass and brick and metal, first from the enemy's rifle fire and then from the truck itself as it plowed through the doors and came to a stop midway through. The driver, after having failed to run us down, backed out. The squeal of twisted metal door frames as they scraped against the truck body was eye-clenching, lip-pressing, cringe-inducing agony. I would rather an overplayed, underwhelming song on the radio be performed by a finger-nails-on-a-chalkboard quartet. And just for good measure, Yoko Ono could sing the lyrics. The truck came to a halt just outside.

Once the initial cacophony died down, we all heard a crazed shout. "Found you!"

"Feroz." I'd got into position at the top of the stairs for their inevitable attack. Yoki was working on Rose. She'd been shot in the thigh. If it had done anything to her femoral artery, there wouldn't be anything we could do. I was extremely worried for her, but there was still the rest of the group to look out for and a maniac on our doorstep. I motioned for Bando to join me. Kirby was helping Yoki get a tourniquet on the leg so they could clean out the wound, maybe dig the bullet out.

I had no idea how many people had been in that truck, but when a man sprinted for the staircase he made it up two steps and we dropped that number by one.

"I'm going to enjoy killing you!" Feroz screamed, it sounded on the edge of lunacy, teetering over the precipice. That was always scary to deal with because you never knew how your opponent was going to react. Insanity made predicting behavior impossible as motivation and self-preservation were out the window. The only good to come out of it was they tended to act rashly, not interested—or capable—of fully weighing options and outcomes.

Daku had crawled to the windows. He looked back our way his eyes growing wide. "*Zombis!*"

I was thinking how fucking awesome this was; our Brazilian party crashers had flung the doors open wide for our mutual enemy. Had a lot going on in my head then I was struck with the crippling thought of: where did they get that truck? Had BT been waylaid? Could it be the truck we'd had to abandon?

"How many? I asked Daku.

"*Nan hyaku mono!*"

All I caught was the *mono* part, that didn't sound so bad.

"Hundreds," Bando said.

"Fuck." I let my head sag to the floor, my forehead touching for a moment. The only bright spot in this whole shit parade was that Feroz was in much more danger than we were. A splintering spray of bullets punched through the wood not more than a few inches from my splayed body. Feroz was directing their firepower into the ceiling, and more than a few bullets were punching through. Not a great tactic, not in a building this big, unless they had unlimited ammo, but again, I was convinced Feroz was insane; she would by default do insane things. Another volley of shots was making fresh air holes in the floor. Most of us up top had made ourselves as small as possible...one tends to do that when concerned about being skewered by lead.

Their directed angle of fire changed abruptly. It seemed the zombies had entered the arena. We had a little bit of time before we were going to be thrust into the middle of it and we needed to take advantage of that.

"You stay here," I told Bando.

I swept my arm to garner some attention then pointed to the couch; not sure that was overly clear, but once I grabbed the arm and began dragging it to the stairs we didn't need an interpreter. We had six couches we could use to clog them up with. Ultimately, I would have liked to go to my tried-and-true stair removal option, but that would take a sledgehammer and a bunch of time, or a large supply of very heavy caliber rounds to cut the stairs up, and neither of those were something we had on hand. I had illusions—delusions? That the right word? Fuck it. I had high hopes of being able to go down the stairs and properly place our obstacles, make ourselves as close to an impenetrable wall as could be done without a contractor. Made it down a step or two when someone down there caught wind of what we were doing and took a potshot. They may have been dealing with zombies, but they weren't above directing some negative energy our way.

Akio and I swung the couch twice, and on the universal "let go of anything heavy at three" we did just that. We were off to an auspicious start, got great distance, made it all the way to the landing, and somehow it landed on its arm. Like a flipped coin landing on its side. Damn near impossible, yet we'd somehow pulled it off. Haruto and Isamu must have been world-class bocce players. Smiling despite our urgency, they tossed their couch which struck ours, knocking it over and wedging itself just right. There were now two fairly snug couches taking up the majority of the landing. It was more of a speed bump at the moment than a blockade, but we had a great foundation. When Akio got back with our next couch, Isamu said something to the man, tapped me on the shoulder then touched his chest. He wanted to toss the couch. It would seem my couch-tossing track record wasn't so good, and I was getting subbed out. Hardly seemed fair after one toss and that had been a trick shot, but I wasn't going to let my over-inflated ego get in the way. Yeah, I grumbled a bit, but they couldn't understand me anyway, so it was all good.

When the cousins tossed that third couch it was like watching Rembrandt paint; I have no idea why they would have the skill they did, but it was beautiful. The couch flipped over twice before coming to a rest against the other two, the front propped in the air and the back supported against a stair, making what could be considered a bastardized abatis. Although, how we could sharpen a couch was beyond me.

"Fuck me," I said as it settled into position. I smacked Akio on the chest and we hurriedly grabbed another. Same results. We now had two couches popped into position with room for one more. "There's no way," I said, stepping back as the cousins spoke rapidly, finishing each other's thoughts. Then like magic, they threw that thing up in the air and it dropped into the opening, wedging tightly. There was no doubt the zombies could eventually get through that, but they were going to pay dearly for that right. We tossed the last two couches down, a bunch of armchairs, end tables, and display cases for good measure. It was a mass of impediments; something a human enemy might not try and breach. Gunfire was at a crescendo below; hazarding a guess I would have said there were at least ten soldiers down there. Heard a high-pitched scream come from the far side near the pantry. Sounded like a male, so whatever had happened, it wasn't good.

"I'm going to check on Rose," I said, Bando, Haruto, and Isamu went with me. Daku remained at the windows, Akio stayed and watched the stairs. Rose was simultaneously sweating and shivering, her pantsless leg had taken on a dark purple color. Not sure exactly what that meant, she was not anywhere near the two-hour threshold for a tourniquet. She had a death grip on Kirby's hand, he hardly seemed to notice; he was intent on alternating between watching her face and watching Yoki work on the wound. He had taken the red lens off his flashlight and was directing it to where Yoki had two fingers two knuckles deep, rooting around for the projectile. Maybe Rose was in shock, that, or the woman had a pain threshold most mere mortals couldn't understand, but besides some heavy breathing and grunting it was impossible to tell she'd been injured. There was a decent amount of blood, but not the deep red arterial gush of a death sentence. It made sense to get the bullet out if we could, to keep it from moving around and doing more damage, but this was about as sanitary as eating off a porta-potty floor after a three-day music festival.

If we could get back to our people we could get her antibiotics...I repeatedly told myself *one thing at a time*. Akio had pulled away some splinters from the floor and was peering downstairs; not sure I would want to put my eye exactly where a bullet had traveled recently, but Akio didn't seem to mind.

"Sir!" Rose gasped. "Bite…down…something!" Her head was tilted back, she was in a great deal of pain. Yoki was talking a mile a minute while Kirby was telling the woman to hurry up and alternating that with telling Rose everything would be all right. He sounded so calm when he spoke to Rose then frantic when talking to Yoki.

I grabbed a handful of pamphlets from the floor and raced over. "I'm here," I told her, she opened her mouth like a baby bird, and I shoved them in there, narrowly missing having my fingers bitten off. Tears were leaking from the corners of her eyes.

"Aha!" Yoki held up a chunk of lead. She washed it off and inspected it thoroughly; she seemed pleased with the results. The head had mushroomed a bit but otherwise looked intact. She spoke rapidly to Rose and Kirby. She headed to the bathroom and came out with the soap dispenser then cleaned out the wound as best she could before tightly wrapping a cloth around the area. When she was satisfied that she had the hole dressed as well as possible, she undid the tourniquet. Blood surged to the area and immediately soaked through the cloth. We all stood there and watched Rose bleed. Yoki adjusted the dressing and it slowed, it didn't stop, but it wasn't rushing to get out of her system either.

Shooting had intensified downstairs. It was strange to have a three-way going on and I wanted nothing to do with it. Those are the kinds of statements that can get you in trouble when you're in a committed relationship. I meant the three-way part only in the abstract. If I thought even for a millisecond that we could combine forces to repel the greater threat I would have jumped into the fray, but I knew the moment we were visible, Feroz and her cronies would shoot at us. No good deed goes unshot at. In a perfect world they would completely take each other out, but this was an imperfect world which meant that ultimately Feroz and the zombies would make some unholy alliance and attack us.

Yoki stood and gave me a bloody thumbs up. Not the most inspiring sign I'd ever seen, but she was smiling so there was that. I looked over at Akio; he pushed up from his spy hole and held up nine fingers then let two drop. I didn't know if he was including the one we'd taken out earlier, didn't matter much, not yet anyway. At least two of the shooters below us were on full auto, the percussions so loud that thoughts were pushed from my mind. I headed for my own spy hole even though I just said I wouldn't, but the Brazilians were immersed in survival; we were of a far distant secondary concern. Bobbing flashlight beams lit up the nightmare—dozens of zombies were in the main lobby with more entering every second. From my angle and the limited diameter of the hole I was looking through, I could not see the soldiers, only their lights and tracer rounds, which were hitting and killing with incredible devastation. Not all that hard, taking proximity into account.

One of the shooters on full auto was definitely of the 5.56 variety, the other I wasn't quite sure. It sounded like a much heavier round, I could feel the whomping vibration where my body was in contact with the floor. With the way it was mangling zombie bodies, I was surprised the zombies hadn't had some sort of peace accords with humans in regards to outlawing using the caliber on the undead or living dead whatever was the politically correct terminology for zombies. The bullets were traveling clean through the first target and sometimes through the second. It was physically forcing them backward, tearing limbs off, or shattering spines, making them flop over. With their sustained rate of fire, they were going to melt barrels and end up getting killed themselves. They were making great strides in mowing down zombies; I just needed the Brazilians to last a little while longer, have those barrels hold up or the rounds hold out. Maybe way back when, I would have felt guilty for that. Not any longer.

There were shouts downstairs in Portuguese, not sure

Bando would have been able to hear it well enough to interpret. Gunfire increased then wound down. Then went silent.

"*Pantori*," Azio looked over at me.

I knew the word; Feroz and the rest were hiding in the pantry. Smart move. She couldn't come up and couldn't or wouldn't get back to the truck to leave. Speaking of which. I moved as silently as I could, thankful the floor didn't squeak as I made my way to the windows. These zombies didn't know we were here, and there was no reason to change that status quo. The ground outside had an ethereal glow as the sun was hinting at coming around for the day. The truck sat there; four zombies were piled onto what I imagine was a previous occupant. There'd been ten little Brazilians, one deviated from the lane and had now lost his brain. Another horrible verse for my Zombie Book of Poetry. That comes from going another night with little sleep.

"I'm going to kill you, Talbot!" Feroz shouted out. She wasn't overly concerned with stealth, the zombies knew exactly where they were. "You're a lying tyrannical piece of shit! You kidnapped my sister and who knows what else you did to her, you vile monster!"

I was getting the feeling she didn't like me. I was fine with verbal insults, it had been a good long while since those had affected me. I suppose she was trying to bait me into responding, take some of the zombie pressure off. The best satisfaction I could get would be the anger I induced by not responding. My mother, Maker rest her soul, thrived on rowdy conflict—I need a better description than "got off" because eww—but for now, yeah she got off on the screaming and yelling. Can't even begin to tell you how many ferocious battles I witnessed between her and my dad and my siblings, especially my sister. I learned a lot. When my turn came up in the rotation, the best course of action was to do nothing, to not rise to the offering. It drove her absolutely bat shit crazy that I would not engage. And it caught her completely off guard, this was something she'd never had to deal with, and had no coping skills for it. She would go louder, her screaming so high pitched as to be considered shrill, then came the slamming of things down and around. My defense would be calmly to agree with everything she said. "Yes, mom. I know, mom. Whatever you say, mom."

She would try harder, making up conflict where none existed, hoping to catch me off guard, and trick me into a shouting match with her. Took about six months before she finally just stopped. My older siblings were all out of the house, my father had one foot out the door. Junior and senior years of high school were among some of my most peaceful times. In terms of household conflict anyway. There was always high school drama to deal with, but it sure was nice to come home and get away from it all. My mother and I didn't have much to talk about for those two years. I had so befuddled her as to have communication come down to the barest of minimums. So where I'm going with this is Feroz was an amateur who in no way could compete with what I'd dealt with previously. For five solid minutes, Feroz shouted all matter of vitriol at me; some of it was wonderfully colorful commentary that I wish I could have recorded to playback for BT, he would have thought it as funny as I did. I was sitting with my back resting against the couch Rose was lying on when she finally stopped.

"Thank God," Rose rasped. "I just want to get a little sleep."

Akio came and sat in front of me; he pointed his rifle toward the floor then flipped his chin toward the pantry. I understood what he meant. Feroz and all her people were holed up in a small room, it would be like shooting fish in a barrel. I didn't have any moral dilemma with that, maybe I should have, I don't know. I guarantee if the roles were reversed, she would have pincushioned the hell out of us. Yes, another verbed noun, I don't care. My journal, my grammar rules. Killing Feroz could solve a lot of problems, the only issue, and it was a biggie, was that once we did that the zombies would know we were here, and so far we had stayed under their radar. Zombies were a lot of things, but curiosity could not be counted among their traits. If we didn't give them a reason to investigate it was unlikely they would. We started shooting....well, that's about as self-explanatory as I need to get. As far as the Japanese went, they had lost one of their own and would want revenge as much as anyone. I don't think I was in any position to deny them that. I could advise against it for the aforementioned reason, but ultimately if they wanted to kill the fuckers, I wasn't going to stand in the way.

Part of the decision was going to come down to how many zombies were here. Funny to think that the only thing standing between Feroz and death was the number of zombies we could deal with safely and escape. I shook my head at Akio, his eyebrows furrowed.

"*Urusai*," I told him. Pretty sure that meant *loud*, but without context that could mean diddly.

Took him a second then it seemed he understood, although I don't know, I could have said donkey to him, like literally the word donkey. It always struck me as strange how different languages could be. It was bad enough with ones that derived from the same roots, but Japanese and English were entirely different trees. Hard to picture Maker getting pissed enough about humanity's hubris in trying to build a tower to heaven that they would have created such divisiveness by altering our languages, cool story, though. (As for Maker, I call him "they" because although he usually appears as an old man to me, I would imagine to a young girl he may be vastly different, maybe a grandmotherly image, or a motherly one, or shit maybe even a unicorn, and in each iteration that is exactly who he, she or it is.)

I read once that less than half of the population have internal running dialogs in their heads. That blew me away when I saw that. I kept thinking, *no fucking way. There are people who don't have runaway thoughts constantly bombarding their brain's ability to think?* And how incredible that must be. Like finally being able to kick that loud, obnoxious, overstaying party crasher from your home. The peacefulness that would ensue afterward would be bliss. Honestly, I can't even imagine what that must be like.

I corralled my inner interloper and went to see if I could get a better idea of the size of the horde. From where I was, I could see somewhere north of fifty zombies milling about, the truck wasn't ten feet from the building. If we fast rappelled down, we could be in and gone in under thirty seconds.

"In your dreams," I countered. Nine of us would need to go down our makeshift rope. We could catch Rose so she didn't come down on her injured leg, hoping for the best, but it was impossible to tell what she might do to her injury making the escape. We might have to try it regardless, but if the truck didn't start right away or the Brazilians had tampered with it so it could not be started without flipping a hidden kill switch or something, then we would be in a fight for our lives with minimal cover. Then it dawned on me. One or two could go down at night in complete stealth, start the truck, get the hell out, and find some help. BT and company with some heavy machineguns could clear the field in a couple of minutes. A lot of presumptions there, like would this number of zombies stay consistent, and would those leaving in the truck find our group, or would the truck break down?

I looked over at the group. Kirby and Bando were my only true choices. As much as I wanted it to be me taking the risk, I had to think of the rest of the people up here with me. I could send one or the other and one of the Japanese crew, but the language barrier concerned me. If there came a moment where they needed to understand each other immediately, it could mean risking harm or death. Yeah, that wouldn't work, but the thought of sending two of my Marines away during an active hostile situation wasn't optimum either. All had been quiet for more than an hour; I'd got the gist of what I wanted to do, and now it was a waiting game. It's amazing how slow time moves when you're doing absolutely nothing. A couple of times my eyes would involuntarily close then I would catch a whiff of the unhygienic zombies or they'd walk into a piece of surviving furniture and the squeal of the scraping leg would startle me awake.

It was after about an hour of this I got my first smile of the day. Took a second as I couldn't figure out why so much coughing was coming from the pantry area, that was until it was accompanied by gagging. Seems Feroz's people had lost the food lottery. I'd like to say there was a part of me that felt bad…you know what? That's a lie. I was genuinely hoping the gases from those cans pushed out the oxygen and they died of asphyxiation. As thick as that smell was, it was just as likely to obstruct their airways. I did have a reflexive gag thinking about it, but it wasn't in sympathy, that's for sure. All that coughing, gagging, and finally retching had garnered unwanted attention from the zombies.

We watched from our sky holes as the zombies moved in closer to the door, even drawing in some from outside. The speeders had made a halfhearted attempt at getting through the pantry door, but it was stout, and the Brazilians had barricaded it. Everyone's head whipped around as rifle fire from below harnessed all our attention. My first inclination was that they were firing at the zombies through the door. That made zero sense and would only deplete their resources. Fine with me, I was only trying to figure out the logic of it. It was when we saw splinters of wood rising into the air and our ceiling taking hits that it became apparent what they were doing.

Akio looked over at me. "*Kuki ana.*"

"Yeah, definitely. Air holes," I replied. He nodded. Must have been worse than I could imagine as they blew through somewhere close to a hundred rounds. I tried for a beat to count, but they were shooting fast and furiously. It had gone on long enough I was worried they were trying to cut an escape hole through our floor. We all heard Feroz order them to stop. She must have realized that their bullets were a finite resource.

"Any chance any of those hit you?" Feroz called up. "I sincerely hope not, as I want to stand over your cooling body as your blood flows down the gutter!"

The sound of her voice had done what the cries of distress and the moans of the sick couldn't do: the zombies were hammering away at the pantry door.

"I hope the zombies have a bulker or two on speed dial," I said angrily but quietly.

"Round one, yes?" Akio asked slowly and deliberately as he thought through his translation. He held his outstretched arms in "I am Santa Claus, gaze upon my magnificent belly" movement.

"Exactly." I gave him a thumbs up.

"Boom." He made the gesture of his fist ramming into the palm of his hand.

I nodded. As much as I wanted a bulker to come and end Feroz's miserable existence, bringing that dangerous zombie into the mix made our survival more difficult. If we were discovered, that behemoth would kick our couch barrier out of the way like a throw pillow.

"Sir," Bando whispered, motioning at me to come. I scooted his way, staying low and making no noise. He moved so I could see down the spy hole he was using.

"Bitch." I was referring to Feroz and the situation she'd now put us in. The bullets that had punched into our floor had caused the zombies to take interest in what might be happening up the stairs, and a few were drifting that way. "Keep an eye out, but don't shoot," I whispered. I went to check on Rose to see if she'd made some medically induced miracle recovery. She was out. Good thing the woman didn't snore.

"How is she?" I asked Yoki.

I got a whole bunch of Japanese words I couldn't even begin to write down much less translate. The only thing I could tell from the tone of Yoki's voice was that she was concerned. It probably had to do with her needing proper medical attention to make sure something wasn't damaged more than she could tell, and that Rose needed to take a heavy dose of antibiotics so she didn't die from infection. Nothing I didn't already know. I was just kind of hoping that wasn't the message.

"How are you doing?" I asked Kirby. He didn't look like he'd slept in the last week. The bags under his eyes looked heavy enough to need help carrying.

"Good, good," he said without taking his eyes off Rose.

"She's going to be fine," I told him. Because that's what commanding officers do, they keep morale up. "We'll get her what she needs." I didn't know about my first statement at all, that was more of a wish, a hope, and the second part? Yeah...I had no idea how we were going to accomplish that either. I suppose I had nothing but wishes to offer. What I could do was distract him from the problem. "I'm going to need you, soon," I told him. "The zombies look like they're going to make a push for the stairs. You up for it?"

Took him a second to respond. "Of course, sir. I'd like to ask one thing though."

"Go ahead."

"I'd like to drop a mag in the pantry first."

I nodded. Feroz had to go. I wasn't concerned at all that it was going to be a less-than-glorious death. When the fish in the barrel are rabid piranhas, you shoot them. If we didn't walk out of here, neither did she. "Don't get shot."

He gave me a face that only a hard-core Marine can when

talking about shooting and killing. It was a matter-of-fact, blood lustful grin. Made no sense when put into words, but looked perfectly readable in real life, especially on someone who had watched a person they loved get injured by the very people's existence he had the opportunity to snuff out. I felt no empathy for those about to die. And I couldn't tell how that made me feel. That was the weirdest part about the whole thing. I guess I thought I was supposed to feel bad about it, can't say I did.

Hard to say exactly why what happened next happened. Later, upon reflection, my guess was that there were some holes in the pantry door and they'd been able to see the zombies on the stairs and were attempting to speed things up. The trapped soldiers began to shoot into our floor again garnering more attention from the zombies. We could hear the zombies rushing the couches, we'd been called up to play in the big leagues.

"One mag!" I yelled over to Kirby.

Bando and I headed to the top of the stairs, two zombies were making their way over our obstacles. A moment later they added their bulk to the obstruction. I'd expected a rapid firing of bullets punctuated by screams from Kirby, but that was not the case. He had crept closer then used one of the many openings to fire down into the pantry. He got off four quick shots before he was pushed back by return fire.

"Fuck you!" he yelled. "Two less of you pieces of shit!"

He'd backed up further, the return fire had been excessive. I was wondering how many rounds they could have left in there. Feroz was not going to take this lightly. I called Kirby over.

"You stay with Bando. Controlled rates of fire, you two."

I was going to watch that floor. I was worried that Feroz was going to force herself or one of her soldiers through an opening and they'd pop up like a whack a mole fueled on revenge after being slammed in the head for so many years with a mallet. Akio stood with me, and Yoki stayed by Rose while Haruto and Isamu drifted closer to the stairs.

"*Motto zombis!*" Isamu shouted as he looked out the window.

Either my understanding of Japanese was getting significantly better, or I was well-versed in shit-anese because I knew exactly what he'd said. More fucking zombies. My pipedream of someone getting into that truck and getting help wasn't looking quite as doable as it had been. Sure, the odds of it being successful had been a dismal twenty-five percent to begin with, but that looked like a sure thing compared to our prospects now. At least we were in little danger from Feroz as they didn't have any decent firing angles to endanger us. I tapped Akio on the shoulder and motioned for him to watch that area. I was going to keep an eye on the staircase where the more immediate threat was coming from. The couches were being pushed with enough force to make the ones we had sitting at half-mast go to completely standing up, which made for a great looking wall but one easily toppled, and now we didn't have clear lines of sight on them. Hadn't been expecting this plot twist. I guess that's the point of them, plot twists, I mean, they appear out of nowhere to twist shit up. I very much disliked the idea of shooting blind, but it was a safe enough assumption that the zombies were directly behind the standing couches and that the bullets would travel through the upholstered furniture easily enough, no matter what lies Hollywood had portrayed about the stopping power of furniture.

When invariably the shooting would slow to a stop, we could hear the pounding at the door downstairs coupled with the creaking of the couches as the zombies fought on two fronts. Unlike the harried Germans of World War II, this seemed like something the zombies could exploit to their benefit. And unlike the tentative accord the Allies had, we had no such agreement with the Brazilians. Enemies of our enemies did in no way make us friends. Plus if you believe in conspiracies, Brazil was in league with the Nazis, enough so to hide Hitler.

"Bando, you and Yoki get the rope ready. If we have to go, it's going to be in a hurry," I said quietly, making sure not to be overheard by our downstairs neighbors. Vaguely certain they would not appreciate us stealing back the ride they took from us. They moved quickly and tied an end off to a support column.

"*Mijikai*," Yoki had been leaning out looking then pulled the rope back in.

"Short," Bando explained.

"How much?" I asked, not taking my eyes from our blockade. Thing was creaking worse than an old bed being used by an amorous couple that had waited through their year-long engagement to consummate the relationship on their wedding night.

Yoki held her hand slightly over her head which stood about five feet from the floor. Not a bad jump, maybe somewhere around ten feet, though, once we tied some of it around Rose. Catching an injured person from that height was bound to cause her a decent amount of pain, but pain equated to being alive, a small price to pay for that gift. I moved to take a glance out. Zombies were appearing out of the woods like wraiths that had been lying in wait for weary Hobbits.

"Where the fuck are they all coming from?" I asked, moving back to my original post.

Akio shouted; I turned to see the barrel of a weapon being forced through an opening in the floor. Seems the steerage passengers on this disastrous cruise wanted payback. I don't blame them the sentiment, but as far as I was concerned, they could eat some hot pepper spoiled burrito ass. The shooter let loose a volley, though again, the angle was far too severe to warrant us any danger. Akio pointed his pistol toward the pantry. I doubted the 9mm rounds would be able to penetrate unless he threaded the needle and sent one through an existing hole. He fired twice, the barrel dropped down. He might not have hit anything, but it was close enough for them to rethink that particular strategy.

"Rose, I'm letting Akio use your rifle." She gave me a thumbs up.

"He breaks it he's buying me a new one." She was in too much discomfort to pull off a smile.

I grabbed the rifle and handed it to the man. He gave it a quick once over, releasing the magazine to check for rounds, then slightly pulled back on the charging handle to make sure there was one in the chamber before slamming the mag back and switching the safety off. It was a very smooth operation. He was familiar with the weapon, giving credence to the assumption I'd made of him being prior military.

For the umpteenth time, I was wondering where BT was. If the Brazilians had found us, why hadn't our people? Wasn't like we were sneaking around. As much as I wanted to believe that help was on the way, I had the sinking feeling we were on our own. This was like that time travel axiom which states that time travel will never be possible because if it was, it would have already happened. Sure, it's a circular argument, and there is one time where it has to be first, but after that, you're looking at an infinity loop, and the odds that you're existing in that very first go around are almost non-existent. Like winning the Powerball jackpot twice on your first two tickets kind of rarity. Okay, so maybe the odds of BT finding us were better than that, but the fact they hadn't already rolled on up here said a lot. We couldn't wait for the cavalry to show. Thought about asking Feroz if the keys were in the truck; might get a few laughs up here, but it probably wouldn't go over too well downstairs.

"*Jibun*," Yoki said as she patted her chest with a finger and then pointed to the truck.

"Then what, Yoki?" I asked.

63

She spoke for close to fifteen seconds straight, maybe saying she'd drive the truck up the stairs or leave and find BT or hell, could have been a recipe for cinnamon buns. Lot of gesticulating with her hands. She was explaining *something* in great detail; would have been fantastic to know what it was.

"*Sore de?*"

She'd asked a question. A deer in the headlights had more of an idea of what was going on than I did. She grabbed hold of the rug rope.

"Wait, I don't even know what you said."

She grabbed my forearm and smiled. "Funny," was all she said.

"Shit," was all I could manage as she got in position to head out. "Kirby, get your ass over here, we need to cover Yoki!"

She was halfway down when he got there. "Don't shoot until she's on the ground, and only if she needs help. I don't want to alert the bastards she's down there." Didn't have to worry about that; a dozen or more of the zombies almost immediately caught sight of her before she let go. She was reaching for her sword just as her feet made contact with the ground. Kirby and I shot at nearly the same time. Two zombies were retired from active duty, but our shots alerted a half dozen or more. She had to move fast because we'd never be able to hold off that mathematic progression of zombies. We could deal fairly easily with the zombies coming from the jungle and those that were already outside, but the ones coming back out were going to be difficult to get a bead on, given the short distances and speed involved. Yoki had taken two out in seconds. Zombie heads rolled down the gently sloping parking lot collecting gravel inside their neck stumps.

I was still trying to figure out how this truck was here. I'd heard the thing in its death throes; a thrown rod isn't a DIY type of repair. They would have had to put a new engine in, and I can't see how that would have been accomplished, given the timeline. There was smeared blood on the passenger side of the windshield, consistent with where Eastman had lost his life. The only thing that made sense was it hadn't been a blown rod. Something to do with the radiator, maybe, not that any of that made any difference now, as long as the thing started. Yoki boarded and pulled the door shut. Kirby and I stayed away from the zombies by the driver's side or the front end, not wanting to hurt the driver or the vehicle. She was quickly becoming encircled.

"Start the fucking thing," I said a half dozen times. I had finished one magazine and was reaching for a second when the truck finally turned over, a plume of thick black smoke rising from the engine compartment. Thing sounded rough. Whatever they'd done to get it running was temporary at best; only so long duct tape could hold.

"Does she know how to drive?" Kirby asked as he continued to offer covering fire.

"Odds are, no." I capitalized on my cheap stereotype and, considering Kirby had no idea about what I meant, it fell silently anyway. Sometimes the humor gods toss you a bone. The truck jumped forward and again smashed into the building. Yoki looked up at us with an apologetic expression on her face before she placed the vehicle in reverse.

"How did you know?" Kirby asked.

"Just a hunch." I smiled as we both watched her back up far enough away then put it in drive and peel out of the parking lot, a couple dozen zombies chasing after her.

The sound of the truck starting and leaving had riled up both sets of guests. Feroz was screaming indignant curses, probably ordering some poor bastard to go after our repossessed ride. I'm not proficient in Portuguese, but I knew enough swears to realize she was spewing out mouthfuls of them, on occasion the juicier ones would be punctuated by bullets. None were coming up, which meant they were shooting at the door.

"They're going to try and bust out," I said aloud. I wasn't quite sure what to do, but Yoki was going to be long gone before they could do anything about it.

"Shoot?" Kirby asked.

I shook my head. "No, we let this play out." My thinking was they'd be far too busy fending off zombies to start shooting at the ceiling again. And the more zombies they killed, the better for us. Then on the off chance that they were able to escape the building, I had no problem shooting them in their backs as they ran for the jungle. The gunfire got intense, a scream pierced the din, and a stream of bullets cut through our floor. It didn't seem intentional, just the last action of a dying person as they were pulled down with a finger still on the trigger.

"Help us, you fool!" Feroz shouted.

"Are you fucking kidding me?" This I said for my ears only. I had no intention of doing anything to help her. She'd done us a solid by attracting all the zombies' attention as they vacated the staircase assault and went to try and get in on sampling some of the local cuisine. Or local-ish.

"Sir?" Bando asked.

I shook my head. Hard to tell if he was relieved or upset.

"*Puta que paria!*" Feroz shouted.

Bando's attention swung to me.

"Don't worry about it. My mother and I had a compli-cated relationship," I told him. Most men will lose their shit if their mothers are dragged into an insult, I wasn't most.

"Got a runner!" Kirby shouted.

Somehow, some way, one of the soldiers had made it through the gauntlet. He was fast, but he had ten zombies right on his heels. I told Kirby not to waste the bullet. The fucker had world-class speed, might have even been a profes-sional; the problem with a human sprinter though is it's a short-term burst. Zombies were unrelenting. He was ten feet away from the tree line when the lead zombie lurched forward and sank its teeth deep into the man's shoulder, clamping tightly so that when its legs ran out from under him and he fell, his unfortunate victim dragged him twenty feet into the trees before he was brought down. Pretty sure that was an illegal tackle; where were the refs when you needed them? I watched as they eviscerated that man, who survived longer than anyone had a right to. The screams were on a register I didn't think a male was capable of, or any human for that matter. Far too late to spare those with me, I rethought the wisdom of not shooting him.

"We could have escaped, Talbot!" Feroz screamed. "Now I will have to kill you!"

I could not figure out how she didn't see the irony in her statement. I mean she had come here with the sole purpose of killing me. It was likely that the moment I'd shown myself to lend aid, any sense of reason she possessed would have flown the coop, and she would have started shooting at me. No more able to help herself than a kid locked in a candy store overnight would have been able to contain themselves from shoveling handfuls of sweet confectionary goodness into their mouths.

I wanted to ask her if the "we" she'd mentioned escaping meant all of us, we, or just her people, we. I kept quiet. For the moment the zombies had forgotten all about us as they slurped their way through the unfortunate bastards below us while others continued their assault on the door to the pantry Feroz and company had retreated back into.

Akio had moved to watch over Rose, now that Yoki was in the wind. He motioned me over. Rose looked rough. He said, *netsu* again and then held his hand above his head. Because I could have been a brain surgeon in some reality, I knew that he meant her fever was higher. Wouldn't have taken more than one look at Rose to realize something was very wrong. Black bags had formed under her eyes, and they looked sunken. Her skin had taken on a sickly pallor and she had dime-sized dollops of sweat forming on her brow. Didn't seem right that an infection could set in so quickly; I was under the impression it took two to three days. Is that why Yoki had decided to make a go for the truck? Was something else happening here? Something she couldn't fix?

"Kirby, keep Rose as comfortable as you can."

The kid was visibly distressed after taking a second to look her over. Akio went back to manning his pantry post. The cousins and Bando were watching the stairs, and I was keeping an eye on the parking lot, making sure to stay as hidden as possible. Between the pounding and the soldiers shouting we could have had a tap recital and gone unnoticed. I mention that because Rose had begun to moan and, on occasion, fever rant. I had the feeling she would have been shouting at the top of her lungs had she the energy to do so. She was very vehement in whatever she was talking about. I put my eye to the floor; she wasn't garnering any attention from below. Not sure what I could have done had she been, anyway.

When I leaned back up I caught movement outside. My face may have drained enough color that Rose and I could have been twins. It was a row of six spiders. More than enough malevolent bulk to kill every human in this building ten times over. The zombies had decided to bring nuclear weapons to the gunfight. They must know my wife. I knee-walked over to the couch.

"Kirby, you're going to have to tie a loose gag on her. Spiders." Didn't need much more explanation than that. I made my way to the rest. What had already been a tense situation, close to being pegged out on the tense-ometer, was now ratcheted into whatever color is past red. If our meter was like a Geiger counter it would have been one long static clicking. I went back to the window. The spider zombies had fanned out and appeared as if they were readying to surround the building. Some of them were going to climb up, I was as sure of that as I was one of my infant children getting sick on a planned night of frisky endeavors. It was a foregone conclusion. The only place we could retreat to was the bathroom, but there were issues with that. First off there was no way to barricade the door and second, if the pantry dwellers wanted to (and why wouldn't they), they would have an angle to shoot at us. Sure, we would as well, but who the hell wants to fight like that? It'd be like two old warships coming broadside at a distance of twenty yards. There would be an equal amount of death and destruction on both sides.

I tapped Isamu and hunched down, hooking my arms then making a lifting motion. I wanted to snag the couch Rose was on and bring the whole thing into the bathroom. Great in theory; the issue was the couch wasn't going to fit. Ripped the cushions free before carrying Rose in. That move alone taxed her, her clothes were soaked through with sweat.

Kirby grabbed the rope. I wasn't sure what we were going to do with it, but better to have it than not.

"Come on, Yoki," I said as more of a prayer, as I was the last to file into the bathroom. I was convinced I wasn't going to die today only because there was no way I was calling it quits in a public bathroom.

4

MIKE JOURNAL ENTRY 4

WHAT GLASS WAS LEFT downstairs was shattered; apparently the spiders were not content to go through any existing openings. Five seconds later the windows on our level exploded. We could hear the tiny shards skittering across the wood floor, then the heavy footfalls of an enormous creature. First one, then another. I leaned against the door, not that it would do much, it was more of a psychological thing, like holding your hands in front of your face when someone is pointing a 45 at your skull, maybe it was instinctive. The spiders were moving around quietly, I mean, as quietly as something close to half a ton can. I expected more noisy destruction, like the windows. It was the shock and awe they provoked that generally would get their prey running.

I stepped back when I heard the door to the other bathroom being opened. I suppose *opened* isn't quite the right word. It was slammed open with enough force that we heard the splintering wood of the disintegrating slab. Had the spider done that to my door first, I would have looked like a fly swatted against a marble countertop. Squished, I mean squished against the subway tiles on the wall. I wasn't sure if it could fit through the narrow opening, and I did my best to back up far enough to make sure it couldn't reach out, snag me then retreat to a more private area where it could enjoy its meal in peace.

We got a movie-level reprieve. I didn't know for sure, but I had to believe that one of the spiders was right outside of our door and about to smash the thing like a balsa wood airplane when gunfire erupted downstairs. We could feel the floor vibrating as the behemoths bounded away to see what all the fuss was about. We had to get out of here. I'm sure the Brazilians would put up a brave fight, but they would lose, and then what? The zombies would in all likelihood mill about while the much smarter spiders would check every nook and cranny for more goodies. Our best chance of escape was going to be while they were distracted. That was the theory anyway. Theories shouldn't get disproved quite so quickly, but here we were. I opened the door once I thought the coast was clear. The coast was not clear, it looked like Waikiki Beach at the height of tourist season. If you've ever been to Oahu during that time, you will realize that at the relatively small Waikiki beach, you can no longer see sand because it is quite literally covered by beach towels. To navigate to the ocean, you will need to walk over dozens of others' marked out territories and make your throat raw with the number of excuse me's you will need to voice. About as relaxing as a day at the jackhammer and tooth extraction expo held annually in the Everglades area.

The spider was standing five feet away, eight eyes were fixed on me. I had no idea how it knew where we were until I saw the red glistening drops of blood that had spilled from Rose's wound on the floor between us. The whole fucking thing had been a ruse. The second spider had never left either, it had only pretended. Outsmarted by a zombie. I'm not sure exactly where that put me on the intelligence scale.

"Not great." These were the words that escaped my mouth as I backed up and the spider surged forward. My rifle was barely hip high when I began to fire. I saw but didn't process that the first bullet sheared off the front half of one of its feet. That impromptu, hastily-made shot most likely saved my life as the step it meant to take forward went askew. As it rolled the foot over, it smashed into the wall. I wasn't on full auto, but with the speed I was pulling that trigger you would have never known. We knew a little about the spiders, mostly that the enormous brain the creature housed would no longer be positioned inside its skulls. And judging by the doughy heads sitting on top, it looked like all the bones had migrated to a different location too. It had to be center mass; that was the most well-protected area. No single round from any normal caliber rifle would kill it. They weren't quite of Terminator resilience, but they were a lot closer to indestructible than we were.

I'd be lucky if my comparatively small 5.56 would even punch through the thick fat layer to strike something moderately vital. Why I'd been dragging my feet on adopting a different rifle with a bigger round was something I hoped I could lament about later. It threw itself at that door; the third time was hard enough to break it free from its hinges. I was lucky enough to catch the bounce off my shins. I was pushed backward then fell forward, just out of reach of a flailing arm leg thing. The pain was sharp and intense, and I couldn't focus on much more than hoping it would ease soon. Someone else had picked up my slack in shooting, tough to see who it was when one's eyes are closed. I was pulled back and into a stall —that's what happens when you're interfering with a military op. Was a solid two minutes before I felt as if I could stand. By this point, I was fairly certain my shins weren't broken, wouldn't know for sure until I stood.

The acoustics of the tight room were such that each shot fired felt like it went off right next to your ears. For whatever reason, it doesn't seem as bad when you're the one shooting, but right now, I was suffering. I wasn't the only one. All of the

Japanese had their hands planted firmly over their ears. Rose was sitting up against the far wall, and Bando was next to Kirby, who was the shooter. The spider was wedged tight, grasping at the door frame, trying to pull its enormous bulk through. Kirby might as well have been tickling it with an ice cream scoop for all the good his shots were doing. When he dropped his expended magazine, we heard the real horror show. The spider thing was crushing its body to squeeze through the opening. Even over my ear damage, I could hear rubbery squelches emanating from inside it as muscles and layers of fat rubbed against each other. Then came the popping of joints being dislocated, then because that wasn't horrific enough, came the sharp snapping of bones being broken. Its own actions were doing more damage than Kirby's machinegun.

I suppose all of us at one point could sympathize with that, but right then I hoped it was enough to kill the bastard, or at the minimum incapacitate it. It had successfully pulled one of the hulking body sections through, though this wretched thing hung slack, the damage sustained from fifty bullets and the doorframe trash compactor was too much. That still left three-quarters of the thing ready, willing, and wanting to kill us at all costs. We were saved from listening to more self-mutilation as gunfire happened below us. The Brazilians, having learned a nifty lesson, were using much heavier rounds. A part of me had to hope they were successful in defeating the spiders because I knew without a doubt Feroz would come up here and kill our attackers—if only for the satisfaction of being able to kill me herself. I was beginning to give myself a complex over how much I could make people hate me. Would that be considered a gift? Not a very useful one. Bando had switched out with Kirby who was working on a jam. Two of the bodies were in, and we for the most part were pressed against the far wall. I'd helped Rose into a stall so she could stay seated.

Akio waited for a break in the action. He had his sword drawn as he tapped Bando on the shoulder. There wasn't much room to safely wield the weapon, but we gave him as much as we could. As a kid I had often fantasized about having a light saber; when I got to adulthood I still wanted one, but I knew without a shadow of a doubt it was a good thing I didn't. I wouldn't have made it five minutes without doing irreversible damage to myself or my valued property. I was even sure I would have taken down a support beam from my parents' house, which wouldn't have gone over too well. I wonder what the grounding would be for making a house cave in? I was still thinking about that sleek, blue-flamed torch sword when a fat, oversized hand slapped against the floor tiles. Akio had neatly sliced through the beast's wrist. Blood spurted out, coating the wall as the arm flailed about, still trying to gain purchase as it had yet to realize it no longer had the ability to grasp things with that arm.

The exposed bones rubbing up against the polished surface of those walls made a sickening sound that had me cringing harder than the most uncomfortable scene I'd ever endured watching Michael Scott in *The Office*. "Ode to Joy" played on a saw and kazoo would have been a soulful rendition of that beloved song in comparison. He made short work of the two arms we could see before slicing at the abdomen. I had no idea what he was doing until five-pound-wads of fat and body batter began to flop to the floor. I'd seen my share of animals being butchered, I can't say I enjoyed the process, but I wasn't squeamish about it. That was not the case here. It was so. Fucking. Vile. Things continued to jiggle long after they should have stopped. It looked as if those pieces were still alive and looking to reincorporate themselves with their host body. It had more to do with the beasts making the floor bounce, but the mind interprets what the eye sees in whatever way it deems fitting.

He had cut a vee of fat and gristle away, at its widest it had to be two feet across and over a foot deep. I think the zombie and I understood what Akio was trying to do at about the same time.

"Bando! Go!" I shouted. The spider was trying to turn the newly exposed area away as Akio stepped back and Bando moved forward. Could just make out the yellowish mass of bone where the thing was trying to keep its operating system safe. The first two shots ricocheted—literally fucking *ricocheted* —off that thing's skull plates, the third made a hairline crack, the fourth and fifth then shattered through like an egg rolling off the kitchen counter, and what flowed out looked a lot like what would come out of a fertilized egg late in the gestation period. Fucking gross is about as descriptive as I wanted to get. This was already going to curtail any egg eating I might do in the future. I needed to stop these comparisons to consumables; I was running low on acceptable foods.

The spider's legs gave out, and if it hadn't been wedged so tightly it would have slid to the ground. We had a moment to take a breather. I mean, as much breathing as one was able to do when confronted with an odor so thick we couldn't suck air through it. For a second I got mixed up as to which horror movie we were living through, thought it might be one of the *Halloween* flicks where Michael Myers, after having suffered through every possible way to die, still came back to life to finish off what he had started. Our spider zombie was shaking back and forth; it looked like it was trying to break free. Slightly ashamed to say it took way longer than it should for me to figure out that it was the spider behind our dead one pulling the carcass free.

"Conserve your ammo," I said aloud. We'd just wait until the new interloper got hopelessly stuck, have Akio do his slice-and-dice routine, and then one of us would finish up with five shots instead of a hundred and five. That was the plan, and a damn good one if I do say so myself. The problem with that was the second spider had learned from its counterpart's mistake. It wasn't trying to pull the dead spider out, it was pushing it in, using it as a half-ton meat shield. With the dead monster out in front, we would be hard-pressed to get any good shooting or cutting angles. As long as it had that thing in its clutches, it would have plenty of protected time to work itself through the opening. And once it was in.... Well, we'd never be able to stop it in time before it ripped all of us apart. We'd offer up no more defense than cotton fuzz stuck on the lint tray.

Akio didn't hesitate, slicing the dead spider so quickly he looked like an experienced sous chef prepping vegetables. Just one more reason to dislike the green things. Then I realized that the dead spider was shaking so violently Akio didn't need to do much more than hold his sword steady as the vibrations sent ribbons of shavings streaming to the ground, his blade a deli meat slicer. Not only the world's fastest deli slicer but also the worst. If I decided to sick up, at least I was situated in the right location. There was three inches of blood, bile, intestines, and undigested body parts littering the ground, and something else—something wriggling with life. With the monsters creating a watertight seal on the door, we might need to worry about drowning in the filthy sludge. It was like looking at the garbage in the trash compactor scene in *Star Wars,* replete with our very own *dianogas.* Sure these worm things were smaller, but I had a sinking feeling they were carnivorous, just like their much larger, supposedly mythical, cousins.

"What are those!" Kirby had backed up, I don't know if I'd ever seen him quite so paralyzed with fear of anything before, and considering the nature of our apocalypse, that was saying something. He was alternating lifting his legs and standing on his tiptoes, it was strange to see ballet dancer moves coming from one wearing combat boots.

The worms, if that's what they were, were roughly the same length as nightcrawlers but easily twice, maybe three times as fat. No eyes that I could detect, but I wasn't getting any closer to look. They had a mouth though, about the same size as the tip of my middle finger, which I wanted to give them. No idea if the opening was lined with razor-sharp teeth —and again, not moving in to investigate.

"*Kiseichu!*" Isamu shouted. Akio was nodding.

"Isamu thinks they're parasites," Bando said. A grimace on his face clued me into how closely our upset stomachs were in unison.

"Fuck. Fuck. *Fuck*—" Kirby kept repeating the word, getting shriller with each iteration. It was Rose that got him to calm down somewhat by having him come into the stall with her.

One of the fat yellow worms rode the crest of a wave that broke over my foot. The slimy goo passed on by, but the parasite stuck to the top of my boot, and not like a leech lying flat, its body was sticking straight up, head down and wriggling back and forth as it tried to burrow through the leather. At least that's what I figured it was trying to do.

I also was repeating the word *fuck*, if only in my head, and it was definitely getting shriller. There are times when, as humans, we make some truly boneheaded mistakes; shit they even have something called the Darwin Awards for those of us that take ourselves out of the gene pool in the most spectacularly stupid ways possible. I pointed my rifle at my foot. I don't even want to know how close to putting a round through it I was. I would not be watching the after-action footage, for just that reason. Look at that, made a pun and didn't even mean to. Bando stomped down, hurt like the dickens but worlds better than a bullet would have felt. The mashed creature fell away dead, dropping down through the muck to the floor where two more of the things attacked, pulling it apart like taffy.

"Sorry, sir," Bando said.

"Yeah, um, no worries, thanks," was all I could manage.

Were the parasites part of the zombie? Maybe a new species that had specifically evolved to feed on zombies? No idea. They existed, that was all that mattered, and now another huge question was: What would happen if they were to feed on a human? They didn't seem too discerning in their diets. The wedged spider loosed a little over a dozen of the fat worm-things. They would pause for a moment, rising vertically as if they were sampling the air, as if they...no. They were definitely looking for their next meal.

"Fuck me," was all I could think to say when those heads swiveled our way, most toward me for some reason. I was much closer to shooting than foot mashing but was saved from either when, after one sickeningly long, bone-grinding moment, the spider was forced through the door. It fell and crushed half of the new invaders. We were now staring at spider number two. As a denizen of the planet, I know in the back of my mind that I am supposed to find beauty in all of God's creatures, that they all have their place, yada yada, blah, blah. Mosquitoes, ticks, horse flies, in fact, every biting insect can fuck right off to extinction. This list would include spiders, whether they bite or not, and while we're traveling down this road, I'm not much of an amphibian person. I mean, I won't kill them, but I'm not looking to pet one either.

Spiders, though, normal run-of-the-mill spiders? I don't like them, they freak me out. All those legs, eyes, intelligence, that web shit. They should have stayed on whatever planet they came from. My point is that no matter how much those spiders give me the willies, they have nothing on their zombie counterparts. It is such a grotesque specimen as to be nearly indescribable. Four humans melded together. All the eyes floated toward one location but in a haphazard way that didn't seem to make any sense. Just randomly placed, like a two-year-old was told to draw them in. Eight arms, eight legs, one amalgamated brain drawn down into the body. With zombies, it's still possible to see the human that once existed, to a degree anyway. The spiders though? They could have been a completely different species, the mutations so great and numerous there wasn't enough in common with us to seemingly have any evolutionary relation.

I was able to blow out one eyeball before it could regroup and grab hold of its shield. A deep rumbling bass sound emanated from its chest, I could only hope it was a savage stab of pain that had caused it. Bando had moved near me; I heard his foot stomp down and then was rewarded with a spray of something I never want identified, all over my right leg.

"They're leaving!" Kirby was still in shriek mode as he looked over the stall, he seemed to be hanging from the door to keep himself off the floor. If he hadn't been pointing down, I wouldn't have known what the hell he was talking about. The worms that hadn't been smashed into what, unfortunately, looked like lumpy mashed potatoes were heading out, not running away from us, but toward something. In an abstract way I found Kirby's reaction to the worms humorous; I say abstract because I was on the verge of flipping out my own damn self. As bad as it was for him, he had nothing on the reaction of the spider. I don't know what those parasites were all about, but the spider we were dealing with wanted nothing to do with them. It flung its dead comrade down, taking out a couple more worms, but when the rhino-sized beast saw some were still coming toward it, I watched as all its eyes grew wide in fear and it just left. It fucking scampered away in a hurry, like, the thing hauled ass outta there. As fantastic as all of that was, it boogied down the stairwell, which sucked because it destroyed our blockade. Sure it crushed a half dozen speeders in the process, but the remaining ones now had a clear path. Our slimy parasitic buddies wavered in indecision as their potential host was no longer in range. I don't know if a worm can sigh, but it sure felt like that.

"Well, I guess we'll eat *them* if we have to." (I was pretty sure that's what they were saying as they again lifted and sampled the air before dropping down and turning back toward us.)

Bando had raised his leg and was ready to stomp down when we heard a good number of speeders making their way up, now that the barricade had been thrown open. As much as I wanted out of this stupid disgusting bathroom, it was still the best defendable position we had. The speeders were barreling toward us, arms pumping, mouths clacking, eyes wide in excitement. Bando and I stood side by side and shot through the opening, taking out the first few of the vanguard. There were too many, and they were moving too fast. I wasn't exactly sure what our ammunition levels were at, but I knew we were dangerously close to being out.

I looked over at Akio; he nodded in what seemed to be him saying he would be ready once we were empty. I nodded back in thanks. We were screwed. We had been so close to escaping, to getting back to the States, back to Colorado… fucking Feroz. I hadn't heard anything from downstairs in a bit. I could only hope that they died before we did. I know that is a whole other level of petty, and I was fine with it. My magazine went dry, giving the speeders time to advance closer as Bando moved forward to pick up the slack.

"Kirby, get your ass out here!" I shouted as I grabbed my last magazine.

"Are they still out there?"

Says a lot about how irrational our fears can be, and how they can control us at the most instinctive levels. Here was a man who would volunteer to take point against an enemy like the hulking zombie spiders, yet was terrified of a baby dwarf graboid. (The little bastards freaked me out too, but it's my journal, so I'll keep that information to myself.)

"Need help!" Bando shouted.

By the time I was loaded and ready to go, the bulk of the

speeders weren't ten feet from the door, we weren't going to be able to stop them in time, even with Kirby. After all we'd been through it was going to be ironic to be taken down by what we now considered the pedestrian zombie. The worms, which had stopped in indecision, were now moving toward the door again. Good piece of information to take to the grave, while they *would* eat from us, they much preferred to feast upon zombie flesh, or zombie internals, anyway. Kirby was coming out of the stall just as I was bringing my weapon to bear—or is it bare, b.a.r.e? But that would mean I was wielding my weapon naked, which has a whole other connotation. Whatever. I was about to shoot at the frontrunner when that snarling drooling sprinting zombie happened to gaze down. Everything about that monster changed the moment he caught sight of those worms.

It couldn't stop, that wasn't going to be possible in the amount of distance it had. What it could do was veer off, which it most assuredly did. It hit the wall next to the door with enough force we heard bones breaking. It must have raised the alarm because all of the trailing zombies were also stepping to the side. The multiple thumps against the wall were enough to break some wall tiles and send the paper towel holder to the floor. It was a solid half-minute of zombies avoiding the door, I couldn't even imagine how many ACLs and MCLs were torn by the abrupt maneuvers. One zombie that had been pinned against the wall fell to the side and forward, its head not more than a foot from the nearest worm. I'm not going to say that fat wriggly thing darted at the zombie, but it moved with a quickness I wouldn't have expected. The zombie groaned, it was unable to move as another zombie, this one heavyset, had fallen on its lower half and pinned it to the ground. For a second I thought the worm was going to enter the zombie's nostril, that would have been horrible to watch, a large writhing snot being sucked back in was more than I thought my stomach could handle. Be careful what you wish for, what really happened was worse.

The worm bit down on the zombie's cheek; couldn't even begin to guess what venom, poison, and / or neurotoxin it injected, but the zombie stilled immediately. Its eyes rolled into the back of its head. Looked like a heroin addict getting its fix the way it immediately calmed down and went slack jawed. I figured this was when the worm would enter the zombie's mouth, head down the gullet, into the stomach, and maybe adhere to the intestines so it could do whatever it was it did. Nope, it went for the eye. By now we'd all stopped shooting. All of us save Rose were grouped together, entranced by what was happening. The zombies that had smashed against the wall or had been able to stop in time were making themselves scarce. Looked like teenagers at a keg party getting busted by the cops, meaning they were flying off in all directions. (That was probably self-evident, but some of you have never been deep in the woods on a cold fall night, bonfire roaring in a clearing, getting plastered with a hundred of your classmates when multiple spotlights illuminate the area and you are being told to halt and it shows.)

Even the big-boned zombie had extracted itself from the situation, abandoning our victim, because that's what it was, though this was one time I wasn't going to advocate for its rights. The worm moved. We could see the round pucker mark where it had bitten, thin black blood trailed down the zombie's cheek. It squirmed up and over to the zombie's right eye then did something I hope I never have to witness again. The worm planted its kisser on the zombie's baby blues, baby *blue* in this case, and with its tail end resting on the lower lid, it stood bang upright, the eyeball still firmly held in its mouth.

At the wet suction pop, we all let loose our versions of a gasp. For Kirby, it was a set of coughs and hiccups as he worked at stifling down what wanted to come up. It had effin' plucked the eyeball straight out of the socket. The optic nerve pulled tight as the worm stretched further up. With the sucker mouth and the eyeball holding still, the back end of the worm adjusted and scooted toward the new opening then wriggled its way into the bloody orifice followed by the squishy slurping sound of something slimy forcing its way through too narrow of an opening. When the white bloated thing was three-quarters in it released the eyeball and it was a race to see which one would get in first, the zombie's eyeball or the worm. I don't think it's a spoiler to say the worm won.

We got the unbelievable joy of getting to watch this same event four more times as the remainder of the worms sought out new lodging. The last two worms did a synchronized version where it looked like a cartoon zombie had just witnessed the most beautiful zombie seductress and both eyes had popped out of its head in a bazooinga moment. When the show was over, I had a moment of clarity.

"Akio cut its arms off!" I shouted. Took a few words from Bando and some charades play from me to get the message across. It's not often you're told to dismember a zombie instead of killing it. Watching the arms get cut off what was once a human being should have been the most disturbing thing any of us had ever seen in our lives, as it was, I'm not sure it cracked the top ten today. It took three good thwacks to amputate both appendages. The zombie didn't seem to care.

"Sir, sorry, but what the fuck are you doing?" Kirby asked when I grabbed the rope, got behind the zombie, and first gagged then tightly tied its legs together.

Akio got it immediately. He clicked his tongue and then helped me, making sure the zombie didn't move and that the bindings were tight. Isamu and Haruto in the meantime had gone back out into the room a couple of feet.

"*Kieta!*" Isamu exclaimed.

"Gone," Bando said flatly, watching me intently.

"Those worms saved our lives," I said, standing and moving away when I was done, not wanting to be any closer to the zombie than I needed to be. And it wasn't the flesh eater I was afraid of, I mean, not the big flesh eater anyway. "Okay, so they didn't save our lives in any conscious way, and I'm sure they would have eaten any of us, given the chance, but…it was the zombies they wanted and the zombies are terrified of them. They know what they are and want nothing to do with them."

"So what are we doing with the zombie?" Bando asked.

"Those worms could be a game changer. We could place them around a perimeter and zombies wouldn't enter. Could you even imagine?"

"Like a mean dog on a leash?" Kirby asked. "I think I'd rather deal with the zombies. What if they got loose?"

"A cage…" I was thinking of how the thing had elongated and stretched out so that the too-wide body could fit through the relatively narrow opening of an eye canal. "A box, a plexiglass cage."

"But…but air holes." Kirby protested.

"I don't know," I told him. "All I know is these vicious little wigglers could change everything." I wasn't sure if that was too bold a statement, but watching those zombies falling over themselves trying to get away was promising. There were always kinks to work out in any great plan.

"But air holes…" he reiterated.

"Listen, I don't know yet.… Sure, it would be great if zombies were terrified of puppies, but that's not the case. We have a potential weapon here that could very well bring us back from the brink of extinction."

"Too dangerous."

"It's a tool, like your rifle. It's a tool. It can be instrumental in saving your life or taking it. It's worth the risk."

He opened his mouth.

"Don't argue with the captain," Rose said. She was bracing herself against the bathroom stall door. Kirby immediately rushed to hold her up. The zombie began to struggle against its bonds. Whatever sedative the worm had given it was beginning to wear off, and it wanted to go about its business. Didn't seem like it was being affected at all by its new passenger—or was it considered being *infected*? I had no idea what the thing did once it was inside, figured I'd let the docs figure that out and a way to safely display our new guard-worms. Who knew? Maybe they could make a pheromone from it that would ward the zees off. Could be like industrial-grade Zombie-Off, I'd pay good money for a can of that. I was trying to figure out what I wanted to do with the newest member of our party when the Brazilians informed us that they were still alive and kicking as they again shot up into our floor.

They didn't seem to be trying to hit us. We tentatively moved out into the main room; whatever message had been broadcast out to the zombies seemed to contain the message that this floor was off-limits because none of them had come back.

"What are they doing?" Bando and I were watching as bullets smacked into the ceiling, splinters of wood were popping up into the air from the floor.

"I think they're trying to come up," I said. It was all I could figure. I mean, what other reason was there? Somehow they knew the zombies weren't here and they wanted in on the inaction. Can't say I blamed them for that at all, but there wasn't a chance in hell I was planning on sharing our space. Feroz was a ruthless enemy who by all accounts seemed incapable of compromise. She wouldn't stop trying to kill us until she was dead, that much was clear.

"Are we going to let them?"

I shook my head. He caught the motion in his peripheral vision, and even if he hadn't, it would have been hard to miss my barrel coming up to the ready. When the shooting stopped the hammering began, not sure what they were using, but it sounded like a sledge. The floor was vibrating from the heavy hits, the planking lifting and splintering away. They were desperate if they thought this was an avenue of escape. I wasn't thrilled with shooting them in their skulls when they popped up like groundhogs, but we'd tried diplomacy, and they weren't interested. Three chunks of flooring crunched and fell over, I had my rifle up against my shoulder, just waiting for the first unlucky soul to show themselves so I could send them on their way.

"Talbot!" Feroz called up. I could feel the hostility in the word as if she'd uttered a swear. To her maybe it was the same thing.

Bando looked over at me to see if I was going to respond, I shook my head slightly, I wasn't going to give our location away. No way to tell what she wanted, could have been she just wanted to make sure that when she tossed her grenade up it got close enough to take me out.

"We need safety, we are claiming…" I heard her mumbling, trying to come up with the right word. "Sanctuary!" she shouted.

I wasn't sure you could "claim" sanctuary. You could ask for it, but that didn't mean it would be granted.

"No," I said.

"No? You cannot say no!"

"Sure I can."

"Sanctuary means you allow us safety!"

"I understand the basics of the word, Feroz, I'm just not offering it to you."

"We're coming up!"

"Whoever pokes their head up will be shot."

"Refusing us sanctuary is a war crime!"

"I'm not sure what Peace Accords version you've read, but we're enemies engaged in active combat. There is nothing that says I need to look out for you and your squad's safety. For sure not if that's detrimental to me and my squad's safety. So I'm telling you, if anyone shows, they're dead. The only quarter from me you'll get is I won't attack you while you're down there, unless we get the opportunity, then that's off the table too. Fuck you, Feroz."

"We'll die down here!" This was followed by enough swears of a variety so colorful it made Bando blush.

"On you. I don't remember asking you to follow us."

"*Diabo!*"

Bando made the sign of the Trinity. "She called you the devil."

"I got that," I told him.

A volley of bullets shot in frustration punched the floor about fifteen feet from where we stood. I generally detested the thought of more people succumbing to zombies, but for Feroz, I was counting the minutes.

"Did I kill you?" she asked. I couldn't see her face to say with certainty, but it sure sounded like she had some mirth in her voice.

I didn't respond. It didn't make much sense to get into a verbal sparring match with her. It wasn't likely we were ever going to see eye to eye, and we had enough going on that I didn't want to waste any more time on her.

"Bando, will you be all right guarding that area?" I asked. I would have asked Kirby, but he was holding an in-pain Rose up, and the Japanese weren't traditionally armed and did not appear to be in any rush to be so; Akio had long ago given Rose her weapon back.

"I'll be fine, sir."

Those were his words, but he didn't look fine. He looked like a little kid on Halloween playing his first game of dunking for apples, but instead there were lemons floating around on the top of that barrel, and he'd bitten deeply into the one he'd grabbed. Odds were pretty high that he would personally know whoever he had to shoot. That would make pulling the trigger difficult.

I was worried now that the worms were housed in our

captured zombie. I almost said *safely* housed, but I had no idea. Maybe they could break through the chest or vault out of its mouth or ass, like a shit that would not be denied. That was secondary though, because the worms within a body did not appear to have the same terrifying effect on the zombies as those free-range ones had, otherwise, that second spider would never have been up close and personal to its buddy. Maybe we were all right up here, maybe we weren't. The zombies could come back. Getting our blockade back into position was important.

"How are you doing?" I asked, moving over to where Rose and Kirby were.

"Doing good, sir, now that those things aren't around."

"I was asking Rose," I told him.

"Been better, sir, but I'm okay."

She didn't look okay, but there wasn't much more we could do for her until we could get some actual medical care. I nodded instead.

"I'm going to see about getting the couches set back up. Kirby, I need you to watch Bando's back."

We helped get Rose as comfortable as we could before he went to back-up the other man. Isamu and Haruto were watching the zombie; Akio followed me without prompting.

"Could be dangerous," I told him. He merely nodded in response. "I could get used to having a friend who doesn't understand what I'm saying."

He grunted.

"In fact, it could be perfect. You'd never give me any shit for something I said. Of course, you're going to have to be the one to tell BT he's been bumped from the top. Sorry about that, can't be helped, occupational hazard and all."

He again nodded.

"Plus, this gives me the chance to talk uninterrupted for as long as I want. That sounds fairly narcissistic...Deneaux must have rubbed off on me. You ready for this?" I asked as we approached the stairs.

"*Hai.*"

I stopped to look at him. "Do you understand me?" I asked.

I don't know how to spell it, but the sound was "eee yah," or near enough. I knew that meant no. It sure did seem like he understood.

"I'm not trying to give you a speeding ticket, it's okay if you speak English."

"Hanbaga." He brought both his hands up to his mouth as if he were holding a sandwich—hands cupped, fingers an inch or two away from the thumb, then he shoved the invisible food into his widening mouth.

"Hamburger?" I asked.

"Hanbaga!" he nodded.

"You're fucking with me aren't you?"

His smile widened.

"I already have enough friends that give me shit. Don't make me regret offering you the number one spot."

"Hanbaga." He was smiling.

"Not cool, Akio, not cool at all."

Of the six couches we'd used, only two remained on the landing, the rest were scattered on the floor below. There wasn't anything we'd be able to do with the two to make the risk of going down there worthwhile. So far, the zombies downstairs didn't feel any reason to come up, and I saw no reason to change the status quo. Someone shot behind us. Smoke drifted up from Bando's weapon.

"Will you watch the stairs?" I asked Akio.

"Hambaga," he nodded.

"They're getting desperate," Kirby said, "trying to come through. Deadeye here put one through someone's hand." Kirby was all smiles, Bando still had that "I bit a lemon" look.

"Going to kill you!" Feroz screamed.

"Was it her hand?" I asked.

"Not unless she has man hands," Kirby replied.

"Like Jerry's date on 'Seinfeld?'" I asked.

"Who?" he replied.

Any humor I found in my statement was lost when I realized I'd dated myself.

"I knew what you were talking about, sir," Rose offered. "My grandfather loved that show. I found a station that ran the reruns for him."

"That doesn't make me feel any better," I muttered.

"Nosoupfoyou! Nosoupfoyou!" Akio made jazz hands and was smiling broadly; this made up for Rose's jab.

The next volley of bullets from our rowdy downstairs neighbors were fewer, although a couple of feet closer.

"We have better firing angles, Feroz. You keep doing that shit and we're going to drop a couple hundred rounds down there. Maybe we get you all, maybe we don't, but some of you will suffer, no way to survive a hail of bullets in such an enclosed space. Give me a reason." We didn't have a hundred bullets to spare on them, and they probably knew it, but that wasn't something you rolled the dice with.

I expected another diatribe, I took it as a good sign when one wasn't forthcoming. Then I remembered...if Feroz was a man, that would be a good sign, but as a woman, that quiet meant she was contemplating something that would be extremely detrimental to me. Hard to say the order of the instant chain of events that happened next.

Akio shouted "*zonbi!*" just as we heard the sound of a *whoosh* from a launched rocket. I may have also heard the sound of an approaching engine somewhere before, during, or after the maelstrom, but fuck all if could recall which had happened first. The visitor center shook violently—I was genuinely concerned about its structural integrity—dying by building collapse made you just as dead as a bullet or a bite.

"Get Rose!" Superfluous words, as Kirby had already been up and heading back.

Rifle fire was intense and moving below us. Feroz and company thought there was a window of opportunity to escape and were going balls to the wall to make good on it. There was no sense in letting their actions go to waste in regard to us. Isamu and Haruto had the zombie up and were waiting to see what we were going to do next. Akio had backed up as a burning speeder came up the stairs, literally burning, its clothes were on fire. I stitched it with a three-round burst. Two nailed it in the head, the third sailed over as the zombie fell away and down into a trio of them. They hesitated, realizing there was food on two sides. One of them jumped the railing and headed toward the fleeing Brazilians, they must have been closer. A second was shot and dropped. I'd have to send them a thank you card at some point. Akio neatly took the head off the third one.

"Bando, help Kirby!" I stayed at the top of the stairs. Outside came the heavy thumping of a fifty-cal machinegun. Yoki had brought help.

"Get some!" I could hear BT yell even over the explosive sounds of the heavy caliber rounds. He was finally drowned out as the chatter of a half dozen or more rifles joined in with his.

I headed to the windows to get an idea of what was happening. My squad had cleared the ground around their trucks of zombies for twenty to thirty feet in any direction. Concentrated fire was blasting into the lower floor. The building continued to shake—I wasn't sure how much more of this it could take. I saw some sparks and holes appear on the trucks as the Brazilians shot back at them.

"Fuck this." I'd had enough of Feroz and her Merry Band of Idiots.

I bounded past Akio who wore a confused expression, I would imagine wondering what the crazy round eye was about to get up to. Is that racist? Can I be racist about myself? Or was that self-deprecation? I should probably be thrilled that those of us left aren't overly concerned with being politically correct. The niceties of society tend to be the first things out the window during an apocalypse. Easy to get upset over inane slights when life isn't difficult. Even going so far as to make drama up when life isn't a struggle.

I got on the first landing. Feroz had five people with her, three were focused on the zombies, she and the remaining two on the trucks. She was partially hidden from me, otherwise I would have taken her out first. I was not expecting them to react as quickly as they had. I put my first round through the lungs of the nearest soldier, and immediately four rifles swung my way, I was mid-dive when bullets sizzled past, one had got close enough to dig a shallow groove across my shoulder blade. It felt as if one had scraped a red-hot poker against my skin. I had gone over the stairs, away from the Brazilians, and had no sooner made an ungraceful landing when I heard one of them scream. It was not in triumph, but rather in piercing pain. By taking their eyes off the zombies and onto a new prize, they'd lost another one. That seemed to be their defacto operating procedure. Made about as much sense as eating a Tide Pod for likes. (Likes! I mean seriously, *LIKES!* What did you trade those in for? Certainly not to regain your health or life. At one point I thought social media was going to be humanity's downfall. I'm convinced that given enough time, it would have been.)

I was now in double enemy territory, not the greatest place to be. I was forgotten for the time being as Feroz finally figured out that her only chance of survival lay in escape. I could tell by their fields of fire where they were headed, it was going to bring them right past me, and at that point I was going to have to decide on what I was going to do about it. If I caught them completely unawares there was a chance I could take them all out, but then I'd be front and center for the zombies. And I was way too low on ammo to even make a decent final stand showing. Honestly, my best course of action was inaction. Bullets were flying from multiple directions as they came inside and from above. If I could have folded in on myself and disappeared, this would be the time. I was seriously considering trying that trick as a trio of bulkers came thundering in. One of them collided with the framing for a window and completely demolished the heavy aluminum column. It slid across the floor and came to a jarring stop not four feet from where I was doing my best to become an inanimate object.

I saw no way that Feroz could get away from the pincer she was in, and just when you think something is impossible, the possible happens. Two of her people came into view, Feroz was next, I didn't think about it, not even for the briefest of moments. Had never been my style to overly contemplate, no matter how many times that had been detrimental to my health, my welfare, and / or my sanity. I raised that rifle and pulled the trigger. Okay, let me back up. I *tried* to pull the trigger. Funny thing about an M-4, it's impossible to pull the trigger on an empty rifle, well, that's not a hundred percent true. I could have pulled the charging handle back and dry-fired, but the result would have been the same, all click, no bang.

I made no sound except maybe a frustrated sigh, but I did not go unnoticed; Feroz caught sight of my movement. A malicious grin split her face as she turned to shoot. I was saved by the two trailing her, one screamed in pain as she was bitten on the shoulder and the man hit Feroz in the side just as she shot, so the bullet punched the wall not four inches from my head, and she was not able to get another shot off as the man forcibly ushered his commander along and to the side, grabbing her to escape. I thought she might shoot *him* to get away, and maybe she would have if she thought she could have got the angle. A heartbeat later zombies followed the Brazilians and right on their heels was what could only be described as a sheet of lead. Blood, bones, wood, glass, bits of couches and furniture were clouding the air as the bullet-fueled wind whipped through the foyer. The assault went on for another two minutes, I'd since dropped to the ground and covered my face, I had this thing about not breathing aerosolized glass.

"Talbot! Where the fuck are you!" I was surprised I could hear BT's voice over the disruption and destruction my eardrums had gone through. "Let's go!"

A hand had grabbed my shoulder and was pulling me up. It was Akio. Kirby and Bando were already down the stairs, chair-carrying Rose toward the trucks. Isamu and Haruto had the struggling zombie. By the way Akio was pulling on me, I could tell we were not out of the woods yet. And considering we'd been in the fucking jungle for months with no end in sight, that made sense. I was a bit out of sorts, the sounds had messed with my equilibrium which in turn seemed to be affecting my ability to think properly. I was patting my body, looking for a full magazine I did not possess. Akio was shouting a string of words at me that I couldn't possibly understand, and at the time I was confused as to why that was. Yeah, that's how out of it I was. BT did not look relieved when he saw us, and that did not bode well. Should have been a lot of high-fiving and the *pssts* of numerous cans of beer being opened in celebration, instead I got shoved and lifted.

I was forced back into my seat as the truck took off. We were rocked from side to side as first one, then two then dozens of zombies struck us on the broadside. I watched faces mash up against the window, teeth chipped and broke, lips split, tongues were severed as they struck. Then a violent head butting not only cracked the skull of the zombie but also sent a spiderweb of lines along the surface of the glass. A couple more hits like that and I was going to be face-to-face with one of them. The engine noise rose and we slowed; I looked out over the seat and the windshield to see the wall of bodies we were contending with. It didn't look good until BT's vehicle pulled up alongside and he went to town on our obstruction, the punishing rounds obliterating everything in their path. They were not falling away so much as being dissipated. Couldn't happen to a nicer enemy. Then we jumped forward and fishtailed as the restrained power was finally freed to do its thing.

We all got jostled around, hard enough that I smacked my head against the window and finished what the zombies had started, looked like a scene from *Night at the Roxbury* when Chris Kattan's character took out the glass in a head-bobbing rave moment.

"Fuck." I put my hand up to my head and it came away with blood.

"Sorry, sir," Stenzel said from the driver's seat, she was looking at me through the rearview mirror. I waved away my response. My head throbbed, probably had a concussion. Twenty minutes later when we came to a stop, the pain had diminished to nearly non-existent, but blood still trickled from the wound. Major Dylan looked over Rose, Catalina came over to me. She grabbed some tweezers and pulled out a few chunks of embedded safety glass. That was fun.

Tracy looked like she was ready to spit nails. I had no idea why; wasn't like I'd planned a sneak attack on myself. Her body was tense, her arms hanging down by her sides, and if I didn't know better, I would have thought a slap was coming. She unexpectedly hugged me, not sure if I was ready for the violence of it. You would think a hug couldn't be violent, I'm here to tell you differently. She pulled me in so tightly I was half expecting a rib to break...or maybe she was going for the long game, making me die by asphyxiation.

"Talbot," was all she said as she let go of the hug. She held me at arm's length and looked into my eyes. "I thought you were dead."

A shit-eating grin and some sarcastic bullshit about how I

couldn't be killed weren't going to cut it, not this time. I wisely did something my dad had clued me in to many moons ago. If you don't know what to say, don't say anything. You can get in far more trouble or make matters worse by saying something you don't mean or that had no basis in truth. It wasn't something I practiced very often, damn near had no experience in it, if I'm being truthful. Still did it. I thought tears had formed in the corner of her eyes, I had a tough time telling because my own had formed. We hugged again, and this time I wasn't in danger of being compacted. I would have kissed her, but without looking in a mirror for confirmation, I was fairly assured I was disgusting.

5

MIKE JOURNAL ENTRY 5

AFTER MAJOR DYLAN had spent some time on Rose and felt satisfied she was in stable condition, we got back underway. It was a relatively quiet ride, the only one talking was Kirby, who would periodically say something in anger. The Brazilians had taken most of his hoarded MREs. He was not taking it well. Stayed on the road a good three hours until I called for a halt —it was all I could take. There was no way Feroz was going to catch up, and I needed to clean up, desperately. As near as I could tell we were in Honduras, another hell hole, but as far as I knew only in terms of weather. It was sweltering. We were outside the city limits of Choluteca, for all that meant to me. We weren't on a sightseeing tour. It was a tiny village, a hamlet maybe. It was fairly nice, or it had once been, and the city off in the distance looked beautiful, but looks could be deceiving. High-population zones were usually havens for zombie hordes and evil people.

We did a quick but thorough investigation of the general area. There were signs of a zombie struggle here, but the dried brown streaks of blood on some of the walls spoke to how long ago it had happened.

"This might have been from the very beginning," BT said.

"Sir!" Justin called from one of the adobe homes BT and I were outside of.

"Is that weird, him calling you sir?" BT asked.

"Can't say I like it," I replied before heading in.

Justin was in the hallway just past the living room, and a kitchen area was off to the right. House couldn't have been more than thirty feet across.

"You all right?" BT asked my son. "You look a little pale."

He pointed behind him and to what I imagined was a bedroom. He wordlessly walked past us and outside. We weren't in immediate danger, that much was clear, but I had a feeling neither of us were going to like what we saw down there.

"Rock, paper, scissors?" I asked.

He smacked my shoulder and started to walk.

"That's not one of the choices," I said rubbing where he'd hit.

"Goddammit. Just goddammit." His frame nearly took up the entire door casing. All I could see was the far wall and the pastel pink shade of the paint.

I echoed his words, and as yet I hadn't seen a goddamn thing.

"Yeah, go back. I've seen enough of the nightmare for the both of us." He backed up, closing the door and making sure to scrape me down the hallway like the last bit of cake topping in a frosting bag.

"What did you see?" I asked when we were back in the living room.

"Three dead zombies and a mother protecting her children with a machete."

I inferred the rest. If she had been successful we would have been asking her where I could take a shower and maybe scare up some homemade tamales. Right then though I had no appetite. "This is one of those instances where it's hard to see a silver lining, but not impossible."

"Careful, Talbot."

"I'm not a monster, I'm merely saying that if there were bodies in there that means there aren't any zombies."

"That's some tarnished silver right there, maybe even slightly green-tinged, but you're not wrong."

I went outside. Justin looked like shit, talk about green-tinged. No sense in asking him how he was doing, that was self-evident. "Are you sure you want to stay on the squad? That won't be the last, um, distasteful thing you'll scout out."

"I'll be fine." He walked away.

"Sir," I called after him.

"*Sir,*" he spit the word out like it was rotten, it had the affectation of a swear.

Got similar reports from Bando and Gary. There had been some fighting here, but it was not widespread, and for once it looked as if people had won, or at the very minimum forced a draw. It was unlikely that the villagers had gone down to the last one standing, but it was strange that the victors had not buried their dead. Maybe they had been evacuated or headed off to somewhere they thought was safer.

Found a well behind the property, and ten pumps later the squeaky arm and aerated mud water flowed out followed quickly by clear, cool almost cold water. Even in the heat of the day it was going to be a bracing shower. I was thinking about how fast I could clean up when BT found me.

"Haven't had much time to talk, and I'm not sure what I'm hearing from Kirby makes any sense; every time I ask him a question about it he starts shivering and his voice rises. So I figured I'd come to you."

"Make it quick. I'm going to want that sun beating down on me while I scrape off layers of grime."

"Why do we have an armless zombie?"

I told him, he didn't believe me. Not completely anyway.

"Are you sure it wasn't something else that had them

spooked?" he asked. "Like maybe they were taking too many casualties?"

"I saw what I saw, we all saw it. The parasites housed inside that zombie could change everything."

"Kirby is of the mind that we should burn it 'and burn it with fire.' I'm not sure what else we could burn it with, but those were his words."

"I don't have any idea what those things do once they're inside, maybe nothing besides siphoning off some food. Could be just the introduction phase the zombies want nothing to do with. Can't blame them either. Getting bitten with a paralyzing neurotoxin so you can get your eye pulled out so a creature can climb in the empty socket it created would be traumatic for anyone. Here's a little bonus I'm just now thinking of, I bet that what the worm thing injects does nothing for pain management." I shivered, which, given the gross state of dried gunk on my body made the gesture unwelcome. "We'll let the docs figure out the details, brother. I need to clean up."

"Yes, let's give dangerous things to the science-y ones. Nothing ever goes wrong in their hands. Nuclear bomb for one!" he shouted as he walked away.

I searched two houses for a new bar of soap with no luck; I had to tamp down my inner germ phobias to grab a used bar. Got a plastic five-gallon water jug and jabbed some small holes into the bottom. Grabbed some clotheslines and sheets and made an impromptu outside shower. Even had a pulley rig to hoist the dripping bucket. The water felt great for the first couple of minutes as I lathered up, then it began to feel like I was getting lanced with tiny icicles as I struggled to rinse off. By the time the bucket was empty, I was clean and freezing. I was about to grab a sheet—because in all my elaborate preparations I'd not thought to grab new clothes—when BT's meaty arm appeared. In his fist were some new threads.

"Thanks, man."

"I didn't want to expose the kids to any new horrors."

A line had begun to form for the fancy accommodations. I filled up the bucket for the next in line.

BT had set up a guard rotation, and we stood looking down the roadway the way we'd come.

"You think she's following?"

"I know she is," I told him.

The night was quiet, peaceful even. The heat of the day was replaced by a surprisingly cool night, and the threat of rain was in the air. Sometime in the wee hours of the morning, the heavens opened up with a thunder and lightning show that looked more like a battle between the gods than a terrestrial storm. I knew going back to sleep after that first sky-pounding was out of the question, seemed it was the same for most of us there. Not Henry though, the pup was sawing logs so loudly I figured he was trying to drown out the surrounding storm cacophony. Smart strategy, wish I'd thought of it. I was looking out the window of the one-bedroom bungalow the entire Talbot clan had taken refuge in. Couldn't see much beyond the sheet of flowing water traveling down the surface of the glass. I felt peaceful right then; for right or wrong I wasn't even expecting the jump scare of some monster slamming up against the house. I was in a contemplative mood as I sat in a wicker chair. I was thinking of the family that lived here and what their lives must have been like. Did they commute into the city, or were they farmers? Maybe bringing their labors into the city to sell every day, or trading with their neighbors for what they needed. Moments before the sun was to make its daily appearance the rain stopped like its shift was over. I didn't get much in the way of traditional sleep, but I felt rested. My internal batteries, which had been in full draining mode for the last few days, were in the process of recharging. Maybe two or three more years like this and I could top them off. We just weren't made to deal with all-the-time, all-encompassing stress, it was entirely too taxing on our systems. Sure, some struggle was necessary for the betterment of an individual, even a society, but keeping full tension on a being's physical and mental strings only led to breaks, and when a person broke there was usually no way back. I don't like being prophetic.

Holly was stirring. The funny thing about that dog, she loves her bed so much she gets angry, actually *angry*, when she has to get up and go take care of some business. It's hilarious if you know what's going on. Otherwise, that deep rumbling growl can be intimidating, and if she's feeling somewhat more ferocious, she'll even lash out at the air, biting it aggressively. First few times she did that she scared the hell out of me, I fully expected to be under attack in moments. Eventually, she will drag herself off of whatever pillow or blanket she's using as bedding and reluctantly make her way to a door so she can go outside. The first time this happened I followed her out, rifle in hand, looking for the danger. When she meandered around to find a spot suitable for soaking, I relaxed somewhat. Same thing the second and third time this happened. It was on the fourth I finally figured it out. I'm not going to say she still doesn't startle the shit out of me, but at least I don't feel like I have to worry about zombies on her every alert.

She was growling, eyes still closed when came the sound of a gunshot. I didn't even take the time to grab my boots before I was out the door, rifle in hand. I was in time to see the birds flying off in droves from where they'd been perched. It was on the second and third shots I figured out where it was coming from. It was closer to the center of the small village, where the majority of the civilians were housed. I'd already been moving quickly to the location, but began sprinting when I heard the screams. A man stumbled out of a picturesque home, one that might be on the cover of any country living magazine. Even after a couple of years of neglect, it was nearly idyllic, even had a decorative white picket fence; I could picture a happy dog running up and down the length, wagging his tail at passersby. Blood was flowing out of the side of him like a tapped maple tree at the height of sap season. He paid no attention to the wound; tears streaked his face, he fell to his knees and he made a long mournful wail as his head dipped to his chest.

I knew the man, Genjie with a hard G sound, whom I called *Ganja* because I'm the mental equivalent of a newly pubescent boy. He was fine with it. There was a bit of a language barrier, but we both loved the sweet leaf, and we'd bonded over talking about different strains. We were always fundamentally going to be at odds, as he was a sativa fan and I was an indica lover. I much preferred a good couch-locking buzz over letting the rabid hamsters in my brain have free rein. That was the best way I could describe the two strains and he seemed to agree, but still preferred the crazies. Normally, I have an issue with someone who smiles continuously—I've said it before, but those are generally the people that are hiding the most. But with him, I never got that feeling. He just so happened to be a "glass may only be half full, but I will enjoy it as if it were overflowing and will share it with all those around me" type of person. It was a rarity back in the days before zombies, and now it was unheard of.

"Genjie?" I asked. I had my rifle trained on him. "Genjie where are your kids? Where's Vedel?" Vedel was his wife. She was affable enough, but compared to her husband she was damn near dour. They had two kids, both still in the phase of needing their asses wiped, so I generally steered clear.

"*Morta!*" he wailed.

"What happened, Genjie?" I moved in on him slowly. No wife, no kids, no zombies, and a bleeding man kneeling outside...easy enough to snap those pieces together. "Fuck." I had his head in my sights. What did we do with a person who had not concluded the suicide part of a murder-suicide? "Fuck, Genjie, what did you do?"

By now nearly all of our troop was there. Major Dylan was pushing forward, a medical bag in hand.

"Hold up, Major," I told her, momentarily taking my forward hand off my rifle to halt her progress.

"He's injured."

"I realize that, Major, I'm still trying to assess the situation. You could potentially be in danger."

All eyes turned when the front door crashed against the wall. It was Vedel, a crazy-haired, googly-eyed Vedel holding a rifle. She was covered in blood as if she'd bathed in it. She raised her rifle and was aiming in at Genjie, I didn't know the specifics, whether she was finishing off what she'd started or whether she was meting out swift justice. Whichever it was, I couldn't have her shooting—not with so many others around.

"Vedel put the gun away!" I shouted, training my weapon on her. It was impossible to tell if she was insane with anguish or just insane. I had a second, maybe less. I shot. I'd not even had the time to process if I was going for a disabling shot. Training took over and I did what I was trained for. I put one straight through her side, blowing out her heart and lungs. She never had the opportunity to pull that trigger. She fell into the ornate metal railing and tipped over and out into what I'm sure was once a beautiful flowerbed, but was now overgrown with weeds.

My heart was pounding, it felt like it was lodged in my throat. I had the sensation that I had just made an enormous mistake, the kind which you cannot come back from. It is a surreal sensation where you mentally feel detached from your body, that what has happened can't possibly have transpired. Your mind runs through it dozens of times in seconds, attempting to make sense of something that makes no sense. Someone pushed my rifle down and me to the side and ran to her, ended up being BT. I think it was Catalina who rushed into the house. Major Dylan went to work on Genjie as Stenzel and Kirby watched over them.

I watched as Catalina came out of the house and gave a terse headshake to BT. Pretty sure I was in shock. I was seeing everything, but processing none of it. It all just seemed like a batch of still images with no context that I could tell.

"Dad?" It was Travis.

I didn't immediately answer as I seemed to be having the same issue with my audio as my visual. I could hear just fine, but words carried no meaning that I could attach in my mind. He could have been speaking in tongues for all the sense he made. He tugged on my arm. The sensation of touch still seemed to work. I turned to look at him.

"Travis?" I asked like sixty years had passed and I did not recognize the aged body he now inhabited.

"Are you okay?"

"I don't know what happened." And right then I didn't. Something had been happening that required immediate action on my part, but fuck all if I could remember what it was.

BT was hustling toward me. "Help me get him away from here." He was talking to Travis as he plucked my rifle from my numb hands.

"What's happened?" Tracy saw the sorry state of me.

BT subtly shook his head. I did not miss it, but again, right then I didn't realize it meant we weren't going to openly discuss it.

I was directed toward a chair residing on a porch, out of sight from where the event had transpired. In one hand I had a bottle of water, in the other a beer, I think Justin had wrangled that up for me. I was alternating each hand, taking large drafts of whatever was in my mouth at the time. It was an hour later when I felt more like myself. That's not saying much. It was like me getting back to my regularly scheduled insanity. Still not optimal. BT had left for a bit, and when he came back he pulled up a chair and was facing me. I think he would have grabbed my hands if they weren't full.

"I shot her, right?"

BT nodded.

"She's dead?"

He nodded again. "Not that this is going to make you feel any better, Mike, but she killed her children and was planning on killing Genjie."

"How's he doing?" I asked.

"Major Dylan is operating now, I had Bando ask about him. She was confident he would make a full recovery physically, but we all know that man lived for his kids."

"Do you know what happened?" I finished the water so I could put it down, then wiped the corners of my eyes with the back of my hand.

"From what I'm gathering it sounds like they were fighting, or Vedel was, I don't think I've ever seen Genjie have a cross word with anyone. She was threatening to leave him. No telling if he said he was going to keep custody of the kids or exactly what happened. Whatever it was, she didn't like the prospective outcome."

"Custody? What the fuck, BT? Wasn't like he was going to be taking them out of the country! Even if they divorced she would see the kids every damn day!"

"I know, Mike, I know. None of this makes sense. She snapped. There's a disassociation when that happens. No rational cognitive thought. You saved Genjie's life."

It's hard to think like that when you take another's away, I thought. To him, I said, "Somehow, I don't think he's going to be all that appreciative of that."

"Maybe, maybe not. Time will tell. You need to know that the shooting itself was justifiable."

"What if it wasn't?" I asked. "What then? What if Vedel had been trying to kill Genjie for killing the children?"

"Still justifiable, that's not how we mete out justice."

"Since fucking when?"

He shrugged. We sat in silence for a while longer before he

stood and gently clapped my shoulder. "I'm going to set up a guard rotation...looks like we're spending the night here again."

I said nothing.

One more day ended up being three more, even then Major Dylan was hesitant to move Genjie, that was until I informed her that we ran the very great risk of the Brazilians catching up to us and then it wouldn't only be her patient's life in danger. Even then she hemmed and hawed.

"Major Dylan, how many more shooting victims can you administer care to?" I asked. That was all the motivation she needed.

It was approaching noon as we departed what I had thought was a perfect little village, and I suppose on its own it was. Wasn't until you threw humans into the mix that paradise went to hell. Seriously, what couldn't we fuck up? Giving intelligence to humans was like giving rifles to cats, no good could come from it. It bothers me sometimes just how country-centric I was. There was no part of me that realized just how vast South America, and now the lower parts of Central America, were. Honestly, I'd just never cared enough to know. It was Catalina who informed me that Mexico was some twelve hundred miles from where we were. I thought about demoting her, that's no less than she would have deserved for bringing me news I didn't want to hear. I would have if that wasn't so damned petty.

I was surly, hot, tired, and still reeling plenty from the deaths of Vedel and the kids. In all likelihood, when Vedel was finished offing Genjie she would have killed herself. For the life of me, I couldn't figure out why people that did murder/suicides didn't just skip over the murder part. Just because they were miserable fucks who no longer desired to live doesn't mean they should take someone else out with them. The anger I harbored for Vedel was all-consuming and getting worse. I already had legions of my own demons; I didn't need outside-sourced ones. I had lobbied for pushing six hundred miles a day for the next two days so we could be in Mexico. That was a lot of time to sit in a car or truck, but I figured the benefit to morale of some serious mileage covered would outweigh the discomfort. We—and by we, I mean the rest of us—came up with a more doable four hundred miles a day.

I was not thrilled with the extra travel day even though I had no clue as to what my rush was, wasn't like I had to get back to the office for a useless conference call. I know I've written about those before, but that was another of those things that should have been banned, right alongside beans. Yeah, I said it, don't even feel bad. Fucking things are like eating wet dirt. Did I mention I was surly? At the end of the day, four hundred miles would have been fantastic; we made it just over a hundred when one of the trucks overheated. Smoke billowed from under the hood, then some rocket scientist had the good idea of popping the radiator cap off, ended up with some burns on their hand. I don't want to name names, but goddammit, Kirby. He had better hope it took a couple of weeks to heal up because BT was waiting in the wings to punish him for the destruction of government property. And for you civilians that didn't know, oh yes, that is indeed a thing. When you are in the service you *are* government property, and as such, if you get hurt in a way that they deem inappropriate, you can be subject to the Uniform Code of Military Justice. Higher-ups get pissed if you break a bone punching a wall instead of catching a bullet in defense of the country's ideals and needs.

Kirby's burnt hand not withstanding, we ended up stopping for an early lunch while the truck cooled down and we could fill it back up with some fluids without it acting like Mount Vesuvius. We'd been on the road another hour or two, I'd just dozed off when we were once again coming to a stop. I kept my comments to myself because I was on the verge of lashing out at anyone close enough to receive it. I got out and stretched, wondering what was going on. A Dodge truck with BT in the passenger seat had banged a u-turn and was heading back down the highway. There were three transports back there from what I could tell.

"Anyone know what's going on?" I asked.

"Hopefully it's not the radiator," Kirby responded holding his wrapped, injured hand close to his body.

It had to be over a hundred. The heat and humidity were stifling; I had some genuine concern for our tires. I was worried about the animals, too. Any of them that had to go outside to take care of bathroom needs I carried or had carried to the side of the road and then back to their ride. Paws would burn quickly on asphalt, could easily have cooked a pizza. I also didn't let any of them linger for too long outside. Only us smart apes stayed out in the un-air-conditioned climate. Henry looked at me like I'd gone bonkers when I asked if he wanted out. Not sure how he did it, but he made himself denser so that he could sink further into the bed of pillows arranged for him. If he could have spoken, he would most assuredly have told me to shut the door because I was letting the heat in. I had my first smile in days.

"Holy shit Rasher," I said as I carried the pig to the side of the road. I had no idea if hooves could burn, but I wasn't willing to risk it. The porker was not only the largest of our animal contingent, he was also the biggest baby. He did not deal well with any type of pain or even the slightest scornful remark. Ben-Ben had barked at him once for chewing his ball, and Rasher had tried to hide behind a kitchen chair—which did nothing to conceal his nearly two-hundred-pound bulk. "What have I been feeding you?" I rose to pop my back after setting him down.

I had just completed the unenviable task of putting him back in his ride when BT pulled up. He rolled down his window.

"Hot out there," he said needlessly, or not so much, if he was busting my balls. "You look flushed."

"Just carried Rasher out to piss. What's going on?"

"Bando thinks it's the transmission."

"And?" I wasn't in the mood for a discussion. The smile I'd had moments earlier had melted away.

"It's a goner. They're transferring everything out of it now, should be back on the road in ten."

"I want that thing permanently disabled. The Brazilians have better mechanics than we do."

He nodded then had Stenzel turn back around. True to his word we were back on the road in under ten. By the time we called it quits I'm not so sure we'd gone more than two hundred miles. I was pissed. And if that isn't the definition of a malcontent. Here we were rolling more miles up in a day than we could have previously done in a week, and that wasn't good enough. The heat, besides screwing with the vehicles, was also having an adverse effect on the personnel, both military and civilian. It was BT who called for a premature stop in another town, much like the previous one. I had a thought of confiscating all the guns not in military hands to avoid another set of unnecessary deaths, but the civilians in this case were as important to the defense of our community as we were. To unarm them risked all of us. Then I started thinking of yellow flag laws that had started creeping in right before our world tanked. How did one determine if someone was too crazy to carry a gun? By that measurement, I should be the first to have mine taken.

I'm not sure what voodoo was happening in whatever sunscorched fuck stain of a country we found ourselves in, but as soon as the blister-bestowing bitch went down, the temperature plummeted. According to the outside thermometer on the deck I found myself on, it was now fifteen degrees Celsius, which I was told meant sixty degrees. I found that oddly chilly; thankfully I had stumbled upon easily the nastiest liquor humankind had ever created. (No, not white wine, tequila.) I absolutely hated the shit, and I had zero in the way of a mixer. I was six shots in when Tommy sat down next to me. He held out a canteen.

"Is this one of those times where you tell me to stay properly hydrated and to take a water break?" I asked.

"Not so much, Mr. T. Open it up."

I did then took a whiff. "That Kool-Aid?"

"The MRE version, I think they call it Red Drink."

"That'll do," I said as I took a big swig. It was debatable which tasted worse, that or the cactus piss. Wasn't sure how the two together were going to be as I tipped the bottle into the canteen.

"Want some?" I asked to be socially polite, but truth be told I didn't want to share, and I wanted to be alone. Or as alone as my pack of furry family would allow, though I never resented them being near. They never judged, and that was what I needed right then.

"No thank you, Mr. T. Just checking up on the family and then I have a turn at guard duty."

"You realize I'm not Mr. T, to you right?" I asked. I found it odd that for a while he had referred to me as "dad" and then reverted back to his old moniker for me.

He smiled but said nothing. My eyes narrowed for a second, then when he turned to go into the house I shrugged and took as much of the mixed cocktail in as I could in one go. It was best to get this buzz on as quickly as possible, otherwise I'd be sipping this garbage all night, and I didn't want to be sober for that long. The taste, instead of getting better as I got more inebriated, got significantly worse, but that was most likely due to the fact that with every gulp I would top the canteen off with more tequila. By the time I passed out my mixed drink had far more liquor than mixer. If I worked as a bartender, I would have been the most popular in town, but I'd be fired after the first party. I was mostly through with the canteen when I got the sobering realization that Tommy wasn't around. He hadn't been since the refinery.

I awoke to the slobbering ministrations of Henry. My face was coated in thick, slimy saliva, which was distressing enough, but I could feel the deep rumbling of a growl in his broad chest.

"I'm up, I'm up." I wasn't. I was sheeted; I had so many sheets to the wind I had to make up a new term. "Oh fuck —*did I shit myself?*" My nose wrinkled. This was going to be a new low for me, drinking to the point I defecated myself, yeah, that's the definition of rock bottom. I sat up. I was afraid to open my eyes; I could feel my brain sloshing around inside its skull cage. I felt a blanket fall away, at some point Tracy had covered me up. I vaguely remembered her trying to wake me, I think I told her I wanted to sleep under the stars so I could see YourAnus. Good to know that even under the influence of alcohol I could hold on to my juvenile attitude. She may have given up at that point. Pretty sure I snored like a lumberjack when I was drunk; I would have left me there too.

I flipped one lid open. The moon was up high and reflecting plenty of light. I thought how fantastic it was that I was going to be able to see myself and what I'd done in all its moonlit glory. I sat up when I saw that it wasn't only Henry that was on alert. Riley was standing, her ears up, and Ben-Ben, Chloe and Holly were making a wall of canine menace. Behind them, Rasher shored up the lines. I was giving him the benefit of the doubt. Patches was at the door scratching to be let in. I tried to stand, fell over to the side instead. I was going to blame that on my feet getting tangled up in the blanket, even if that had already fallen away. There was a possibility I had not shit myself, although I didn't have enough faculties about me to realize what may have actually been going on. Riley began to snarl and bark, strings of drool were dripping from her muzzle. I turned to reach out for my rifle and fell over the chair I'd been passed out on. I tried to climb back into it, didn't quite work out.

"Ouch," I said more out of reflex than pain. "I might be a little ineepiated." I let out a small laugh at my crappy verbalization. "What am I doing?" I was looking at a stone paver up close and personal, as if I were inspecting it for damage. The smell of boiled liver grew. "That's not my shit." I came to that realization because I never ate liver. For all that insight, it was astoundingly insane how much trouble I was having putting a two-piece puzzle together.

"There you are." I reached further for my rifle and slid completely off the chair and thudded to the ground. "Ow." This time I meant it when my hip landed on my holstered pistol. "Oh yeah," I said, twisting my body so I could grab the weapon, although my wispy grasp on higher functioning had no idea of why. Still, habit was kicking in; instinctually I knew I was in a fuck ton of trouble. Hard to fight for your life when you're ineepiated.

"Help." It came out conversationally toned and was immediately followed by my laughing. To anyone listening, it wasn't going to sound like I was in any great distress. Henry had turned and butted his head against mine. I was wondering when he had gotten so tall. "Oh yeah, I'm on the ground." I laughed again. Henry barked in my face, coating me with a decent amount of slobber. "You're harshing my high." I sat up and dragged a sleeve across my face.

"Dad?" Travis was at the door. "Damn!" Patches startled him as she bolted inside. My son, who had been smart enough to not get falling down drunk, was on it immediately. "Zombies!" he shouted loud enough to wake the undead.

"Ohhhhh!" I was in the process of pushing myself up. "So I didn't shat myself. That's good news." Although those two things weren't mutually exclusive, I could still have done so *and* zombies were in the area. I was going to go with the odds that these weren't corollary statements, not an "if A then B" type of thing. I was pretty smart when I was drunk. "Help. I've fallen and I can't get up." I again hit the chair and sat down hard upon it. "Don't tell the trademark police I used that line. Shh." I went to hold a finger up by my mouth, ended up inadvertently digging for gold. "Fucking ow." That was not the first thing that I had hurt that night. Activity was happening all around after Travis had sounded the alarm. I would be angry with myself in the morning for not being the one to do that. I was so polluted this was a fight I should by all rights be sitting out. Then my hand was forced as one of the stinky bastards that was trying to make it look like I'd crapped myself came around the corner.

Travis must have gone back to retrieve a weapon and get everyone else up. I was alone with my fur shield, but fucked up or not, I was not going to allow them to be in harm's way for my dumb ass. I yanked on my pistol, giving myself a wedgie as I pulled. It would not come free. I was on my tiptoes trying to free the welded-in-place gun—the snap finally let go and my hand flew into the air like I just didn't care. Even wasted I knew this comedy of errors was going to have some very real consequences soon enough if I didn't attempt to gather my scattered wits into a usable pile. It was kind of like trying to show a squirrel how to hammer a nail. I brought my gun down to aiming level.

"Which one do I shoot?" I asked as I tried first with both eyes open then only my left, then my right. There always seemed to be three of them. The not-so-funny thing about it was there ended up being three of them. I shot, the gun recoiled, and my arm went back like it was boneless.

"Four!" I shouted as the zombie, or mirage, on the left fell over, a chunk of its skull twirling away in the moonlight, glittering wetly as it did so. "Why do golfers shout a number before they swing? If you're going to go that route might as well say sixty-nine!" I shouted the last part then fired again. Two for two, as the zombie on the right's head swelled then popped. The side of its face sheered away, and teeth tinkled to the ground. I thought I was getting sober as my attacking trio had become one lone stinker. I was having more fun than I had a right to. "I should be dead." The zombies had come around the side of the house not more than twenty feet away. Speeders could cover that distance in a second or two; I could guarantee it had been many times that amount of time.

Before I could stop the last one, another shot came out, it was a rifle. I followed the devastation back from the brained zombie to the door of the house. Travis was standing there, the barrel of his heavy caliber hunting rifle smoking.

"Nice shooting, Tex."

He looked at me funny. Even if that came out perfectly, it was still a weird thing to say. He walked all the way outside, Justin and Dallas right behind.

"Shufflers," Travis said.

"Shufflers?" That was like finding an actual leprechaun in your Lucky Charms. As far as any of us knew they were rarer than people, much more so, as they were mortal enemies with the many other varieties of zombies. They were the equivalent of Cro-Magnon in a homo-sapiens dominated world.

"Whoa," was all I could manage when it became apparent there were more of them, a lot more of them, shuffling out from the shadows. "Tally ho!" I was full of wit as I took another shot. It was not a kill shot, straight in the heart, if I wasn't mistaken.

Tracy was at the door and after taking a millisecond to assess the situation, she seized control. Thank God. "Henry, let's go!" She held the door wide; where he went the rest of the pack would follow. He looked up at me, I nodded that it was okay, he went in, Rasher collided with him at the door, causing a momentary bottleneck. The pig had stood his ground, but now that the sober humans were involved, he was more than happy to relinquish his post. Showing bravery when all you want to do is run is as close to a pure definition of the word courage as can be made. "Mike, you can't fight."

One would think one's ego would be bruised from the comment, but I had no such compunction. "Truer words could not be speaked." Then I hiccupped.

"Everyone in," she commanded.

"Dad it's f.o.r.e. Not the number four," Travis corrected.

"That makes a lot more sense," I told him as I followed *La Jefa* in.

Sure I held rank in the military, but it was never in discussion who the big boss was. She was the commander-in-chief, as far as this group went. Again, I was fine with that. She'd once got me a shirt that said: "Adult Supervision Required." (I'd caught it on fire the second time I wore it. I'd been working on my Jeep, couldn't even say with any degree of confidence what had happened; one second everything is fine the next I'm peeling that blazing cotton blend tee free.) I was going to wait until everyone else got in, but who knows how that would have turned out. Justin grabbed my shoulder and yanked me in. Travis pulled the door shut, and a second or two later the glass on the storm door shattered. Wasn't long before other windows on the first floor were broken, curtains were ripped down, and outstretched arms waved within.

"*Night of the Living Dead*," I said in disbelief. We were living the scene that had terrified me as a youth, and even as an adult it had the same effect. Wouldn't be long before the first of them either fell inside or were pushed in. "Anyone got a hammer?" I asked, looking at the stairs.

"You're a one-trick pony, Talbot," Tracy said.

"But it's a good trick," I answered."

"Justin," the boss ordered, "there's tools in the basement."

The basement in this case was more of a shallow dugout under the house used for storage. When we'd scoped the place out earlier I had noped out of walking down the three earthen steps into the blackness below and placed a heavy table across the hatch. Not sure when Tracy had checked. Justin came back with a pickaxe. I went to reach for it and stumbled.

"Upstairs." Tracy pushed my shoulder. We were all up there, watching Justin as he went to town on the stairs. Travis and Dallas were watching his back; so far only two shufflers had found their way in. We could hear more battles around us.

"I'm going to check out what's happening," I told Tracy as I stood, wavered, used the wall to steady myself, then went into one of the bedrooms to look out a window. I wasn't even sure what I was looking at. Below me looked like the Woodstock music festival was about to get underway, not the yuppy '99 festival, but like a scene from the original one, as everyone was dead, but not very grateful. There were zombies everywhere, a sea of them. Had I more coordination and a bit deeper death wish, I could have jumped from the window and run along their heads, never having to worry about touching the ground. We'd been protected from the worst of the smell inside, but now that I had my head poking out a window and was gawking, it punched me full force in the nose.

"Pull your stairs up!" I shouted a few times. I had to yank my head inside to get a relatively fresh breath of air for every repetition. I don't know who, if anybody, heard me, but it was the best I could do. I wisely forced the window down, glad I didn't smash the pane with how hard I'd slammed it. I knew there were a few homes in the area that did not have second stories, I could only hope that no one had shacked up in those. We'd told people to stay close, but other than that we'd given no further direction. "Fuck."

"Got three steps removed," a sweaty Justin informed me.

"Great job, everyone up here?"

"Of course."

It wasn't one of the smartest questions, but it was still one that needed to be asked. Tracy gasped as she came up alongside me, she was looking out at the horror below.

"Dad, I don't think your trick is going to work!" Travis shouted right before either he or Dallas took a shot.

"I'm going to check on everyone," Tracy said, heading to the bedroom at the end of the hall. I went back to the stairs as fast as I could without having to worry about spilling down them.

"What's going on?" I asked. He and Dallas were side by side at the top. A dead zombie was on the landing at the bottom.

"The opening doesn't lead anywhere, it's boarded over."

"Shit." The little fact that there wasn't a real basement in this house had never factored into my plan. Of course, the hole led nowhere, there was nowhere to go. Or not far, anyway. "Clover me." Not only did I use the wrong word, it was the wrong pronunciation. Instead of a short O sound, I'd gone with the long, screwed it up completely. Sounded like I wanted to be surrounded by ground cover, which in hindsight sounds nice.

"Clover?" Travis asked.

"Did you know what I meant?"

"I mean, sure Dad, but still. Do you think you should be going down there?" he asked as I scooted past him. The gap in the steps was halfway down. The opening looked dark enough like maybe it led into an alternate reality, but upon closer examination, I could see wood. I tentatively stepped through. It was firm but yielding. There was some flexibility in what I think was a piece of plywood, but I couldn't tell if it was a quarter-inch or three-quarter-inches thick. Doesn't sound like much of a difference, but it would be significantly harder to break through that thicker board. I wasn't even sure if the return on investment was worth the reward. If the entire sheet didn't fall away, the only zombies that would be in trouble would be those wearing high heels as their stilettos got stuck in the holes. I pulled my leg up and stomped down as hard as I could. A stabbing bolt of pain shot up my foot, twirled a few times around my knee, lingered on my hip then rocketed up my spine to blow out the top of my head.

Did it again, because how dare that inanimate piece of lumber defy my will! I was rewarded with a cracking sound, but not much else.

"Dad!" Travis shouted. I looked up at him because that's what dumb drunk asses do, they miss cues. He was pointing back the other way. A shuffler had made the landing and had one foot on the first step. Minimum of twice I would have bitten the farm if these were speeders. Third time's the charm, and don't worry, that was right around the corner. I must have still been thinking about how difficult it was to get my sidearm out the last time because this time I pulled at it like it was a fifty-pound dumbbell. Clean jerked that fucker right out. It flew from my hand, hit the ceiling then thwacked two steps down from me. Any takers on whether I went to retrieve it? Oh, it gets better—maybe I should stop telling you and just show you—is that the way that saying goes? Hard to think straight when you're drunk. Hard to think of it as a comedy of errors when you're smack dab in the middle of a nightmare. I was going to make for the next step down so that I could bend and grab my gun; I'd not taken into account I was in a hole, caught my shin, and toppled downward. My head struck the approaching zombie square in the chest, sending him backward. Where the back of his head struck the wall there was a loud crack as both the plasterboard and his neck gave way. Sometimes the stupid can get lucky. He was still alive, but his ability to heal broken components wasn't nearly as proficient as his descendants'.

"Fruck me," I said as I stood. "Flanned that!" I was going to blame this whole night on a concussion, should I survive, that was going to be the only way to save face. We all know pride is the most important aspect in a survival situation. Travis had raced down to help me back up. I was feeling a little woozy; maybe if I tried hard enough, I could make myself believe I'd banged the hell out of my noggin. Justin made sure we were going to make it back before he finished the zombie off. He gave a quick try at the stair gap to see if the underlying wood would give, but he realized a lot sooner than I had that it wasn't going anywhere. The gap would delay them, it was not going to stop them. We could take shifts watching the stairs, but wasn't like anyone was going to be able to sleep with intermittent rifle shots going off because zombies were coming up the stairs. This was going to be a war of attrition, as each hour passed by.

Avalyn could help, but she was a short-term last-ditch effort we would have to save for an escape attempt once, and if, one presented itself. Even if we got to our vehicles there wasn't a chance we'd be able to roll them through this horde.

"Dad, maybe you should see if you can get some rest. Travis and I can watch the stairs."

I was feeling some shame for getting so blistered I could barely function and was a danger to myself and those around me. Pride poked its head up and wanted me to stick it out and tell him he weres absorutely wrong. So yeah, when even your inner voice can't say shit right it's time to call it a day.

"I, uh, I'm sorry." And I was. "If you need help…"

"We'll come get you, and dad, it's all right. You didn't know."

He was right I didn't know, maybe couldn't have known, but short of being in an underground bunker, I *should* have known. I should never have allowed myself to get to the point I couldn't function properly. Want to know how to sleep through rifle fire? Bet you already figured that out. Besides, didn't seem like there were more than three or four of them; this I knew because of the punctuating blasts of thunder that rocked my dreams. It was the sun shining across my eyes that woke me. That and the smell. I wanted it to be bacon, to be a Sunday morning in Denver, a wholesome breakfast cooking downstairs, the siren scent of crisping bacon traveling the nose ways. Nope. It was the putrid stench of the dead, coupled with my roiling stomach and blistering headache. I knew I was in for a fantastically bad day.

I rolled my legs out and sat there, head hung low, rubbing my temples. If I moved too quickly there could be a revolt in my gut, and I didn't want to take that chance.

"Here." Tommy came into the room holding a bottle of water.

"Tommy?"

6

MIKE JOURNAL ENTRY 6

Not sure how hard I'd hit my head the night before, but it was Justin who had come in with the water.

"Sorry. I guess I rattled something harder than I thought." I don't think he believed me. I didn't believe myself. I had seen Tommy like he had overlaid his image upon Justin. I wasn't entirely sure what it meant. Was that his way of reaching out and letting me know he was all right? Or maybe it was a call for help; maybe he was pissed we hadn't come to find him. Ah, nothing like the joys of being human and having the ability to carry guilt with you everywhere, expanding as you go. "The zombies?" I moved my head far too quickly for my condition. "Oof."

"Travis and I blocked it off with a dresser. Surprised it didn't wake you; we pushed it off the top of the stairs, and the whole house shook as it pounded down. It's wedged tight. Once the zombies couldn't see us, they lost interest."

"Nice to be dealing with stupid zombies for a change."

He nodded.

"What's it looking like out there?" I asked instead of exposing my sensitive eyes to the blazing of the early morning sun which was likely to fry my retinas and imprint on my brain due to its mushiness.

"Only got a peek."

"Out of sight, out of mind," I answered.

"Dad, they're everywhere."

"Where did a horde of shufflers come from? Rhetorical," I added when Justin stared at me blank-faced wondering if he was supposed to have an answer. "Any news from any of the other houses?" BT was across the alley; Justin had told me he'd checked in at some point before I passed out. Their house was nearly identical, though they had a full basement, so the stair removal worked much better for them.

"BT, Aunt Lyndsey, Jesse, and the baby are fine. I checked again before I brought you some water. Other than that, we don't have great views. The ones we can see aren't signaling and I didn't want to start shouting."

"Good, good. Now the second I can feel like I'm not going to coat my boots in bile, we need to figure out a way out of this mess. Where's Avalyn?"

"Why?" He got angry quickly. I looked at him curiously.

"Because he wants to know if I can help somehow," she said from the doorway.

"Help? What could you possibly do?" he asked. He looked back and forth between the two of us. "Dad?"

"It's not my information to tell," I told him.

"She's a kid, she can't be expected to hold on to important secrets."

I wanted to tell him she was a lot of things but a kid wasn't one of them. "Regardless, she told me something in good faith. If she wants to tell you she will."

"Could you leave us alone please?" Avalyn asked.

Thought he might get whiplash the way his head swept back and forth. "This is bullshit."

"He's angry," Avalyn told me as Justin huffed out of the room.

They might not be blood-related, but they shared at least that one trait. I smiled at the notion.

"To answer your question, I cannot," she said before I even opened my mouth. "They are not the same."

The girl gave me the willies, and with my overreaching imagination, I could sense double speak in everything she said, whether it was meant to be there or not. That last statement for instance. Were the shufflers not the same as the speeders? Not the same as her? Or both? She gave just enough of an answer without giving up too much information. I did not know if it was on purpose to hide just how foreign she was, or that perhaps she believed she had answered the question satisfactorily and did not need to expound.

"How far is your reach?" I asked.

"Why?" Her eyebrows drew down in suspicion.

"I can see no clear way out of this." I felt like I had to tread lightly, wondering exactly where her allegiances were. That, and I wasn't thrilled I was relying on her to help get us out of this. "Speeders and shufflers don't get along, I'd like to use that to our advantage."

"They don't call themselves 'speeders.'"

"What?" That caught me by surprise, though it shouldn't have. For whatever reason, I never considered the bastards self-aware. But if they had a name for themselves then yeah, it went without saying that they were.

"What do they call themselves?" I was somewhat intrigued and terrified. It was not a great feeling. Like maybe I was on the Price is Right, and the prize I could win was either a brand new Jeep Wrangler or a Bengal Tiger with rabies.

"The closest translation would be *the unified*."

"The unified." I rolled the word in my head. Sounded like something from a B Sci-Fi movie.

"It is much longer in their language, and more complex. That is only as close as I can get it in English."

"I'm going to stick with speeders, keeps them less threatening. Can you get in touch with them?"

"Perhaps. One would need to be close enough to hear me."

"Hear?" I asked.

"Not literally. I wouldn't be shouting."

"Ah, gotcha. So how far can your not-shouting travel?" There was an awkward silence.

"Not far enough," she said after a moment. "And before you ask how far I can shout, I cannot answer that."

Hoo boy. I had "Can't?" or "Won't?" all locked and loaded in the vocal chamber, instead I grunted.

"I will keep trying, though."

I wanted to believe her, and I suppose there was a part that did, but I couldn't leave it up to her whether she may or may not help. Or even could. Waiting for outside forces to get you out of a jam was always problematic, especially if you could only hope that someone cared enough and was capable of showing up. She left the room without saying another word. I stayed low and headed over to the window.

The day was moving slower than a turtle with crippling arthritis crawling through thick molasses. Does that convey just how slow it was clicking off? We heard a few gunshots throughout the day, but by now people were either well protected and hidden, or dead. There wouldn't be much in the way of gray area. We generated our own excitement from time to time. Our house was chock full of kids and animals, so there was only so much quiet that could be expected. I felt as if they were moving toward being conditioned for quiet; it was fast becoming necessary for survival. Would future generations of people and animals be born without the ability to vocalize their communication? Would it all be telepathic? Selective Darwinism. I shivered thinking about it. Sure, it would be cool in some respects, but can you imagine if your significant other was pissed at you, and you couldn't go to another room to get away from his or her scolding because they were inside your fucking head?

Sometimes I travel so far off the beaten path I don't even know where I was originally headed. Then Ben-Ben barked, and I remembered. It was a hard enough time keeping adults quiet for an extended period of time, it was impossible with kids and animals. Even Patches would meow on occasion, probably just to display her fangs, but still. And every time we made a noise it triggered something in the zombies. We could hear them get restless, and oftentimes they went for the stairs, not all the time, but enough that we were doing our best to minimize the risk of it. If I had some doggie downers, Ben-Ben would have been the recipient of a handful. It was like he couldn't help himself. He would get excited at seemingly mundane things, I think hoping against hope that bacon would somehow magically be involved in the end. Tracy, at one point, had reached into her bag to get a pair of socks for Nicole, and I guess he was convinced she was going to pull out a package of bacon. He'd shoved his nose in alongside her hand and wrapped his mouth around the cloth and wouldn't let go until he was convinced it wasn't his all-time favorite food, or any food. He'd barked twice in apparent frustration before a well-placed nip from Riley shut him up. And kids? Well they'll laugh and cry out at inopportune times, it's in their nature. What I'm getting at is, staying in a black hole of quiet was an impossibility.

"How long do you think we'll have to stay here?" Tracy asked.

It didn't sound accusatory, I was just in a mood. I held my tongue for a bit; a few seconds of restraint would save potential hours in back pedaling. "I don't know." It was the best I could come up with. The problem was that Tracy was in a mood as well, and not the good kind. Cooped up is one thing that can have its own set of issues, but cooped up and quiet? Not a combo anyone wanted.

"We need to get out of here. You need to get us out of here."

I knew she was angry and scared, again, another bad combo. But fuck all, if she didn't make it sound like I'd got us into this mess. Breathe, Talbot, breathe. Getting in a fight wasn't going to do us any favors. I knew if I so much as looked at her sideways we were going to verbally spar. In her eyes that was probably a better option than sitting there and worrying about shit none of us had any control over. I thought about telling her I was working on it. But I didn't think a useless circular escape plan that only involved us getting killed and eaten was an option.

"You don't believe she's really going to get us out of here, do you?" She'd seen me talking to Avalyn, it would be easy enough to deduce the topic.

"I don't have anything else, Trace. We're surrounded by hundreds, maybe thousands of zombies. We won't be able to shoot our way out of this."

"Why doesn't she just tell them to stand still and we'll walk out."

"She says she can't."

"That's convenient."

Maybe my wife was right to doubt the kid. She had maybe not *every* right, but yeah, there should be some doubt there. Tracy had been very vocal in her distrust of Avalyn, and I hated going against her, especially since she was uncannily correct most of the time. Even on those few instances where I was right, she'd still make me feel as if that were the wrong choice, or that I could only have come up with it based on what she had said. I think it's a talent among women. Or...is it gaslighting? I was going to have to look that up when I could find some reference books.

"For whatever reason, you will not believe the fact that she is a zombie first, and a human second, if she's human at all.

Have you looked at her recently? There's more life in Wesley's stuffed toys than in her eyes."

"She'll hear you," I hissed.

"I'm sick of dancing around this."

"She's different, I agree with you there. But she's helped us."

"So you say, but it seems that no matter where we stop, we get surrounded by zombies."

That did give me pause, but I charged forward. "And you think that's her doing? What about it's just maybe living in a world where they're the dominant species?"

"Wake up, Talbot. Even if I'm wrong, and she's not summoning them here deliberately, she's still a beacon. A zombie lighthouse, only she's not warning them away, but rather toward her rocky shores."

"Are you listening to yourself?" I almost added, *she's just a kid*, but that was not a valid argument. "If she wanted us dead, we'd already be chum." Not sure if that was the best avenue of approach, but it was out there now.

"And what happens if she decides that now she does?"

I knew that one was coming back around, that's what happens when you lob your attacks, they get volleyed into your lap.

I wanted to tell her she was being paranoid, but it wasn't anything I hadn't thought a thousand times before, and if I thought it myself, I couldn't then argue against it. Hypocrites drive me nuts, I would not add myself to their ranks. Tracy and I fundamentally shared the same values, and when we didn't, I was sure to compromise mine to be more in line with hers, mostly. Even when we didn't agree, we did our best to present a united front. I was extremely worried where this conversation was headed.

"What exactly are you saying?" I asked. We agreed the kid was different, we agreed that there was great potential for her doing our group great harm. After that it began to get a bit fuzzy.

"I think you know exactly what I'm saying."

"No, I have a good idea what you're thinking, but this is far too important for me to be interpretating your thoughts."

"She can't stay with us anymore."

"You want me to kick her out?"

She remained silent.

"Ah.... So kick her out permanently. No."

"You don't understand. I spend more time with her than anybody except Justin. She looks at us, at all of us, like a cat staring into a bird cage. She's puzzling out how to get her prize."

"What do you think Justin would say about all this?"

"He's turned a blind eye. He may love the...girl," she had a hard time with that last word, "but has he told you that he is locking the door to his bedroom at night?"

That was news to me. If something had fundamentally changed with my son and his feelings regarding Avalyn, how did that bode for the rest of us? If we were to exile Avalyn, which I couldn't imagine doing, I had a feeling she would be just fine. There was no reason to think the zombies wouldn't embrace her as their new queen, and where would that leave us? Would she be thankful to be with her own kind and still have fondness for us, thus steering our greatest enemy in a new direction? Or would she be bitter and vengeful and wish to destroy those who had made her an outcast? I had a great many shortcomings, and I've erred as many times as I've made the right call. I'd let Eliza, Deneaux, and now Feroz go free after I, at one point, had them firmly in my grasp. All of those had bit me in the ass. Now I was being presented with another choice. All three I had let go were homicidal, but in my defense, Eliza had initially helped us, Deneaux helped when it suited her, and I had hoped that Feroz would. Ended up all of them had done what they had only with the hope that one day soon they would be able to kill me on their own terms. I can be as oblivious as the next guy, but that kind of intense focal hatred had not gone unnoticed. I did not like at all that so many wanted me dead, and not in the abstract, but in a very personal way. Shit like that was bound to give someone with more self-awareness a complex; good thing I wasn't that person.

"Whatever you're dancing around, I'm not going to do it. Maybe she's not a little girl, okay, probably not *just* a little girl, but she has helped us and has yet to do anything to us that would warrant us taking severe action."

"I don't think this should be a time we wait to be reactionary, Mike. What are you going to do if she attacks Wesley, or any of the other kids?"

If that happened, I would never be able to forgive myself, that much was certain, but killing Avalyn with nothing other than suspicion and weird looks was something I also would not be able to forgive myself for.

"We have other things going on right now, can we discuss this later?"

"Sure. Or we can wait until something irrevocable happens."

That was not a fair statement, but as I've come right out and said before, women don't argue for the sake of a debate, they argue with the sole intent of winning, and I'd thoroughly been put on notice. I didn't call her on it, there was no sense. This day sucked. I sat in an uncomfortable chair for most of the time, staring off into space, contemplating what we were going to do. I'd not come up with anything that was worth its weight in fired synapses. As night descended, I was still in the chair. I hadn't offered more than a few grunts to anyone that tried to speak with me. My kids had seen enough conflicts between Tracy and myself that they knew something was going on. Unlike my wife, whatever it was, was usually all I could focus on, while she was able to completely compartmentalize the conflict, and could go on with other people and thoughts as if nothing had happened or was happening. I hadn't the foggiest clue as to how she accomplished that, but it was irritating.

The evening was progressing as slowly as the day had. Tracy had since left the room, getting the kids bedded down for the night. The majority of the animals had gone with her, save Henry, who was resting comfortably by the side of my chair, and Patches, who was staying close to Avalyn, which seemed like it might be cause for concern. Why, though, I didn't know. My heart got a nice dose of adrenaline as Avalyn turned toward me; a sliver of moonlight had caught her eyes and they illuminated like she had a light source behind them. I instinctively grabbed at my chest to rub out the sharp pang that had struck.

"Grandpa..." she was gliding across the floor like a wraith, her arms were outstretched and her mouth wide, a set of blood-dripping fangs on full display. I was welded to my chair, that's what happens when you don't move around for eight hours. Henry stood, his chest puffed out as he readied himself for a savage barking. Patches rode atop Avalyn's shoulder like a parrot on a pirate.

"What is happening?" I struggled against my invisible bonds. She'd somehow found a way to keep me immobile, then ropes wrapped around my forearms. "It's a dream!" I shouted. Startling myself awake. Avalyn was inches from my face as I jerked awake. I barked out "Fuck!" Henry snorted in protest as I'd lessened the depth of his repose, not awoken him, not even close, his beauty required a breadth of slumber the average sleeper cannot achieve without years of practice.

"You were having a bad dream."

We were having some issues with personal space right then, and if my chair had wheels I would have pushed back and scooted across the floor. I had that uncomfortable flighty feeling one gets when something has squeezed their adrenal gland.

"They're coming," was all she said as she turned and went to the other side of the room. She was looking out the window, it didn't seem like she was looking at anything particular, just off into the distance.

I stood and moved her way. "How much time?" It would be bad if we all slept through the battle. Wasn't like there would be explosions, rifle fire, and blood curdling screams of terror and pain; might not be much louder than the tearing of some clothes.

"Before morning." She clasped her hands behind her back like a concerned president might while she waits for news of her SEAL team's success on a vital and delicate mission she has sent them on. "A lot of them will die."

There was no sense in asking if she thought that was a problem—she wouldn't have brought it up if it wasn't. A lot of zombies dying sounded A-ok with me. "How many are coming?"

"Not enough. They will be sacrificing themselves for me, for us."

I had a hard time thinking that the zombies were doing a selfless act. "Are they coming because you asked?" I was trying my damnedest to figure out what was going on while also not infuriating Avalyn or shutting down communication.

"Yes."

"And what do they believe they are getting out of this?" There was no way they were being altruistic...that had been bred out of zombies.

"All of you."

Want to guess when Tracy walked into the room? I'll wait while you wrestle with that easy question.

She gasped like an 1800's debutante, one hand to mouth, one to her chest, it was as alien a maneuver as me putting on a brave face while suffering the debilitating effects of one of the most brutal afflictions, a man-cold. "How many times are you going to dance with the devil, Talbot, before you realize she's taken the lead?"

"There are speeders coming to help." I could only hope this was a misunderstanding, that she'd walked in late on a conversation and missed the context. But she kind of didn't. Avalyn was bringing zombies here with the promise of eating. That was truth, and there wasn't any way to sugar-coat it. And besides, who wants Frosted Feces Flakes? Or Sugar Shit Smacks?

"Help?"

"Maybe not on purpose, but their distraction should give us a way to sneak out of here."

"She's setting you up, and you're letting her."

"I'm letting her? If you know something I don't, please feel free to enlighten me, because as I see it right now, we are hopelessly stuck."

"We're trading out one problem for another."

She was saying things I couldn't necessarily argue against. *Yes, honey, but these ones are nice zombies! They'll tear us apart fast so we don't feel as much pain.* I'm sure that'd go over big.

"What happens if they bring their friends?"

Never even dawned on me to think that the speeders would bring others. But why not? There could be shriekers, greavers, reavers, spiders, melders, bulkers, super bulkers.... And who knows what other nightmare they could conjure up?

"Avalyn?"

She didn't turn to face me, I did see her wring her hands though. I didn't take that as a good sign. Impossible to say what she was feeling, anger that Tracy didn't believe her? Or anger that her plan had been discovered?

"I cannot differentiate," she answered.

She was lying, I felt it in my bones. But was it for my bene-fit, or Tracy's? The only problem was I wasn't the greatest at sniffing out deceit, so if I could tell, then it was a guarantee that Tracy could.

"It might be the only chance we have to get away," I told Tracy. Pre-z-poc, when I used to daydream about a zombie invasion—well, first off it always involved the slow bastards—but secondly I knew beyond a shadow of a doubt I would never get myself into the situation I now found myself in. How does one get hemmed in by an enemy that took their walking lessons from male penguins balancing their mate's egg on the top of their feet? I was going to use Tim Conway's Oldest Man character as a comparison, but it's likely that anyone picking up this journal would have no clue about the slow shuffling funny man.

Tracy levelled a gaze on Avalyn then turned it my way before she left the room.

"A hundred and forty-seven are coming. Ten are what you call bulkers, seven are spiders."

"Greavers or reavers?"

"I have no dominion over them."

That answer was a partial truth, a lie by omission, maybe. "An understanding, then?"

"It will be happening soon." Wasn't so much a deft side-step as it was a clear-cut avoidance to answering my question.

"You're not making this easy."

"I'm not?" She spun quickly and faced me. Her face was a mask of pain, silent tears leaked from her eyes. "You've asked me to kill some to save others."

I was never going to have a problem with this particular equation, but I could not tell her that. She had one foot firmly planted in each camp. Deaths on either side were going to affect her, I could only hope that for this particular moment in time, losses on humanity's side would hurt more than the losses of zombies. It shouldn't have been that close; she was surrounded by people who she knew and cared for, or I think cared for, and for the most part those feelings were reciprocated. The zombies were nameless, faceless beings she'd never met. If this was a photo finish right now, what would it be like a month from now?

Like always, it was looking like Tracy was right. Now I had to figure out what I was going to do about it. First thing was getting out of this village. I'd worry about it or ignore it thoroughly later on until I was forced to act. Maybe procrastination wasn't the best strategy, but it had its perks. Finishing a school project on a Sunday night that you've known about for two months is not one of them. Yeah, I'm calling you out, Travis. Want to know how many stores are open at nine pm that sell poster boards? Like, one, and it's always across town.

"Aren't you going to say something?" she asked.

"What do you want me to say, Avalyn? Thank you for your sacrifice? They're zombies, for fu…dges sake. I care less about them than a mosquito I squash against my arm. They're the enemy. True, I feel bad for the person they once were, but for the monster that tries to kill me and mine? No. My heart soars with every one of their deaths."

"Then that's the difference between us."

"No shit." It was out long before I thought to stop it. "You know what I am, Avalyn; do you think I war with where my allegiances lie?"

"I'm doing it, aren't I!?" she screamed. It was loud enough she woke not only us, but the zombies. I could hear them shuffling around downstairs. I wasn't sure if they'd do anything, though; they tended to be more visually stimulated than auditory. Hearing things brought them to a location, but sight was what triggered their hunting response.

"What's going on?" It was Justin's turn to join in.

"Your father is laying the groundwork for my removal from the group."

Little fucker was astute.

"Dad?"

I thought I was going to have more time to work on this

135

problem. As I said earlier, I'm not the greatest BS detector, and I'm far worse dishing it out. Sometimes the best way forward is the direct and honest way, then deal with the fallout in real time. There was a second where I thought about throwing Tracy under the bus, and saying it was all her idea to get rid of the kid. Not sure what good favor that was going to buy me though, from either party. Perfectly acceptable reason when your friends want to go out on a Tuesday night, and you don't have the money or the inclination. "Yeah, guys, I'd love to, but the missus says I can't." Some minor ribbing about being whipped is to be expected, still saves you from ringing up your credit card and showing up to work the next morning hung over.

"She's having a hard time figuring out what team she's playing for. I'm worried about what's going to happen when she walks into Fenway with a Yankees cap."

"Baseball, dad? You're using a baseball analogy right now?"

"Not my best, but besides her potentially getting us killed, I can't think of a more apt one."

"If you kick her out, I'm going with her."

"And Dallas? She's cool with that?" I asked. I had a feeling that the locked bedroom door had more to do with Dallas's feelings than Justin's.

If push came to shove, Justin would choose Avalyn over Dallas, not because he loved one more than the other, but rather that he would always defend the defenseless. It was an admirable trait, if not woefully misguided in this instance. Might not be any among us more able to defend themselves than her. She could rule over nations, if given the chance. Who would be able to stop her once she was surrounded by her legions? I'd let so many dangerous females go.... Would I finally learn my lesson? I wasn't feeling confident.

Justin hesitated for a second before answering. "She will go where I do."

This wasn't going anywhere I wanted it to. I didn't think that was true in this case, but Justin would dig in if I pressed him. "Ask her yourself." Avalyn wouldn't lie, it wasn't who she was.

"Avalyn, sweetie," he squatted down in front of her, "I love you."

"I care for you," was her tepid response. He gave me a side eye to see if I had caught the not so subtle difference in the exchange.

"If it came down to us or them, who would you choose?" he asked.

"I would choose us over them," she said.

Justin was all smiles. Maybe he wasn't used to the girl's double speak, but she'd answered nothing.

"Who exactly is 'us?'" I asked.

The anger on my son's face was evident.

I cut off any response he was ready to deliver. "—I'm talking to her."

"What does that mean?" he asked.

"Let her answer the question."

Avalyn was having a hard time with that one. Maybe testing out whether she could lie or not, or maybe she just didn't know which side of the yard she would land in once she fell off the fence.

"Avalyn?" Justin looked back at her when she didn't immediately say anything. "I don't understand."

"She considers you one of them."

"I'm not a zombie!" he shouted.

"No, you're not, but you have enough of the virus within you that you could pass muster, should you need to."

"Tell him that's not true!" he shouted as he gripped her shoulders. If he was placing too much pressure on them, she didn't complain.

She remained quiet. My heart cracked as I watched my son break down. He dropped back onto his haunches then pulled Avalyn in close for a hug. She did not reach around to complete the gesture. I'd seen kids with severe autism display more affection. She was staring directly at me. Her face was blank.

"Engine!" Travis had come into the room. "Sounded like a truck started."

Justin stood and, as discretely as he could, wiped his eyes, making sure to keep his back to his brother. I followed Travis to another room; he had the window cracked open and we heard the engine sound as it faded. There was no way to tell who exactly it was, but sourly I figured if they were leaving it had to be Hammer and the doctors. A fair segment of the shufflers were being drawn to the noise. From past experience, we could expect a third of them to go after the lure. A large percentage, but not enough to change our circumstances much. And even out of that third, many would return once the truck was out of range. The others would wander in the direction they'd been going until they came across another group or were distracted by another sound, sight, or smell.

"Where are they going?" Dallas asked turning to look at me. She looked like a kid on Christmas morning who had just realized that the one gift she'd wanted above all others was not there.

I could not answer her question, couldn't even take a guess. If it was Hammer, they might even now be flying down the highway with nary a glance backward. If it was BT, he'd be thinking of a way to come back and get everyone. A villager? Who could say. Odds were they were halfway home. Who could blame them? I mean, I could, but if we got out of here, I wasn't going to chase them down and make them pay. Hard to describe what we were hearing outside now as a commotion, but it wasn't nothing. There wore a series of grunted *kiais* coming from the house next to us.

"That where Yoki's staying?" I asked. No one knew for sure. Oftentimes her martial art cries were punctuated with what sounded like a foot stomping on the ground. She was on the offensive, with a sword. The woman had brass balls bigger than that bull on Wall Street. Couldn't see a damn thing. Something was happening for sure, a plan was unfolding...probably a good thing I wasn't involved. It was too coincidental that a truck would be started, and now Yoki was what? What was she actually doing? How could she possibly defeat the press of zombies with a sword?

Haruto showed up at the window opposite us. "*Zanshu wa zonbi o kowagara seru!*" He shouted it twice like on the second time we'd be able to decipher the foreign language. Possibly if he spoke louder and slower I'd get it.

I gave him a shrug, with my palms held upward. He smiled and held a finger up as he thought, then he took that finger and swept it across his neck, then with his pointer and middle finger he flicked them back and forth, moving them away from his body in what I figured was the universal meaning for running away.

"The fuck does that mean?" I asked. He repeated it three more times, each one getting more animated, letting his head lean far to the side. "Charades sucks."

"Cut zombie heads off and run?" Travis asked.

"Run where, though?" We were bouncing questions off each other, never offering answers. Haruto disappeared from the window. Someone down on the first floor had shouted something—it looked as if his help was needed. We watched intently as a lone zombie pushed his way out of the house and into the throng that was trying to enter. I had no explanation for that.

"Another one." Travis was pointing as yet another zombie was hitting the exit. It had a difficult time, as the crowd trying to gain entry was adamant. Then two pushed their way through, and the in-seeking crowd became less insistent, hesitant even. Then because we'd not quite seen everything the zombie apocalypse had to offer, the mob turned away from the door and were actively pushing against those further out who still wanted to get inside and see if any flatscreens were still available. (Black Friday reference, used it before, but in this case, shoppers were exiting the store like the place was on fire *and* the TVs were gone. I'd say like there was an active shooter, but first off, there *were* loud reports from gunfire, and zombies gave not one shit about it. In fact, they were actively drawn to it like dung beetles to an elephant's droppings.)

Yoki's focusing cries were joined by another, sounded like Akio, then another, though I couldn't tell who the third was.

"What are they doing? Swords?" It was all I could think of, but how did they have enough room to swing not only one, but at least three? The zombies exiting were now walking over others who were slower so that they could get away.

The enemy was in full retreat. It wasn't that we hadn't seen that before, but it usually involved overwhelming and withering gunfire. Yoki had somehow turned the tide with one piece of steel. A signal was being passed through the zombies, and those close to her dwelling were moving away. The ones around our house had not moved, either not having received the message yet or believing the distance they had from the event gave them a measure of safety. I equated the zombies losing their heads to the chemical smell of distress grass puts off when it gets mowed. I was all in.

"Time to join in the fun." I wore a grin which, had I seen it, was more creepy than mirthful, but I was moving to behead zombies, not befriend them. To be safe, because one must be safe when one is swinging sharpened steel around, I made sure my rifle was securely attached to my back, but still within easy reach.

"What are you doing?" Tracy asked as I headed out of the bedroom. I had the sword out in front of me like I actually knew what I was doing.

"It's time to get out of here."

"With that?" she asked.

She had every right to be worried. I couldn't think of any instances, but I'm sure there was one, where I ended up in the emergency room after a cardboard sword fight. There are just some people that should not have access to three feet of sharpened steel or...sharpened anything.

"It repels them."

"Like bug spray?"

"I guess," was all I could think to answer. She was going to want something more than that before she moved aside. "I don't really know, something about potentially having their heads lopped off has the zombies in a tizzy," I told her.

"Are you sure?"

"A hundred percent? No, but the gambling odds are favorable."

"Mike."

"I know, I know, let me just try it out."

She reluctantly moved. I went to the top of the stairs. It was going to be awkward getting around our barrier, but there was a zombie on the top stair, right before the barricade. It was not facing us, so he was my perfect test subject. I got up on the bottom of the couch quietly, ninja-like. I ended up being more like Chris Farley in *Beverly Hills Ninja*, though. I was positioning myself for the best swing when I adjusted my left foot and went straight through the black felt lining on the bottom of the upturned piece of furniture. I fell over to the side, narrowly missing smacking my head against the railing.

The zombie's head evaporated under the assault of a 45 slug. "Jesus, Mike." Tracy was on the step behind me, the barrel from her pistol smoking.

"Minor set back," I grunted as I extracted myself from the grip of the cushions and springs my foot had gone through.

"Get back here, they're coming!" She fired again. Another zombie fell to the side. By now, Travis was standing next to his mother, ready to assist.

"Give me a second," I told them as I jumped down a step

to where my original target had been. The directionless zombies now had something to focus on, and they were coming.

"Hold..." I told myself, wondering if that was the best strategy. How the fuck the early Americans stood their ground from the impressive and much more skilled British, I'll never know. No wonder so many of the colonists broke ranks and ran for cover. "Hold!" I shouted as I swung. I didn't adjust properly and ended up taking off the top of the zombie's skull like a botched scalping. Gray brain glistened dully as the monster went down. I don't know exactly what I was expecting, but all the other zombies looking at me in abject terror and then bolting for the door would have been preferred. That did not occur.

"Hold!" I shouted again, this time adjusting my swing. The shock to my arms was much less as the steel sliced through the skin, muscle then bone of the neck. The head struck the wall, wound side first and slid down, leaving a slimy trail much like a slug would have. Whatever emergency broadcast they'd sent out next door had yet to be sounded. Took three more Old Testament killings before I was able to advance down one more step. The zombies were still coming, but they didn't seem to be in as much a rush. Travis had climbed up onto the couch and was offering me cover fire.

"*Hold*" became a bastardized Japanese *kihap* of "*Hai!*" which I shouted with each swing. I could feel it focus my energy and force itself into the strikes. At some point, I was going to tire and the shock traveling the length of my arms was going to cause pain and weariness, but that was not the case yet. The classic outstretched arms of the shufflers had dropped to the sides of those nearest, yet still they came forward, though this now seemed more of a reluctant gesture. They broke when my next swing took off two heads. It was a good thing too, because I'd wound up as hard as I could, and the resistance had been far less than I'd anticipated. I spun off to the side. The moment I went down, Travis's rifle picked up the slack, but now he was shooting them in the backs of their skulls as they fled.

When I got my feet under me I held up my hand for him to stop firing. The stampede had started. I wasn't sure what would stop it, but there was no sense in having those outside come in to investigate all the racket. I'd already had an appreciation for what the sword could do, that had since been elevated to King Arthur level. Not sure if the same results could be attained with the speeders—plus I don't think I would have been fast enough to deal with them—but for the shufflers, it was nice to have such a game changer in our arsenal, even if the slow bastards were rarer than a Pikachu Illustrator card. (This I knew because when Travis was much younger it was something he wanted for Christmas. I was all gung-ho to get him one, until I realized they were going for about a grand at the time, and that would have blown our entire holiday budget twice over. I ended up finding one for twenty bucks on a less than reputable site, pretty sure it was a counterfeit, but my seven-year-old had no idea, and the smile on his face was priceless. Come to find out two years later he sold it to another kid for a hundred bucks. I was so proud I got a tear in my eye when he told me.)

Five minutes later the first floor of the house was empty, save me. The place was destroyed. There was shit everywhere, and by shit, I mean literal shit. The furniture that wasn't crushed was coated in all manner of ill fluids, it was smeared on the walls, and somehow some of it had been flung onto the ceiling like the zombies were angry chimps.

"What the fuck?" I asked when a solid glob of it splatted to the floor on the other side of the room. I did not look above my head because I had a pretty good idea of how that would work out, seen enough Three Stooges episodes in my day. I made my way to the door. The shufflers were in full retreat. Yoki was following a group, taking out some pent-up frustration one swing at a time, and not once did any of them turn to confront her.

"Yoki!" I called out before she could go further. She turned, the fury and determination on her face quickly melted away. I made a steering wheel motion with my hands, but given that one had a sword in it, it was an awkward movement. Surprised I didn't slice my cheek open. There was commotion off to my left, the opposite side from Yoki. She looked at me, then past, then darted back to the door and shouted something in. I'm sure it was something along the lines of: "Get your asses moving, we're getting out of here!"

Travis had just come out to witness a zombie getting tossed into the air. Had to be close to fifteen feet. The next zombie had been torn in two, but also went for a short flight. The strength of whatever was coming was immense. It had not only torn a zombie in two, it was sending them into low orbit. Bulkers were incredibly strong, but they didn't have the dexterity to do something like that. Their arms tended to be nearly welded to the sides of their body, absorbed by, well, the bulk. Wasn't grabbers, not with the sun just coming out; grievers might toss things into the air like a raging bull, but tearing them apart wasn't likely to happen. Had to be spiders. Not sure of the reason behind the display, other than a signal for the shufflers to get gone.

There were four houses: mine, Yoki's, her neighbor, and the one across the street, where BT emerged in what looked like 70s basketball attire, meaning tight short shorts and a sleeveless jersey.

"Don't ask!" he roared when I gave him a questioning look. He must have caught sight of what Yoki or myself were doing; he was carrying an aluminum bat that had seen more than a few skulls. He gave me a quick thumbs up to let me know everyone was all right and I returned the gesture. Justin was ushering people into the truck. Travis was keeping guard. Kirby and Rose had come out of the other house. He stood there, scratched his nuts and then stretched like he'd just been awakened.

"Must be nice," I muttered. "Welcome to the apocalypse!" I shouted at him.

He waved back. "Thank you, sir." The thing about it was, he meant it. I could only shake my head. I didn't see Stenzel or my brother. I'd asked him if he wanted to stay with us, but he'd declined. For the moment this seemed to be the only patch that was clear of fighting. The eye of the storm. Our ride was packed, and I would have sent it on down the road and to safety while we secured the rest of the people, but there wasn't a clear avenue of escape. It was touch and go as the zombie battle ebbed and flowed. There was no way I was going to have us stuck in a truck with limited ability to defend ourselves. Swinging a sword in enclosed spaces is generally prohibited, or at the minimum frowned upon.

"Come on, come on." I wasn't a fan of displaying favoritism, especially not as the designated leader of this band of people, but I was desperately looking for my brother and Stenzel. Of course I was concerned for the welfare of everyone, but some were more equal than others, and some less. That's only natural, right? I was partly human, and that part was not exactly a canonized saint, at that. I feel like it would have been some sort of psychosis if you cared about everyone equally. That was what I was going to go with anyway. Makes my baseline more reasonable.

Somehow Justin was behind the wheel. There were dangers you avoid in life, like putting your hand down the kitchen sink when the garbage disposal is running, or licking the blades of a turning metal fan (at least after the first time), or getting toast unstuck with a knife, things like that. Riding as a passenger in a Justin-driven vehicle was on that list. He has a bad rep, but that's what happens when I had him out for a driving lesson and he smacked the front end of my Jeep into a light pole. For context, we were in an empty parking lot. That kind of trauma tends to stick with you.

"There's an opening!" Justin was looking off to his left. I was toward the rear of the truck, outside, waiting for someone, anyone, to show.

"Get them out of here." There were too many animals and kids in that truck. If there was a way to get them to safety then we needed to take it. "Go a mile or two down the highway; we'll catch up."

"Oh hell no." I watched the truck raise up a foot and a half as BT exited. The springs sighed in relief. "Every time I leave you to your own devices there's trouble."

He wasn't budging, and I didn't want to waste precious time trying to budge him. Yoki nodded at me; she was going to look out for the welfare of those in the truck. My rampant panic eased slightly when they drove away without any incident. We were still alone, although we could hear other people either shouting, shooting or shutting the hell up, but "people," by definition, are a noisy animal and were far louder than the zombies, even though they were in a pitched battle. So fucking strange to bear witness to a quiet war.

"This was dumb," BT said, I suppose just now realizing it was only us two, and our only means of escape was on foot. That window was in the process of closing as zombies surged into the empty area. "This is why I hate being impulsive. I blame you for this!" He turned and pointed his finger at me.

The shufflers were being pushed back by their deadlier and more aggressive cousins. BT and myself were still standing quietly within the swirling eye of the storm. As we stood there, I realized the tactical mistake we'd made. Yeah, I know I was the one who made it, but I'm all about sharing the blame because there was plenty of it to go around. The better play would have been to leave with the truck when the leaving was good, then coming back at it from the outside. We would have had a better perspective of the whole thing instead of being smack dab in the middle of it. Here, we couldn't see the horde for the zombies.

"Right now you're realizing the stupidity of this move, aren't you?"

I didn't say anything.

"Now, Talbot? Now is when you realize it?"

No matter what we did, hanging out in the middle of the road was not the best option.

"Let's go." We were moving closer toward the zombie line, as I wanted to get to the house that Kirby and Rose had exited. On that side of the street the homes were much closer to each other—I don't know if they were swashbucklingly close so we could jump from roof to roof—but the opportunity looked decent enough. Just as we entered came the sound of a truck engine turning over.

"That the tanker?" BT asked.

"Definitely sounded like it." I'd just stepped into the living room and was heading for the stairs. A trio of shufflers came out from where I figured the kitchen was. One of them looked at us, but they headed to the door and went out. "Did that just happen?" was all I could think to ask.

"Who was driving the tanker?" BT asked as he moved past me and up.

"Fuck me. It was Hammer." I'd not been thrilled about the arrangement. He'd argued that the doctors responsible for the production of the fuel should be in one of the safer means of transport. In terms of size and gun emplacements, that was true, but it was still a large container of fuel. In the end I'd said yes because the people on the emplacements were loyal to the group as a whole, and it wasn't like the tanker was going to outrun any of us. Ultimately, I did not think Hammer would actively seek a way to leave us. Just wasn't his nature. What was his nature, though, was to exalt the safety of the doctors far above the rest of the group to where if he could get them out right now, he would do so, and it was highly unlikely he would stop up ahead and wait for the rest of us, and he sure as shit wasn't going to come back and help us because that would mean his precious cargo was left unguarded.

"Mike, if he takes off, he can outdistance all of us."

This I knew. We had a lot of fuel in cans in the trucks; if we condensed everyone into as few vehicles as possible there was a chance that we could get to Colorado with what we had, barely. But Hammer, hell he could give Colorado the finger as he drove by, no reason to think he couldn't make it all the way to Alaska as long as mechanically the truck stayed sound.

"Fuck it."

BT stopped at the top of the stairs. "Fuck it? Your response is *fuck it?*"

"The fuel was always temporary. We probably have enough gas to get home."

"Probably?"

"I'm not really in the mood to do the maths, brother, but yeah, I think with some rationing and cramming we could just about make it. Maybe even have a gallon or two left to fill up a lawnmower. Even with that tanker, how long were we going to have diesel? A year at the most. Don't get me wrong, it'd be great to run a generator or two for that length of time, but then what? We grow dependent on that fuel and poof it's gone, again. The readjustment period will be a pain in the ass. It will be much better when we get to wherever we're going to set up something that's going to be more permanent. Solar, wind farm, bike power generated by a gaggle of convicts."

"You get weirder every day."

"Just think, we could trump up some charges on Kirby and have him peddle power our air conditioners."

"I could get on board with that." We were in the bedroom I figured Rose and Kirby had used. This we could tell by how the mattress was on the floor, the box spring was leaning up against the wall and the sheets were draped over the bed frame. Angry cops with search warrants wouldn't have made this big a mess. "Smell funny in here?" he asked.

"Don't, man, we don't want to know."

The house next to us was nearly close enough to reach out and touch. If we could get on the roof, it wouldn't be more than a seven-foot leap, which was definitely doable. The roofs here tended to be on the flat side—when you didn't have to worry about snow why go with peeked toppers?

"Do they have an attic?" I was going from room to room looking for an access. I'd just made the observation that the roofs were flat here, and I'd not made the connection that flat roof equals zero attic.

"Get me a chair." BT was looking straight up. The only chair on the second floor was in the tossed bedroom, and it was broken, and even if it wasn't, I wasn't grabbing it. It looked sticky. I bolted downstairs and grabbed a red and blue vinyl covered tube type chair. Thing looked like it was from the seventies. BT grabbed it without looking. He placed it down then stooped to get on it. With his shoulder he pressed up against the plywood above him, there was some initial creaking—tough to tell if it was coming from the floor, the chair, BT's shoulder or the ceiling. Best guess would have been E, all of the above. I was waiting for the thin, chrome plated legs on that old chair to buckle. I knew without a shadow of a doubt I was going to laugh when BT tumbled to the ground. That's what happens when your intellect is stunted.

The seat of the chair was on the verge of giving out when a crack of splintering wood echoed down the hallway signifying the ceiling had given first. I was slightly annoyed that a chuckle at BT's expense had been denied. He pushed until his head and shoulders were outside. Someone flying a drone overhead would have thought the house was birthing him. I mean, most likely not, but I needed to get my smiles in somehow. Studies show that smiling regularly promotes a healthy body, and smiling at others is even better. I don't make this shit up, that's science.

BT pulled some more of the plywood down before he hoisted himself up and through the opening he'd made.

"That's gonna fuck up the resale value," I told him as I stood on the chair and reached a hand up, he hoisted me right out. When you're looking straight ahead, seven feet doesn't seem like anything, but when you're looking across at another roofline with a twenty-foot drop between, it takes on a whole other slant. BT didn't say anything, didn't even hesitate. The moment my feet touched down on the roof he took three quick strides and leapt. Thought it would have been pretty cool if he had done the superhero landing. You know the one, bent legs, one hand on the ground, one splayed out behind, head dipped down, he didn't so that. He just stood there like he'd jumped off the bottom step onto the floor.

"You coming?" he asked.

"I don't like heights."

"This about your brother?"

"Of fucking course it is," I told him. I've put this in earlier journals, but since most of them are scattered to the four corners of the world, here's a quick recap. When I was seven or eight, my brother Glen was tasked with babysitting me. That was akin to a mama gazelle dropping her kids off with a pack of ravenous hyenas while she went off and grazed at some of the more succulent grasslands on the other side of the savannah. My sister wasn't a fan of being relegated to babysitting duty, but Glenn took it as a personal affront. I mean, that's the way it seemed, anyway. Why else would he have felt the need to make me hike up Blue Hills and then suspend me by my ankles outside of the forest ranger observation tower? So yeah, I had a serious issue with heights. Proportionality-wise, now that I was an adult and this was a significantly shorter fall, all should have been well within, but alas, that's not the way the human mind works. As far as I was concerned, I was looking down into the abyss of the Grand Canyon. Then to make sure there's a moldy cherry sitting atop my shit filled pie, at the bottom of this particular canyon there were flesh eating zombies. So maybe the height wasn't enough to kill someone, but the landing spot definitely would.

"Come on, I'll catch you." This was no idle promise. He had the wingspan, he could just about pluck me off from where I launched, and he had the strength to snatch me, should I not make it quite across the span of the chasm. I forced myself into higher reasoning, which, given me as a person, is not an easy thing. Then because that didn't work with stellar results, I shut down all thinking and went primal, running and jumping like my ancestors. Cleared the gap easily.

BT smiled as he got out of my way then pointed along the line of houses. "One down seven to go."

"Fan fucking tastic."

7

MIKE JOURNAL ENTRY 7

ONCE WE MADE the jump to the next house we made sure to thump on the roof; no one answered.

Then, "Hey, could you guys keep the racket down?" Gary poked his head out of a window in the next house. "Hey, Mike! What are you doing up on the roof?" He waved at BT.

"Is he serious right now?" BT asked.

"You do realize we're in the middle of a war, right?" I asked my brother.

"Hello, Captain." Major Dylan came to the window. She had a sheet wrapped around her and she had quite the case of bedhead.

"I, uh, thought she played for the other team?" BT asked as quietly as he could.

"I'm leaving it alone, I suggest you do the same." The gap from us to where they were staying was a bit wider, twelve feet or there abouts. Not undoable, just not nearly as acrophobia-friendly as the previous two.

"How'd you get up there?" Gary twisted around to look up.

"BT pulled a Kool-Aid man and went through the roof."

"I would have liked to have seen that," Gary replied.

Major Dylan retreated for a few seconds before coming back, she was winding up a coil of rope.

"Why is our entire squad comprised of freaks?" BT asked.

I hadn't made that leap until he said something. Now I got to have the wonderful imagery of my brother into bondage games. Of course, in the skewed version inside my head it involved a lot of straps and exposed asses. "Goddammit." I shook my head.

"Are you seeing leather hoods and spiked collars?"

"Fuck you man, I wasn't."

"Now you are, am I right?" If his grin got any larger the top half of his head would flop over like he was Canadian. (*South Park* reference, it won't be the only one.)

"Jerk."

He smacked my chest. "Come on, let's do this, we can grab the rope then pull them up."

BT made the jump with little effort. I, on the other hand, did not. With a further span I decided I needed more speed. I backed up as far as I could before beginning my approach. The problem lay in the takeoff: I misjudged my last step. I lost roughly half of my thrust. Wasn't anywhere on this planet I made that jump. Gary later told me that had we been on the lunar surface I would have cleared the house entirely. I did not feel better about it. My mind flashed to *Die Hard* when Hans was flailing at the end of the movie as he was falling from the top of the Nakatomi building. My chest slammed against the edge of the roof. The pain of the beating was bad enough, then add on that I forced all the air from my lungs *and* I was on the verge of dropping into the deadly abyss below. I was immediately in panic mode. The first meaty hand of BT's that smacked down on me latched on to my ear. I'm not a doctor, and I never played one on TV, although I was very familiar with WebMD, and I was completely sure that there wasn't any way he could suspend my weight by the fleshy appendage. Thought he was going to pull a Van Gogh on me until the next hand slapped my back hard enough that I wouldn't be able to choke on future food due to the remembrance of the strike. He grabbed the back of my shirt; it rode up and was forcing my head down and I found myself staring straight down Major Dylan's towel. Even out of air, in great discomfort, fearing for my very life and concerned about losing an ear, I could admire the view. If men were any more basic, we'd wear Uggs.

"I've got you," Gary shouted. I couldn't tell for sure, as I had other things going on, but I don't know by what definition of "I've got you" Gary was going by. Best I could tell he had his outstretched hands wrapped around the heels of my boots. If BT lost hold of me, the best I could hope for from Gary was that he would have just enough of me to make me fall backwards and headfirst. His *help* was only going to get me killed faster.

"Mike, I'm slipping!" Those are close to the last words you want to hear from the one person holding you in place, the only thing that tops that is, "oops," or possibly "sorry." BT was leaning dangerously far forward, his head thrown back, the veins on his neck pulsed like the raging flood waters of the Amazon. His teeth clenched hard enough I thought they were going to shatter. None of these things were what was going through my head at that time. I was dealing with pain from the point of contact and the inability to breath and the idea of falling. Somehow, incredibly, concern about the zombies had dropped to fourth place. They didn't even medal, although that would change immediately if I landed in their midst.

"BT, we've got him!" Gary shouted.

I'm not sure what that meant until I felt the rope loop around my right leg.

"Are you sure?" BT hissed through his closed mouth.

"We've got him!" Major Dylan reiterated.

"Sorry, Mike." BT let go and stepped back before he ended up falling with me. I didn't blame him for that, no sense in both of us dying. I fell. The funny thing about it is, as I was doing the Nestea Plunge—old iced tea commercial, you're going to have to take my word for it—I was able to take a full breath. It felt so good but was oh so short lived. I sent every last bit of that hard fought for air back out into the wild as my back struck the house with enough force to rattle the windows. My entire back was on fire like I'd been slapped with a broad cattle prod. The rope slipped a few inches, to where my hair was brushing against a zombie's; if we had found ourselves on the world of Pandora, it would have been the beginning of a mating ritual. Before the zombie could figure out what was going on I could feel myself being hoisted up like a game animal onto a rack.

I couldn't do much more than hang there like a limp noodle. Hands grabbed at my lower leg, and I was unceremoniously dumped onto the bedroom floor. It was a couple of minutes before I could say more than, "Ow" followed by, "Thank you."

Major Dylan was checking me over for injuries, and as of yet she'd not had time to put some clothes on. The sheet had long ago been lost, and I had full-sighted access to her and her body. I'll say it again because it bears repeating. Funny thing about men, we can have just moments before cheated death and feel like we'd been hit by a train but that still won't deter us from appreciating the female form. I don't know what was going on between her and my brother, but he was a lucky man. I'd never really spent a thought on what was underneath her uniform. But yeah, my brother was one lucky son of a bitch. Gonna leave it there because there's always the chance my wife sees this, and Major Dylan was with my brother. I may have said *ow*, a few more times just so she had more to check out, but you weren't there, and if you were, you wouldn't be judging me. Once she deemed I was medically sound she didn't gasp and realize she was naked, but rather stood, her toned and sinewy body strode to the other side of the room and she grabbed her clothes. She dressed quickly, but not with any embarrassment. She was a doctor, after all. I suppose nudity isn't such a big deal in her profession.

"You all right?" Gary asked, getting right in my face. I'm sure it was to thwart any more of my ogling. Not that I was gonna, but if I had the strength I might have pushed him out of the way. Just saying. Once Major Dylan was dressed, Gary stood and turned so that he could put his clothes on as well. He unabashedly showed me his lily-white ass, I bet in an effort to overwrite my previous viewing experience. I sat up and groaned. The only part of me that didn't hurt was my left leg.

"We need to get on the roof," I said as I finally got to my feet with the help of some serious propping from the bed and my brother.

"Why?" Gary asked grunting as he helped me. "We've got Thrasher right outside."

Thrasher was the name Gary called the truck he'd modified. It didn't quite live up to the moniker, but besides the tanker it was the most well protected of our fleet. It had a plow retrofitted from an old Ford, so it was a bit undersized for the deuce and a half. The wheels were protected by diamond plating—it wasn't overly thick metal, but would deter sharp objects and small calibers. As for the cab and bed, he'd used three-quarter-inch plywood and encased almost the entire vehicle. He'd left the windshield exposed, but had placed a thick panel of plexiglass over it for added protection. It wouldn't stand up in a heated battle, but it might be just perfect for what we needed it to do.

"It's accessible?"

"Yeah, I parked it right up against the door and left the window down so we could crawl in if we needed to. Not our first rodeo," Gary said.

I was thinking of the ropes they just happened to have in their bedroom and was wondering just how many rodeos there had been. Gary hadn't said a word about this, not that he was one to kiss and tell, but still, I'm his brother. Then I realized that was probably exactly why he didn't tell me...I was his brother.

"Next problem..." before I could finish, BT spoke.

"What's going on down there? Not really time for high tea!"

"Yeah, I'm fine, thanks for asking!" I shouted.

"I watched. I saw you get dragged into the window like a tuna."

"Not making it any better!" To Gary and the Major I asked, "How do we get him down here?"

"BT, is there a place up there to anchor a rope?" Major Dylan asked, sticking her head out the window.

"You all planning on climbing up? I could hoist you."

"Like you hoisted me?" I asked, I wasn't bitter.

"Maybe if you stopped shoveling every cupcake you stumbled across into your pie hole I would have been able to hold on."

"Could you two possibly focus on the problem at hand?" the major asked.

"No promises," I told her.

"We can get to our truck from here, we need you to come down," Gary said.

"Mike?" BT was asking if that was the best plan available. Don't know what the hell he was thinking, he was trying to confirm a Talbot plan with another Talbot. That was a gas on a fire situation.

"Yeah, it's Thrasher, and we can get into it."

He paused, I knew what he was thinking. The truck looked every bit the part of a cheap knock off tank one might have purchased on any number of suspect web sites. I once saw a bullet proof vest sold on one of those sites, upon further inspection it was deemed the only projectile the thing could stop was an airsoft pellet, and even that could be felt through the "specially woven" layers of what ended up consisting of rayon.

"Can you see any better options?" I asked.

He spent a few minutes walking around the perimeter of the roof. He took a lot longer than he should have, safe to say he wasn't too keen on being a passenger on a truck stress test drive.

"Toss the rope up." It was easy enough to hear the reluctance in his voice. He was soon inside the bedroom with us.

Gary grabbed a backpack and was hurriedly running around the room packing away a couple dozen candles. It was then I noticed a cooled puddle of wax, or what I pray to all the gods was wax, on the middle of the bed. BT shook his head, then we headed down. Three out of the four of us weren't going to have any problem with that truck window. We all turned back to BT; it would be like forcing a full can of Play-Doh through a straw mold.

"We could pull forward then back up," Gary offered.

The house was surrounded by zombies, it was a risky maneuver, but the zombies weren't displaying any signs of aggression. They weren't even acknowledging our presence.

"I'll wait with him," I said.

Major Dylan got in first. I made it painfully obvious I was not staring at her well-shaped ass as she wriggled in. Gary was next.

"That was strange," BT said as Gary rolled the window up and started the truck.

"What was?"

"I'm surprised you didn't start whistling while you looked around. You couldn't have been any more obvious. The question is, why you weren't looking at her."

"When she was helping me, she was completely naked."

"And?" BT asked in genuine curiosity.

The only thing I could think to do was make a fist and bite at my pointer finger.

"Seriously?" he asked.

I nodded my head as I bit down harder. Gary's pursed lips and hard squinted eyes were watching.

"Fuck me." I stopped then shut the front door as he pulled away.

"He's not going to come back," BT said.

"Probably not," I lamented.

We watched from the window; he was moving slowly, sort of forcing the zombies out of the way like cows instead of just trying to bowl over them. The strategy seemed to be working and they still weren't paying us any attention. It got a little dicey when he finally got into position to back up, as he was forcing the zombies into the house and the door, two crashed through the window on the other side.

"Open the door then stand back."

"Is it so you can hear your own voice, or do you think me an idiot?" BT asked.

"Huh?"

"You have a long piece of sharpened steel cocked back and ready to fly; why would you think I need any kind of directions on stepping back? When you hand me a rifle, do you feel the need to tell me which end to point downrange? Or maybe remind yourself not to stand in front of me?"

"Huh?" I asked again.

He sighed and rubbed his forehead. "I'm saying, do I look like the type of person that would eat a lobster, shell and all?"

"Hey man, I've seen you eat. I don't think that last one is that far out of the realm of possibilities."

BT shook his head. "I'm going to open this door, then I am going to take a giant step backward before the uncoordinated man wielding Excalibur slices the heads off of the zombies. Happy now?"

"And they say you can't teach a dumb dog new tricks."

"It's 'old dog.'"

"I know," I told him.

He flipped me off.

I nodded at him to go. I wanted to get the fuck out of here, but I'm not entirely sure what happened when he opened that door. It got stuck and only made it halfway. A zombie was falling in backward, I was in mid swing, and BT hadn't jumped clear, despite my unappreciated warning. If not for the fact I buried the blade deep into the solid wood of the door, I would have taken his arm clean off. As it was, my sword was embedded in the oak and it wasn't going to be extracted without some serious effort and a bit of time that I did not possess. The first zombie fell by my feet, the second stumbled and fell over the first.

"Shit." BT was staring at the blade. "Shouldn't have said that."

"I know what I'm doing," I said sarcastically, mimicking BT's voice as I pulled my sidearm free. Just because the zombies hadn't been paying attention to us didn't mean they had completely forgotten about how delicious we were. It was like having eaten a very filling and fulfilling, rib sticking meal, the kind where you need to unbutton your pants to feel more comfortable. Even if you said you couldn't eat another bite, once that lattice apple pie was dropped on the table it was game on. The first zombie tried to roll over and bite at my calves. I fired the pistol, obliterating its head easily from this distance. I finished off the second much like I had the first, then wrestled my blade free, just as Gary got into position.

We were in the back of the truck, looking through the cut outs in the plywood as Gary drove. Although it was tough to call it that when we weren't moving much faster than a baby crawling. The flap between the bed and the front seat was pushed to the side.

"The sergeant says the other zombies are up ahead," Major Dylan said.

"Let's go to as many other houses as we can before we deal

with the upgraded fuckers." I was referring to the next generation of the deadly beasts.

The truck turned so slowly it felt like a barge out at sea.

"This is going to take all fucking day," I said. By the time we got on the open road, if we did get there, we might never catch up to Hammer.

BT didn't say anything; I think he was still reliving how close he had come to being called Lefty or Righty, I'm not sure what the naming convention is. Are you named for the one you lost or the one you have remaining? Why that was going through my head, I don't know.

"Does that open?" BT was pointing above my head.

I try to be observant of my surroundings, but I miss things. In my defense, it was dark in the back of that truck. Above me was a hatch, it had a slide lock and a handle. I slid it back and popped it open.

"Well that's handy. Why didn't we use that to come in?" I asked.

"No window above the front door," Gary answered without looking back. "And the same problem as the window, BT wasn't going to fit."

"I think I need to get more size-appropriate friends," I said as I stood up looking around.

"I could punch you in the nuts right now," BT said.

I leaned down, "I take back what I said."

"I thought you might."

"Gary, to the right...that blue house with the red shutters. Someone is upstairs." I stood back up as the window was thrown open. It was Stenzel with Bando behind her. "Is my entire squad hooking up?" While I appreciated the bonds they were forming, this was insane. Then I realized there were other people in the room as well. Either they were into orgies, or they'd grouped together for safety, before or after the zombies had come. But then again, this was my squad—more than likely it was the orgy explanation.

"Will this plywood hold up with people jumping down?"

"It's plywood, Mike, not a trampoline," Gary answered.

I liked it much better when I was the only smart ass. It wasn't that I could only dish it out and not take it, but who *wants* to take it? It's like saying, sure, I could survive a BT shot to the nuts, but again, I'd prefer not to.

"Stenzel, have people hang down, we can't have their full weight hit this roof from height. And good to see you."

"You too, sir." She nodded then pulled back in to relay the information. An older man from the village was the first to crawl out the window. If I thought Gary had been driving slowly, comparatively, he'd been an F1 racer. I could feel myself aging as the man got into position. I wanted to tell him to get his ass in gear and was just about to when Major Dylan spoke.

"Spider."

I reflexively brushed my shoulder, trying to get it off. Can't change a lifetime's worth of habits overnight. Even if I knew she didn't mean some exotic and deadly jungle spider, it evoked a moment of blind panic. Seriously, why does something already so scary need to be venomous? I was about to ask where, when I noticed shufflers being tossed into the air. The zombie beast was clearing a path and heading directly for us. Looked like a predator wading through tall grass to get to its prey. I mean, if the grass was getting ripped up in clumps and tossed twenty feet to either side, then yeah, it was exactly like that.

"Let go!" I yelled at the man. Bando and another man each had one of the older gentleman's arms and were leaning out the window to the point that the old man's legs were less than a foot from the top of the truck. I had my hands around his thighs. It was going to be extremely difficult for him to reach terminal velocity with all the help he was receiving, but still he would not let his death grip go from the two above.

"You're going to get others killed! Let go!" I shouted at

him. Had a spider bearing down on us and I was playing nurse maid.

The man shouted back a string of what I would imagine were curses. No idea the language but the meaning was clear enough.

"Bando peel his fucking hand off!"

"Trying, sir. He's incredibly strong."

I looked sideways at BT. "Sir, if you don't let go, I am going to punch you in the nuts right now."

No language barrier there. He landed lightly, like a fleet footed dancer. I pulled him in tight and yanked him with me down the hidey hole. When the window was clear, Stenzel took a shot, which did little to dissuade our rampaging beast's approach. If anything, it was flinging shufflers away with more fervent vigor. We were playing a dangerous timing game now, getting people out of the house while also giving Stenzel an opportunity to shoot at the spider. We had to kill it, or seriously deter it, there was no other choice—it would rip the plywood exoskeleton off of this truck easily, and devour the succulent meat nestled within like we were a can of all you can eat crab.

"How many more up there?" I called out. The shufflers were converging down on the spider, slowing it slightly, but it was only about ten yards away at this point and would be upon us in under a minute. Even if Gary took off now with how slow he had to travel we wouldn't outpace the thing.

"Five!" Bando shouted.

Now came the executive decision. Did I leave those five there, where they were arguably safer than we were? And did I tell Gary to get moving with the last-ditch effort that we could get away? Leadership is for the birds. I was still trying to figure out what to do when another person came down. The answer came to me from a source not my own. We all died, or we all lived, simple as that.

"You," I had ducked back down, I couldn't see anything in

the dark of the truck, I was randomly pointing. "You help the rest of the people down." I climbed out of the hole and placed my feet as best could on the roof so I could get some quality shots off. I could hear the creaking of the wood and sometimes some cracking. I would adjust accordingly. Stenzel had a better angle, but the thing was close enough now that I could clearly make out the grotesque features of the amalgamated zombie. The right side of its heads had been pulverized by Stenzel's shots. Neither of us had clear angles to the brains of the thing, that would be housed mid-body, but we could take some of its senses off the table.

I aimed in on that bulbous blistering infection of greenish yellow oozing heads on the left, as did Stenzel. It was stomach turning watching ribbons of the viscous liquid churn in the air like rancid, congealed butter. Five yards away, it was lifting shufflers up and cracking them in half and discarding their broken bodies to the side like an angry teacher might a stack of pencils kept ready for when his students pushed him to the edge. The spider turned what was left of its one head toward us. It had five stumps of ragged flesh and blood-oozing holes with shattering bits of bone sticking up. How it was still alive was a testament to its redundancy. Easier to kill a tick with a Q-tip. Its arms were outstretched when I tossed a volley of bullets into that infected melon. It seemed I had softened the thing up for Stenzel's explosive round. Its face expanded like it had just been stung by a bee and it was deathly allergic. No epi pen for that fucker. I rejoiced when the head burst, and the resultant spray of viscera thankfully missed me.

This world. This world and its fucking need to balance out good with bad. I felt someone land on the roof behind me just as what was left of the spider crashed into the side of the truck. I fell backward into the arms of the man whose nuts I'd threatened to punch. That was a bit of karmic justice I suppose, but not what I was referring to. As I was caught, the person who had just landed was tossed onto the ground. He or she was long out of my reach as I twisted and made a try. The shufflers weren't actively attempting to get at us, but if you hold a blueberry muffin up to someone's nose long enough, they're going to eat it. Heard the first scream before I could scrabble away from the old man and get to the far side of the roof in a bid to help. It was far too late for that. The shufflers had dogpiled on the unlucky bastard. I couldn't see the person at all. I was terrified to look up and not see Stenzel or Bando.

Been through this. Yes, any loss was unacceptable, but some losses were more so. That's humanity in a nutshell. You have your sphere of caring, for some like Deneaux that sphere is small and only one inhabits it; for others the sphere is a bit bigger, and it encompasses family and friends. That's not to say I wouldn't grieve for the loss of whoever that was, it's just easier to deal with when you don't know the person well. I'm not saying it's right. Just saying that's the way we work. How many news articles have we all read where someone, by all accounts a very decent someone, dies violently, wrongfully. It sucks and it may cause anger or sadness at the injustice, but you will still go about your day. Now bring that loss in much closer, and yeah, you're going to have a bad several years.

Another thump to my side. I looked over to see Bando. I grabbed him as the truck swayed again. The spider had no hearing, no sight, and no sense of smell as it slid down the length of the truck doing what, I don't know, but it still had the heft to bandy us about like we were at shock absorber testing facility lined with deep potholes. He thanked me as the old man ushered him inside. When I looked up, Stenzel was helping the next in line. The old man had an iron grip around my calf while also getting ready to help the next person. I felt abundantly bad about the threat I'd made to his manhood. Luckily, he didn't seem to be taking it personally. Two minutes later we were all crammed in the truck bed and Gary was pulling away. We were going to need to offload these people before we could try and rescue more.

"Gary, get us onto the highway!" I told him over the strain of the engine trying to plow through the zombies.

We were jerked sideways hard, I knocked heads with someone, whom, I couldn't tell through the stars swirling above me, might have had a tweeting bird or two up there as well. Could hear the screeching of metal, sounded like the frame was being bent. Then we were moving again.

"What was that?" BT asked.

I was still mentally going through concussion protocol.

"Spider ripped the bumper off!" Major Dylan replied.

Took north of twenty minutes to escape the horde and another five to pull up alongside Justin, two other trucks, and surprise surprise, the tanker. I noticed that Lina was driving, and a very disgruntled Hammer was standing outside by her door. Wasn't a doubt in my mind he had been trying to persuade her to keep going.

"Let's go," I told him once Gary's truck was empty.

"Where?" Hammer asked suspiciously.

"Back in, we're going to rescue who we can."

He stepped up on the truck siderail and spoke to Lina. She got out. He got in. "Let's go," he told me. "Going to be easier and safer in this than that rolling cardboard box."

"Hey!" Gary said, offended.

I wanted to tell him that Hammer wasn't wrong, but we had made it out, so there was that. Stenzel, Rose, Kirby, and Bando each mounted one of the turrets.

"I was expecting a fight," I told Hammer. BT shoved himself in next and I was so wedged against it I could barely shut the door of the passenger seat.

"The other doctors are still inside."

"Ah," I replied that explained everything.

"What?"

"I figured once you got out you would have been halfway to the states by now. Makes sense why you aren't."

"You think so little of me?" he asked.

BT shook his head at me.

I thought for a bit about what I wanted to say, getting into a knockdown drag-out fight at this very moment wouldn't do any of us any good.

"I think your complete fixation on the safety of the doctors leaves little room for any others. I've seen horny men who haven't got any in a bit because they were deployed, have less single-track mindedness when they get home to their beautiful wives."

"That's oddly specific," he said.

"I said what I said."

I was surprised when he answered with. "You might be right."

We weren't on the path to everlasting peace and friendship, but we were well aware of where each other stood, and that was all I could ask for right then. His hands gripped the steering wheel tightly when I directed him to the nearest occupied house. It was not where the doctors were staying.

"They have no protection," he mumbled.

"We save those we come across first. They're either okay or they're not. We need to get out of this soup as quickly and efficiently as we can."

"They're important."

Of course I knew they were important, but whoever was in the next house was important as well, at the minimum to the people they were housed with. We could not set up a hierarchy to who was the most important—this wasn't a triage. But then again, it sort of was. I was worried I was making the wrong decision, and that was right up until a young woman and what I assume was her kid were helped down onto the top of the tanker. There was a catwalk up there. It wasn't going to be a comfortable ride, but as long as they sat down and used a strapdown to tie themselves in, they should be fine. Provided we didn't run into any second-and-beyond generation zombies that could climb. Even as weighted down as we were, the tanker was jostling about a bit as Hammer was running over as many zombies as he was pushing out of the way.

"You're going too fast."

He glanced at me. No need to write down what that look expressed. I was previously unaware that someone could flip you off with a look. I consider myself properly schooled.

"I'm surprised you drove off without them." I didn't mean it as a dig, just a thought, but considering every conversation Hammer and I had bordered on hostility I really should have known that would be the way he interpreted my words.

He glared at me. "I didn't abandon them."

"I wasn't implying that."

"Then what were you implying?"

He didn't give me an opportunity to answer.

"Lina is the most significant person in my life. Getting her to safety was of the utmost importance. Isn't that exactly what you did?"

He was partially right, and I could see his point. This outburst may have had more to do with the guilt he was feeling for leaving the others, but I'd be good and goddammed if I was going to be anyone's punching bag.

"We had animals and children. Are you implying I should have left them here in this shit?"

"Convenient."

"What the fuck is convenient about that? You know, Hammer, I figured at some point we would get over whatever this is, and maybe not become friends, but have some sort of professional relationship. But I think I'm going to have to throw in the towel on any sort of salvage mission. I hate to say this, but there were times when I actually enjoyed being around Deneaux, as fucked as that sounds. I can say in all honesty that I've never felt the least bit glad to have you around. Normally that is something that develops after someone has known me for a bit, but I'd barely opened my mouth over in England and you'd already made up your mind to be a pain in my ass. I've checked, I do not have a resting bitch face, which leads me to believe that nearly all of our problems are the direct result of you."

"Is that so?" he sneered, though he did not deny it, which I found telling. "Have you idioted your way to the top?"

BT placed his hand up to his mouth and leaned back. "Wait, can you make that a verb?"

"What?" I think I asked both of them. "Idiot my way to the top? What does that even mean?"

"You know, like you're a fucking idiot with a sword or something and you just twirl around the room saying oh my, oh dear, as you accidentally lop the heads off your enemies." He was making a high-pitched lolling sound as he mimed the maneuver.

"Why do you sound like Cam from *Modern Family* when he's afraid?" I asked.

"Oh shit!" BT placed his hand up by his mouth again. "He does!" He was pointing with his free hand.

I gave BT what I hoped was a withering gaze to make him keep quiet. He pfffted me.

We were three houses in when Stenzel called down. "Got twelve up here, sir, getting a bit cramped!"

I was careful as I stuck my head out the window. "How many more can you fit?"

"Half dozen at most before it starts getting interesting, sir."

"That's it, we're going for them now," Hammer said.

I wasn't sure who had shouted it, but it would have been impossible to miss.

"Bulkers!"

A wall of the brutes was coming our way straight down the road we found ourselves on. A few tons of zombie propelled flesh marched along towards us, mowing down the shufflers, trampling them underfoot like a harvester to its crop. Brass was flying past my window like copper colored rain as Rose opened up with the machinegun. I don't know what she had for rounds up there, but she wasn't in conservation mode.

"Do you think the truck can take that?" Hammer asked. If the bulkers could get a full gallop going, I didn't think so, but the shufflers were slowing them up considerably. The better question would be once they reached us, would we be able to push through them?

"Spiders!"

I twisted around looking for the more dangerous of the attackers.

"Where?!" I shouted.

"Seven o'clock."

Couldn't have been hidden any better from my view, on the rear driver's side.

"How many?"

"Three, sir!" Kirby answered back.

"Should have stayed back. I've had all the excitement I can take today. Glad we're doing the reverse Oreo thing though," BT said.

"Reverse Oreo?" I asked, not sure why. Sometimes if you shut the hell up you can't walk right into shit.

"You know, vanilla wafers encasing a sexy chocolate filling."

"BT, what are you talking about?" I was looking from mirror to mirror for our threats.

"I'm saying that if we die today it's not going to be the brother that goes down first! I've got a couple of crackers protecting either side of me."

"And that's important somehow?" Hammer asked.

"Of course it is!" he thundered. "Been watching movies for decades where the Black man is always the first to go. It'll be nice to make it to the second act once in awhile."

I offered my fist because he wasn't wrong. He returned the gesture.

"Buddy, if we're about to get torn to shreds like a slow-roasted pig, I'd be honored to go first."

"You always go just a bit too far, man," BT replied.

"Blame it on Tracy. I'm so used to her using a flame thrower to light a candle I don't know how to respond appropriately anymore."

"Truth." We fist bumped again.

It was back to the thick of it. Those nine super zombies were far scarier than the horde of a thousand or more shufflers we were entangled in. When I watched those old zombie flicks way back when, I couldn't imagine a scarier thing than those undead shufflers walking about moaning. How wrong I had been.

Two bulkers had dropped under Rose's withering assault, but she had to be getting close to running through her stores. And if we were going to prioritize, the spiders needed to be dealt with first. Bulkers, last I checked were incapable of climbing.

"Hammer, you're going to have to get us out of here."

"You're running away?"

"What the fuck do you want me to tell you? Yeah, we're running away, we can't deal with those spiders. We escape, drop off who we picked up, and then figure out a new way to come in."

"They're two houses away. We could grab them quick and go."

"Kirby, how much time do we have?"

"Maybe a minute, sir, they look pissed!"

"Fuck," Hammer growled. He pressed down on the gas. I didn't have a chance to warn people to hold on, but if they weren't already gripping that catwalk like their lives depended on it then they deserved to be phased out of the gene pool. I'm not sure what I would have done if Hammer hadn't realized the futility of our current situation. I could have pulled my gun on him, then what? He could have easily delayed long enough until we were under attack, even if I pulled and fired without giving him a chance to respond, by the time I shoved his carcass out of the truck it would have been too late. Then I would have had to tell Lina what happened, or a skewed version, anyway. My squad wouldn't rat me out, but there would be questions. You would think in an apocalypse getting away with murder would be easier.

When I was in boot camp many moons ago, they would truck us out to the shooting range in cattle cars, which was bad enough, but they would pack in three platoons, to the point that the India Railway system, after having viewed film of us, thought it was a brilliant business model. The kicker though was the final stretch of road. Knowing the Marine Corps as I did, I was a hundred percent sure this last couple of miles was purposefully built to have as many potholes as could be feasible and still be considered a road. If not for the fact that we were packed in so tight, there would have been grievous injuries as we got tossed around in the back of that rolling steel cage. I was having flashbacks as Hammer plowed through every obstacle in his way. The people in the turrets were somewhat safe, as they had a steel barricade welded around them, but those on the catwalk were fucked. Anybody that had to assist holding another, like kids or the elderly, were in heaps of trouble.

"Hammer, you're going to knock people off!" I was braced as best I could be, feet on the dash, one hand on the door, the other gripping my seatbelt. I was doing my best to minimize the whiplash like movements. I fundamentally knew that bracing and fighting against the torque was the worst thing I could do; going floppy would save me a great many aches and pains if we made it through this. Way easier said than done. Difficult to go against human nature, self-preservation and all.

"Those spiders get to us and none of them will survive!" Twin thick plumes of black diesel exhaust roared up the stacks and choked the air as he stomped down harder on the accelerator.

We were again plunged into the darkness of saving the many at the expense of the few. In terms of the black and white on a ledger, it was the right thing to do, there were always expenses you needed to write off, but this wasn't ones and zeros, these were people, and every goddamn one of them was precious to someone. I did not have a viable solution. I was angry at the portion of myself that was thankful I wasn't driving and didn't need to make that call. I could only hope Maker would forgive me; I could plead I was helpless to change anything, but I wasn't. I could have sacrificed Hammer at the end of my .45.

"Fucking dark, Mike," I said aloud.

Hammer spared me the smallest glance. He'd heard me, but there was no way he could have known what I was referring to, right?

Screams came from atop. Didn't see exactly what happened, but when booze goes missing from your liquor cabinet and you only have one teenager in the house there isn't much need for visual evidence of the crime. Sometimes vomit hidden under a pile of clothing that smells suspiciously like gin can sew up the case. I tried to look through the rearview mirror, but without ultra-sophisticated anti-shaking technology, that was useless. Might as well have been trying to look through a kaleidoscope within a paint shaker.

Hammer's knuckles whitened as he gripped the steering wheel tighter, safe to say he'd heard the scream as well. What was telling was what we *didn't* hear. No one was shooting; they couldn't.

"Twenty feet!" Kirby shouted then he yelled out; my guess was he'd pinched his tongue between his teeth.

Twenty feet—an unencumbered spider could probably make that in one leap—we were that close to ruin, and then we were out, and the truck sped forward. My organs took a few seconds to settle down as I sat up straight in the seat. When I looked in the mirror, I saw three spiders break through the crowd of zombies and gallop our way. For a terrifying few seconds they were making up the distance—then one jumped.

"Holy shit!" I was sure it was going to make it. I jolted. Then came three or four shots, not enough to kill the thing, but they had been enough to alter its trajectory. It landed hard on the pavement, rolled a few times then resumed its run, but by then, unless we had a mechanical issue, it wasn't going to catch us. Why the hell I wanted to mess around and give the gods an idea of how to thwart us, I don't know, but they must have been busy screwing around with someone else. A few minutes later we pulled up alongside Justin and the other evacuees.

Hammer bolted out of that truck like he'd had an ejection seat and headed over to Lina. I got out slower, knowing I was going to have to deal with the wailing that was coming from the top. I saw Stenzel looking down at me, she nodded slightly, she was letting me know that our squad was all right. Two people had been pitched off into the maelstrom, a two-year-old kid and his fifty-something grandfather who dove to try and catch him when the baby slipped from his mother's grasp. Understandably, the mother was inconsolable. My heart was breaking as I watched her anguish. She was gently helped down, unable to do it on her own. There was a small huddle of people around her doing their best to console her. There was no amount of "it'll be all rights" in the world that were going to make a difference.

"Goddammit," BT hissed next to me.

I hadn't a clue what I could do except bear silent witness to her sobs. Tracy lightly touched me on the arm before she breezed past and offered what she could in terms of solace. She was so much braver than me. I wanted to get the fuck out of there, truth be told. Find a bottle of grain alcohol and see if I could make myself blind to it all. How quickly I had forgotten about my tequila debacle. There's being a glutton for punishment. What's after that? Big fat stupid fuck? Major Dylan came in after a bit, she had a sedative; the woman was having difficulty catching her breath between sobs. I turned to see my squad behind me, they moved aside as I walked past them with my head hanging low. Half of our people were still stuck in that accursed village, and I didn't know how we were going to get them back. We had no viable way to deal with the dual threats of the warring zombie factions. Staying in the middle of the roadway also wasn't the best tactical maneuver; it was likely that something unsavory would find us. People, shufflers, spiders, a pride of panthers, it was only a matter of time.

8

MIKE JOURNAL ENTRY 8

We'd gotten off the road by traveling another ten miles to the next village. Although, even using that word was a stretch. This place gave shanty towns a bad name. It was more like boxes and old tents under a highway crossing, if there had been a highway crossing. Wasn't any of us that didn't decide to sleep in or on our vehicle. It sucked more than it sounded. Sleeping in a car alone or with another person is bad enough, but cramped quarters on uncomfortable accommodations is worse, way worse. I think Henry and Patches were the only two to get anything nearing quality downtime. And even Patches lost some as Henry repeatedly and often stunk up the joint. Eighteen hours had passed, and we were no closer to getting the rest of our people back. Short of an M1 Abrams tank, I was fresh out of ideas. I had walked out to the roadway and was looking back the way we needed to go. I'd love to say I hadn't thought about it, but just leaving was an option. A horrible one, but an option, nonetheless. At what point did you keep risking lives for the lost? I wisely kept that abomination of a thought to myself. It was hard enough holding on to my humanity, no sense in letting people think it had already slipped through my fingers. Avalyn had come up

176

next to me and slid her hand into mine. Startled me, though I think I was able to keep from showing it. I'd not heard her approach.

"I might be able to help."

"I thought we went over this?" From what I knew she could "suggest" things to the newer zombies, but held little to no sway with the shufflers. And her limited control of the second genners was hampered because they were distracted. It was like we were trying to screw decking down and all we had was a hammer as a tool. It could be done, but there would be damage, and it could fall apart when you walked on it. And again it was all we had.

"I can do it." She was looking the same way I was. I glanced down, she had her tongue firmly planted in her cheek. For a heartbeat she looked like any second grader contemplating kicking in a run during recess kickball. What sucked was she would never know what that innocence was like, those days when the most horrible thing in your life was when Bratty Billy Simpkins said your sneakers looked funny.

There was a racket back by where we had slept. Most of my squad and Gary were gathering up some corrugated sheet metal, the preferred building material of shanty towns everywhere.

"Going to make this a fortress." Gary smacked the side of his plywood tank. He was securing sheets of the stuff over the plywood. It would be marginally better, like covering up construction paper with cardboard better. Even if a bulker didn't break straight through, it would still destroy the framing.

"Can you do anything about the two by fours?" I asked. We were going to do this, and this stupid truck was our best option. Even if it was like shooting a bear with a spitball. Best we could hope for was he wouldn't notice it, wouldn't do a damn thing if it was charging.

"I can wrap them up in some of this." He bent the corrugated tinfoil, it broke where the rust had eaten through. My confidence level was not increasing.

"Sounds good," was all I could offer. I was contemplating finding a secluded spot so I could say my final prayers. Maybe make a confession or seventeen so I could enter the afterlife with a clear conscience. Probably couldn't do that; I didn't really have the time for a full confessional, and if I could find a priest, I don't think it would be fair to unload all of that onto any one person, they'd be bound to break under the strain. Shit, I think I'm responsible for the mass therapist quitting of oh-nine, and I've added to my mental arsenal considerably since then.

We spent nearly the entire day doing all we could to make Gary's truck as fortress like as possible. Sure it looked decent enough; on the outside, paper mâché looks strong, then you whack it with a stick and it shatters. Sometimes the illusion of strength can win the day, but this was not that day. There's only so much you can do with half rotten corrugated steel and rope. We found enormous lengths of the stuff and had wrapped everything in a cocoon of the fiber. No doubt in my mind that was much stronger than the steel we'd covered up.

"Are we leaving?" Hammer asked. When we figured the thing was as good as it was going to get.

I popped my back as I looked up to the sky, my guess was somewhere north of six pm. "Tomorrow, first light." I started to walk away. Not sure why I hadn't figured out yet that Hammer needed to get in the final word. I'd encountered less tenacious Chihuahuas.

"Now. We leave now."

"It's going to be dark soon, we leave at first light."

"Awww...what's the matter, are you afraid of the dark?"

"You know what? Yeah, I am a little bit. It's an evolutionary thing. You see when we first climbed down from the trees we were living in, we realized mighty quickly that there were a whole shitload of predators better able to see in the dark than we could. If we hadn't figured out how to harness fire and have our own light source for those long dark nights, odds are I wouldn't have to be listening to your stupid ass because we wouldn't have made it as a species."

"Oh man, you went back to pre-history to diss him!" BT leaned back.

I was glad BT got a kick out of it, but I was tired and worried, and I didn't need any of Hammer's shit right then.

"Just let me take the truck. You can stay here, find a nice table to hide under while you bite your nails."

Did I mention he was relentless? I walked away. My only other choice was to kill him, and then we'd need to bury the body to keep any predators away, including zombies, and I was just too exhausted to deal with all of that.

BT was outside my car as the sun shone through the windshield the following morning.

"How long have you been there?" I asked once I extracted myself as quietly as I could and we walked a few feet away.

"Couple of hours. I knew Hammer was going to be up your ass to get moving. Barely beat him here, told him to get lost."

"And he did?"

"He didn't stray too far, that's why I stayed here."

"Ah, I'm sorry man."

"Don't be, you've got the hard part today."

We'd decided yesterday who was going and was staying back. Out of necessity for as much space as we could save, we figured on only four people. Three up front and one in the back to help with the extractions. Gary had made it extremely clear that the truck was his baby, and he wasn't going to entrust it to anyone else. I'd made it clear to BT's protests that as commanding officer I was ordering myself to be part of the detail. He told me that it didn't work that way, but Captain Talbot can be an obstinate SOB, and he wasn't listening. He's a friggen jerk like that. I would have taken BT in a heartbeat if he didn't take up three spots. One of the people coming was Hammer, because of course it was. He wasn't going to take no for an answer, probably steal another vehicle and follow us in. We had somewhat of a backup plan. Rose and Kirby were going to follow us and wait on the outskirts. Not entirely sure what good that was going to do. If the truck broke down or was overrun, it wasn't like we were going to be able to run out and get in another. The only decent thing about this rescue attempt was Hammer was going to be in the back and me in the front. BT gave me a hug then walked next to me as I headed over to where Gary was.

"Sir," Kirby said from the other truck, he was behind the wheel.

"Morning," I told him.

Gary was beaming as he looked over his creation in the light of day. To me it Looked more like something Frankenstein would have created. Although this didn't look nearly as hardy as that monster had been.

Hammer kept looking at a watch he wasn't wearing as he silently urged me to hurry up. I wanted to get those people to safety, I did, but willingly going back into that cluster was not something I was actively looking forward to. The zombies had really taken the shine off this apocalypse. It might almost be decent if they weren't around. I got in the truck with little fanfare, no cheering masses hoping for our victory and speedy return. We were all so tired of it. How could we not be? To know death was the price of being sentient, being immersed in it at all times was an abomination that befuddled the senses. We'd constantly been shifting from being alive and living, to surviving and not dying, and every time we turned around, someone else failed at it. It was no way to walk through this life.

"Hey kid? How are you doing?" I asked Avalyn, who had already been inside the truck and was sitting in the middle of the bench seat.

She gave me a vacant, vapid look. Then gave me a weak smile that did nothing to dispel the immense joy I wasn't feeling.

"Tally ho," I told Gary pointing out the windshield.

"It's going to be fine," he said rubbing the dash. I noticed he wasn't talking to me.

Kirby hung back a mile or so.

My head hung as we came up to the village. I had hoped that maybe there was a chance the bastards had all left, gone to a rave in the city or something.

"I'm not sensing anything." Avalyn startled me again, her voice was octaves lower than normal, as if she had entered a pre-teen BT Sound Alike contest. Wouldn't even know how to voice it, if I were a narrator. I'll leave that to the professionals. All I do know was it creeped me the hell out. Worse than that *Redrum* kid, and his stupid talking finger.

Like everything in life, that declaration was both good and bad, or I suppose there was the third option, which would be: catastrophic. Good because it would mean the second genners weren't around, or had been defeated. Bad because the shufflers would not have any distractions. Catastrophic came in if Avalyn no longer held sway over any type of zombie, then I'd just brought a kid into a war zone. As it was, I was far past what I felt comfortable with.

"Are you still too far?" I asked. I was reaching. We were less than a quarter mile from the horde. Distorted, grotesque faces began to turn our way.

Gary looked over at me. We'd been counting on Avalyn to lead a zombie-on-zombie assault to create openings for us, and now that that wasn't on the table.

"What's the hold up?" Hammer called out.

"We're getting takeout. Want something?" It's my default operating mode, especially in high stress situations.

"Just go in and get those people." I could hear the sneer.

"Our ringer doesn't detect any zombies," I explained the delay.

Hammer was quiet. We'd gone over the plan a half dozen times, and our success had resided squarely on Avalyn's small shoulders. Now I was wondering if we should head back and drop her off. My fear was that once we did, would I come back?

"Mike?" Gary asked. I was stuck, like my transmission had seized. The engine was running but I couldn't move. I looked in the rearview mirror; Kirby was about a quarter mile behind us. I'm sure he was wondering what the hell we were doing.

"They're moving," Gary said, referring to the nearest shufflers, which were coming to check us out. I was looking in that direction, but in an absent way, where I wasn't actually seeing anything, or more aptly, I wasn't processing any external stimuli.

I don't know if Hammer was keyed into my mood somehow, but if he had said anything to try and get me moving I would have likely told Gary to turn around and get us out of there. I was hoping for an excuse to do just that, if I'm being honest with myself. The truck itself with the plow was stout, but was it stout enough? We were talking about potentially plowing through multiple tons of zombie flesh.

"I'd kill for a Terex right now." I was referring to the enormous mining trucks that Eliza had used during the attack on Etna Station. Although at less than a half mile per gallon, probably not the most fuel-efficient vehicle we could have used.

"Think they have a rental facility nearby?" Gary asked. It was tough to tell if he was serious or not.

Funny either way, I suppose. "I'm going to go with no," I told him.

"Pity. They're eventually going to get here."

The zombies weren't in any rush because, well, they

couldn't be in a rush, per their design limitations. It was like we were watching an occurring disaster in super slo-mo.

"Leaving?" he asked. He seemed to be acutely aware that I didn't know.

"Yup, get us out of here."

Gary waited to make sure I wasn't going to change my mind then did as I said.

"Lose your nerve, Talbot?" Hammer shouted from the back.

"I can't believe we're on the same side." I was thinking it, but Gary had said it.

"We're going to go back and regroup, Avalyn is no longer part of the plan," I told Kirby when we pulled up alongside. I'm sure he wanted to know more, but I wanted to get back. There were two people in this truck that shouldn't be here and I needed them gone.

BT and Stenzel were on the roadway when we came back. Before I could tell them what was going on, Hammer had jumped out and come around to the passenger side.

I stepped out as calmly as I could. "Either get the fuck out of my sight or prepare to be eating out of a straw for a few months." I was wholly committed to that course of action, I don't make many idle threats. I don't think Hammer gave two shits about my soon to become reality threat, but when BT placed his massive chest up against the other man's shoulder, he rethought his next set of actions. He looked up at the big man before turning and walking away.

"He's got to go. I've taken all of him that I can."

"What happened?" BT asked.

"Besides him reminding me of the times I was using single ply and my finger punched straight through?"

"Fuck, Mike, yeah besides that. Now I get to live the rest of the day with that visual."

I clued him in quickly on what had happened, restraining myself to just the day's incursions.

"Do I dare ask what the plan is?"

"It's shufflers, and we know they're averse to overwhelming losses. I think we need to do some shock and awe."

"Did I hear shock and awe?" Rose had joined the conversation. "Those are my middle names."

"What? You said it was Alice, after your mom's mom." Kirby was confused.

"Son, did you have someone else take your military entrance exam?" BT asked. "When did recruiting boxes of rocks become a thing?"

If I had let him be, he might have gone on for an hour.

"Whatcha got?" I asked Rose.

"I have a 203."

"The grenade launcher?" I asked, referring to the attachment that went below the barrel of an M16. "You have rounds? I thought all you found were dummy ones." Dummy rounds were like blanks, they would go bang and shoot out a grenade that would not explode upon impact, nor distance traveled. They were a training aid. Sure, you could kill someone if you shot the damn thing at their chest, but other than that they were relatively harmless. I suppose if you thonked someone on the head with it downrange that could cause issues, or for sure hit them straight in the eye, but they were mostly safe. Kind of like a butter knife. Unless you were my son Justin, then they were considered a dangerous weapon. (A story I wrote in one of my other journals: butter knife, apple, ER, stitches, that about covers the basics.)

"Well, they *were* dummy rounds."

"Do I even want to know?"

"I made sure to work on them far enough away from people that if there was an accident…" she tailed off due to my look.

"Rose, I'm as concerned for your safety as I am for everyone else's."

"Wait, I was next to you. You said they were inert," Kirby said.

"I mean they were right up until I placed the charge up against the primer," she told him.

"Do they work?" I asked.

"I haven't really had a chance to test them. And sir...I'm hesitant to."

"NO!" BT spun and pointed at me. "If Reckless Rosie is hesitant than there's a reason."

"Reckless Rosie?" she asked.

"Sorry," he told her but never stopped looking at me.

"Rose?" I asked.

"In theory they should do their job, but I've never worked with rifle primers."

There was no chance I was going to ask her what was the worst that could happen because that was a foregone conclusion.

"How strong is the charge?" I asked.

"This right here. This is the definition of white people doing white shit. Literally the whitest shit I've ever heard! Like putting corn kernels on white bread and calling it cornbread, white shit! Ever read those Darwin awards? Pretty sure you've never read about a brother being awarded the prize." He was pacing a small circle.

"The good news is there's no one left to read about it," I said.

"Yes, Mike, that's the good news. Fucking fucker."

"The cornbread thing, that real?" I asked.

"Of course it is! Haven't you ever been to Florida?" BT was still in full rage mode.

"He looks angry," Kirby said to Rose. "I should probably get going."

"How many do you have?"

"Are you serious? Are you not listening to me?" BT stepped in between me and Rose. I was staring at his chest.

"Not sure how that would be possible," I told him. "Listen, man, half our people need rescuing. I don't have anything better than this."

"We'll see." He walked away in a huff.

"Twenty-seven, sir. I have twenty-seven grenades."

"And how strong are they?" I don't know if I was hoping they were like loud firecrackers or small nukes. Tough to say. Small nukes if they worked, loud noise makers if they didn't— in case that wasn't clear.

"The shell on the dummy rounds is a lot thinner than on a normal grenade, so I made up for it by packing an extra charge. And ball bearings."

"Like a claymore?" I asked shuddering. Still had nightmares about those.

"Pretty much." She winced, I would imagine remembering the time she tried to make shredded cheese out of me.

"Sir, I might not be known for my smarts, but is this wise?" Kirby asked.

"Oh, I think you and I both know the answer to that," I said.

"I do?" He thought about it for a moment. "I don't think I do," he said to Rose.

"Go grab them," I told Rose.

"Sir, I'll shoot them," she volunteered.

"And deny me all the fun? I don't think so."

I was standing there wondering how to word my good-byes when I saw BT moving quickly in my direction. By the set of his features, I was worried he was going to cold cock me, so that I went unconscious. Rose must have seen him too as she veered off. The man was scarier than iffy explosives, and if that doesn't say something, I don't know what does.

"One day, Talbot. That's all we need. Rose, get your ass over here!" BT beckoned.

"What's going on?" I asked.

"I talked to my brother-in-law and we came up with an idea."

"I'm your brother-in-law, I'm confused."

"You do realize I have two of you crazy bastards, don't you? Remember your brother, Gary?"

"I, umm, yeah I remember him. I just kind of never really thought of that relationship until just now."

"Screwed up thing about it was, he said the exact same thing. Maybe I'm giving white people a bad rap when it's really just Talbots, and you just happen to be white. The Asian community would flat out kick you out of their club. You'd be a stupid brother, too. I'm telling you, if you were Black and were pulling this shit, my grandmother would have given you a 'come to Jesus' moment, until you figured it out. Hallelujah and praise the lord! I would have paid good money to see her size fifteen slipper being repeatedly smacked upside your head."

"Size fifteen?"

"All the Tines on her side were large people."

In my head I was seeing a frail old white-haired woman with flippers for feet, but in all likelihood, she would be as statuesque as an Amazonian Goddess. Then I was thinking of her wielding that deadly slipper.

"I mean, I wish I had rhythm and could dance worth a shit and had a firm grasp on southern cooking, but other than that, no way man, I'm glad I didn't know your grandmother."

BT's face softened and he grabbed my shoulders. "For some reason, she would have loved you." His eyes watered at the corners as he thought of her. "Just give us a day. You, with me," he told Rose, and they both walked away.

I didn't feel like I had any choice in the matter. When I find myself in these moments of downtime, I do what any normal person would. I headed for a dog pile. In this case, a dog pack that included a confused pig and a cat that pretends her best to not be a part of the action but always stays close.

9

MIKE JOURNAL ENTRY 9

"WHAT THE FUCK IS THIS THING?" I asked the next morning as I stood outside Gary's truck.

"It's an anti-Rose device," BT was beaming as he said the words.

"Jesus, man, did you get any sleep?" He had carryon sized bags under his eyes.

"Some, but I wanted to make sure this got done."

The rifle was on a sturdy tripod, and that was about the only normal part of the configuration. Attached to the tripod was a round piece of steel heading straight back, it was about six feet long, and diameter-wise close to a broom handle. At the end of the connector was a plate of steel, three feet wide by the same height and roughly a quarter inch-thick. The pole allowed us to move the barrel back and forth, the legs kept it steady, and the plate maybe offered protection.

"Are you kidding me with this thing? How heavy is it?"

"I figure a bit over a hundred pounds," BT said still beaming.

"A hundred pounds? Not very wieldy."

"Wieldy isn't the point, safety is."

"And that plate will stop a misfired grenade?" I asked.

"I have every faith," Rose said.

"In the steel or the grenade?" I asked. Found it telling she didn't respond. The more I looked, the less I liked the contraption, a heavy piece of string was attached to the trigger and fed through a drilled hole in the steel. "How do I aim if I'm blindly pulling a string?"

"It's a grenade, how much aiming do you need to do?" Gary asked.

"Fair point." I smacked my lips.

"There's um one more thing," BT stated.

"Of course there is," I sighed.

"When you get to the village, you're going to have to go in backwards."

"The what now?"

"To keep Gary safe, you're going to have to enter in back-wards. The launcher can't be forward facing."

"I can't believe how much shit I get for my redneck engi-neering when this thing looks like it came from the Appalachian Community College." I was going to ask if the Appalachian Community College had an Idiot Outreach program and that maybe they'd overseen this project. Decided against it. "Fine. Let's get this show on the road because apparently these are my monkeys and this is my circus. Fuck me."

"Where's Hammer?" Gary asked.

That was when I saw Lina approaching with a note in her hand. I didn't need to read it to know what it said. I was partially right. She gave a tight smile as she handed it over. "Captain."

It was a simple note, "Went to get them, fuck off."

"So personable," BT said as he read over my shoulder.

"How long ago?" I asked.

"I'm not sure," she said. "When I woke up, he was gone."

"Check the guards."

That was when we caught sight of Kirby leading Bando over.

"I'm sorry, sir," Bando said holding a hand over his left eye.

"What happened?" BT asked.

"Fucker sucker punched him!" Kirby was pissed.

"He said he was coming to relieve me. When I told him I'd just started, he popped me in the eye, tied my hands and feet before I could get back up, and drove past in one of the cars."

I was more pissed than Kirby. The man had to go. Not only did he assault a guard and take off without orders, he'd left us exposed. Had an enemy taken that moment to attack through that avenue we would have taken casualties before we'd had a chance to muster our defense. Disobeying an order was one thing, lord knew I did it enough times, but leaving us unguarded a whole other. I had all the ammunition I needed to either exile him from the group, or place him up against a wall. The firing squad would be for the best because it would assure me that I could keep the scientists. If he was exiled, Lina would for sure go, the others could be touch and go.

"How long ago, was that?" I asked.

"Just over two hours," Bando said. "Kirby was just now coming to relieve me."

"That's enough time that if he were successful, he'd already be back," BT said, then apologized when he realized Lina was still there.

"I'm going to…" Probably wasn't a good thing to say I was going to kill him in front of his wife because this wasn't a figure of speech. I would have been perfectly fine with his expiration date coming due today. "Let's go."

"Help me with this," BT Motioned to Kirby. They hefted the strange cannon configuration into place in the back of the truck.

"Munitions are inside, I'm coming with you," Rose stated.

Kirby liked that about as much as someone finding out they had a colonoscopy scheduled for the day of a lunch date they'd been asking for since Christmas.

"Are the grenades that unsafe?" I asked her as we got in.

She slapped a hand against the steel plate, she didn't need to say a word.

"Unreal. Can you imagine that statistically the most dangerous job I worked before this was at the Post Office? Since the Corps," I elaborated.

Rose smiled. "Good thing this isn't a job then, but a way of life."

"Let's go, brother." I smacked the protective shell we were under.

"Godspeed," Lina said as she waved.

"Beer will be waiting!" BT yelled.

"You think Hammer is still alive?" Rose asked once we were underway.

"It would be a lot easier if he wasn't."

"Sir?" she asked.

I was thinking that maybe I shouldn't have said that aloud. "I mean, we're going to have to be careful where we start lobbing grenades."

I think that mollified her, but it's tough to think of too many things at once when you're babysitting temperamental explosives.

"Getting close!" Gary shouted, wasn't like he needed to inform us, the smell had already wafted in. Second gen zees didn't smell like roses, that was for sure, but there was something about the first genners that was a bit more pungent. The stink of death wafted around them more so than the newbies. He began to slow down, and then we could feel the movement to the side as the truck was turning around. Rose undid slide locks for the rear panel as I got in position to push the barrel out. There was a joke picture on the internet, when that was still a thing, it was of a backpack larger than the person carrying it—it was big enough to convert into a sleeper sofa when it wasn't being hefted around. This fucking rifle was less wieldy than that. The other problem with the M203 grenade launcher was it was one round at a time, like a black powder rifle, meaning we would fire one off, then have to pull the entire thing in so Rose could slide another in place, wash, rinse, repeat. Not sure yet what our rate of fire was going to be but *unimpressive* came to mind.

"Loaded, sir," Rose said as we both peeked over the top before doing our best to completely close off the back of the truck.

"Stay low, brother!" I shouted.

"Already looking up at the steering column!" he assured me.

Rose nodded. The thing I didn't like was the usual gleam in her eyes was missing. She was generally pretty thrilled to blow shit up.

"Here goes nothing—or everything," I said as I gave the thin rope a slow steady tug like I'd been instructed to. Wasn't long before we heard the *whomp* sound as the firing pin struck the primer and launched the grenade. We didn't get to see the initial explosion, but we heard it, and then when we went to reset, we saw what it had done.

"Holy fuck, Rose." Looked sort of like those pictures of the Tunguska explosion site, the trees all blown over for seemingly miles. It had been either a meteor strike or a Tesla experiment gone awry. The grenade had had gone thirty yards past their front lines and had made a circle of meat byproduct some forty feet around. I'd seen government documents look less shredded. The issue now was that the stinky bastards had seen us.

"Ready, sir," she said as she plopped down next to me, and we pushed the whole assembly forward.

"Still down, brother?"

"Amazing all the wires under the dash!" he replied.

"I'll take that as a yes. Fire in the hole." I pulled, pulled some more, then felt the release of tension, but no subsequent sound of a primer going off, and certainly not a grenade. "Uh oh. Dud?" I asked.

Rose looked genuinely offended; she took great pride in her explosives.

"Slow roller," she replied.

"What's that even mean?"

Five seconds went by. "We can't wait forever." I'd been briefed that the effective range on the military version of the grenades was in excess of a thousand feet; Rose had changed things up. She'd packed the things so heavy with projectiles she figured we only had about half that. To be safe, I'd told Gary to get us somewhere in the neighborhood of a football field away. He'd argued with me about whether I'd meant a US football field or an English football field.

"Details matter," he'd explained.

"Aren't they the same?" I'd asked. (If you're reading this and you're a fan of the inferior sport known as soccer in the US, I'm sorry, I just didn't care to know that particular piece of information. Kind of like I don't give a fuck about the nutritional value of ham, because I'm never eating it.)

"I wonder if it's easier being that ignorant." He'd shaken his head "I'm going with the Futbol length, gives us more space." He'd made sure to pronounce the word *futbol* with a French accent, so I knew what he was talking about.

Right then I was happy he'd gone with the longer distance, I just wish I could remember how much longer it was. Shufflers were slow, but they weren't laden down snails, slow. It was likely we only had another twenty seconds before we were surrounded.

"Hey, I don't want to be a nag, but they're coming!" Gary shouted.

"Keep your head down!" I warned.

"I am! I angled the side mirror so I can see, and at the

bottom of the mirror it warns that objects are closer than they appear, and no shit, Mike, they already appear pretty close."

There was a screech as Rose was pulling back on the rifle assembly.

"What are you doing? I thought this was a slow roller?" I didn't know exactly what that meant, but I assumed it had something to do with a slow burning fuse, or primer, in this case.

"Can't wait any longer."

We both yanked the contraption back. The zombies had passed the halfway mark and were on the homestretch.

Rose slid the barrel forward, then pulled it back quickly. "Recharged, try it again," she said as we pushed it back into place.

The time for a slow and steady pull was over. I yanked the line like I was trying to set a hook in a fish. This time we were rewarded with the *whoosh* sound and the resultant earthquake inducing explosion. Problem was, the grenade had sailed clear over the heads of those immediately threatening us. But if I had Gary move, all we would be doing was killing a small percentage of the zombies chasing us. We needed to get them spooked, cause a stampede; not sure if shuffling zombies could be considered a stampede, but for this explanation, the analogy fits.

"Mike!" Gary yelled, it wasn't phrased as a question, but it was one. He was wondering when I was going to give him the order to drive us out of here.

"Hold!" I told him.

"This isn't an old timey Civil War musket line, brother! Something doesn't start happening soon, we have to go."

"Ready." Rose nodded as we completed the reload procedure.

I lifted up slightly on the plating, not thrilled that we were exposed, but this grenade needed to detonate a lot closer if we had any hopes of standing our ground. The trigger pull went off without a hitch, not sure about the primer part, there wasn't so much a *whoosh* as a *whomp*. The grenade was fired, that part was true, but calling what happened next "a launch" was like calling the Challenger Shuttle a successful test on the tensile strength of a space-craft. Too soon? It hit the ground some twenty feet away and skittered a bit, as if a toddler had tossed a rock, so, basically, not much *oomph* behind it. I dropped the plate down right before the explosion took place. Holy bells if that plate didn't ring like a dinner triangle struck by a stout and angry farmer's wife.

"Are my ears bleeding?" I shout asked Rose.

Her mouth was moving, but I couldn't hear anything except the high whine of tinnitus. Pretty sure that wasn't her voice, but not absolutely positive it could have been she'd taken on a parental role in a Charlie Brown segment.

Caught snippets from Gary that involved a lot of "bastard child" and "dickless demon." That was new, probably going to hold onto that one. He used some of the old standbys too, fucker was predominant, and "mistake" came up once or twice. When I could finally hear somewhat decently, come to find out the ball bearings had taken out both sideview mirrors. As far as I was concerned that was a win, because what he couldn't see he couldn't complain about. Rose and I were going through the motions of reloading, although my head was ringing so loudly it felt like I was flying a drone. Would have been hard to feel any more detached from my body than at that point.

Rose took the string from my hand. Not sure how much I'd been addled, but I wasn't exactly sure what to do with it right then. Another pull, a distant explosion...I mean, I guess it was distant. Could have been five feet away and sounded distant. I was on autopilot, muscle memorying my way through another reload. We were up to the seventh or eighth time when pathways began lining up again in my head.

Thinking became as clear as it ever does up there. Not saying a ton, but you work with what you have.

"Huzzah!" Gary shouted as we finished another reload. "They're running!" We were moving backwards, toward the enemy.

Rose and I both looked over the plate and out. The thing about shufflers is, for them, running isn't so much about running, as it is leaving an area in a geriatric type of way. Gary wasn't going much faster than five miles an hour, which was double what the shufflers could pull off on a good day, which meant he was going to plow straight into their ass. If this wasn't my brother and they weren't zombies, that would be a vaguely veiled sexual innuendo. What the fuck is wrong with men that we can take almost anything and make it sexual? Right before we'd left the refinery, Tracy and I had been cleaning up in the cafeteria, she'd asked if I could help her dry the dishes. Want to know my response?

"Oh yeah, baby...I'm gonna dry them real good." This done in as sultry a voice as I could pull off, as I erotically wiped a towel over a dinner plate.

"That's about as appealing as a potato," she replied. Funny thing, though? We fooled around that night. Maybe she had a thing for clean dinnerware. I was going to have to keep that in mind.

"Slow up!" Rose shouted, so maybe I didn't have quite as firm a grasp on my faculties as I'd thought. Only so many times you can have your salad tossed and not spill the tomatoes. Wait...doesn't having your salad tossed mean something else? Maybe I'll leave that one right there.

My thoughts crystallized when my brother gave a one-word answer. "Can't!"

She hadn't been talking to me, she was talking to my brother, as he was about to do some zombie ass plowing.

"Drop it in neutral!" I shouted. Some of the blow back must have taken out the brake line.

"Already did."

We were slowing and would be more so when we encountered bodies on the road, but right then we were still making headway.

"Gary, duck down! Keep the wheel straight!"

"Fire, Rose, we have to keep them moving."

Making shit blow up was never going to be an issue for her. She pulled the trigger. We had started the reload process when the truck bumped all over the place, safe to say we'd struck the debris field. It was all we could do to keep from planting our faces into the metal plating or the floorboards. It was a low-speed teeth cracker. We'd come to a shuddering stop as the echoes of our latest explosive offering came to a close. There was a knock on the side of the truck.

"Just me! Coming around! Don't shoot anything!" Gary yelled. "Including me," he said quieter.

The shufflers were pulling back as quickly as something with that name can.

"I'm going to see what I can do about the brakes," Gary said as Rose and I came from behind the shield wall.

Even if he stopped the leak, if that was what it was, I had no idea what he was going to do to fill the reservoir back up with. Wasn't like you could piss in the master cylinder like you could a radiator. Yes, I've done that. A bunch of us were heading down to Cape Cod on a Friday, during the height of summer. Traffic was as close to a standstill as it could be without being called a parking lot. My car was not dealing well with the heat, the temperature gauge was firmly in the red when I was finally able to sneak my way over into the breakdown lane. It was Dennis who had the brilliant notion of popping the radiator lid. Seemed like a good idea, right? Let some of the heat out? Kirby would know. It's a wonder any teenager makes it into their twenties. Thing took off like a bottle rocket. Bounced off the hood of a nearby Porsche. The owner wasn't thrilled about it, but when you see six juvenile delinquents, you have to start thinking about personal safety.

The geyser that burst forth from my car looked like someone had unbolted a fire hydrant in Brooklyn in July. Luckily, we'd all been drinking on the car ride down. I know, right? Lucky we'd been drinking and driving, refer back to the part where I wonder how dipshit teens make it out of those years. We all ended up pissing in the radiator to the numerous beeps and curses of those trying to pass by. Finally got down to the Cape a couple of hours later but we had the unfortunate displeasure of smelling super-heated piss the entire way. That was the tangent I was on as Rose and I began making our way down the roadway.

"Sir?" Rose asked, I got the distinct feeling it wasn't the first go around to get my attention.

"Present and accounted for," was the first thing out of my mouth, which would lead me to believe I was not present, and far from accounted. "I'm good. I'm good."

I couldn't blame her for being hesitant. It wasn't like we were sitting around the pool having a couple of beers and she wanted me to pass the pretzels. This was a rescue mission with hostiles in the area. I was doing my best internally to convince myself to get it together.

Maybe she gave me a squirrelly look, I didn't check, I was okay with ignorance. "I hope the gen threes aren't here." Two Marines, even with automatic weapons, would be hard pressed to turn just one of the super zombies away. A couple dozen gen two speeders would be bad enough, considering our mode of transportation.

"Where is everyone?" Rose asked.

I'd thought about calling out, but if someone had somehow slept through the maelstrom we'd just created, then me playing town crier wasn't going to do anything. With the zombies emptying the area like concert goers at the end of the show, people—the living kind—should have been checking out what was going on.

"This isn't good." There was no sound; even the ringing in my ears had subsided. Gary could be heard swearing off in the distance. Brakes were probably a bit worse off than we thought.

"Good fucking job, Mike, just ruin our only means of travel!" Gary was losing his shit. Most likely he'd not intended me to hear his rant, but within a cone of silence, all sound is magnified.

"Not sure how that was my fault. If anyone he should be talking about you," I told Rose.

"He's knows better."

I nodded.

"That's the car Hammer took," Rose was looking down a side alley.

"How'd he get this far in?" I asked as we scanned the area, forward, back and side to side. Nothing, no zombies and no people. We knew it was possible to gently push the zombies out of the way, but he would have been fully encased in the stinky fucks, and at some point they would have realized there was a human around.

"And where is he?" There were four dead zombies nearby and a fifth with no ability for locomotion, though that didn't stop its shitty biting disposition and desire to eat us. Rose raised her rifle, I shook my head. I don't think it would have mattered, but I didn't want to pierce the quiet just then. I was afraid that it might signal the beginning of new hostilities, and we were way too far away from our ride. We came up on either side of the car. I ducked down to take a look. No one was in it, although there were a few weapons and a backpack, probably had some ammo and maybe med supplies and food. If we found no signs of people or only dead bodies, I'd snag it on the way back. Rose's eyebrows furrowed. I shrugged, I had no answers to her questions.

Only two things could have happened here. Either he'd got the survivors out of here somehow, or they'd all succumbed. The loss of so many souls would be as close to insurmountable as anything we'd faced thus far. Hard to build a community with no people.

"You hear that?" Rose asked.

"Hilarious," I replied, thinking she was making a reference to the lack of any sound.

"Someone's yelling."

I couldn't hear anything. The sound of metal bacon sizzling on an oiled-up pan, aka tinnitus, had come back to say hi.

I followed Rose's lead, not liking the fact we were moving further away from my brother who would be paying zero attention to anything besides the repair he was attempting to make. Rose was moving faster; whatever she was hearing had yet to break through my compromised system.

"Rose, what's going on?"

"Someone is shouting for help."

"How loud is it? I can't hear it."

"Half as loud as this conversation."

I should have been able to hear that. I was more than a bit worried about that. Any handicap was detrimental to one's continued existence, and as far as existences went, I wanted to keep mine. My innards were roiling, something was wrong, I mean besides the obvious.

"We have to go back." I stopped.

"Sir, the sound is up ahead." She hadn't stopped.

"Sergeant, stop, that's an order." I hardly ever pulled rank, wasn't my normal means of leadership. Most of my squad were professionals and did their job as well as they could with minimal direction from me. The way it should be. It was no surprise she turned back with a confused look.

"I've got nothing better than a rumbling gut feeling, but something's wrong. We need to get back to the truck."

She looked back in the direction she had been traveling. "Don't make me order you, again."

She relented at that.

I don't have the power of premonition, oh sure, there were a few times in life where I sensed something and it was dead on. I feel like everyone does that a couple of times throughout their life. Nothing I could have pulled a career from though. Or maybe I could have, lord knows meteorologists had been doing it for decades. Just so happens that this time my gut intuition and what the Universe was throwing at me were aligning, and not in the I just picked the Powerball type of way. My adrenal gland had been getting a decent work out, and it wasn't letting up. Without a word we began to jog back—I wasn't quite at the panic point of a sprint yet. When we rounded a corner and could see the truck, I don't know if sprinting would have made a difference.

"Fuck." I raised my rifle only to realize I was as jittery as if I'd shotgunned a pot of coffee. A zombie that would have been able to apply for a handicap sticker was dragging the remaining top half of its body toward my unsuspecting brother. It might have been an assless asshole, but its mouth would work just fine. "Gary!" I shredded my voice. Not sure how loud it would be at a hundred yards. With Stenzel here the problem would have already been dealt with, but we didn't have that luxury. "Nothing to it, but to do it," I said because to do nothing sealed a horrible fate for my brother. I opened fire. If nothing else the sound of bullets slapping the pavement near his legs would get him moving. I didn't feel confident going for a head shot from this distance with my brother's feet inches from the zombie's teeth. I had to have hit it a couple of times, but if being torn in half wasn't enough to do it in, a few shots from a round not much bigger than a .22 wasn't going to do a whole bunch more. The zombie was still crawling, half its body (a quarter of its body, as it was) was under the truck as

Rose and I now made a run for it. There was a single shot as we neared.

"Gary?" I asked tentatively as we drew near.

There was movement and then my brother pulled himself out from under. I let out a sigh of relief.

"You're going to have to get my wrench," he said as he dusted himself off. "It's laying on it, and hurry up, its brains are leaking and that'll cause it to rust."

"If I get that wrench, will you be able to fix the truck? Because otherwise I'm getting you another one."

"Are there other cars in the village I could siphon off some brake fluid?"

Hammer's car was there; would I be screwing him over if I had the brakes bled? Funny how big a part of me was like, well, that's just too doggone bad. Shucks. The issue now was we didn't know where Hammer was, or if he was even alive. Gary either fixed the truck or we took the car, either alternative took a working vehicle away from the man. We were going to have to find him or find what happened to him. Then I'd feel comfortable doing what we needed to do.

The zombie was almost completely under the truck, the only thing that was within reach was its spine, and that was a hard nope from me. I wasn't grabbing the thing by its exposed tailbone. I think that might have violated some public decency laws anyway.

"Better be the best fucking wrench in the world," I said as I got onto my knees and stuck my upper torso underneath so I could grab onto some of the zombie's tattered clothes. Did not help at all that its head was caved in from where Gary had shot it. Throwing the thing through a meat grinder would have been more appealing. I heard metal scraping as I pulled the zombie free. I stood and backed up quickly, needing to turn my head to keep from yacking. The zombie had been a female once, and what remained of her concert shirt alluded to her being on the younger side. Sure, there were older folks that were Swifties, but the over-whelming majority were teens, I think. I did my best to depersonalize zombies from humanity, but it didn't always work.

Gary and Rose pushed the truck back a couple of feet to move away from the death stain on the roadway. There was no wrench. It was still trapped under the congealing mass of rotting flesh.

"It's from Harbor Freight, Mike, it's probably already rusted!"

"Harbor Freight?" I looked up. For those not familiar, that is basically the Dollar General of tool stores. Cheap tools straight from China. When Nationality meant something, I did my best to support local businesses and products made in the US, but I also liked to eat and make sure there was a roof over my family's head, so when I needed a particular tool and it was going to cost seventy dollars at a large box store and twenty five at Harbor Freight...well, you see where this is going. "Don't you have another one?" I asked hopefully.

"A whole set, just not in the exact size I need to complete this job."

"I feel like the job is already done and this has more to do with your obsessive compulsive need to have the entire set back in its holder."

He didn't reply.

"Never thought it was fair that you couldn't pick your family." I grimaced as I bent over, I had turned away as I rolled the carcass over. Would have been impossible not to hear the eww from Rose, or the gagging from Gary. Decom-posing Debbie had left a thick layer of gel behind as I rolled her over. Of course I could see the wrench, unfortunately it looked just like as if Jim Halpert had placed Dwight's stapler in a brick of cherry Jell-O as a practical joke, nothing prac-tical or jokey about this though. "Right there." I pointed with the toe of my boot.

"Going to need you to get it." Gary wouldn't look my way. "And, and it's going to need to be clean."

I mumbled some choice words. I had been thinking about kicking the wrench over. I had boots on so it wasn't going to touch skin, but still, I wouldn't step into a steaming fresh pile of dog shit because I had boots on, either. And this was worse, way worse.

"Rose," I called.

"Patrolling, sir." She moved away. "Can't leave my post."

"I'm the commanding officer."

"And you're very commanding," Gary offered.

I browned out for a bit as I kicked the wrench loose, found a piece of cloth in the truck, and did my best to clean it off. I was holding my hands up looking for the mega germs I was sure were crawling all over me getting ready to run up my arms and into my nasal cavity.

"I have a lighter," Gary said.

"What do you want me to do, hold my hands over the flame?"

"It would kill whatever you have on them." He had picked up the wrench by a corner and was waving the lighter back and forth over it.

"Alcohol wipes in the med kit," Rose offered but did not approach.

Once I was cleaned up, I made a declaration. "Gary, you need to fix the truck. Rose, you have to keep watch over him while he has his ass flapping in the breeze."

Gary's face flushed.

"Figure of speech, brother."

"And you, sir?"

"I'm going to keep looking for survivors."

"Alone? Top will kill me if he finds out I didn't escort you."

"Hopefully someone turns up soon and I won't be alone for long."

"That sounds dubious," Gary said, pulling a two-inch by two-inch folded piece of paper from his pocket. He licked the tip of his pencil and made a check mark. One can only assume it was a page from his word of the day calendar, and he had used it successfully in a sentence. I mean I think he did, sounded reasonable to me.

"Don't like this," Rose said.

"Not a fan myself, but at least I'll be able to see trouble coming."

"As if that ever stopped you," Gary grunted as he got back under the truck. "And Mike, bring back some brake fluid. And a cheeseburger wouldn't be bad either, and some fries. But not the curly cue ones, I don't like when sometimes the inside of the curl isn't cooked properly."

I could only shake my head as I went back down the road-way. "This sucks." I only said the words so I wouldn't feel so alone, sort of like when you whistle inside a home you hope you are by yourself in. If something whistles back its time to skedaddle. Gave myself the creeps just thinking about that. Like I needed something else. I was going in alone to investigate an abandoned vehicle in a ghost town that had moments before been vacated by a zombie horde for some unknown reason; not sure how much creepier than that you could get. I suppose dealing with a clown invasion would be worse. All those red noses and giant feet, it would be terrifying.

"Dude, cut it out man. What the fuck is wrong with you?"

"Oh, and now we're back to the third person, this is perfect. Plenty of nuts to go around, might as well share them. Do you prefer dry roasted or honey?"

It was so quiet that from fifty yards I heard Gary drop his wrench as clear as a bell. I almost thought about heading back to hand it to him. Anything to keep me from going on this Hero's Quest, or more commonly known as the fool's errand. I stopped when I got to where I needed to take a right turn where Hammer's car was, and where Rose had heard cries for help. I looked back, Rose was staring in my direction. She waved an arm. I headed down. Got to the car, peeked in because who knows what crazy crap can be thrown at you during a horror movie in the making. I still didn't hear anything. Yes, my hearing had suffered greatly through the years, but I wasn't deaf. Had it all been in her head? A zombie psychically linking to her psyche? For all I knew it could be Payne. That was not a welcome thought; meeting her one on one was not likely to go my way. Maybe one of these days I would lean into the whole vampiric thing...or maybe I wouldn't.

"I wonder if Gary picked up his wrench yet." Again said out loud to not feel so alone. Somehow, though, hearing your own words only reiterated how alone you were.

Smoke drifted left to right past my field of vision, thought it might have been some ephemeral fog, or something to signify a new direction for my nightmare, but it smelled like wood, though I had my doubts it was a campfire. I had no idea what was on fire, but looking around the town it was easy to discern it was going to be the entire place soon enough. Nothing here was made from bricks or anything that would have at least slowed the onslaught of the fire storm coming.

"Where the hell is everyone?" I kept moving forward, listening for anything out of the ordinary and also making sure that I knew where my avenues of escape were. I was forty yards past where Rose had said she had heard cries for help. If the sound had come from this far, I would have heard it by now. I could feel the seconds I had left clicking off in loud percussive booms.

Footsteps coming from behind startled me out of my paranoia. I whirled, millimeters from putting a round in Rose's midsection. I almost laid into her for not warning me of her approach.

"Came for the brake fluid," she had a knife and a two-liter soda bottle.

"Fixed?"

"Almost."

"Hold up. Before we put another car out of commission —" Not sure why I hadn't thought of it previously; I guess I can blame being distracted with the thought of having my innards spilled. Those types of concerns tend to get in the way of one's higher reasoning. I bet Socrates wasn't concerned daily with the notion of violently getting disassembled. This is also why gazelles aren't great philosophers. "Check for keys," I told her as I made my way back. She rooted around as I kept a watch.

"Nothing," she said as she stood up.

One more reason Hammer irked the shit out of me. My guess it was just habit that he took the keys with him, but we'd drilled people repeatedly to leave keys in the car, that there was no telling what might happen to an individual, or who might make it to one first, and without keys the thing was basically an anchor. How sucktastic would it be to get away from the zombies, make it safely to a vehicle, only to find out you were trapped inside the fishbowl, or worse, couldn't get into the bowl?

"He afraid these zombies boost cars?" she asked. She was looking for a laugh, best I could offer up was a facsimile of a smile. Something was off here, I couldn't put my finger on it. I was jittery, a pot of coffee on too little sleep jittery. I didn't like the sensation then and didn't now. Even less so now because back then I could blame it on the coffee and the insomnia, what was my excuse now?

"Are you a hundred percent the Staff Sergeant is going to be able to fix the truck?"

She looked at me for a bit. First off, I rarely called my brother by his rank, and right then this car was as good as a busted truck, as neither were going anywhere. Okay, that wasn't fair about the truck, it could move, the problem lay in stopping. Were you really having any fun if you couldn't get into a high-speed crash with an immoveable object?

"As soon as I bring back a length of line and the fluid, he's pretty confident. Sir, do you want to come back with me? We'll wait until the truck gets fixed and we'll look around together."

"I'm fine," I answered without answering anything.

"You seem distracted, sir."

"Do you hear anything?"

"I do not, that's kind of why I want to hurry."

"Yup, sorry, get what you need. I'll watch your six."

She crawled under the car. I heard some noise then the sound of fluid falling into a container. I fully expected Hammer to come bolting out of a house, the scientists in tow, and a few dozen zombies right on their heels. That's normally the way this stuff works. The car would still work, he would just have the same problem we had. Must be catchy. I was still off wherever I'd gone when Rose crawled out from under.

"Done, sir. I should be back in a couple of minutes."

"I'll be here," I said, absently realizing that made no sense. If I was going to stand right there and wait, what was the point? "Um, yeah, I mean the village." *Good save*, I berated internally.

"Be right back." She took off.

"Ah, indecision, my old friend." Go back or stay right here made no sense; what was the point? I had to move forward. Where to and to what end, and what would be waiting for me there, who could tell? The questions begged to be answered, even if I didn't want to know the answers. There was movement farther down the alley, the casted shadows making it impossible to figure out exactly what it was. Trash bags and cans were being jostled and shoved aside. Too big to be a rodent, cat, or a dog. There was a jerky lurch, then it sprang. A speeder or a very exuberant person having just placed highly in the Olympic trials for hide and seek. It had been hiding, of that there was little doubt. It must have known I was nearby and lost its patience as it lay in wait. The hunter had blown his cover and was now trying to make up for his mistake.

I was going to shoot it, but the odds were way too high that this fucker wasn't alone, and the second I fired that they would spring whatever trap they had laid. As I glanced around, I saw so many potential hiding spots: abandoned cars, overturned tables, piles of trash, deep shadows, fences. Backing up slowly was off the table, running was my only option, and I took it and ran with it. Super punny. Again, refer back to higher reasoning and getting torn asunder. (You come up with better shit when you're trying to break the record for the fastest mile.)

"Coming in hot!" I shouted as I rounded third and was making for the home stretch. Gary poked his head out from under the truck, Rose was watching, bringing her rifle up to aim. Gary looked for a couple more seconds then resumed what he'd been doing. I spared a glance over my shoulder; the zombie had stopped right at the mouth of the alleyway. In terms of running away from an enemy, this was on the side of pathetic. It wasn't even chasing. I was in danger of having my man-card revoked, or at least a corner bent.

"Fucker," I said as I slowed and turned at the halfway point between Gary and Rose and the zombie.

"Are you going to shoot it, or should I?" Rose asked, seemingly bored with the whole encounter.

"I think there's more lying in wait." I attempted to make the situation seem more dangerous than it currently was. Kind of jacked up when a single zombie no longer raises an alarm. If Rose was the type to do her nails, she would have returned to the arduous work of filing them. "Now what?" I asked, but I didn't have an answer.

"Huzzah!" Gary clapped triumphantly as he stood.

"Who says huzzah?" I said it quietly so he wouldn't hear it, was his win but there are better words to express it.

He was busy pouring the captured fluid into the master cylinder, I'd taken my eyes off my stalker for a few seconds, it didn't matter, he wasn't coming. Maybe he thought it was a trap of my making. When Gary closed the hood, started the truck up and then gave Rose a thumbs up after pressing the pedal until it stiffened, she began to make her way back to me.

"Are we going back, sir?" she asked.

"They're waiting for us." I could only hope that didn't come across as shakily as it sounded in my head. Last thing I needed was for my squad to think I was losing my confidence. For her part, if she noticed something, she didn't react. Kudos to her; we all have our moments.

"Sir?"

"Our buddy over there came out from under some trash bags. Got a pretty good feeling that there's a whole bunch of them in that alley."

"Wouldn't we have smelled them?"

She had me there. You could get nose blind to a lot of things, and even as bad as the zombies were, you could block out a fair portion of the stench. But if they were close and in numbers, your olfactory system could only filter out so much, sort of like a full CO_2 scrubber on a spacecraft.

I scratched my head. Reality had me thinking one thing and my hinky gut another. I trusted my gut, as one should, but there were times it had shouted its warnings only to come up shooting blanks. Sometimes my head would get involved and foul the works, and I wasn't able to differentiate when this occurred. Sometimes the sub-conscious had no desire to check the validity of things and would throw red flags up in a bid to get you to quit doing whatever you were thinking of doing.

Rose raised her rifle to get rid of the zombie. It pulled back as quickly as if it were attached to a stunt harness and had been kicked by Bruce Lee. She kept her rifle up as she advanced tactically. I followed as I wrestled with what I was going to do. This was important. There were three possible things: people were in trouble, people were dead, or people were safe. The last was the least likely, just the nature of this behemoth beast. Dead or safe, got us off the hook for the most part, at least in terms of action needed. It was that pesky in trouble option that meant we couldn't stand here and do nothing. I read once that the police were *not* required to place their lives in jeopardy for another. That had blown me away at the time. As a kid you just always figured that this was exactly what they did, and for right or wrong, I'd brought that notion into adulthood. So when the lawsuit came because someone's loved one hadn't been saved because the cop had not gone above and beyond, and he'd been acquitted, I was thrown for a loop. Why the tangent, you ask? Right then I was wondering if military personnel could use that defense. Hero complexes can suck an egg.

"Gone," Rose said, looking down the alleyway. I caught up quickly.

She said "gone" while I was looking at dozens of hiding spots. "Not gone." I shook my head slightly. "Fucker's here, and he has his buddies with him." I knew that. I knew that with conviction.

Rose was a non-believer, not worshipping at the altar of the Talbot cult-like Church of the mighty God Paranoia. Maybe she didn't see things the way I did, but flirting with death is still not something to be taken lightly. She walked in a few more paces. I stayed close. She went toward the side of the alley where there was an old piece of corrugated steel conveniently leaning up against a moldy rusted-out dishwasher. She used the barrel of her rifle to push at the edge of the steel; she flipped it over and jumped.

"Jumping Jehoshaphat!"

I was about to ask her if she and my brother had been working on old-timey crosswords or something when I saw the reason why she'd exclaimed in Olde English and bounded into the air. Two zombies were nestled underneath in the classic spooning style to conserve space. I could only for the love of all that was holy hope that was the only reason. They didn't move initially, like their operating system was on standby. My gut had some more precognitive insight.

"Put the metal back."

Rose was pretty close to telling me to fuck off, or some close variant of that. But when the zombies didn't move, she gingerly stepped forward and flipped the metal back into position, then moved even further away from their resting—or nesting spot—as the case may have unfortunately been.

"Do you know what's going on?" she asked, never taking her eyes off the spot.

"It's an ambush."

"Why aren't they bushing then?"

I knew what she was trying to convey, and in seriousness, still found it funny. She didn't appreciate that this was where I found humor.

"Sorry." I held up a hand to ward away her scowl. "This is something new, like they're remote-controlled or something." I had no idea what was happening, but for now, my theory held water.

"There was no smell." Rose stepped closer and took in a big whiff. "There should be something."

Wasn't sure how close I wanted to get to confirm what she was saying, be kind of like when your friend asks if you smell something weird, so you take in a big whiff only to realize they'd just sent particulates of shit into the air, and you've pulled it into your nose and down into your lungs. With all the things people had sued each other over, I was surprised that wasn't one. You could open with emotional and physical distress, exposure to harmful chemicals might be a stretch, but worthy of attaching to the lawsuit. I'd not put it together because if you've seen one speeder you've seen them all, but I had an idea.

"They washed." It was a revelation, and I was convinced I was right. "I thought their hair was just greasier than normal, but no...I think it was the wet of bathing."

"The clothes, they looked newer too. I didn't say anything because who cares," Rose said. "Isn't their smell just part of who they are?" she asked.

We were getting into advanced Zombie Theoretics here. I was more a grade school teacher rather than a university professor, but like all Talbots everywhere, I was willing to give it the old college try. Or at the minimum the Bostonian bullshit.

"The shufflers, yeah, they're decaying masses of stink and goo, but the speeders though, they don't die like we traditionally think. So besides having blood and shit all over themselves, I think it's reasonable they could clean up. Maybe not shiny penny clean up."

"Is it reasonable, sir?" she asked.

"Fuck no," I told her. "It's not reasonable. Zombies should be making Brick Tamland a Mensa candidate."

"Who?"

"Brick Tamland, weather man from *Anchorman*."

"Is that the movie with Will Ferrell? My great grandfather loved that one."

I gave her the finger, an expression of love throughout the military.

"What now?" she asked.

What now was right. Had what she heard been part of the trap, or were there people in trouble? It was impossible to know how many zombies were here. There were a bunch of ancillary questions as well, like how in the hell did the speeders get here so fast? When did they clean up? How did they know for sure we were coming—I mean besides the explosions?

None of those mattered for the here and now. We were two people willingly stepping into the steel teeth of a trap, and no matter what it was baited with, that was not a good idea.

"We have to go back and get some help. I don't see any way around it."

"Help," drifted from down the alleyway, because of course it did.

"Is that timing a little suspect, sir?"

"Just a little," came out as more of a sneer.

"We going to check?"

I hesitated during the downtime of no conversation. "Please," came next from our disembodied voice.

"Okay, we're going to be methodical about this. Pop the top," I told her as I pointed to the nearby steel.

"Typical military crap...move the barrier, put the barrier back in place, move the barrier," she groused. I motioned with my head for her to get on with it, she could complain on her own time. She flipped the lid. I aimed in just as the closest zombie's eyes opened wide. Put one straight through his skull. The second was on the move, but was too entangled to get far. Popped a round in that one's skull as well. Rose was keeping an eye out for any others who thought this might be a good time to have a go at us. Nothing.

"Next." I ushered her forward and over to a pile of old tires.

"Is this what Kirby feels like on point? I don't like it."

"I'm going around the far side." Got that gut clenching thing, like I'd eaten at my sister's as I came around the back. Seven zombies in similar spooning fashion. Of course my fucked up thoughts went to zombie orgy, because yeah, who doesn't want in on that action. Dammit. Eyes opened up and the festivities began. Would have been in trouble if Rose hadn't joined in. In less than thirty seconds we'd put them down. In that time, we'd not been watching our backs, luckily they'd still not attacked. I wasn't sure I wanted to continue;

seven sleeping zombies had nearly been more than the two of us could deal with in a timely manner. What if we hit a den of a dozen or two dozen? I switched out my magazine for a fresh one.

"Someone is directing this bloody little play." I looked around. "They're getting a signal to wake up when we expose them."

"Why not just wake them all up?"

"Might as well ask me why a woman says she's hungry but shoots down every idea you toss out, ends up eating wherever you go, but complains no matter what."

"I'm telling your wife that."

"Go further down the alley, I'll keep an eye on you from here. There can be no witnesses to my words."

She smiled, assuaging the nervousness for a brief time.

"We're going back."

"Sir?"

"Can't see them, can't smell them, but they're out there, and in numbers you and I can't contend with, I'm sure of it. Or as reasonably sure of it as I can be. I won't risk your life on this."

"Or yours."

"I figured that was implied."

A horn came from the end of the alleyway. Gary was waving frantically. "Let's go!"

There were times to ask questions, and there were times you hauled ass, no questions asked. An apocalypse was a good time to shut the hell up and run. He kept urging us on, which was alarming considering we were already on our way. Wasn't like we were going to stop if he stopped waving. As we neared the mouth of the alley, he pulled ahead slightly, making the rear hatch closer. I wasn't sure the extra ten feet of running was going to make a difference until I realized it was. I slowed enough to let Rose get ahead. She was moving plenty fast as she headed in, just not fast enough, I pushed on her ass, probably launched her halfway into the truck bed, I banged on the wall of the truck before I'd even made it completely in. My brother must have had his foot on the gas pedal because we were off before the sound faded. Rose was kind enough to grab my outstretched hand. Not sure if I would have toppled out, but it could have been closer than one would have appreciated.

"Sorry about the push and thanks for the save."

"No problem and you're welcome." We both watched the few hundred speeders as they chased after us. I needlessly pointed to the alley where more, a lot more, were streaming out.

"Is there anyone alive in there?" Rose asked.

I didn't think so, but I wasn't telling her that. Thought I'd seen some of our people in that horde, but I couldn't say for sure. Might have even seen Hammer, or the body of him anyway. The guy was a royal pain in my ass, but I wouldn't wish that on anyone, and I meant it. Except Deneaux I suppose. Whatever that woman had coming her way was justified.

10

MIKE JOURNAL ENTRY 10

LINA WAS WAITING for us as Rose and I exited the truck. Gary must have seen her too because he wisely stayed inside until he was sure she saw me and was coming closer. He boogied away quickly. No one wants to give that type of shit news. And here I was front and center.

She didn't ask anything, and I didn't say anything. All that was needed to be communicated was done through that silence. She turned and headed away, her head held high and her shoulders back. Stoic. BT waited until she was gone from view.

"Where are they, Mike?" He was angry, though not at me. I wasn't angry so much as crushed. That was half of our group wiped from the face of the planet. A fifty percent reduction in population was going to be an enormous hurdle to overcome.

"I can't confirm it, but I'm partially convinced they're gone."

"Partially?"

"Some of the horde that chased us out looked very familiar. I think I even saw Hammer."

"Are we going back?"

There was the rub. Cutting and running seemed the best course of action, but when you cut off half of yourself, it's not like you're running anywhere.

"I'd like to get everyone further down the road. I don't think those speeders are going to stop chasing us, and we need to rethink a strategy."

An hour later we were another thirty miles away. My squad and I were sitting at a picnic table looking at a map and a way to skirt the highway and get back to the village. I was as positive as I could be that we weren't going to be happy with what we found, but we still needed to see it. If not, there would always be questions and accusations that we didn't do enough. The suck was high with this mission.

When Mainers say: "You can't get there from here," in that Upper New England twang, they are referring to exactly this. Getting back to that cursed village without using the highway was impossible. As a crow flies it was about forty-five miles, but with all of the lefts, rights, backtracks, tunnels, bridges, ferries, dirt roads and dead ends, it was going to be about ninety miles. The day was long in the tooth. I wanted to get this distasteful thing done as soon as possible, but rolling in under a cloudy night sky was a bad idea. First thing in the morning was agreed upon. The next problem was if the speeders kept running they would find us before our departure. We were all going, all of us that were still alive, anyway. It made sense to start now. They would not come down the ancillary roads without reason. The sun was far down the horizon when we stopped and decided this was our home for the night. It was going to be another night of uncomfortableness. There wasn't much grousing about that, a lot of crying over those we potentially lost though, heard a great many sobs. My heart physically hurt. There was zero chance of sleep. I was walking around the impromptu encampment, possibly because I was a glutton for punishment and wanted to make sure I heard every cry. I could not help but think that this was my burden, that my leadership or lack of had led us to this moment.

Caught a whiff of sweet smoke, my initial irrational fear had been that it was Deneaux and her cigarettes. I couldn't say why, but she had been on my mind too much lately, and it was only a matter of time until that crone's vengeful wraith found me. Then I realized that wasn't the harshness of a cigarette but rather the smell of an expensive cigar. I was no aficionado, but I would have gone so far as to say it was of Cuban origin. And from there it wasn't too hard to extrapolate the answer, considering BT was the one holding on to them with a death grip. Got caught more than a few times trying to find his stash.

"Figured you'd find your way here." I could just make him out as the cherry brightened. He was slouched in an oversized chair. Where he'd found the thing and what lived in it, I had no idea. He had his head resting back as he let go of a long plume of smoke, looking up into a small sliver of sky that was opened to the stars. "Sit. Take a load off and I'll share one with you."

"I don't know if I'm up for taking a load off."

"Funny how you Catholics like to corner the market on guilt."

I remained silent.

"I know you, man," he said. "Right about now you want to take that fancy sword of yours and fall on it. How this horrible thing is all your fault. Got some news my friend, it's not. This is war, people die in wars, combatants and innocent civilians alike. There is no differentiation when He comes calling."

Had a fist sized lump in my throat. If I tried to say anything it would come out like a croak. He patted the seat of a chair I'd not seen. I had a feeling that if it were light enough, I'd have caught a cloud of dust rising from the thing. Considering I was choking on the mildewy scent, I knew I was right. Still sat; a Cuban is a Cuban. Back when I was younger and was attempting to look sophisticated, there was a point where I smoked cigars. Started with Swisher Sweets; looking back couldn't have been any more low rent if I tried. Couldn't think of a soul those were going to impress, except the board members of that tobacco company. After realizing that those were leafy garbage, I graduated to Macanudos, they were from Nicaragua or Honduras somewhere like that. Figured I had graduated to the big leagues of cigars. At that point in my life, I smoked them for the enjoyment, a way to unwind.

I don't recall how I eventually ended up with a Cuban cigar in my hand, but there was no comparison. The difference was like stew meat compared to filet mignon. Yes, they were similar because they were both tobacco and meat, per the example, but that was it. The taste, the smoothness, they were unparalleled and coupled with the fact that they were illegal in the States was all the impetus I needed to secure a black market means of getting more. So yeah, I was going to sit in that scuzzy seat and enjoy the fuck out of that cigar. For a half hour we said nothing while enjoying each other's company, and that of the cigar. I'm not going to say it was bliss, but it was as close as I'd been in a while. The ability to completely quiet one's mind is something that should be cherished. It's so fucking easy to lose your sanity, but good luck trying to recover it, not sure if it's even possible. You're always going to have that damage; the best you can do is to keep from sliding further.

"Thank you," I told him when I was done. I stood and squeezed his shoulder tight.

He placed his hand over mine. "Not your fault, remember that, Talbot. I need you to remember that."

There was a plea in that statement. You can get so wrapped up in yourself that sometimes it's difficult to empathize with what others are going through. BT and I standing tall only worked when both of us were standing. Knock one over and it would be like dominoes.

I clapped my free hand over his. "I love you, brother."

"Of course you do, fool...how could you not?"

I leaned down and kissed the top of his head. "I couldn't do this shit without you."

"No kidding. Do you have any more obvious statements you want to get off your chest?"

"I'm sure I could come up with some, but I'd like to leave on a high note."

"Three days, Mike. In three days we're going to be in Colorado. Full circle. We'll rebuild, we can do this."

His words were meant for both of us. "I know, man, I know."

I felt better as I walked away, how could I not? The feeling diminished as the night wore on, but it didn't go too far. I was able to hold on to the afterglow far longer than I would have thought possible. I would mourn for those souls we lost, possibly for the rest of my life, and that was something I was going to have to find a way to live with, and BT had just shown me that I could. That the small special things in life could add up and push the enormous nightmares away. Sleep wasn't something I even bothered to attempt. Each of the kids as babies had taken their fair measure of sleep from Tracy and I, but that had nothing on what a zombie apocalypse had done. The next morning as I watched the sun come up, I thought I might have caught the smell of coconuts roasting in the sun. That was mysterious for a couple of minutes, until I deduced it could possibly be the zombies, and their new hygiene regiment passing by on the highway. I'd have to look at the map to see how close we were, but for the time being we were going to keep quiet until we could all get boarded up and either get this dreadful fact-finding mission (or elation inducing rescue) underway.

We made good time. The sun was midway on the horizon

as we looked at the village off in the distance. I was standing on the tanker, binoculars in hand. I'd been staring and scanning for five minutes straight, hadn't seen so much as a piece of garbage fluttering in the wind. It was too still, very much had the ghost town or ambush feeling to it. We were going to take Gary's truck again, this time with myself, Rose, Kirby and Bando.

"The commanding officer does not go out on missions, Mike." BT had his hands resting on the tailgate, "especially leaving me behind to babysit."

I was surprised he was able to talk so intelligibly, with how tightly his jaw was clenched.

"You know with absolute certainty, Top, that the people we have back here mean everything and more to me. You're the only person I trust more than myself to keep them safe."

"What's that mean for us?" Kirby asked Rose.

"Expendable," she said around a mouthful of jerky.

Bando dragged a finger across his neck then reached for a piece of the dried beef, or deer. Or deer-like, it was a weird gazelle thing. I don't know, it was tasty as hell, though.

"Expandable? Like we're fat?" Kirby asked.

"Is his dick bigger than his brain?" Bando asked Rose.

"Wouldn't you like to know." She waggled her eyebrows.

"No, not really," he told her.

I tapped the side of the truck wall. "Let's go brother, slow." I had a handhold and was standing so I could look out. If he went too fast there was a chance I'd end up in the roadway, and once you've fallen hard on your tailbone, it is not a sensation you wish to ever repeat. If given the choice I think I'd take a punch to the nuts over a concussive blow to my ass. Maybe it would be best if I left the entire region alone, far too many nerve endings to be tampered with.

Gary came to a stop at the mouth of that stupid alleyway. As far as I was concerned this place was the root of all evil. Couldn't be money anymore, as that was useless. I suppose gold would eventually make a comeback, but not for centuries. There was already so much of it mined and easily accessible to anyone looking, that it was on the verge of useless with the limited number of people still alive. I used to watch some show they had up in Alaska, *Gold Rush* maybe, don't know, anyway, they threw this fact out, that roughly two hundred thousand tons of the stuff had been mined since man discovered the shiny metal. That meant what, four hundred million pounds? Now taking into account the lack of people, let's say there was only one percent of us left out of seven billion, that leaves roughly what, seventy million people? I shook my head, that seemed optimistic, but I'll go with that, means everyone still left could have more than five pounds of the stuff. Right now, tin foil was far more valuable due to its practicality for use, and something like antibiotics? Actual gold.

I guarantee there were already people hording gold, ripping off every jewelry store they could get to, foregoing all that time they could have accumulated resources much more inclined to help one survive. I wouldn't trade a pound of jerky for a pound of gold. Shiny shit was fun to look at, but it couldn't feed you, keep you warm or safe. It could make you extremely paranoid though, might actually be detrimental in that regard. That thought had shot through my head in far less time than it had taken to write it all down. I jumped down from the truck, the other three followed.

"Rose, you stay with Staff Sergeant Talbot. Bando, Kirby, you're with me."

"It's because you're a woman," Kirby told her.

"Son, you're stupider than toes on a tulip," Gary said.

"What's that even mean?" Kirby asked.

"Point proven," Gary told him.

"Zip it," I said, I wanted this distasteful thing done as quickly as possible. None of our people were here, not alive, anyway. They would have either already greeted us or taken off when the zombies left. No, this was merely visual confirmation of those that had gone before us, in the philosophical way.

I caught Rose sticking her tongue out at her boyfriend; she looked pretty sheepish when I caught her, and instead of reeling the appendage in, she doubled down and licked a piece of the jerky as if that was what she had intended on doing the whole time instead of acting like a five-year-old.

"Bando, flip the metal," I told him, pointing to the same pile that Rose and I had been at yesterday. I didn't have to tell Kirby to watch our back, not what we were doing; the kid wasn't going to be assembling rockets anytime soon, but he was a hell of a Marine, and that was all I cared about. Bando flipped the sheet metal and did not jump back, there was nothing to jump back from. The zombies we killed were gone, all that remained was the stain of their existence. Why the metal had been placed back into position I could only guess at. A mind fuck? A delaying tactic? A zombie with rampant obsessive-compulsive disorder? Who knows? We made our way slowly down that alley, checking every possible hiding spot. Nothing, not so much as a discarded brain candy wrapper. If the zombies do secure the evolutionary spot atop this shit heap, it is a foregone conclusion that they will begin to sell sugar coated brain snacks. Not sure whose brains they would be, but there it is. What was I saying about lost sanity?

We were coming up to the end of the alley, beyond us only stood a field with overgrown grass. Looking at that, an army of zombies could be lying in wait. It was a possibility, though I didn't think so. I just didn't have that feeling of foreboding like I had yesterday. Didn't mean I wasn't going to keep an eye on it. Gary had backed up his truck halfway down, in case we needed a hasty exit. If they ended up coming from the front, he could back up and into the field. It would be a bumpy ride, but nothing the truck couldn't handle, I hoped. Wasn't like I was going to go and scope out the terrain. Even if there weren't zombies, venomous snakes were likely. They'd kill just as easily as a zombie, though it would be weird to be in the middle of a z-poc and go out in a relatively mundane way. You would become the butt of innumerable jokes from the inhabitants of whatever realm you ended up in.

The only place left to check was a picket fence off to our left. The gate was slightly ajar and there was a smell, not potent, but it was there. This was what I was dreading. Kirby went to open the gate and take a look.

"I've got this," I told him.

I'm sure he wanted to know why, but he didn't ask as he stepped away. Good chance he could sense it as well.

"This sucks," I said as I pushed it open with my barrel. I had to swallow hard and keep my lips pressed tightly together to keep the gorge residing within from violently blowing out. You'd think after all this time, in a world full zombies, I would have seen just about everything, barring that, I would be prepared for just about anything. You'd think that. Then you stumble across a backyard drenched in the blood and body parts of people you know...

"*Me dios*," Bando had come up behind. I pulled the gate shut. I was going to have enough nightmares for us all, no need to share, although it was too late for Bando.

"Let's go," I told them. Without some serious forensics work, it was going to be impossible to tell who, if anybody, was still alive. We'd have to send multiple samples off to labs for DNA testing. I was hearing that the turnaround for results was nearing eternity.

"What's in there?" Rose asked. It would have been easy enough to tell from my face alone that something was wrong, but Bando, who was darker toned than the rest of us, had flushed all the color from his face as well, to the point that Kirby came over to his friend to lend support.

"*Todos mortos*," he said as Kirby led him back to Gary.

"He alright?" Gary had stepped out. "Are you alright?" he asked when he saw me.

"No and no and let's go."

Gary knew enough not to ask what we'd seen. You could have nightmares by proxy, but if you hadn't seen it then there was no material for your psyche to use to produce images. The poet laureate that came up with "ignorance is bliss," nailed it.

I gave BT a slight shake of my head when I got out of the truck upon our return. Must have been the look in my eyes that convinced him not to press further. I was glad the majority of that day was spent on the open road; couldn't hear the sobbing from the people in the other vehicles. Not sure how many miles we traversed that day. I was lost in the hum of the tires. I think the same poet that came up with the ignorance saying also penned, "you can't run from your problems." This was a prime example. Had to be six hundred miles away from the slaughter and it was still with me, like an open festering wound carved into the niches of my brain, with me. I would have got blinded drunk if I was in a truck with booze. We stopped three times that day, bathroom and refueling and also debris removal. We were on high alert as we all pitched in to move a tree, but the placement and the twisted trunk leaned more toward a natural fall than a trap concocted by highway men. And who would lay a trap on a highway these days anyway? We had to be the first cars to pass in over a year or more. Hard to survive on the spoils of others when there are no others.

People were exhausted, washed out, wrung out, take your pick. I forced us another two hours on the road, to the point if we didn't stop soon we were going to need our headlights on, and that was something I wasn't keen on doing. Engine and tire noise was as much as I was willing to risk being noticed. Headlights could be seen for miles. The reason I'd wanted to go just a little further was so we could get into Texas. Being on US soil was not going to change anything except my mental state, but right then it needed some changing.

"Oh shit," Gary uncharacteristically swore. I'd been busy

looking out the side window not focused on anything. Strange to have so much data streaming past your eyes and not annotate any of it. Reminded me of calculus.

When I looked out at what he saw, I changed *shit* to *fuck*, but it was the same sentiment. We were idling next to a sign that said the United States border was two miles away and that was the last bit of good news we were going to get that night because up ahead was an endless tangle of cars that got swallowed up by the encroaching darkness.

"How are we going to get through that?" he asked.

It was a great question, and I didn't have the foggiest notion.

"That's going to be a problem," BT said after stretching and coming over to find me.

"You don't say?" I asked.

"Sorry, that's what happens when I'm with your son all day."

"Get the vehicles in a circle, everyone stays inside their ride or the circle, guards stay atop the tanker."

BT nodded. Ten minutes later I was sitting on the hood of the tanker looking out at the vast ocean of cars like a sea captain. It would take Rose with her entire arsenal of explosive gadgetry a week or more to get through this mess. We didn't have the ordnance anyway. I couldn't see much, but there was a bit of a shoulder here, we'd be able to push some of the cars out of the way, but I had to figure as we got closer to the actual crossing, the number of cars trying to force their way through would have become one solid mass of rolling steel and the shoulder would disappear as the authorities would want to make sure that those making the crossing were being herded into the check point slots. How many cars were we going to have to muscle out of the way? A hundred, three hundred, a thousand? Was it even possible? Like immigrants of old, traversing thousands of miles, losing nearly everything in our desperate quest to cross this line drawn randomly in the dirt by those in power centuries ago: Had we come so close to only be turned away?

I was tempted to grab my pillow and make the two-mile trek merely so I could sleep on my beloved US soil. But honestly, I didn't really like Texas. I'm sure the people were nice, I still wasn't a fan of the heat, and that distance wasn't going to change much, latitude wise. Gary joined me on the hood and tapped my arm with his canteen.

"Kool-Aid again? I'm good." I waved him off.

"It's the purple one, Mike, no one passes on the purple. Just give it a go."

I reluctantly took it from him. I'd planned on keeping my lips closed and letting the liquid splash against them just to satisfy my brother, but that was until I spun the top off and got a distinct whiff of alcohol.

"Vodka. Tito's, as a matter of fact. They make that two miles from here."

I had no idea where he'd procured it from, but I wasn't going to ask questions. I took a big swig. He wasn't lying, purple was now my favorite. Didn't end up drinking enough to forget the day, but enough that, coupled with the previous night of not sleeping, I crashed hard. So the person I was lauding as the most brilliant human of all time, given his or her words of wisdom, was now an idiot as far as I was concerned because they'd also said that "everything looks better in the light of day." It did not. Cars stretched past the curvature of the earth, yes exaggeration, but not as much as you might think. I don't know what happened in Mexico and why the citizens thought the US was a better option, but it looked like the entire country was trying to empty out.

Had to be nearly fifty lanes of highway to and from, and they were all packed heading north. If we waited ten or twelve years the things should be pretty rusted out, would be a lot easier to move then. This was one of those projects that was so huge and daunting, like cleaning my garage in Colorado, that I didn't even know where to start. BT had Kirby and Bando and they were a few cars deep in the mess, looking inside. He shielded his eyes and turned around, waving at me to join them. Thought about giving him the finger just out of principle. Instead I jumped down from my perch and reluctantly made my way toward him. We met right at the beginning of the jam.

"There's zombies in a lot of these cars."

"Good morning to you too. Any chance you still have blueberry muffins?"

"This is serious, Mike."

"I know it is, that's why I'm doing my best to ignore it and you. I'm guessing shufflers?"

"No real way to know, but if they've been here since the beginning, that's safe enough to say."

"Still alive?"

He gave me a, *for real?* look. Head cocked to the side, lips pursed, shoulders hunched.

"You know what I meant."

"Emaciated looking, but very much alive. If they had the opportunity, they ate through the rest of the passengers that were with them. Sometimes it's kid zombies, and sometimes it's what we figure were parents."

"Fuck me. This is no way to start a day." I was infinitely better with kids eating their parents, the other way around just struck a nerve. As parents, our primary purpose in this life is to see to the wellbeing of our offspring, to raise them, keep them safe, give them the skills necessary to navigate life. Nowhere in there does it talk about eating them. This was going to make an already impossible task that much worse. To move cars, we were going to have to gain entry and put the transmission in neutral. The idea of also having to dispatch any number of combatants made the work that much more dangerous, plus the noise of it all. It was likely we'd have to break a fair number of windows, which was bad enough, but then you start tossing in rifle shots. "Where's Yoki?"

BT was already shaking his head. "I know what you're thinking, but first off there's too many of them, and I'm not sure the things in those cars are capable of coming out on their own. I'm telling you, Mike, all this time not eating and baking in the heat has made them corpsified like, like Halloween prop corpses."

"Are you sure they're not? Dead-dead, I mean.

"Their eyes are very much alive, they track movement, and they clack their teeth when they see us."

"You ever think we're bit players in someone else's tragicomedy?"

"Do I look like a bit player?"

"Size notwithstanding, the question remains."

"What are you talking about?" I could see BT looking around, planning how he was going to organize his work detail. He was listening to me with half an ear.

"It's all a play, on a world stage. A dream, maybe some god's dream, a nightmare really, a long, twisted nightmare. I mean it has to be, right? We're just figments of some schmo's indigestion. Like maybe he ate tainted crab cakes before bed, and we're the figments his soon to be purging stomach has conjured up. 'More gravy than grave,' you know?"

"Mike, there's a lot of work that needs to be done today."

I wanted to tell him, what was the point of any of it? When soon enough we were going to be flushed down a toilet after being violently expelled from some poor asshole's one end or the other. I didn't. Instead I went to meander down the length of cars and...trucks. That was another obstacle we were going to have to work around. Pushing a car out of the way was one thing, a semi? That wasn't happening, and there were plenty of them peppered throughout the tangled parade. We'd have to clear the cars around them. Fine and dandy until we got to the front and there were two next to each other or something.

"Already mapped out a route!" BT shouted to my retreating form. I was feeling a bit redundant. I deliberately kept myself from looking in the cars I passed. I didn't know what I was doing until I did. I couldn't fix my mind on anything other than that two miles between what I realized I viewed as Hell and Heaven, and it was quickly becoming a question of a real test, as if St Peter was literally standing in one of those border booths, having denied entry to every one of these people, families, exporters, tourists...they all failed. They all died two miles from salvation. I couldn't allow myself that self-absorbing tangent right now, because I knew the more I thought about my life, the more certain I would be that I wouldn't pass Peter's muster. I would never be allowed to walk over that line, through that gate, but I wasn't ready to give up just yet.

Last night I'd thought it wouldn't make any difference, but as the sun rose, I figured it kind of did. I was going to place my boots over the border; in a way, I'd be home. I could prove to myself that it was just another invisible boundary line, one made mythical only in my mind. I'd gone maybe a tenth of a mile in the real world when I began to debate the merits of this maneuver. How smart would it actually be to go two miles by myself through hostile territory?

"I'll go and be right back. Less than an hour." How many times had I grossly misjudged the time it would take to complete a mission? Even if it had only been once, that was one too many, that's the beauty of being an obstinate idiot. I walked on. I tried, but finally couldn't help staring at the horror on both sides, how many hands and mouths pressed up against glass as I passed. In dozens of instances hands stuck out, reaching, and if the window was open far enough, zombies would end up sticking their entire heads out. At a few choke points I felt like a pro athlete running down the tunnel to enter the game, and dozens of people would have their arms outstretched in the hopes of high fiving their favorite athletes. So maybe this had more to do with them wanting to nosh my soft bits, but same idea. Not really, but it made it slightly more appealing, and I'm pretty sure this is how the insane deal with issues. Because here we are, and I don't know in what world anyone would consider me of sound mind.

I was coming up on a white school bus that had Texas Correctional Transportation in large black lettering on the rear and sides. Must have taken some convicts down into Mexico for some R&R, or maybe some medical care because it was a whole bunch cheaper. Smart racket, too. Charge American taxpayers the going US rate for medical care and bring the convicts down to Mexico for a fifth of the price. That's a lot of pockets being lined. Wish I'd thought of it, would have been nice to have a few million, would have definitely had a bunker built in the mountains of Colorado. I mean what could have possibly gone wrong up there? I was dreaming about what I would have done with my ill-gotten booty, when I heard the crash of glass then the solid *thwack* of a body hitting the ground. I spun around to see an enormous monster of a man getting up. If Hollywood was looking for their prototypical cartel enforcer, I could save them the trouble. He wasn't BT big, not anymore, the ensuing time of not eating had left him diminished, but not emaciated. Must have had a fair amount of protein in that rolling lunch box. He stood, thing had to be over seven feet with a wingspan to match. Fucker looked like he could crush bowling balls in his Yeti-sized hands. (On a side note, I have no idea how big a Yeti's hands are but I would imagine they're in proportion to its feet, which given that it's likely related to Bigfoot....you see my point.)

I had my rifle ready, but the moment I shot that, BT was going to figure out I wasn't around and send a massive search party out. I didn't feel like being dressed down by my Top and that was surely what was going to happen. And if not him, then my wife. Even if she didn't get angry she would wonder why I continually put myself into dangerous situations when I didn't have to. More than once I'd been accused of having a death wish, and that might have been true. Only so many times you could flirt with it before it got its measure of flesh, or those you commanded decided they needed someone a bit more stable in the saddle. I had my sword, but the zombie was so tall I was afraid I wouldn't get a killing blow in before those abnormally long arms grabbed hold of me. I was debating my options; I could just walk away at a brisk pace, avoid conflict altogether.

"Yeah, that's not going to happen." I let my rifle hang on its tactical harness and heard the steel of my sword sing as I pulled it free from its scabbard. Was sort of hoping a bolt of lightning would strike the tip and the name Anduril, Flame of the West would echo across the skies, it did not.

There was the soft crack of a suppressed round and the cartel enforcer zombie staggered to the side, two more sounds of an exploding water balloon and the zombie dragged its head down the side of the bus, leaving a red and gray smear as it descended.

It was Kirby. He was approaching, a suppressed 22 caliber rifle in his hands. "You all right, sir?" he asked, never taking his eyes from his downed target.

I put my sword back, not sure why I'd not taken one of the quiet rifles with me.

"I'm good, thank you. Are you following me?"

"Top ordered me, I'm your guard detail."

"Top thinks I need a guard detail?"

"Sir, no disrespect, but we all think you need a guard detail."

I nodded in agreement. No sense in protesting against reality, it didn't care, and you weren't going to change its mind anyway.

"Well, let's go then," I said as I continued. Kirby was the consummate traveling companion. He didn't say a thing, didn't ask a question. Wasn't wondering where we were going or when we were going to get there. He was perfectly content to let things unfold as they may. Still plenty of faces mashed against windows and arms waving out of windows, but no more fell out, of their rides. Soon enough I was looking at the enormous sign that said Welcome to the United States. Can't describe the sensation in the pit of my stomach. I just stared for what seemed like five minutes.

"Not sure I ever thought we'd do this, sir," Kirby said as he looked up.

I stepped right past the less than pearly gates and over onto the States side, unbuttoned my cami pants. I had nothing against our southern neighbors, this was more a symbolic act as I pissed from Texas onto Mexican soil, or Heaven into Hell, if you will. In five seconds, Kirby was a respectable distance away doing the same thing.

"You ready to go back?" I asked as I did the basically useless three jiggles to rid myself of excess flowage only to have a stubborn few drops get the inside of my pants damp as I buttoned back up. "Every damn time." I shook my leg.

"That's it?" Kirby asked.

"That's it," I told him. "I'm not a complicated man."

We walked back much like we had walked out, companiable silence. Wasn't too long before we came upon a clean-up detail. It was Rose, Stenzel, Yoki and Bando.

"Sir," Rose said as Bando and Kirby fist bumped. I nodded to her.

"My dick is so big I pissed into another country," Kirby told his friend.

"Were you playing Risk?" Stenzel asked, "because that's the only way that could happen."

"Board game," I explained. "World domination. Has a miniature map of the world on it."

"I know what Risk is," Kirby said. "I just don't know when she thinks we could have played, and everyone knows it's not a two-person game."

"If you didn't join the Marines, I think you could have had a great career as a flagger, provided you only had to display one side of the sign," Stenzel said.

I held up my hand for her to ease up on Kirby; joking around with your fellow service members was a time-honored tradition, but giving crap to one that had little chance of retaliating as good as he got, was like kicking puppies.

"How many have you killed?" I asked, looking at the long line of broken glass and gore that trailed them. "Damn." My eyes watered as the direction of the wind changed. I should have used the visual cue of the bandannas around their mouths as a warning.

Stenzel pulled one from her pocket. "It has a bit of camphor on it to mask the smell. It helps."

Bando gave one to Kirby. Rose had a special hammer, the kind designed specifically for breaking car windows. It was red handled, the claw had a razor blade built into it, used for cutting quickly through a seatbelt, and the hammer part was pointed steel that broke windows with not much more than a tap. She gave the window a decent tap then stepped away, most of the glass blasted into the car but did little to deter the zombie from reaching out and trying to get at her. Stenzel waited until Rose was clear then popped a suppressed twenty-two into the skull of what looked like a teenager, although the passage of time, the virus, the baking heat and lack of food had taken its toll. She took a quick look inside to make sure nothing else was unalive in there before nodding at Bando. He opened the door and pulled the dead zombie free, then dragged it out of the way. Yoki's job was to place the car in neutral. It was hard not to notice the other three passengers. They had been picked clean, wasn't a scrap of meat on them. It was then I saw the thick layer of what looked like solidified mud on the floor of the car, thick enough it was leaking out over the lip and onto the pavement where it sizzled like it was radioactive.

"You have got to be kidding me." I turned away quickly as I figured out exactly what it was. Processed zombie excrement created by the consumption of human meat. Would have been perfectly content to live a vast array of lives having never borne witness to that. I needed to find myself a science fiction reality with the ability to have my mind wiped.

"Stay safe, heading back," I eventually managed. Not sure how many times you had to see that before you were unaffected, but the group seemed fine.

"Do you want me to come with you?" Kirby asked. We could see the car moving detail not that far behind, tenth of a mile maybe. Looked like every able body was playing their part. And then there was me, pissing away the day. I was going to blame Kirby, wasn't like he was going to be there to defend himself.

A sweat-soaked BT rubbed a towel across his forehead as I came close to the work detail.

"Have a nice stroll?" he asked.

"I thought you'd be further along." I was giving him shit, but they'd done a great job. Had to be a cleared lane some hundred cars long. Not quite a half mile, but it was a hell of a start. Of course, the closer they got to the border, the worse it got, and the longer it would take, but Rome wasn't razed in a day. And that's razed as in destroyed, as opposed to raised like built. (Just in case there's some of you listening to this story out loud around a campfire.)

"Where's everyone putting their weapons?" I asked, taking off my rifle and sword.

"There's a ski doo trailer we're using." He pointed back.

"Ah," I said as I peered over the heads of some of the laborers. I was impressed; BT had this working like a well-oiled machine—with one giant flaw. "Listen man, far be it for me to criticize what you've got going on here…"

"But?" He stood, took a long swig from his canteen, then glared at me.

"I see that you have our caravan following." There was a line of cars behind us.

"Yes," he said, not sure how you could make that sound suspicious, but it did. "I want everyone to stay close, you know, not go wandering off on their own." This obviously meant for me.

"Be that as it may. What's the evacuation plan, should zombies come?"

He turned and saw what I did. If zombies came from the rear, there wasn't anywhere for our vehicles to escape. It would be a free for all run to Colorado, and it was unlikely any of us could outrun speeders for that kind of distance. Wasn't like we could cross the border then turn and give them the finger. Zombies weren't known to carry passports but then again no one was checking them.

He spun. "This is your fucking fault," he hissed, his finger so close to my face it looked like a tree trunk.

"*My* fault?" Lord knew there were plenty of things that could be laid at my feet, wasn't sure how this one got placed there until it did.

"Your extremely paranoid self went on a little nature hike, check out the sights, I suppose, kiss the soil of your mother-land. You left me in charge. The problem with that is I'm not nearly as unreasonably paranoid as you are. I don't think there's a monster behind every door. If you had been here, that would have been addressed."

And there it was. I even looked down to see the bruised and bloody blame laying astride my boot tops. "Huh. Didn't think that was going to happen, not so quickly anyway. I'll fix it," I told him.

11

MIKE JOURNAL ENTRY 11

I WALKED BACK to the last car in line, as fate would have it, it was Gary and Travis. The latter was standing at the back, keeping a lookout.

"Hey brother." I tapped on the door, he was fast asleep. I'd not meant to startle him.

"Not sleeping!" He sat up straight.

"The drool says otherwise."

"It's hot and boring, what else was I supposed to do?"

Part of me couldn't fault him, another part was pissed. He was the first line of defense, he should have been keeping a sharp eye out for trouble. It was times like this that command had its problems. I should have berated him until he started crying, maybe had him do enough push-ups he couldn't feel his arms. Then I had to overlay that with the fact that he was my big brother. "Stay awake," was what I told him. I hope my tone conveyed the importance of those two words.

"Hey dad," Travis said as I headed to the back. Did not at all like him being back here alone. He had good sight lines, and it was unlikely anything was going to sneak up on him, and help was feet away, but still, this was my offspring. As parents, our whole life shifts, and our primary reason for being is to do our utmost to ensure their safety and well-being, and here he was, our early warning system. Statistical fact: early warning systems don't generally last long.

"Hey kiddo, would you rather push cars?" I liked the idea of him being within eyeshot of BT a whole lot better. It was like having a friendly grizzly bear babysit, ain't nobody going to mess with you.

"Let's see, it's got to be ninety something and you're asking if I'd rather do hard, physical labor instead of standing here doing my best to stay in the shade of the truck?"

"More or less."

"I'm surprised Tracy hasn't been canonized yet," Gary came out of the truck and stretched. "Patron saint of...."

"Nope, you don't get a free one right now, you're on my shit list," I told him. "Get back in. We're going to back up to the beginning of the jam." I went down the line of parked cars and told them we were backing up and to spread out. Within fifteen minutes we were in our new configuration, twelve cars and trucks and one tanker spread out fairly evenly along the line. I got some backup for Travis in the form of Dallas and Stenzel. Felt decent enough that I headed back to help out with the cars. As the day wore on, finding room became more and more difficult, as I thought it would. At first we could roll cars completely off the roadway into the woods, and we'd use these outlets until they became completely clogged up, then we'd move things around to create another space. Sometimes it would take as much as pushing over twenty side vehicles out of the way to get the next in line out of the road. Wasn't too much further up where off-road access was impossible, first there was a guard rail a tank would have had difficulty navigating, then a wall.

I was soaked. I was sweating so heavily that I looked like one of those cartoon characters shot full of holes. Water going in was coming out just as quickly. I wiped my head and looked up; the sun was far past its zenith. We weren't getting this cord untangled today, probably not tomorrow either. We would have to leave this channel and find a place to rest for the night that we could defend or evacuate on a moment's notice.

"We're going to have to call it soon," I told BT who had just leaned back to pop his spine.

"I need to talk to you." He went to grab my shoulder, I dipped away before he could.

"Sorry man, I'm so fucking gross right now I don't think I can manage to have anyone touch me."

"I get it." He led me a few feet away. When we were relatively out of earshot he spoke. "There's a problem."

"It would be more surprising if there wasn't." I wasn't trying to be trite, state the obvious, or be sarcastic, just dropping facts.

He grunted. "We've got room to move maybe fifty more cars out of the way and that's max. After that…" He shook his head.

He looked back down the lengthening roadway. I'm going to blame it on the heat and exhaustion, but it took me a lot longer to figure out where he was going with that than it should have. Smacked me upside the head like my wife did that one time we were on vacation driving through a resort town and a woman in arguably the smallest bikini on the planet was walking down the sidewalk. For fuck's sake! She was looking too, but I didn't say anything to her about it.

Pushing a car fifty feet was a chore even on level terrain, which most of this was. Your legs would thrum with the exertion when the task was done, and each subsequent vehicle only added to the strain. To think we were getting close to the point where we would have to push cars a mile or more to the mouth of the jam and beyond was almost too much to even think about.

"I've got an idea, though," he said after he let me go through the whole nightmarish thoughts of the "Great Push," as it would historically become known.

"You enjoy my panic?"

"Oh, very much so. You never really believe the descriptions in books when they say someone turned as white as a sheet of paper. I now have living proof."

"Just tell me, before I feel the need to sit down. My legs feel like they've gone to sleep, got that weird pins and needles feeling."

"Going to be more noise, but I don't see why we couldn't use the tanker to tow the cars out. I would think we could tie several together. Should be able to pull five or six out at a time."

"Maybe more, but no."

"What do you mean, no?"

"Do you agree the tanker is the most valuable commodity we own?"

"Yes..." he said hesitantly, because if we were in court, his lawyer would object saying I was leading the witness. I guess, not really sure how that worked, I usually did plea agreements to avoid trial.

"I don't think we should place that kind of strain on it. It'll be slower, but we could use Gary's truck, should be able to pull two easily enough, three? I don't know."

"Mike, there's a lot of cars. This is already going to be a slow process."

I was doing the math. Tying the cars together, hooking them to the truck, towing them out and returning. "Fifteen minutes a round-trip sound about right?"

BT looked off down the road. "Twelve cars an hour? That's slower than what we're managing now. Looking at over thirty hours of work."

"Good thing we're not under a time crunch." I smiled.

"Aren't we?" he asked in all seriousness.

Zombies would always find us, and Feroz was somewhere behind, unlikely to stop. She was like that fucking snail I referenced in one of these damn journals. You know, the one where she knows exactly where you are and will follow you for all time, killing you upon contact. That snail.

"We halve that time using the tanker."

"We'll get faster with each run. That tanker breaks down, we're dead in the water."

"Lot of ways to die here."

"I know man, I know, I'm trying to weigh the best options, but it's in degrees of shittiness as opposed to 'best available.' It's sort of like voting; the candidates usually all suck, it is your job to pick the one that sucks the least. Not an easy thing to do."

"That's one nice thing about the apocalypse."

"What's that?" I asked as he clapped me on my shoulder, signifying that the break was over.

"Not having to worry about who to vote for."

"Ah."

"There's another problem we need to work through." He grunted as we pushed a vintage DeSoto, an example of the other meaning of "heavy metal." Guess this would have been even worse had we been doing it in the 1950s.

"Do tell. I was hoping for more hurdles. I'm in a hurdling type of mood. Oh, you know what? Fuck hurdles, let's do that insane steeple chase shit, weird wall jumps, water hazards, don't they have mine fields too?"

"Yes, Mike, high school track meets were famous for blowing their athletes up. That's how they packed the stands."

"Lost a lot of good friends that way," I said wistfully.

"So full of shit," he blew a laugh through his puffed-up cheeks as we got that hulking tank of a car moving. "People are going to have to get in those cars to steer."

"The fuck you say?" I stood up to look at him as he kept ambling by.

"Can't you protest and push at the same time?"

"Sure, I could, I just don't want to. I feel like maybe I'm getting the man-flu."

"Get your ass over here."

"Not it," was all I could think to say.

"Real mature."

"As my enforcer, you realize it's your duty to assign the people that have to sit in whatever layers of filth those cars have." I was doing my best to think of alternatives because I wouldn't wish that on any of the people we had with us. I mean sure there were plenty of people in my life *previously* I would have paid good money to put in that position, but at this point, I couldn't afford to make any enemies. "What about jogging next to?" I offered.

"Too slow and dangerous."

"What about standing on the running board holding on to the steering wheel?"

"Slightly less dangerous...there's a couple of choke points where an open door could become a problem, that door whacks a car and then smacks the person steering."

"Do we have any hazmat suits left from the refinery?"

BT paused. "No shit. I always thought that saying 'even a broken watch is right twice a day' was a crock of shit, but here we are."

"Thanks? I guess. Where are they at?"

"Oh hell no, I send you to go look you won't come back."

"I'm the C.O. that's my prerogative."

"You, there!" BT bellowed.

"You there? That's Kirby."

"I can't tell, all you crackers look the same."

"That's how people get cancelled," I told him.

"I dare you."

I could only raise my hands up in mock defense.

"Top?" Kirby came hustling over.

"Go grab the hazmat suits."

"You okay, Top?" Kirby looked concerned. BT leaned against the car we'd just got off the road. He did look flushed and the beads of sweat on his forehead were large enough for ducks to land in.

"Help me." I motioned for Kirby, and we got BT to sit in the shade the car made. That BT didn't protest was telling in and of itself. "Go grab some water." Kirby nodded and darted off.

"Think I might have overdone it," he said after he got orientated.

Kirby hustled back with a gallon jug; I watched as BT chugged half of it.

"Anything else, sir?" Kirby asked.

"If you could find those hazmat suits that would be great."

"On it." He gave one look back at Top.

"I'm going to have to discipline him now."

"What?"

"He's seen weakness, blood in the water. Going to have to show him I'm still at the top of the food chain."

"You mean command chain."

"Sure," BT said as he took another large swig.

12

MIKE JOURNAL ENTRY 12

It took BT about a half hour to rebound, it was just as the sun was setting, he stood. I thought the timing was a little suspect; I'm no dummy—most of the time—or some of the time, anyway. Kept my mouth shut. We stayed close together at the mouth of the open lane for the night, again circling the wagons and keeping guards atop the tanker. It was a viable defense against a small force of shufflers and one honey badger; if those little bastards ever decided to team up we'd be screwed. I sometimes wondered if my mind drifted around so much so that I couldn't fixate on any of the scar tissue chiseled in there. Possible and someday maybe I'd think about it in more than a cursory way, but most likely not as my mind would never give me that type of opportunity. I'm not even sure I know what contemplative means.

We had a quick meeting on tomorrow's clearing strategy. We'd just about tapped out all the extra space. We could maybe cram two or three more cars somewhere, but that avenue was exhausted. It was onto the towing phase. Gary had assured us that his truck could tow three average cars. We'd have to adjust when we came across trucks and vans, and there was also one trailer-toting semi in our way. We either figured out how to get that behemoth out of the way or we cut a fifteen-car detour path around it. We did have one major point of contention: we only had two hazmat suits. Some of the cars were much cleaner than others, some even had been completely evacuated, but those were the exception to the rule. More times than not, the three cars were filthy cesspools of disgusting human debris. There was absolutely no way we could ask or order anyone to sit in that filth, especially not without any viable means to shower off and disinfect.

That meant most of the pulls were going to be two cars at a time. Dropped us down to somewhere around eight cars an hour, so somewhere in the forty-eight-hour range to complete. It was going to be much less labor intensive than it had been, but we were still looking at four heavy workdays to get the job done. That was a looooooong time to have our asses in the breeze, to turn a phrase, not even sure if that's how it goes, but not like I can ask someone. Or I could, but that would involve getting up and seeking someone. Hard to remember when we had an entire clear week free from d-bags and zombies. It was so fucking frustrating. How could we be both so close and so far away?

It was like traveling home on Christmas. You'd waded through the crowds, waited in security for hours, finally boarded your weather delayed flight, made it to your connection with minutes to spare. You're running through the airport desperate to make it before they close the gates. Somehow you just beat the bell and sit down in your seat as the door closes and you pull away from the terminal, feeling somewhat giddy and victorious. A smile spreads across your face as you realize you've done it, and now you're sitting on the tarmac, third from taking off, when the pilot announces that the plane is being called back to the gate because the crew has timed out. After deboarding, airport staff assures you that another crew was hustling to the airport to take all the weary travelers to their final destination. As a person who has flown a fair amount of time, I know the smoke screen for what it is, but you always hold onto that hope. Nothing worse than realizing you are stuck midway between where you were and where you want to be with no viable alternative to go backwards, to where you live or forwards, where you were headed.

This was a little different because I wanted out of Mexico and into the US, but still had enough similarities to the already lived through analogy. You look at travel much differently when you spend Christmas Day on an airport floor. Even a free flight as a comp loses its luster when you get back a day later. They tried to reenact the celebrations, but most everyone else had gone back to their lives, the magic is gone, and you're stuck eating leftovers while your parents' incredibly ancient dog watches you with rheumy eyes, wondering when you are going to pay him appropriate tribute through food snacks.

Tough to say which came first, the first ray of light striking the side of my closed eyelid, or the lone rifle shot that cracked through the still air. I was awake and outside in under five seconds, that's the benefit of going to sleep fully clothed. Hard to call that a bennie, but there it is, nonetheless.

"Shuffler," Stenzel said without looking back at me.

"Just the one?" I was preparing to climb the tanker to get a look.

"That's all I saw." She was scanning the area.

A lone shuffler was as likely as a lone ant. Less so, as shufflers weren't known to send out scouts, they didn't have the sophistication their counterparts did. They could communicate on some level, and liked to congregate, but tactical planning was not their strong suit. We spent a solid ten minutes looking. Nothing. By now everyone was up; it was time to get this show on the road. Funny how fitting the saying was because we really couldn't get on the road.

"How much time do you have left on your shift?" I asked before I headed back down.

"It was over a half hour ago. Just had a feeling, you know?" This time she did look at me.

I can't say I was overly thrilled with the information her eyes conveyed. She was tired, we all were, that wasn't it. I'm not sure if she knew, but whatever part of her nervous system was being triggered as an early warning system it was on high alert. We held each other's gaze for what was seemingly an awkward amount of time, me searching for any answers regarding the scope of the attack, and when it was coming, and her for reassurances that what her subconscious was feeling was incorrect. I'd never tell someone to go against their hunches; I could only hope we played out our part before the hunch could play out its. Four days, though, what type of slow burning hunch took four days? I was debating pulling up stakes and hiding out somewhere for a few days, maybe a couple of weeks. We could come back and restart the escape efforts once the coast was clear. Shit, Andy Dufresne waited eight months until he got his solo cell back before digging again. (*Shawshank Redemption* reference for any of you near savages that don't know what I'm talking about. For the more sophisticated among you, it was originally a novella entitled: *Rita Hayworth and the Shawshank Redemption*, arguably Stephen King's finest work—or finest movie adaptation.)

Thing about that story, though, was Andy had nothing but time. A life's sentence worth, to be specific. I knew enough about myself to know that waiting eight months was out of the question. Eight weeks was too much to ask, eight days was on the peripheral, and eight hours wouldn't make a difference one way or the other. We had a meeting, made sure groups stayed in tight with their rides; we were going to bug out at the first sign of trouble, even had a rally point in mind, should we get separated. Those not part of the work crew were responsible for guard duty, the more eyes the better. Some good ideas came out of that meeting; any time added to the evac would be negligible, which I was good with. Instead of haphazardly disposing of the towed cars, crews waiting at the end were going to arrange them as best they could as a barricade. As long as it was shufflers that were coming, any wall would be extremely effective. Of course a time would come that they had the horde numbers they were famous for to push everything out of the way, but until then, yeah, cars were as effective as a foot-tall bush in a video game where the developers didn't want you to so easily escape a setting. Frustrating as shit when you can't lift your leg above a one-foot impediment. (Yeah, I'm talking about you, Zelda!)

Somehow the day being less strenuous took more out of me. I could only figure it was the stress of the cars not getting the fuck out of the way quick enough while we waited for the approach of the zombie storm. We actually ended up close to ten cars an hour, after figuring some stuff out and streamlining the process. Tomorrow, should it come, would even be better. We worked until it was no longer safe to do so. If the moon had played along and decided to shine brightly, I think we would have gone long into the night. There was no way I was going to authorize headlights in a dark world, I couldn't even imagine from how far away they would be seen. Stenzel stayed up on the tanker the entire time; someone had wrangled her up a sunshade made from an old tarp.

"The sun's a mean drunk," I said to BT as I took a rest while we waited for Gary to return. I wiped my brow.

"I hate that I have a curious streak." He sat down near me —we were fighting for a sliver of shade Henry wouldn't have been content with. "Tell me." He motioned with his hands.

"It's beating down on us."

"What? That's it? I thought it would be a bit better, I mean, sure, it's true and all, still not funny."

"You're just tired or something, that's gold right there."

"Domestic violence is funny to you?"

"Well, I mean no, it was the reference."

"So referencing domestic violence is funny to you?"

My mouth was opening and closing as I fought to look for the right words to make this conversation go away. It had not at all turned out like I'd thought.

"You know how many battered women calls I ended up going on, Mike?"

"Hey man." I held up my hands. "It was an attempt at a joke, nothing more. I'm truly sorry." And I meant it, it wasn't just an attempt to placate an enormous angry man.

No matter how many times I lived through the truth of my mouth getting me in trouble, I still managed to find a way to do it again. It wasn't until we saw Gary backing up to get into position that BT spoke again.

"I think maybe your drunk sun is getting to me. Ready to get back at it?"

"Of course," I told him.

"We good?" he asked.

"I could ask the same. BT, anything short of you murdering me or someone I love, we'll always be good."

"Where does *wanting* to murder *you* fall?"

"Still in the acceptable realm. If I cut everyone out of my life that had wanted to murder me at one time or another, I'd be living a very solitary existence." What I didn't tell him, and wouldn't, was that I wouldn't be living at all, as I'd wanted to off myself more times than probably all of my enemies combined. Who needs enemies when you have yourself?

Trying to sleep that night was an act of futility. I was amped up with how close we were to getting out of this trap, and my body had just enough aches and pains that finding a comfortable position to sleep was eluding me. The encampment received a two-shot wake up alarm. I was surprised to see Catalina's gun barrel smoking when I got outside. She was atop the tanker, tracking targets.

"How many?" I called up, wasn't much of a reason to be quiet about it at this point.

"There were eleven." She turned to look.

"And now?"

"Four. No, three."

Apparently getting any meaningful information out of Catalina was going to be an effort, I climbed the tanker, because even with some incredibly well timed and placed shots, there was no way she'd taken out eight zombies with two bullets. Would that be amazing? Sure, but highly unlikely. I watched as Yoki was threading her way through cars, taking down zombies as she came up on them.

"I shot before I knew she was out there," Catalina said.

"Did you shoot at her?" I asked.

"No, but I could have." She sounded concerned.

"Did she tell you she was going out?"

"No."

"I'll talk to her. You did what you were supposed to do. Yoki put herself in added danger." Although as I watched the assassin dispatch of the remaining three, I was wondering if we were going about this the wrong way. She wasn't fifty feet from us, and I'd barely heard a grunt as she decapitated the bastards. It was nice to create that kind of silent void. The less we put ourselves and our noises out there, the less likely we were to be discovered. Shufflers versus a sword was like playing a video game where you traveled back to a forest on the first level where you could kill a deer-like creature for five hit points of experience so you could level up. Sure it would take a thousand of the bastards, but you had beer, edibles, and pizza pockets galore to get the job done.

BT waited until we gave the all-clear before we got the day's work underway. I thought about those eleven zombies for the better part of the day. What was going on? Why had there been one yesterday and eleven today? Were we in for a horde tomorrow? I hitched a ride back with Gary after the first load of cars was dropped off.

"You planning on doing any work today?" BT asked.

"Don't think so, man. I was planning on using a mental health day," I told him.

"It's not right how many of those things you've allotted yourself."

"You live in this head and tell all the voices that. Listen, on a serious note, was thinking of grabbing someone and a car and doing a little scouting. Figure out where these things are coming from, and how many more are on the way. I don't want to get stuck here when a thousand of the bastards show up on our doorstep."

"There are risks."

"I know, man, there's the noise of the car, there's being out there relatively alone, no comms. Yeah I know, I won't go far, but this not knowing what's over the horizon is troubling."

"Ten miles."

"What?"

"You're going to give me the mileage on whichever car you take. You have ten miles to work with, five out, five back."

"My mom used to do that when I first got my license and told her I would head to the store for bread. She was getting pissed when the three point eight-mile round trip somehow took over fifty."

"*Fifty?* What the hell were you doing?"

"Hey man, it takes a while to smoke through a fattie, get to a fast-food joint and eat it all while driving around and cranking tunes, and then, man, you need to drive around longer to air out the skunk and burger smell."

"Maybe if you had invested in some higher quality weed it wouldn't have smelled like skunk."

"I was sixteen, I got whatever was available."

"I'm serious, five miles out max, because when we invariably have to go and rescue your ass, I don't want to have to go too far to do it."

"Sure, I get it. I'd hate to have my rescue be an inconvenience."

"Don't pull that shit."

I was smiling.

"No side roads, either. Stay on the highway. Ride out, take a look, ride back. If you leave now you should beat Gary back with his next load."

I wanted to give him a hard time, but he was so sincere. I'm sure some of it had to do with my safety or the safety of whichever poor bastard I made drive me around, but more of his concern would have to do with him being pulled away from this task. It could be monitored by another, but he'd taken complete control of this project, and wanted to oversee every step. I understood that level of commitment and micro-management. My issues with authority are legendary in my own mind, but what is one to do when they themselves are the authority? I suppose I have plenty of issues with myself; that was going to have to do.

"Five miles," I told him and I meant it. Would something happen out there that would necessitate altering that? Odds were likely, but for that moment, I was good with the five-mile curfew radius.

"Ten minutes, Mike. If we have to spend time looking for you, it's more time it'll take to finish this and that much more time to get back to Colorado."

"Right for the jugular, nice. You been taking lessons from Tracy?"

"Just hurry up."

I again rode with Gary, this time back to the off-loading.

"Want to go for a ride?" I asked Yoki as I came up to the ancient Toyota Corolla she was leaning up against.

"*Doraibu?*" she asked, rocking her fists back and forth in a driving motion. Like she didn't want to go for a ride so much as drive.

"I don't know, Yoki, you're um, how do I put this delicately?"

253

"Drive fine, round eye," she said angrily, then she gave me the finger.

"I suppose that's warranted. Let's go then." I swept my hand toward the driver's door. "Five miles." I held out my splayed fingers. "We're only going five miles to take a look."

She put the car in reverse, stepped on the gas far too heavily and braked far too quickly. My head rocked back and forth. I don't know if the bad start was on purpose to teach me a lesson or if she was indeed the stereotype I'd been so close to pointing out. Got my answer soon enough when she was looking far to her right and on the left side-swiped a parked car. That was one less headlight we weren't going to have to worry about giving our position away. She flipped me off again. I was having a hard time figuring out how this was my fault. It was smooth sailing once we got onto the highway proper, I sure as shit wasn't going to say anything about the amount of lane drift she had going on. We were doing more side-to-side movement than forward, but again, there was no point in riling her any further. She stopped at four point nine miles, a bead of sweat on her brow.

"*Shojo!*" she cried, smiling.

"Shojo?" I asked.

Her eyes went high as she searched for the answer. "Virgin," she managed.

"Um, what?" I didn't think this was some weird proposal, first off because I was married, and secondly, I wasn't her type. Still, here we were in a car, alone. I wasn't sure what the fuck she was talking about, or meant, for that matter. I was about as uncomfortable as one could be, given the circumstances.

"Virgin.... Second time!" She was now smiling broadly.

"What? Oh, you sneaky fuck. That was your second time driving? And not for nothing you can't be a virgin the second time around."

She was nodding her head, smiling, then gave me double eagles. "Virgin mothafuckah."

"I'm driving back."

She nodded.

As I got out of the car, I looked further down the roadway. A lone zombie stood there, watching. Tough to definitively say, but it sure looked like it was dressed all in black, and from there, how hard would it be to extrapolate that it was excessively tall and thin? No idea what this new wrinkle was, but it sure would feel good to iron it out.

"We're going to kill that fuck," I told Yoki as I slid in, and she scooted over. Would have been way cooler if I had a turbo-charged Mustang to peel out with, leaving scorch marks on the roadway as we raced to end a danger. Instead, we had the slow and steady acceleration of a four-cylinder dinosaur. If I had any input when the movie was made, we were switching out for something with a V8. The zombie thing began walking toward the tree line as we approached. Didn't seem to be in any particular rush, but by the time we got to where it had been, it was gone. I smacked the steering wheel, and Yoki smacked the dashboard. I thought maybe at first she was making fun of my outburst, but she seemed genuinely as pissed as I did. We were both staring into the woods, couldn't see shit past two feet deep. Had a pretty good feeling our target was waiting in there with a couple dozen or more of his bestest buds. Hell, for all we knew could be a hundred. Could be ten thousand. Anything not wearing blinking neon signs was going to be impossible to spot. Yoki opened her door, I reached and lightly touched her arm and shook my head.

"I don't know how I know this, but that thing wants us to go in there after it. And I think for once I'm going to listen to that little voice in my head that's telling me to go back."

"Ha! BT is voice! Not little."

"I suppose his voice wouldn't be so little. Not sure that's the voice I was referring to but I suppose maybe I'm listening to him too." I accelerated responsibly once she shut her door, but merely because it was the only option available to me.

"No way. I kind of feel that surreal feeling others must get when they win the lottery. Like the odds of it happening are so vastly against it that you can't believe it when it happens."

"Bite me," I told BT when I got out of Gary's truck.

"Lay it on me."

"They're out there, led by everyone's newest favorite scary zombie."

"The Thin Man?"

"One and the same."

"How far?"

"Just a bit over five miles." Never really did the math. Shufflers traveled somewhere in the speed range between a three-legged desert tortoise and a Red Bull fueled slug. But two or three miles an hour would be well within their ability, especially if we were making it worth their while, which meant if they were headed right for here, we had around two hours to clear over two hundred cars. It wasn't happening. We could probably make a pretty decent barricade to keep them out, but then what? We wouldn't have any room to put the cars we were towing. This was it, decision time. Abandon our cars and make a go for the border on foot, or retreat and wait it out somewhere.

"Let's go! Doubletime, you lazy, sorry ass excuses for meat bags!" BT yelled.

"What are you doing?" I asked.

"I'm not walking to Colorado. Gary, send the tanker down with a few extra people, we're going for maximum pulls."

My brother nodded.

"We only have two hazmat suits."

"Dirty pants are the least of our problems."

"Says the person that's not getting in any of the cars. Fuck." I knew where this was going. While BT was busy setting up more tow ropes, I was checking out trunks of cars for spare clothes and blankets. Then I had the idea of ripping out the carpet lining the trunks. There were going to be plenty of those, even if we only did a one and done with the material. Beauty of that job was that I'd made myself a vital gatherer and wouldn't be called upon for transport. I was more than fine with that. Took a little longer to get set up, but that tanker dragged ten cars out without a problem. BT pushed the next go up to an even dozen, this time the truck did lurch and exert itself as black plumes of exhaust were pushed high out of the exhaust pipes. I was continually moving down the line, making piles of impromptu seat covers.

I kept doing the math in my head; this was going to be a photo finish, I could feel it in my bones. At this pace, we had somewhere in the neighborhood of seventeen more pulls left. It was taking a bit longer per pull because of set-up and tear down, so right now we were averaging fifteen minutes per round trip, which put the caravan into the US in roughly four hours. We'd made our estimate about the shufflers with the thoughts that they would start immediately and would come straight here. Neither of those things were known. In addition, there was a slim chance it was only a half dozen zombies. Unlikely as all get out, but not completely out of the realm of possibilities.

"Stenzel, go back with the tanker, grab a car and someone you trust. Head out about a mile, and as soon as you see the smelly bastards, come back."

She nodded.

"Well that's a nice surprise," I said when the trunk I opened held a cache of weapons. "Where the hell were you when I was running around with only my wits for a weapon?" I pulled out a sleek H&K submachinegun.

"Nice gun. Less gawking, more carpeting!" BT yelled at me.

I put the gun back in its case, this stuff was coming with us. Grabbed the ammo cans and gun cases and briskly walked over to the tanker truck and opened up one of the storage areas Gary had welded on. It was a tight fit, but I got everything in there. I turned to see BT watching me, his arms folded across his chest.

"Don't make me put you in one of these cars."

"Nope, nope, sorry." I threw my hands up. "Won't get distracted again."

There was constant movement as we all had our assigned jobs. It would have been easy to lose track of time, but in this case, I wanted there to be *more* time, not less of it. I would have been alright with that Monday workday phenomenon where no matter how much time you thought had elapsed, it was always a few minutes earlier than the previous time you looked at the clock. We'd improved our speed, at least. I think it had more to do with the tanker pulling faster, but you know, fear of being eaten will make anyone's foot a little heavier on the gas. It was a tick over twelve minutes a pull. It had been six pulls since I'd sent Stenzel out. Nine pulls left, and a bit under two hours to get it completed. I don't think I'd ever wished for someone I cared for not to appear more than this time. It was two pulls later I saw her hop off the truck.

"Fuck," I muttered. "Numbers?"

"Hundreds for sure, could be thousands."

"How far out?"

"Mile and a half at the most. We hightailed it back here but had to wait a few minutes while the tanker off-loaded." The logistics now were a nightmare.

"BT we need to do a side pull!" I called over, I was moving toward him as another set of cars were prepped for movement.

"What are you talking about?"

"We need to pull a set of cars away on the side so that we can bring our working cars and people down here. We're going to need to evacuate as quickly as possible."

I thought I might get a bit of pushback on that idea, but he was onboard. Hard not to be when your family would be part of the group brought down. Within a half an hour, all the people we had remaining were down in the thick of the work zone. We had six pulls left, an hour and twelve minutes—if we could keep the pace up. The zombies would be at the front of this clusterfuck in half that.

"Got an idea." BT was frantically looking around. "Adds time to our escape but might give us the time we need to do it."

I understood the logic. We added another fully loaded pull onto the docket, right behind the running cars we'd just parked. The idea was once we saw the zombies, we'd have the tanker park in the cutout, we'd use people power to push the next set of cars into place, and instead of pulling, the tanker would push them out. Thus staying far enough away from the horde that the "drivers" could escape unmolested and head back with the truck. We would lose a lot of time manually pushing the cars into place, but we'd make some of that up because now the tanker wouldn't need to pull all the way to the mouth of the traffic jam, plus we'd be bolstering the barricade the shufflers would need to navigate. I can't remember the last time I would have used the word *giddy* to describe how I was feeling. Maybe when I was a kid and it was Christmas Eve, other than that I couldn't say, but I was traveling mighty close to that blindly joyful place. If the scale went from roid rage to ecstatic, I had far passed the midrange point of meh and was firmly entrenched in hopefully happy.

That was tempered a bit by nerves when there was one more normal trip after the tanker parking spot was made then it came back and parked in its assigned spot. That was our cue. All able-bodied people were on the clock, lot of adrenaline to start off with as we pushed cars forward. There were forty-two cars in our way, keeping us from escaping this hell, and we had placed every egg we had in one basket. Escape by driving only happened if we got the cars out. My dad was a good man, hardworking and as honest as the day was long. The thing about him though that none of us had known at the time and didn't realize until we were older, was he had some serious, undiagnosed OCD tendencies. I'd worked construction with the man for a few years, and I'd marvel at some of the things he would do. I think it irritated the hell out of him that I didn't think twice about calling him out on it. The rest of the crew wasn't comfortable doing that, and besides, I had gotten somewhat used to dealing with his idiosyncrasies. You could say that I was okay pointing it out because I was family, but all of my brothers had worked for him at one time or another, and none of them had ever said boo. But I'd never been one to keep my mouth shut, and let him have it. Had plenty of NCOs and officers from the Corps that would testify to that statement.

Anyway, for whatever reason I'll never be able to fathom, the man could not abide by idleness. A lot of the jobs we worked on called for heavy machinery, but my dad just couldn't stand people standing around watching this multi-ton machine do what fifteen grunting men could. Seriously, I wish what I was relating was fabricated fiction merely for the sake of the readers' enjoyment...sadly, that is not the case. Too many times to count we would be muscling our work under the shadow of the behemoth. Swinging picks, sledgehammers or shoveling piles of debris into trucks. The operators of these rented machines, sometimes making as much as fifteen hundred bucks a day, could only scratch their heads while my dad told them to back away so the crew could go about their work. My dad, as hard a worker as he was, was not the greatest businessman. There were those times when we worked alongside equipment, and then there were the *other* times, when we should have had a machine do the heavy lifting, but my dad would opt not to. Consequently, something that would have taken a decent operator half a day to complete would take a crew of ten, two days and a workers comp claim to finish. Okay, too far off topic, I suppose. What I'm getting at was I wanted to pull a page from my dad's book. Get the tanker out of the mix and have everyone push a car. In this instance I was convinced we'd be faster, and I argued the point until I got my way.

Stenzel was at the end of our new line to hold. I'd just started pushing the car I'd been assigned to when I heard her rifle fire. I was with Bando; we had to travel a bit over a thousand feet. Three hundred yards doesn't sound like a bunch until you're pushing a ton of metal on tires with low air pressure. The first hundred yards went fairly smoothly, it was after that the lactic acid began to affect my muscles and the burn traveled up my thighs. By the last hundred yards, I had my ass pressed against the bumper, my teeth gritted, and my head thrown back. I wouldn't have doubted the fucking emergency brake being on. When we gave our last heave, Bando pulled me to the side just as another car came. I took a few steps until I could completely straighten out and get back in the game helping those behind us.

We had a column of moving cars and a horde of approaching zombies. I wondered what an aerial view of the scene would have looked like: the slow-moving horde inevitably gaining on the slightly slower moving humans. Cool effect for a movie, bad for real life.

"Need more guns up here!" Stenzel called out.

Heads turned my way. Guns to hold back the enemy or hands to move the cars, couldn't have both. God forbid you actually got to eat that cake you'd received. From now on I wasn't even going to accept the dessert, would turn my head as the plate passed me right by. Wasn't worth getting my hopes up. I did what I could and split the group.

"Let's go!" I shouted as half of us headed back to push more cars. "Fifteen. Fifteen cars stand between us and getting out of here." There were sixteen of us on push duty, which meant we could get rid of just over half the cars each round. It was going to be more difficult because only one would be pushing from the ass end while the other was half-pushing and steering from the open driver's side door. Behind us, the fighting had gotten intense. I couldn't see the action because my eyes were clenched tight as I fought through the muscle-binding pain in my legs. I was fairly certain I was going to have enough in me to get this car out of the way, but after that I wasn't sure I could make the walk back to the next in line.

"Switch out! Switch out!" I shouted, Dallas headed back in my stead, as I did my best to stand tall like my evolutionary predecessors when I looked more like the third figure in the chart—you know the one, hunched back, arms hanging low. Once I got to the front I wished I'd sucked it up and gone back for another car. The zombies weren't coming in a uniform line, they'd spread out once they'd encountered obstacles. We had a wonderful hundred-and-eighty-degree view of the undead as they fought for a way through traffic. The absolute only reason we hadn't been overrun yet was that these were shufflers. Had they been speeders or anything else, I would have had to completely rethink my strategy of staying or fleeing when we had the opportunity. Actually, no, that's a lie. We would have already succumbed.

"So many," I said as I randomly picked targets and shot. I say random, but mainly it was the ones that had somehow threaded the needle and found an access point. These were the trailblazers. Problem with those bastards was that they had a way to pass this information along so once one got through, all their buddies would start funneling in. We needed another fifty soldiers on the front line to at the minimum create a stale-mate. With the thin green line I commanded we were losing ground every second. Ground we couldn't afford to lose. We were minutes from having to abandon our posts, a full-on retreat. I'd be going home, not victorious, but tail tucked firmly between my legs as we made the arduous journey away from this disaster on foot.

I had an imaginary line in my head which, once the zombies passed over, I would make the order, and that was already going to be closer than I wanted it to be. I had to figure in the animals, kids and older folks who were going to need assistance at least for the first few miles as we put distance between us and them. My back let out involuntary sobs just thinking of the hefting I was going to need to do with Henry. The best boy ever was a great dog, talented eater, even more skilled napper, but as a walker, he failed hard. Chloe and Holly were better, but anything more than a mile and they were also going to need help. The boys would help there, but it wasn't like either of those bullies were svelte Chihuahuas. Was it my hubris that had led us to this ruin? I don't think that's the right word to use, it wasn't like I'd thumbed my nose at the zombies, not believing them capable of harming us. But come on, it was shufflers. I always yelled at the TV when I saw victims being eaten by the slow bastards, and here we were, trapped and about to be eaten.

As my bolt froze open, so did my mouth about to shout for the withdrawal. I turned as I heard the engine to the tanker start up. I whipped my head around to the border, where I could still see two or three cars in the way. I wasn't sure who was behind the wheel of the semi, but I knew what they were intending to do.

"Move, move, move!" I shouted at the top of my lungs, holding my rifle in the air to garner more attention. A few shots later and those of us who had been trying to hold the zombies at bay were running to get into rides. All the cars had started up and were falling in line behind the semi, which was picking up speed. We were staying back a respectable distance in case debris came flying back—or worse, the semi came to a sudden screeching halt. After the sound of a firing line ended, the world was always a whole lot quieter, though there was still the sound of wind coming in, the sound of multiple engines, but dominating it all was the heavy diesel sound of the tanker revving up for its car plowing duties.

"This is going to work," I said as many times as I could in the ensuing thirty seconds before the screeching thunderous sound of metal-on-metal impact dominated. The semi shook violently and slowed considerably; I held my breath waiting for it to stall out. Started to see stars in my field of vision as we breezed past the checkpoint. Not all is right in your head when you have to remind yourself to breathe.

We. Were. Clear! I thought about having Gary pull over so I could get out and twirl around like Julie Andrews in *The Sound of Music*. (It was years later I found out she was actually in a studio and not on the side of a mountain when they filmed that scene, totally ruined it for me. Well, that, plus by then I was much more into action flicks than musicals.) We were fifty yards from where we had been, yet the weight that had been wrapped around my shoulders and pressing on my chest had been lifted. I wanted to cry from the relief of it. Henry took that moment to paw my arm and give me a slobbering lick on my ear.

"We did it." I had grabbed his jowls and was looking him square in the face.

"I'm not sure how much he had to do with it." Tracy had the widest smile on her face I'd seen in ages. She was lit up like an angel.

"Moral support," I told her. I was so happy right then I'd not thought to look up and see if a shoe was preparing to drop. Why would I? Because it's life and there's always a Shaq-sized shoe hanging out, waiting to smoosh the unsuspecting.

"What the hell?" Gary said from up front. It had more of a perplexed feel than an, I'm terrified tone, so while we slowed, I wasn't in a panic, but my blood pressure had picked up. What good was a win if you couldn't even enjoy the moment you cross the finish line? This was like being twenty seconds from winning a playoff game and knowing you were positively headed to the championships only to lose your starting quarterback to an injury on the last play. And by all accounts he should have been pulled midway through the last quarter anyway because of the comfortable lead we'd already secured.

Henry was miffed when I moved away and headed out of the truck. Instead of asking what the hell, I went with *what the fuck?* Way more fitting. I checked behind us quickly to make sure that the zombies weren't somehow keeping up with us. How long had we been on the road? Five minutes? Maybe a bit more, certainly not ten. So that gave us that much of a lead to deal with the problem ahead. A hulking, twenty-foot-tall, rust colored, solid steel wall that spanned across the entire highway sat there like a smug motherfucker denying us that final point. It even went over the median.

"Who put that there?" Tracy asked.

"Great question. Feds or some Texas militia maybe. Doesn't look like anything the average citizenry could have pulled off," I answered.

I was moving closer, checking the heights to see if anyone was watching. It looked abandoned. Got a decent chuckle when I saw the oversized white letters spray painted on the side. They weren't fresh, but they'd not been up there for too long either. It read, "They took our jobs!" I thought it in my best Cartman from *South Park* voice that I could muster.

"Someone's a real comedian," BT pointed out.

I found out it had been Stenzel who had piloted the big rig, securing our escape. She was already at the wall and look-ing. "It's on a track!" she called back as we made our way toward her.

"That thing rolls?" I asked. "How? It's got to be like…a bunch of tons."

"Bunch of tons? You do that math all on your own?" BT asked.

I gave his back the finger.

"I felt that," he said.

"Bullshit, how?"

"You're as predictable as a three-year-old with a candy bar."

"There's a door," Stenzel said, opening it and stepping through before I could tell her to wait until we got there to back her up.

"I always considered her one of our smarter Marines; just goes to show you can't always trust your instinct," BT said as we hustled to follow her through.

"Whoa," was all I could manage as I stepped through. There were enormous steel wheels sitting on a track, and there was a hodgepodge of cables and pulleys and a few oversized motors that I would imagine were responsible for moving the wall. There was also a brace work of steel I-beams that were in place to keep the wall from toppling over. These were also wheeled, but they did not have a dedicated track. I braced myself against one of the beams and gave it a heave. Would have had an easier time pushing a mountain. It didn't budge, didn't so much as creak to give me an inkling it could be moved.

"Could be locked in place," Stenzel said as she studied the motors.

"Let's hope it isn't *frozen* in place." BT tossed that tidbit out, now that he mentioned it, there was a fair amount of rust.

"What are the chances we brought along a fifty-gallon drum of WD-40?" I asked.

"Not helpful," BT said.

"When are my quips ever helpful?"

He grunted in acknowledgement.

"Need a ladder." Stenzel was shielding her eyes and looking straight up.

"Has to be a way up." I pointed at the catwalk which, at some time, must have been patrolled.

I looked down to the far side of the wall hoping for a staircase, of course there was nothing.

"I'm going to get a rope," Stenzel said as she headed back to the other side.

"Who did this?" I wasn't asking BT, it was more of an open question to myself.

"Those motors look electric," he answered anyway.

"That good or bad?"

"Tough to say. Less things to go wrong than a normal combustion engine, but sitting here outside like this without maintenance, electric motors could be just as seized as anything else."

"Of all the friggen' things I thought we could encounter on this journey, an enormous steel wall wasn't on the list."

"I'll have to check the betting grid, but I don't think this was on there."

"There's a grid? Why wasn't I asked to play?"

"Because you would have asked to have dragons added on."

"Not seeing the problem." I walked to the far side of the highway, I could see to the other side with ease. "Saws!" I shouted. "Do we have any?" I was still loud as I came back.

"We'd need a plasma torch and a ton of fuel we don't have to cut an opening big enough for that semi to fit through."

"I meant for the trees."

"Oh." That got the wheel in my friend's head turning. He looked at the woods that were on either side. "That is a lot of trees we'd have to take down, and they'd have to be taken down right near the ground for the cars to clear. Would at minimum be a few dozen."

We'd gravitated toward the edge. I was as certain as I

could be that we didn't have a chainsaw. It was possible we had some hand saws, but looking at the task at hand, that would be like digging out from an avalanche with a kid's plastic beach shovel. We had some time, but it was far from unlimited. The shufflers would come, and who knew what else was out there? The wall would delay the shufflers for a bit, but as they came up against it they would invariably spread out and find that the edges were easily passable by foot. And because this z-poc was like a broken record, we could keep ahead of them on foot, but not forever. Without the cars we were as vulnerable as we had ever been. I thought the good old US was supposed to offer safe harbor to all those entering her borders? Or did that only apply to those coming in via Ellis Island?

"Sick of this shit."

"We'll figure it out," BT said.

"How very optimistic of you."

Stenzel came back with a rope and a crudely fashioned hook.

"That going to hold your weight?" I asked.

"I'm not climbing it, he is." She pointed over her shoulder to Kirby who had just come through the door. He was busy shoveling some bagged food into his mouth. When he smiled it looked like dry oats spilled out.

"Why do people like oatmeal?" he asked once he was done choking it down.

"You're, um, supposed to cook it in liquid. It comes out like gruel or porridge, or something equally as disgustingly mushy," I said.

"Oh, that makes sense." He tilted the bag up to get the rest of the contents. He struggled to swallow as the food sucked all of the moisture from his mouth. Stenzel handed him her canteen. Water spilled out the sides of his mouth at first as the liquid attempted to make it past the oat blockade.

"I swear to God if he starts choking I'm going to let him

pass out before I save him. Maybe he'll learn something," BT said.

"He's a Marine, how much do you think is going to sink in? And if he passes out, that means you have a one in three chance of having to make that climb," I told him.

"Drink up, boy!" BT bellowed.

Stenzel's ability to shoot targets from unimaginable distances did not at all translate to tossing a rope. It was genuinely bizarre how horrible her aim was with that hook. I was about to show her how bad I could be at it when Dallas came through the door.

"I've got it," she said as she immediately sized up the situation. That was when I remembered she grew up on a farm. I suppose at one time or another she'd learned how to rope a calf.

"First try," BT said as an aside.

"You're on, what's the bet?"

"Ten diaper changes."

"Get fucked." The words bypassed any thought process and launched forth from my mouth immediately.

"You take my guard duty for a week."

"And if I win?"

"I'd say I'd take your guard duty, but you don't do it anymore."

"You're the one that told me I shouldn't."

"Your call. I'll go with whatever you recommend."

"Deal." I stuck out my hand which he shook just as Dallas let go of the rope. "Son of a bitch." As it arced up and out it was easy enough to see that she was dead on. The hook struck the steel and resonated with a gratifying gonging sound.

BT was all smiles. "That was easy."

Dallas tugged on the rope. When she was satisfied that she'd set the hook, she kept tension on it.

"Ri'm rup!" Kirby had produced another packet of oat paste and was halfway through it as he grabbed the rope.

"Double or nothing he chokes and passes out while he's climbing?"

"I don't make foolish bets," BT answered.

I honestly didn't mind guard duty; sleep, on many occasions, was futile anyway. I spent more time looking up at the ceiling or the stars than I did slumbering away in a fantasy world of my mind's making. I'd read once—okay, that's horseshit, sounded like I was an expert, I'd skimmed the headline—that there were scientists somewhere who had concluded that since we spent nearly a third of our lives in these sleep worlds that they were as much a part of our lives as our fully aware existence, thus making them just as real. Should have maybe read the article in its entirety, because what a cool ass theory. (Of course, I was probably busy looking for videos of bulldogs playing or something like cats being assholes, there were plenty of those. Between me and me, it could have been porn I was looking for.)

Kirby climbed that rope like he was half monkey. "That's all those push-ups I made him do," BT said proudly. The proud papa smacked a hand against his forehead when Kirby stopped three quarters up to get another bite of food.

"Tape worm? Has to be," I said. "Like watching a whale eat krill."

Kirby grabbed the railing and hauled himself over. He walked around a bit and unfurled a rope ladder.

"Good job!" I told him, giving a thumbs up.

"There's bodies up here," he said, leaning over the railing and looking down. "Shot," he answered before any of us could ask how they'd died.

Stenzel tested her weight on the ladder and when she deemed it safe enough, she headed up. I know for those of you that might read this, that this might come as a shock, but I don't like ladders. Or I suppose it's not so much the ladder as to where it leads, which is up. Another hang-up that gets to live in the crowded skull cave with the rest of them. Jiggly rope ladders topped that list. We'd had them in all our homes in case of a fire, but my guess was if we were ever presented with a situation where it was needed, I was just going to jump and let the chips and broken ankles fall where they may.

"They were shot from this side," Stenzel said after a minute up top.

"That sucks," I said to BT. "Here you are, thinking you're protected from the enemy ahead of you, only to catch hell from those behind."

"How long have they been there?" BT asked.

That was a question I should have thought to ask, but then I remembered that being a good leader was making sure you surrounded yourself with people who knew their shit. I'd honestly been expecting her to say, "a few months," possibly a year. But that didn't make sense. They would have since lique-fied, leaving telltale signs of their existence dripping down onto the wall and the road.

"Couple of days."

BT and I immediately looked at each other. That changed things. We turned to look down the roadway. Were the people that had done this still around and watching us? Or had they traveled into Mexico, and we had streamed past them in our vehicles? That would give them pause. Having a car would be worth more than having a roomful of gold. Wasn't any person alive that wouldn't want what we had. In a perfect world they'd join up and we could bolster our forces, but more than likely this would come down to a battle for resources, and they would try and take what we had. That was how the world had worked since the first time Uukalook the clan leader had seen the cave that his rival Banaboo was living in, it had a little better view, so he banged the other over the head with a rock and took it. People had been assholes since before we had a name for the orifice, before we could even verbalize a word for the orifice.

Movement above caught my attention, Stenzel was

271

walking across an I-beam to get to where the motor was mounted. I was going to give her hell about it, but then noticed she had fashioned a rope harness and tied the other end off on the railing.

"Dallas, head up there and bring Kirby his rifle. You two keep a look out," BT said.

"On it, Top," she replied.

I was slipping. These were things I should have been thinking of. The second we'd stepped onto US soil, I'd let my guard down thinking that the worst of everything was behind us. Not the best way of thinking, considering we'd been run out of the country. Was I like the victim of domestic abuse that kept coming back for more?

"I'm going up."

"Are you sure?" BT asked. "You've told anyone that will listen how much you hate ladders."

"Would like to get a lay of the land."

"It's Texas. It's almost as flat as Kansas."

I played the part of a very stringent quality control supervisor as I tested the tensile strength of that ladder as best I could before I put myself more than a foot and a half in the air. In terms of how much it could hold, my bodyweight was well within its design, the problem was it moved around. I wasn't a fan of things that moved, not while I was climbing them, anyway. You never realize how high twenty feet is until you're looking down, swaying.

"Bet you wish you weren't up there!" BT called out.

Must have been how the white of my knuckles was glowing from the grip on the railing that was giving me away. I looked out the way we'd come, nothing, no zombies, always a good sign, then to where we wanted to go, same results. I didn't even get the feeling I was being watched. It was nice that my paranoia had taken the afternoon off, or was it? What if my jovial mood had placed us in danger by not allowing me to sense the danger? Wow, paranoia can be its own reverb loop. There were five bodies scattered on the parapet. Four of them still had their rifles shouldered, the fifth must have been sitting down, hers was propped against the wall behind her. The firefight had been a blindside, had to have been at least five shooters, each assigned a different target. That was the only way I could explain the appearance of a lack of response.

The angle and the distance to any meaningful cover didn't make the shots impossible, but the likelihood of one volley doing this from five different shooters was suspect—or made them pros. Not necessarily military, but most likely. Even possibly some of the elites, SEALs, Force Recon Marines, Green Berets. Didn't like that one bit, not unless the dead people were evil and had it coming.

"How's it looking?" I asked Stenzel, pulling my gaze away from the lost souls.

From where I was, I couldn't exactly see what she was doing, I heard a click then a humming noise before she came back. "It's on."

"I'm not complaining, but how?"

She pointed to the far side of the road. Why I'd not taken note of the solar panel array...I'm going to blame it on my total lack of situational awareness for the day.

"Everyone hold on!" she shouted as she went around me to a small panel. It had two buttons, and arrows were scratched into the metal to show in which direction the door would travel when the corresponding button was pressed.

I could only hope this thing didn't take off like a carnival ride and send us hurtling through space. I needn't have worried. Shufflers would have been able to lap the thing. There was hesitation at first as the slack in the cable was pulled taut, then a high-pitched whine as the full weight of the doors was transferred to the motors, then it seemed to struggle some more as it fought against the inertia that idle steel would create. There were a few hot seconds were I fully expected the motors to start vibrating uncontrollably before bursting into flames as they were denied the one job they were created to do, then we moved. You'd think that when something quickly unfroze, you'd lurch forward and we'd all be desperately seeking to get our hands onto something. Wasn't the case at all, could barely tell we were traveling. If it weren't for the unnerving shrieking the contraption was making, it might have been pleasant. As it was, it felt like we were at a violin recital for children that had less than zero musical inclination. Discordant, jazz-like even.

I thought the door moving was cause for celebration, everyone seemed to share in that view except for Stenzel. She was watching the machinery closely, not sure what she was seeing that was different from the rest of us, but safe to say she'd saved the lives of those of us on the catwalk.

"Down! Everyone down!" she shouted. My first thought was she'd seen shooters, must have been BT's too because he spun, going down onto one knee while simultaneously getting his rifle ready. In a normal world, such as it was ever considered normal, if someone yelled, *down!* out of the blue, your first instinct would be to look around. I don't know the why of that instinctual response, just what's going to happen with ninety nine out of a hundred people. In this new world, not doing immediately and without hesitation what those you trusted warned about got you dead, plain and simple. If you wanted to survive this time in our existence, you acted first and thought about it later. I heard the loud twang of a cable snapping, then came the cracking of an impossibly angry, seven-inch-thick whip as it sliced through the air at supersonic speeds. It would have easily ripped every one of us in half. Our last few moments on the earth would be punctuated by pain and a complete lack of understanding as to why we were sailing through the air without our legs.

"That's going to be a problem." BT had stood and was looking at the damage. The door had moved a total of three feet. Would have been perfect if we had a fleet of motorcycles, although we would have already been fine with the doorway, so we'd gained nothing. Actually lost time, because we'd given the zombies a quicker way through.

The cable was a goner. No amount of duct tape was going to hold those two frayed ends together, and that would be if we could even get it in place. Thing had to weigh over a ton, and I meant that literally. We'd need a crane. I sat on the walkway, letting my legs dangle over the edge. I let my head rest against the crossbar. "So fucking close." We'd get past this, but it was going to take a while. When you string that many losses in a row, it takes its toll. You don't feel like you're ever going to be able to crawl out of that never ending deepening and expanding hole. Been a while since I'd felt completely defeated. Giving up crossed my mind, it didn't settle down and take root, but it had crossed my neural pathways and landed in my expression, and that was more than it ever had. Then my forehead scraped a bit against the metal, yet I had not moved.

"Beast mode!" Kirby said in as deep a voice as he could. He was looking down toward the side of the wall.

"What is going on?" I stood; we were moving. We weren't going to break any land speed records, but we were moving.

"Top is pushing the door!" Kirby looked like he was experiencing rapture.

I headed over quickly to see this impossible feat of strength. Wasn't sure what I expected, but watching my musclebound friend somehow able to push open a multi ton piece of steel seemed unlikely. And yet there he was. I was staring down at his broad back and heavily muscled arms as they rippled under the strain of what they were doing. I realize as I write this, that those last couple of sentences might fit perfectly in a romance novel. I would most assuredly title the book *Sexual Chocolate*. The man by all rights should have been lounging atop Mount Olympus, laughing down at us mere mortals, while stunningly beautiful goddesses poured him wine and fed him grapes.

"Go, you glorious bastard!" I shouted down at him.

He leaned his shoulder in so he could free an arm to give me the finger. If that's not boss level, then I'm going to need a new understanding of the term. He went further, pressed his chest into the wall and gave me the double eagle before he quickly turned around, slapped his ass at me, then pressed his cheeks against the wall.

"What is happening right now?" Kirby asked.

"I'm thinking this thing was frozen in place and the cable did just enough to break that seal, and now our mighty Top is taking advantage of the fact that this rolling steel is perfectly balanced, and that Ben-Ben might be able to push it—definitely would be able to if he thought there was bacon at the end."

He'd got it open about fifteen feet wide when we came to a sudden stop. None of us were in danger of being tossed free as the thing just wasn't moving that fast, and fifteen feet was plenty wide enough.

"Stenzel, could you please stay up here until we're through?"

She nodded as Kirby, Dallas, and I headed down.

"Fuck me, man. What even made you try that?" I asked, all smiles.

"Figured why not. It was either risk a hernia and get it open or prepare to walk twelve hundred miles. If it opened, I'd be able to rest my injury while we drove."

"And if you got the hernia and it didn't open?"

"Good thing it did, or I would have made sure you were on litter duty the entire way."

I don't know what world BT inhabited that he thought four regular people could carry him around like he was King Xerxes, but luckily it did not come to pass. Wasn't a couple of minutes later we were all on the side we desired to be. I was still a bit nervous, hoping that this wasn't just one of many hurdles put in place. I'd feel a whole bunch better once we passed some off ramps, at least that way we'd have more choices for our travel plans.

"We're going to push the wall back!" I was talking to Stenzel. "Come on down whenever you want," I told her.

"I'll wait until it's all the way back."

I gave her a thumbs up. If she honored her words, she would never be coming down. The door had slid up and over the snapped cable that was resting on the ground. We gave it one unified push just for the sake of the good old college try, then as a group we all decided against doing anything hernia inducing. Looked like NAFTA was back in business: Mr. Talbot, tear down that wall! Not nearly as earth shattering as when President Reagan demanded Gorbachev take down the Berlin Wall. (Which, by the way, did you know that a number of people in the US were randomly asked and had said the wall was in Kentucky? No wonder so many countries felt disdain for us.)

In the grand scheme of things, it wasn't that big a deal. The wall not closing. As far as we knew there weren't any other fuel operated vehicles on the roads, the zombies would have eventually found a way around, and humans on foot would have hardly been delayed. Still irked the hell out of me because this left an avenue of approach if Feroz had those stupid pedal tanks. They would not have been able to navigate them around, not without some serious road construction through the woods. Or I guess they could disassemble them and rebuild them on the other side, I suppose that was an option. I was really going to have to hope that Feroz lost us in the vastness that was the United States. I wasn't sure if she knew about Colorado, but even then, I don't think odds would be posted on the chances of her finding us. Finding a needle in a haystack during a blizzard would have been easier.

Feroz was insane enough to crisscross that state for the

next twenty years looking for us, but how many of those with her were disturbed enough to commit to that level, depth, and breadth of madness? Cults dissolve, especially during great droughts of dissatisfaction during which they never achieve their goal. My bet would be they'd have a mutiny and Feroz would die a gruesome death. Maybe there were people out there more deserving, but that's not to say she didn't have it coming. Drove for a bit more that day and from my understanding that put us smack dab in the middle of Texas, just north of Austin.

"I'm so done with this state," I said as I stretched my back then wiped my brow. It was ungodly how hot it was. Couldn't even use that lie about it being a dry heat, which I'd figured would have applied to Texas, but no. Swamps had less moisture in the air.

"Yeah, but look at these!" BT was beaming, he was wearing a pair of red cowboy boots that had a fancy, white-stitched design. On his head he donned what was supposed to be a ten-gallon hat, but given the size of the man, had to have been a fifty-five gallon wide brimmer.

"Do you think it took the entire cow to make those?" I asked Kirby. "And that hat. You could shade a cruise liner."

Poor kid looked like he wanted to be anywhere but there. When your commanding officer asks you a question, the best course of action is to answer immediately, but when the answer could anger your punishment-inflicting Top, sometimes it was best to remain quiet.

"I don't want to get involved." He hustled away.

"Shows what you know! These are snakeskin."

"Oh, so you're the reason for the great rattler shortage."

"There's no shortage of rattlers, and oh yeah, fuck you." He was leaning down and rubbing a hand across the surface of his boots.

"You don't even like snakes."

"What's liking them have to do with how much style I now

possess? I also have no desire to ever pet a cow, but I'll eat one all day long. Tecovas sure knows how to make a boot." He was referring to the store he'd made us detour to as he sat and held his leg in the air to get a better look at his footwear.

"You're ridiculous," I told him. "You're too big to be a cowboy; you'd be making all the bulls feel inadequate. Poor bastards wouldn't be able to perform due to their feelings of inadequacy. And where do you think you're going to find a horse to ride? Although you would look pretty impressive on a Clydesdale."

"You just wish you could pull this off, and that's the bull's problem not mine."

"Those don't look all that comfortable to run in."

"Don't plan on running." He stood up and walked around, beginning the arduous process of breaking the boots in.

"Don't get blisters," was the last thing I said to him that night before heading off to pretend to get some shut eye.

13

MIKE JOURNAL ENTRY 13

THE NEXT MORNING he was doing his best to hide his pronounced gingerly steps.

"Where are your boots, Tex?" I asked, looking at the fuzzy slippers he was wearing.

"Just going to take a bit longer to break in." He winced with each step which about coincided with each word spoken. Went something like, "Just (sharp intake of air), going (sharp intake of air) and so on. Easier for you and for me if you imagine the rest.

"He wore them to bed," Lyndsey said, coming up behind us. He wanted to glare at her but that would have required a few painful footfalls to turn around and direct it.

"Swollen feet or swollen head?" I asked.

"A bit of both," my sister replied. "About four am he woke me up, sweating and in pain, said he needed help getting them off, that he'd been trying for half an hour."

"You done, woman?" He'd found an open car door so he could sit.

"I couldn't budge them. I mean, look at him...if he couldn't do it, what chance did I have?"

"I mean, it's a good thing, too, sis. You could have really

hurt your back trying to hold on to that leg. Be like carrying a steel canoe."

"Y'all can fuck off."

"Y'all? Have some of the chemicals in the boots leaked into your bloodstream? Starting to sound like a local," I told him.

He gave me the finger before resuming to rub tenderly on his hurting appendages.

"Did you have to cut them off?" I asked.

"I wanted to. I was afraid he was going to cut off the circulation to his feet. Gary was walking by on patrol, I got him to help."

"I saw some things." I'd not realized Gary was lurking nearby. "I'm never going to be able to unsee them." He had a haunted expression on his face. "Like trying to peel casing off a sausage."

"Isn't there a limit to how many Talbots can be in one gathering?" BT had angrily slammed his Stetson onto his head.

I felt a wee bit bad for the man. Growing up, Talbots were brutal with each other, it was woe to outsiders who might find themselves in the crossfire, or worse yet, the actual target.

"All kidding aside, you should have Major Dylan take a look at your feet," I told him.

"That's where I got the slippers."

I didn't ask when she had stocked up on the Yeti-sized footwear, he already seemed to be in enough discomfort. I harbored a bit of anger because he'd needlessly hurt himself, and if something happened, he could jeopardize himself or others who tried to help. It was then that I walked past the side-view mirror of a truck, catching a glimpse of myself, the person who did that exact same thing constantly. That came full circle a lot faster than I'd been expecting. The ire was based more on my concern for his well-being than being mission ready. Today, if we put some serious miles behind us, there was no reason to think we couldn't enter the bottommost part of Colorado. We'd be an hour or two south of Colorado Springs. It was surreal even thinking about it. I'd been fantasizing about this for so long, and to think it was a fingernail away from becoming reality was making it difficult to focus on anything else. I made sure to be a passenger, because if I was behind the wheel, it was likely that the defunct state police would reform with the sole purpose of pulling me over to issue a speeding ticket that would travel over into the realm of criminal, due to the speeds involved.

"Come on," I said as I sat up straighter. According to the signs, we were two miles away from the Oklahoma border when we saw the tail end of another traffic jam. Texas was one hell of a giant state to be shutting off all its access points, but we were now two for two, and I had to think we'd not been that unlucky to hit the only ones. It wasn't nearly the mess that the Mexican border had been, but it was still going to require some offroad navigation. Didn't know that little fact until we tried to skirt the thing by staying on the shoulder. I had high hopes for about a mile before that too became clogged up with rusting hulks. Before we began the arduous work of pushing cars out of the way again, I sent a small detachment to scout the way ahead: Justin, who had volunteered, plus Kirby and Bando. There was a lot more open space around this pileup, and maybe we could even use a frontage road or something.

Was pretty sure I was never going to be okay with sending Justin out on missions, but it was bad optics if I always kept him by my side. He'd resent me, and my squad would resent him. Maybe not *resent*, but something in that realm of thesaurus words. Besides, I had Stenzel perched atop the tanker watching their back, and there was no one more qualified to do that than her.

"They're on their way back, sir!" Stenzel called down. She wasn't shooting at anything so I took that as a good sign. They hadn't been gone for more than fifteen minutes. It was either good news or bad. I sometimes like to stretch the legs on my psychic gifts; I'd just with one hundred percent accuracy predicted the immediate future.

"Someone already did the heavy lifting, sir," Kirby said as he approached.

"Yeah, da...sir. Up ahead the guard rail has been torn down and cars shoved to the side, looks like they used a snowplow."

"Where would they get a snowplow in Texas? Gary asked. "Too hot."

"You found one a thousand miles south of here." BT still seemed a bit salty about the humor used at his expense. Or laid at his feet, might be better, more humorous anyway.

"There's tracks in the scrub grass," Kirby said, pointing to the side of the road. Tough to see anything from where we were. Anything that had traveled there had grown over. We had another decision to make: whoever had done the impromptu path had to have been part of the traffic jam because we were looking at a few hundred yards of jam in front of us.

"Stenzel," I called up to the tanker. "Can you see where the guardrail starts?"

She turned and looked through her scope. "Little less than a half mile," she replied when she pulled the rifle from her cheek.

"Anyone have a problem with backing up, or do I have volunteers to start pushing shit out of the way?" I asked.

"I'll do it," Kirby raised his hand.

"Just drop down and give me twenty," BT said as he shook his head.

Kirby didn't question it.

"I'd tell him why, but I don't think he'd understand." He was adjusting his hat; I moved closer so I could stand in the shade it produced. I wondered for a moment if the hat got heavy from all the sunshine it was holding up.

"Okay folks. When Kirby is done, we're going to back up to where the guard rail starts! When we get offroad, proceed slowly. No telling what hazards could be hidden in that brush." As we got to the Oklahoma border and back onto the road, we saw the aftermath of a hefty sized battle. Couldn't tell by body count, as those had been scattered to the winds. Either zombies had come by and scavenged through the ruins, or animals had, or just mother nature cleaning up after her wayward children. The amount of expended rounds would have been sufficient to supply a great many colleges' brass bands.

"What happened here?" BT asked as we rolled over the bullets. It made a tinkling sound like fairy bells were constantly being rung. And yes, it was just as strange as it sounds. A lot of angels were getting their wings, if Clarence was to be believed. If you don't know the *It's a Wonderful Life* reference…I just can't with you right now.

I shook my head, trying to figure out what it was about Texas that people had been fighting to get in on one side and out the other. Personally, I wasn't a fan of the state. Maybe it was the department of commerce, they were pretty full of themselves with the "Everything is bigger and better in Texas" slogan, but that wasn't it for me. The people were fine, in so much as any people are. It all boiled down to the heat. Couldn't stand it. Even Dallas, who had grown up here, hadn't shown any desire to stay. She didn't look around wistfully with a sense of underlying melancholy. Surprised I'd not yet found myself a way to stay in the mountains of Alaska. Saw some pictures of a beautiful mountain called Devils Desk, and had always wanted to visit. Place looked idyllic. You always wanted what you couldn't have the most. I sighed, thinking about sitting on some deck, a cool breeze crossing over as I drank a beer and looked over at the majestic views.

I'd even wave at some abominable snowmen if they passed by. I was cool like that. Probably give me the finger, but I wouldn't retaliate. I'd just take another sip of beer to ease the pain.

We breezed in and out of Oklahoma, the land looked scoured clean, like they'd been expecting a visit from some foreign dignitary and wanted the place to look as acceptable and hospitable as possible. I was not complaining, not verbally, I just always became suspicious when things are too clean, too easy. Must have got that from my mom when she knew I'd thrown a party because the house was too clean. How's that for absurd? Grounded because she couldn't find anything. I'd argued a bit because I had to make a good showing, in the end I'd let it drop, took my minimal punishment, and was let out for good behavior early when she must have had the thought that I'd tried to do something nice. I mean, she was wrong, but I wasn't going to tell her. I think had I been alone I would have sobbed when we saw the sign that we were entering Colorful Colorado. The damned elephant that had been sitting on my chest finally stood up and walked away.

We parked in the middle of the road as the sun set. Cloud cover was minimal, but we were in the new moon phase. It was as dark as if we were out in the middle of the Atlantic on a cruise ship and the deck lights had gone out. It was eerie. Seeing anything approaching was out of the question. All we were going to be able to rely on was the wildlife around us to signal that something was amiss. They'd been quiet when we first rolled in, I would imagine they were trying to figure out what we were. It was likely that there were whole new generations of animals that had never seen a human. They wouldn't have any innate fear of us, not unless they had a mother or father around that remembered the old ways. When you saw people, you ran. We were the dickheads of the animal kingdom, reigning from on high and dispensing a haphazard judgement, when we even thought of our lower subjects at all. Heard the yips from what sounded like a large pack of coyotes, they didn't get much closer than a quarter of a mile. Must have been some in the group that knew all about us and they weren't curious or hungry enough to explore any closer. After them came the howls of wolves. Not sure if they were closer or their sounds traveled further, but that is its own sort of unnerving. They moved on after a while and we were all a bit relieved when that happened. The rest of the night went by uneventfully, crickets and other bugs kept up a chorus of sound. It was a symphony, as far as I was concerned. The more they chirped and chittered, the safer we felt.

It was in the deepest dark of predawn that they stopped suddenly. I'd been drifting in and out of sleep, at first a little pissed with just how loud the bugs could be before I finally incorporated them into my subconscious and fell asleep. It was like having an alarm clock blare when they stopped. Not sure how the absence of sound could do that, but it had. I sat up. There was a chuffing sound, a heavy animal sniffing at something nearby. I was fully awake now as I sat up in the truck and quickly extracted myself. A greaver in this inky blackness could be the undoing to a great many of us before we could rally. I was a heartbeat away from waking everyone up. Our best defense was leaving—I didn't like the idea of using the headlights, but when picking your poison, you have to go with the one that's not going to get you killed immediately, and that meant running.

I turned when I heard more of the sound to my side. There were at least two of the killing machines out there. The time for inaction was over. I had pulled air into my lungs preparing to yell, rifle at my shoulder as I was sure to garner some unwanted attention, just as the sun poked its head over the distant horizon. I'd forgotten how far you could see when you weren't surrounded by forest. I saw brown, lots and lots of shaggy brown. My alarm turned to wonder.

"Bison," I said softly. Or buffalo, I wasn't sure of the difference or if there even was one. I did not want to startle them; death by stampede seemed like a bad way to go. Now I had to pass the word of what was going on before someone got too excited. I didn't know much about the animal other than they were tasty, but the one I was looking at was the same height as me and looked to be about ten times heavier, that put it close to a ton. It would easily mess up a human, and likely the vehicle he or she was in. I would have loved to secure some meat, but in a safer manner.

I spun when I heard metal getting crinkled. It wasn't a violent crunching, more like the bison was trying to move something out of its way to get to a succulent growth. That was when Gary laid on his horn and started yelling out the window.

"Get your ass out of here!" he yelled at the bison. "Messing up my ride!" He was genuinely pissed. The horn hadn't done much to dissuade the herd, the tiny two-legger who was now outside and waving his hands over his head though, that they took notice of.

"Gary, what are you doing?" I was trying to get him to calm down.

The thing about my brother was, he was slow, I mean *extremely* slow, to anger, but once he got there it was the kind of a storm that you just had to weather until it had blown through. There was no room for reasoning.

For their part, the bison weren't alarmed, I'd say more on the curious side. Most had stopped their grazing to look at the small squeaking thing, many still chewing what they had in their mouths.

"Shit, shit, shit," I mumbled as I went to stop my brother from pushing on the flanks of the animals, because that's exactly what it looked like he was planning on doing. Just because bison were cow-like did in no way make them safe to approach. Anything that had to deal with bears and wolves for survival was nothing to be trifled with.

"Piss off!" he told it, still waving his hands above his head.

If he was trying to look imposing, he was failing spectacularly. By now most everyone was awake and, unlike my friggen' brother, they had the wherewithal to not poke the enormous animals. It was one of the smallest among us that got the job done. Not sure what in the hell Ben-Ben thought he was doing, but he hustled out of the car he'd been in and made a beeline straight for the herd. I'd run to stop him but missed, plowing my face into the ground as I dove.

The dog was like twenty-five pounds, my guess was those bison took heavier shits on the regular. Bison were known to stomp rattlers to death, I couldn't imagine why they wouldn't employ that same tactic on a small angry dog. Except they didn't. At first they were curious, turning and stooping their necks to get a look at the yapper, then Ben-Ben pulled a move that officially made him a Talbot, meaning it was dumber than fuck and should have got him killed. He bit the nose of the closest bison. The animal recoiled in surprise, maybe a bit of pain. But it decided it didn't like the rough treatment, not one bit. Its head popped up, it bellowed then hustled off. This triggered something in the rest of the herd. They didn't try and figure out what was wrong, just that for whatever reason, this place wasn't safe anymore. Not much in the wild was going to get in the middle of a mob of galloping beasts that weighed nearly a ton each. Ben-Ben chased for a bit, barking and smiling the whole time. When he came back, he was prancing like he was King Sheba shit, which I guess he was.

"That'll do, pig," my brother said.

"Dammit dog! Scared the crap out of me." I'd stooped down and petted him vigorously as he approached, his tail going so fast one would have thought bacon was sizzling nearby, which he no doubt expected as his reward. A shot rang out. That got my attention. Stenzel's barrel was smoking, and when I looked up and out, I realized we were going to be eating well tonight. The bison now had reason to fear us. I was saddened a bit by that, but the safety of both our species required that measure of caution. We lost most of the morning butchering the animal. We smoked some of the meat and then had an impromptu barbecue. It would have been nicer with a cold beer and a bed to take nap on after eating, but it was thoroughly enjoyable.

It was a couple hours after noon when the highway took us through Colorado Springs. There were abandoned cars littering the highway, but a pathway had long ago been cut through. The moment we left the city limits anxiety welled up in my chest. This was quite literally the home stretch to home, but the thing of it was, I knew you couldn't go home. Not ever. I was about to come face to face with this notion. Then what? Would I feel more at home in Maine? Was any physical location going to live up to my ideals? I bet even if I made it up to Alaska I would find something about it lacking. I had the group stop about fifteen miles south of Denver proper in an area that used to be called the Tech Center. Basically, the business area of the city. I'd worked down there for a bit before I found holding onto a white-collar job was a difficult proposition. The place was a shell of itself. Most of the office buildings were burned out husks. This hadn't been a wildfire burning out of control. The buildings were too far spaced apart for it to have been something natural. A pyro that just wanted to watch the world burn was a possibility, a turf war, maybe? Didn't like either of those explanations. People-on-people violence never boded well for people. Last thing humanity needed was some megalomaniac despot crowning themselves king or queen and forcing everyone to bend the knee or lose their heads.

Without going to investigate, this could've happened back at the beginning. Shit, even if we did investigate, unless it was still smoldering, we'd never be able to accurately tell when it had happened, none of us were forensic scientists, no matter how many episodes of cop shows we'd collectively watched. Nothing happened as we rolled past, and I was fine with that.

I had concerns about going through Denver; the highway I-25 bisected the city, and although the city had not been among the largest populated in the nation, it was still a major city. Then there was I-225, that skirted the city and straddled the line between Denver and Aurora. This had been my commute road most days, and if you timed it wrong it looked a lot like the Mexican border had. Then there was the toll road E-470. That roadway made a long looping detour around the worst of the city, and the traffic it afforded, the only problem was it had been an expensive option. When you're a struggling family working hard to pull those ends together, you do your best to not spend money wastefully. Had we sat down and thought about it, I wonder how much money I wasted per day with my engine idling waiting to move. Less than the tolls probably, but by how much?

I directed the convoy onto the toll road. If there were bad elements ahead, whether zombie or human, it was unlikely they would set up shop on the barren wasteland that was the toll road. My guess was though, knowing bureaucracy as I did, that there would be people staffing the toll booths. I knew the IRS had measures in place to collect taxes after a nuclear war; didn't see much difference here. Maybe they'd just have cameras instead of people at the booths, and we'd receive a bill in the mail in a week with a picture of our license plates— no matter where we set up shop—for the amount due. The beauty of 470 was we could also skip I-70, which traveled east to west across the state. I don't know if I'd ever traveled that roadway and not been stuck in some sort of jam, whether due to an accident, a cop giving a ticket or weather related. Thing was constantly plugged up like a morbidly obese man that avoided fiber. E-470, even during the early days of the apocalypse when people would have been leaving the city in droves, the roadway was mostly clear; habits aren't broken easily, and panicking people would travel routes they knew. The only upsetting thing I'd seen in the last ten miles was a broken-down ice cream truck. No, I was not saddened by the loss of the ice cream, it was the oversized plastic clown head that sat atop the roof. Nothing about that plasticene shine, shock of red hair and bulbous nose made it look like an inviting entity. Looked more like something that would bite kids at birthday parties. "Tim's Treats Truck" could fuck right off. There was no way you were going to convince me that thing wasn't a harbinger of evil.

We were on high alert the entire time around the city, but hadn't seen or smelled anything the entire ride as we began our westward journey into the mountains. It was incredible to see the sparkling Rockies so vividly without having to peer through the haze of smog that Denver was famous for. It wasn't that Denver was a heavy pollution place, but rather due to where it sat, the mountains tended to trap all the car exhaust, leaving a layer of brown on the skyline. Without people to screw things up, nature was breathtaking. Once we passed the city limits, I knew we were about an hour from Estes Park. I wasn't sure if that was going to be our final destination or whether we should go further into the mountains where there would be far less people. Estes Park was a fairly popular tourist destination in the summer, not so much in the winter, as there were no ski resorts nearby and the main draw, Rocky Mountain National Park, would have large swaths of the place closed off because the roads would not be maintained. There's a reason that the Stanley Hotel was the inspiration for Stephen King's *The Shining*. I'd read the book long before I'd ever laid eyes on the place, and I'd expected a much more isolated building. Was surprised to see that it was damn near smack dab in the middle of things, and Estes may have lost all the tourists during the off season, but Estes Park by no means emptied out. Hell, if Danny Torrance had just run out the front door he could have boogied his way across the street to the Safeway grocery store and got some help. Hard to feel the same terror once you saw behind the curtain, but still, the place is definitely haunted, so there's that.

My heart was thumping double time as we pulled into town. We'd lost so many good people, crossed so many miles, lived and died through so many events—it hardly seemed real that we could be here. The place where, when our family was much younger, we had come up and vacationed at. It represented hands-down among the greatest times we'd enjoyed as a family. We weren't that far from Denver, but in those instances, we'd left all our troubles behind, even if for only a week. We were home, as far as I was concerned. We'd made it!

14

A POSSIBLE FUTURE –
SUPPLEMENTAL JOURNAL
ENTRY 14

I WAITED until the entire family was together inside the house. They should be safe from Tommy; he could not enter, not without my express permission. There was always the chance he'd try to burn the house down, but he wanted to force me to do something, and he couldn't do that without leverage, and Dallas, Justin's wife—whom he had kidnapped—was his perceived leverage. She was actually his doom, and he'd learn that soon enough. I would make sure of that. Justin was understandably beside himself.

"She'd just gone to the garden, dad, to grab some chives. I heard her scream, and when I got outside, Tommy told me to tell you he'd taken her, and they were heading to America's Stonehenge. What even is that?"

"Strange rock structure in New Hampshire." I was thinking about the why of it, and how much fun it was going to be to reach down that fucker's throat and pull his Adam's apple out.

"America's Stonehenge is a maze of man-made stone chambers, stone walls, and standing stones that align with the sun on the solstices, equinoxes, and cross-quarter days. At over 4,000 years old, it is most likely the oldest human-caused construction in the United States, and is thought by some to be a portal."

"A portal to what?" I asked.

It was at this point that the talking encyclopedia decided to shrug his shoulders.

"Do you know what Tommy's doing?" I'd spun to Azile.

"I don't know, but if it is a portal, this makes sense," she replied.

"What part of this makes sense?" I was thinking of all she'd revealed to me. The convergent points coming to a head, the ability to rewrite past events, or not so much rewrite as relive—I hadn't figured out the distinction yet, either. The gist being I could not alter what had transpired, but I could create new pathways to be lived. Once saw a movie called *The Butterfly Effect*, this sounded very much like that. Although this version of me could only enter the alternate versions of me as a voice inside my head. So that *other* me could still do what ended up being a mistake, or listen to that shrieking voice in his head telling him not to fuck this up. Not sure how well that was going to work, as I'd constantly ignored the warnings I'd given myself. And who knows, those two things aren't mutually exclusive; the other me could listen and still do something wrong or I could steer him wrong, so many avenues for a bad outcome, it was mind-boggling.

The headache inducing part came with the finer points. How did I travel to these other realms, which ones did I go to, and which ones did I try to alter without just making matters worse? Would my tinkering only serve to push over that first domino, starting a chain reaction that would only have an explosive conclusion? I felt like the odds highly favored that second outcome. No good could come from this. This was akin to stumbling across a Jinn's bottle and asking for riches beyond description only to be given an express trip to the heavens. You would literally receive what you asked for, genies were asses like that. I'm not sure you could ever be specific enough to ensure they didn't take liberties with your request. Like if you asked for a larger penis, but that it remained proportional to the rest of you. This said to ensure you didn't have an elephant-sized schlong you continually tripped over. When the genie did his thing, you discovered that your little man was the exact same size, but you as a person had shrunk. Yup, proportionally-wise it was bigger...fucking genies.

How in the fuck was I going to direct another me's mind when I couldn't even focus my own? Simple, I wasn't going to. I was going to hunt Tommy down long before he reached New Hampshire, and we were going to end this Cold War with some hot blood. I'd bring Dallas home and kick the rest to the curb, Azile and Wilkes because they were witches, and I didn't trust either of them, not one bit. Mac would be welcome to stay, but he wouldn't, and I was okay with that. I'd only do it out of a sense of civility, but all while knowing he wouldn't accept, so what was it really? Barely a token gesture. Elam I wasn't sure of. He might be the most dangerous of them all, or he could be a meek, mild-mannered man. Best to get rid of him too...Tommy had come into our lives wearing that very disguise. I went to grab some supplies, the whole time thinking about what I may or may not have done in this lifetime to alter its course. Given what I know now, and the loss I was about to endure soon enough, would I have made Tracy a vampire years ago? What would I have done differently?

"Dangerous path," I said this out loud. Because next it would have been my kids, my friends. Henry? Was it possible to make dogs into vampires? I hitched at the wonderful thought of seeing that magnificent beast again. Soon I would have had an army of undead loved ones. No one person, no one group of people, no society that ever walked this earth should have the kind of power I was being told was at my fingertips. And now Tommy was going to try and force my hand. It didn't take much to home in on what he wanted, what he'd always wanted. What he didn't know, was I would sacrifice Dallas's life to ensure Eliza never made a return. How many thousands of deaths had she been responsible for? I could not bring her forth into a world where she would reign supreme, no longer feeding and killing in the shadows because she wouldn't need to. There weren't many left that could oppose her.

I had no idea how long this was going to take, but it was already too long. Any time spent away from those I loved was time I could not get back, and that clock was ticking loudly, always ticking. It was imperative that I caught up to him this very night, ripped his skull free from the rest of his body, and brought Dallas home, so when Justin met me at the door with his pack, I had to tell him no.

"She's my wife." This was spoken somewhere between a growl and a sob.

"I'm faster alone," I told him as gently as I could. Last thing I wanted to do was make him feel like less of a man.

"I won't stop."

"It's over a hundred miles, Justin. Can you do that in one go?" Every second I had to argue with him was a second Tommy pulled ahead.

"He'll have to stop. Dallas can't make that."

"Justin, she won't be walking." There was no doubt in my mind that Tommy, you know what, screw that. *Tomas*. There's no way Tomas didn't swing the waif of a woman over his shoulder like a sack of potatoes. He could easily make it to New Hampshire with her that way. I felt bad for her, that was a truly uncomfortable way to travel and, if and when I rescued her, she was going to be sore for days. Another reason why I didn't want Justin to come along was, as I'd said before, I would let her perish if it meant Eliza stayed exactly where she was. I loved Dallas like a daughter, but she would be the first to agree with me that her life was not worth the hundreds, perhaps thousands, that Eliza would cut short. Justin would never see it that way. Maybe he'd believe whatever story I spun, or maybe he'd forever hold animosity toward me as he saw through the tale. That couldn't be helped.

"Can't you carry me?"

He kept pressing. Had he sensed that I'd made a decision regarding his wife? "Tomas is bigger and stronger than I am. If I'm weighted down, he moves faster. Right now, the edge is mine to exploit."

Justin realized he was running short on arguments to use. I knew the feeling of sitting and waiting, and it was horrible. Having anxiety coursing through your body 24/7, tight chest, tingly limbs, a mind that won't stop spinning like a hamster wheel. Good times.

"Get her back, dad."

I nodded. It was more an acknowledgment of his words rather than a promise. I couldn't give him one.

"Say the words." He held my arm fast before I could head out the door.

"I can't promise that," I told him.

"Promise me!"

Reluctantly I did promise, the caveat was I never promised whether she would be dead or alive. Sometimes promises are better left unfulfilled. Justin followed me out to where Azile, Mac, and Wilkes were waiting.

"I'm coming with you," Azile said.

Mac and Wilkes looked shocked, like they'd not been let in on the secret.

"No." I brushed past.

"Once off your land, and away from whatever magic-dampening affects you have going on here, you'll be able to do little to stop me."

"You do you, Azile. If you keep up fine, if you don't even better."

"I'll go grab my things," Wilkes said.

"No," Azile and I said in unison.

"You explain it. I'm not waiting any longer." Heard a bit of an exchange, but by then I was at a slight jog, trying to make as much distance as I could from my home and toward the enemy. As I jogged, I was doing the math in my head. Tomas had about a half hour lead. He would have sprinted at first to garner some distance, but with Dallas on his back, he would slow down, if only to keep her from protesting too much about how much pain she was in. Maybe. He'd proved repeatedly he was a dick, but he wasn't Superman; even as a vampire he had limits. Could he carry Dallas all the way to New Hampshire? Yes, I didn't doubt that one bit. The questions were at what speed would he be traveling, and would he stop to rest at all. I figured he was two miles ahead of me, two and a half at the very most. It would be great if I could catch him tonight, eviscerate him, then come home and be back in time for the Tonight Show with Johnny Carson. That's how much of a fantasy that notion was.

I was three miles into my jog, was just coming up on what remained of the dilapidated Tozier's grocery store. My mouth watered just a bit, on the right was Dino's Pizza restaurant. The pizza had been okay, but their steak bombs were legendary. Wasn't a nun I wouldn't throat punch to get one of those. Oh, don't go feeling all bad about it, most nuns I'd ever encountered were sadistic crones that loved to dole out punishment in the name of their lord and savior. I always found it strange how twisted His message became when it was funneled through the inferior minds of people. Maker exists, that I know; perhaps you don't, I'll leave that up to whoever discovers this journal. But if they exist, they really should have used a better delivery system for their words. People suck far too much to be trusted with those words. Should have given it to dogs to pass on. Can you imagine how much better the world would have been if canines were responsible for the passing of the message? There would never have been holy wars...there might have been some disputes over tennis balls and cookies, but all could have been resolved simply with more of both.

My mind tends to drift on runs, that was a coping mechanism I learned in the Corps and had never let go. Much easier to deal with pain when you're not cognizant of it. Hoofbeats. I was hearing hoofbeats. I turned to see Azile atop a horse. Not sure where she dredged the beast up from. The mare looked gaunt; if the animals lived roughly twenty-five years, this one was thirty.

"You're going to kill it," I told her as she pulled up alongside.

"I'm just riding her until I can secure another, and I'm funneling some magic into her. She probably hasn't felt this good in years."

"And what happens when you pull your feel-good drugs from her?"

She stayed quiet.

I didn't necessarily want her on this trip, but she could help. One-on-one with Tomas was a dicey proposition, especially when I no longer had the homefield advantage. There were portents in place at home that gave me a distinct edge; I wasn't omnipotent, but I was a lot harder to kill, and still, Tomas had made it interesting. Dallas might not be the only one sacrificed on this quest. I could not welcome death because I knew it would not be a peaceful venture, lollygagging about the heavenly landscape. I would be continually wandering along the gray blandness of a never-ending purgatory as I searched fruitlessly for my soul. I'd not yet aged out of my normal existence, and I was weary; I had seen too much death, which tends to prematurely age someone. Unfortunately, my time wasn't up, and as far as I knew there wasn't an expiration date stamped on me anywhere. I'm sure there was a Best Used By date, but not a toss it in the trash before it turns green and moldy date.

We'd hit the Belfast line, so about ten miles in, still no sign of Tomas. There was no reason to think he wouldn't travel the most express route, like I was, or hide, for that matter, as he'd already said where he was going. No, he was out there, still ahead, I could feel him, possibly only because he wanted me to.

"We've gained a little," Azile said. She brought her mare to a stop, spoke some words into her ear and gently petted the horse as she sat astride the new one that had shown up a hundred yards or so ago. I noticed Azile looked a bit ragged. The magic she was using was exhausting her. When we caught up to Tomas, she might not be much more than a shiny distraction. I was going to tell her to head back and then I thought that even a distraction had its uses. Yup, I was that callous. She meant nothing to me, a tool to be used as I saw fit. It was as we hit the bridge crossing over the Passagassawakeag River that I saw the blood. Three quarters across was what remained of Tomas's kill. A young woman maybe a couple of years older than Wilkes, hard to say with how shriveled and sickly she appeared. That tended to be what happened when you had every bit of blood drained from you. The fucker had fed, meaning he was in it for the long haul. He was going to stay close enough to keep us enticed and on the line, but he'd never allow a showdown before he was ready. He'd scooped up a victim and carried her along while he'd fed, all the while with Dallas on his shoulder, and my guess was he'd barely lost a stride. Any ground we'd gained had strictly been on purpose.

"I can get you a horse," Azile said as we both looked at the poor girl. What she was doing out here was anyone's guess. I debated tossing her into the river so that any loved ones she might have would not have to come across this scene. But then they would lack closure, always wondering if the blood had belonged to her, or would she one day come walking through the front door. That was its own kind of hell, and I didn't want to put them through that. We kept going.

"How long would you be able to keep two horses going at a gallop?" I asked. "You already look like you could take an extended nap." If the light were better, I'm sure I could have watched the bags under her eyes gain weight. I didn't tell her that last part, women get mad when you point out things like that. See? I've learned a thing or two over the course of my life. I wasn't quite as thick as most might believe.

"I can do it for a bit more. Could be enough of a push for you to catch up."

I doubted it. If we could feel Tomas, odds were that he could feel our presence, might even be the reason for the tenuous link. I would have severed the connection if I knew how, but sadly that wasn't in my retinue of tricks.

"If we don't catch him soon, I'm going to need to stop."

The wheel in my head began to spin. "Tomas knows we're out here."

She peered at me—for the name change, if I had to take a guess.

"Yes, I can feel it as well. I can hide myself from him, but I cannot extend that to you, not without further exhausting myself."

"If we stop, he will too."

"We can't be sure of that."

"Can't we? He wants me to follow him all the way to New Hampshire to find a reality where he can free his sister."

"It doesn't work like that."

"Maybe it does, maybe it doesn't."

"It doesn't."

"Regardless, at the minimum he would want me to place his consciousness in a reality where she lives, or where, with a few key moves, could live."

"That's a fair enough statement," she replied.

"He does not get what he wants if I don't go."

"What about Dallas?"

"If he senses me going back home, she's dead. But if we stop to rest…"

"I could regain my strength, and perhaps be more than a tired lump when we finally confront him."

She'd been thinking along the same lines as I had, hopefully she hadn't realized *exactly* what I'd been thinking. Not too many people are okay with being thought of as chattel. I would sacrifice Azile quick enough, Dallas, if absolutely necessary, and myself because that was the bounce of the ball I'd tossed by coming on this adventure.

"Azile, I need to talk to you." She turned, I could see the beauty she possessed even as it shone through the worried determination and exhaustion she wore on her face. There was also something else there; I was hesitant to call it a longing, expectation, maybe? But something more than curiosity.

"Yes?" she asked. Oh yeah, definitely expectation of something, something more was going on here than I was privy too. Another time, another place, maybe I probed the depth, not this time, not this place.

"My land has protections set up for most known, and a fair number of unknown dangers." It was easy enough to see that this was not what the woman had hoped for. I continued on, not having the time nor the temperament to explore. "Even with the protection in place, Tomas is an ancient evil—"

She looked like she wanted to interrupt me. I held up my hand. "We can agree to disagree," I said. "Has your opinion of him taken this latest transgression into account?"

She shook her head slightly.

"What I'm getting at," I continued, "is that Tomas is stronger and faster than me, and even with the advantages my land afforded, he nearly killed me. Out here the advantage is his. I need a promise from you."

She peered at me for a second. "I won't make a promise before I know the details."

"That makes sense. Odds aren't great for me here." I held my hands out. "I'll hurt him, I know this in my soul, but I'm going to need the luck of an entire Irish battalion of leprechauns to defeat him. When he's at his most vulnerable, you need to finish the job."

"You want me to kill Tommy?"

"I want you to kill him."

She choked back a sob. I thought at first it was for Tomas, then got suspicious it was for someone else. I let it drop in the dirt; I wasn't even going to look in its direction because she clearly knew something I did not, and I wanted to remain ignorant. Needed to remain ignorant.

"Azile?"

"I'm fine." The tears that rimmed her eyes said otherwise, a normal caring altruistic person would ask what troubled her. I did not.

"I need you to promise me that when he is lying there doing his best to recover, that you finish him, that you do not allow him to continue to roam this world. You might think that once I'm dead the chance of him yanking his sister out of whatever hole in the ground she's in will be nullified, maybe you're right, maybe not. One thing about Tomas is he's relentless, and he has eternity to find a way to get what he wants. He does not care who he uses or sacrifices to accomplish his goal. Tell me you will do this—or leave now."

"What? Why would I do that?"

"You're a witch. Do you not think he will find a way to use you or Wilkes?"

"I don't think you know Tommy like I do."

"I know Tommy, but it is Tomas we are dealing with. That is a completely different, feral, rabid entity. You will promise to kill him, or I lose you here."

"You cannot lose me."

"You'd be surprised what I can do. The power you wield right now is not strong enough to challenge me, and I will not wait until morning for your answer when we are more evenly matched."

She pinched her lips, I'm guessing that was a plan she'd been working on. "Are you sure about this? You are asking me to kill someone I trust, and perhaps we are not friends, but we are allies."

"Words can be cheap, and any tale of utter nonsense can be strung together, whether it is true or fabricated. Touch my forehead, I will give you my unfettered thoughts, and you will see what I have seen."

"Thoughts can be manipulated." She shivered slightly as I took her hand.

"Yes, though it is much more difficult to disguise and easily seen through, if you know where to look." I placed her fingertips against my forehead. I felt a burst of cold as I allowed her to penetrate my thoughts. She recoiled as I expelled everything I knew about Tomas, and everything I had borne witness too. Possibly all the manipulation beforehand wouldn't have been enough to sway her to murder. I saved the worst for last. Tomas had to feed, it was the nature of the beast; you couldn't hate the grizzly bear for taking down an elk. But how would you feel if that bear first tortured its victims? I'd gone out to meet Tomas years previously. He'd rounded up a family. Mother, father and three children. Had them all chained up inside an old hunters' cabin. The three children had been hung upside down by their feet, two were clearly dead, having been eviscerated—their innards could no longer be called that. The third he was lazily feeding from. The parents had long ago lost the ability to cry or grieve. The utter horror of what they had witnessed was so severe they'd thankfully gone into shock. Possibly the mother still held the slightest hope that her child would somehow be spared, but the father had checked out, his eyes not focusing on anything. This I'd seen through a slit in the rough curtains. I quickly pulled back and made sufficient noise to ensure that he would hear me coming.

He wiped his chin as he stepped out into the day, making sure to close the door to the cabin behind him.

"New digs?" I'd asked.

"Temporary quarters," he'd said. "I find comfort in there."

"It was then, Azile, I realized he was more like his sister than I'd realized. It wasn't too much longer after that that I went the next step and reasoned that she was more a product of his influence than the other way around. With the two of them running around doing whatever they please, it is unlikely humanity will ever be able to come back. Normally, I might be okay with that, people suck, but when he's done with me, Tomas is going to take his wrath out on those I left behind. I will not sacrifice myself, if I do not have your promise. I can't. There's too much at stake."

Azile cradled her hand as if it physically hurt from what had been communicated through it. "I swear it," she said. "I swear that I will kill Tomas if the opportunity presents itself."

I wasn't sure how I felt about that qualifier, it did offer her some wiggle room.

"That is not doublespeak, Michael. If you hurt him as much as you say, and I can kill him without being overpowered, I will sacrifice myself to accomplish that goal."

"Fair enough." I reached into my pocket. "When this is done, you can read this."

"Trip's note?"

"One and the same, and you cannot read it beforehand," I said before she took possession.

She nodded. "What does it say?"

I smiled. "That would defeat the purpose of me telling you not to read it beforehand."

She smiled, but it was a sad one. "Sounds like a swan song." She was probing, but I would not give her anything to build a narrative. "Get some rest, that's why we stopped, after all. It won't be long before he realizes we've stopped, and when we stay here for longer than what he expects, he will come back to investigate. For my part, I would like to enjoy the night, and the peace and quiet it affords...to some, at least."

I could feel the charge in the air. She wanted to say something, took about fifteen minutes before that energy dissipated and she succumbed to exhaustion. I waited another fifteen minutes then patrolled the area hastily, preparing it with as much protection as I could. It was woefully inadequate. It wouldn't be enough, but I just needed a little bit, enough to give Azile her opportunity. This had to work; the lives of my family were in jeopardy. I'd allowed myself to walk straight into his trap. If I thought I could make it back, I would have, but he would immediately realize it, and dying was one thing —dying tired a whole other. And besides, if I ran and got caught from behind, I wouldn't have Azile's help. If I dragged her with me, she'd be much weaker and wouldn't be able to do much of anything. No, I was already in the cage. The best I could do was lay my own trap within his. He might be suspicious, but he was fully committed, as I was, and he would not think me capable of any sort of successful campaign against him.

I was angry it had come to this; how had I missed him for the villain he was? I'd had numerous opportunities through the years to kill him. But you cannot act on what you do not know. If I'd had the gift of foresight, I wouldn't have been waiting complacently at Little Turtle for the zombies to come.

15

A POSSIBLE FUTURE –
SUPPLEMENTAL JOURNAL
ENTRY 15

THE SUN WAS JUST COMING up. Mike had walked back into camp, Azile was sitting, stretching, when their gazes turned. Tomas had not made a sound as he stepped into the clearing.

"Again with the wards?" he asked as he held his outstretched arms to the side, palms upward.

"Where's Dallas?" Azile asked.

Mike didn't bother. He should have realized it; she was dead the moment he'd taken her.

Tomas smiled as he placed a hand against his stomach. "She's with me."

Mike wanted to rush him right then, but that's what Tomas wanted, anger clouded judgment. He would use instinctive reactions and adrenaline against him. He would be making Tomas's job easier if he'd tried. He had to think that Tomas's first instinct wouldn't be to kill him; he wondered if he could be subdued and forced to do Tomas's bidding. He supposed that was possible, even likely. Michael did what Tomas wanted, or he would keep going back, taking people Mike loved one at a time. He would become that poor father in the cabin. It wouldn't be easy hitting a hardened Talbot encampment, but Mike had no illusions that Tomas would or could be stopped. The vampire was immensely powerful.

"I won't help you get your bitch of a sister." Mike watched Tomas sneer as he said that. While he himself didn't want to act in anger, watching Tomas get angry was not settling well in his stomach either. Tomas looked like he could uproot trees. Whereas if Mike used anger to fight, he figured it would be to his detriment; he was most assuredly not getting that same vibe from Tomas. And this childish baiting was like telling Superman that Lois was a slut, because that's something that will make fighting the man easier. There are a great many ways to die, some are way suckier than others. Out of the corner of Mike's eye, he saw Azile stand.

"Tommy, what are you doing?" she asked.

Mike didn't think she was questioning what she'd seen, but sometimes people wanted to hear confirmation straight from the source.

"You're insufferable, Azile. Killing you is going to be a pleasure. Witch blood tends to be sweeter." There was a pause. "What's the matter, Michael? You're ruining my line."

"Your line?" Mike asked.

"I was expecting your chivalrous self to proclaim that I would only be able to kill her over your dead body, to which I was going to say, that is what I intended."

Michael was not sure exactly what Azile did, but there was a crackle of electricity and a baseball sized sphere of blistering lightning shot out toward Tomas. It struck him square in the chest. Mike was on the move before it had a chance to dissipate. Tomas stumbled back from Azile's strike just as Mike attacked. Mike was awkwardly reaching for his knife with his right hand while with his left, he connected squarely on Tomas's chin. He now had a pretty good idea of what striking granite would feel like. Tomas went back two more steps as Mike's follow through brought him to Tomas's side. Had he not stumbled and nearly fallen over, the punch Tomas delivered would have planted him in the ground permanently. As it was, Mike's vision began to tunnel before he ever struck the ground. The best he could hope for as his face struck the dirt was a standing eight count, but that would mean he needed to stand, and this wasn't a sanctioned fight there was nothing preventing Tomas from completing what he'd intended.

"Stay down," Tomas growled.

The electrical impulses in Mike's head were jumbled. He wasn't sure he could even respond, much less use his motor skills to move.

"I am going to kill the witch, then you and I are going on a little adventure."

Mike could do little more than bleed onto the dirt. He could hear more crackling then came a litany of swears from Tomas. He didn't sound hurt, so Mike figured Azile had gone on the defensive, and Tomas had not yet been successful in murdering her.

That was confirmed soon enough when next Tomas spoke. "You won't be able to keep this up much longer, witch. I can feel you weakening. Surrender now and I will make your ending less painful. But some pain, you will feel, must feel."

Mike placed his hands to either side and pushed up, first sitting and then wobbling to a stand. "I'm in a bit of trouble," he whispered as he swayed. "Tomas," he croaked, cleared his throat, then spat the name out again.

"Gods, you are thick," Tomas turned slightly. "I give you an opportunity to not suffer needlessly, but you just can't help yourself. It's a good thing you Talbots breed like rabbits because your mortality rate from stupidity is much higher than the average of your pathetic species."

"Our species? You're human." Mike was stalling. If Tomas launched now, he'd not be getting up again, most likely not until he was at the entrance to New Hampshire's low rent version of Stonehenge.

"Your skill at stalling is on par with your ability to fight."

Azile was chanting, her hands moving in fluid motions. Mike was convinced she was preparing to launch a salvo that would either be the death of her or of Tomas, if she was given the chance to launch it. If the vampire turned back toward her, he might see what she was doing and put an end to it. Azile was tapping into everything she had left; she'd let her defenses drop completely. If Tomas attacked now she would die before she had a chance to use her spell. Michael must have sensed this as well.

"Did I ever tell you how I heard the knife as it crashed through your sister's breast plate? It sounded like a brittle plastic toy crushed under the wheel of a truck."

Tomas turned completely toward Mike, anger making him bare his teeth. His canines elongated completely, his eyes narrowing as his pupils dilated.

"I imagined the rest as the blade sliced through the fibrous muscle of her black heart." Mike shivered to express his delight at the memory. "I wanted it to be me who delivered that killing strike, to know the sensation of a mind orgasm at each retelling."

"When I force you to bring my sister forth, we're going to keep you alive just long enough that you get to watch every person that you love tortured and killed. Maybe we let you live for a few years to enjoy those memories, then you will die in the most excruciating way we can come up with."

"Were you two fucking?" Mike asked.

"What?" Tomas recoiled.

"Yeah, never mind. I already know the answer. I get having love for a sibling, but this, this is unnatural. Clearly there's something more going on."

"We weren't incestual!" Tomas shouted.

"But not because you didn't want to. Maybe you saw what your father did to her and hoped you could get in on the action."

Tomas moved so quickly, Mike had little time to do more

than hold his blade at his side as Tomas ran headlong into him, grabbing the sides of his head and snapping it to the side with a violent cracking sound. He stood for a moment, but only because Tomas still held the man's head in his hands. When he let go, Mike fell to the ground, as alive as the rock he smashed against.

"Fuck," Tomas said, not sure if it was because he'd just killed his best chance at getting his sister back, or for the blessed blade that had pierced his stomach and bowels. Most likely both, as he dropped to his knees, both hands wrapped around the blade. He pulled it free and gasped.

"NOOOOO!" Azile cried out as she released the burst of power she'd been creating. A bright green filament, no wider than a laser, raced toward Tomas. It circled around and burst into his left eye. The optic nerve sizzled, burnt and withered, the eye a shattered gelatinous ruin. Blood poured from the socket.

"You can't kill—" Tomas had turned toward her before falling over and remaining still.

Azile ran over to Mike, slid by his side and touched the side of his face. Tears streamed from her eyes, coursed down her face and dripped heavily. "No, no, no—you can't be dead. My sweet Michael! We were to have a life together, children. I saw it. I SAW IT!" she screamed. "This is not how the story ends!"

It wasn't until the next morning that she was able to travel. She'd cried until she had nothing more to give, then she'd called on a horse to carry Michael's body back to his family so they could bury him and grieve. She could barely register the anguish they would suffer through as they'd not only lost their patriarch, but also Dallas. It had been a significant blow. She stayed long enough for the burial before leaving, so lost in her own grief she'd not registered much of what had been said that day. Mac, Wilkes and Elam surrounded her, constantly fearful of the near catatonic state she was in.

Had she been more aware, she might have pushed them away.

"I don't understand," Mac said, "she barely knew him."

"Are all men this thick, or is it just you?" Wilkes asked.

"What are you talking about?"

"Not all men are as clueless as this one," Elam said pointing at the other. "Mac, she loved him deeply."

"How?" Mac was clearly confused.

"We have learned a great deal in our time with her," Elam said. "Is it not likely that in some world we cannot see, and do not know, that they were together?"

"That doesn't make sense. Because if that were the case, a world exists where my beloved is still alive, and we have built a life together."

"Mac, there most definitely is," Elam told him.

Mac rocked back as if he'd been physically struck before he found the nearest place to sit. "I…I have to find her."

"I don't think it works like that." Wilkes went over to him and placed a hand gently on his shoulder. He looked up at her, tears brimming in his eyes.

"But, but it can, right? If Azile had a life with him and… and Tommy was trying to get his sister back, it's possible."

"No," Wilkes said as tenderly as she could.

"When Michael died, any chance to alter other futures went with him," Elam said.

Mac hung his head as tears fell to the ground. He felt as if he'd lost her all over again.

"I'm so sorry," Wilkes said as she rubbed his back.

"Do you wish to come in?" Tracy had come over; she wore a small smile upon her face. "I can get you some cobbler. Cobbler always helps on days like this when so much pain is hovering. Dallas was a lovely woman, a wonderful wife to my son, and an even better mother to my grandchildren. It will be difficult for Justin, for a long while, I fear, but eventually he will come to understand that in the end we will all be reunited."

"Is that what you believe about Michael as well?" Elam asked.

Wilkes smacked him hard in the shoulder. "Shh," she shushed hard.

"Don't fret, child." Tracy turned a warm smile on her. "I didn't have an...episode and forgot. Michael does not have a soul, but that won't stop him from entering. He has a single mindedness that cannot be denied; he will find a way. Come, come, I believe Azile has a note to read."

Azile was not sure when she'd been left alone; she looked up. "A note?" she said aloud. She touched her pocket, and pulled out the rolled piece of paper that looked suspiciously like something she would have smoked in her youth.

It read in scrawled purple crayon: "Mike, I am truly sorry, there was no other choice. Your sacrifice was necessary to throw a demigod (won't mention names here, but it's someone we both know well) off your trail. The Michael you spared is the one that can make the difference. Azile, you know what to do."

"Where's my horse?" Azile said, looking renewed and anxious.

16

TALBOTSODE 1

"Want to hear a theory of mine?" I asked BT, we had just got off guard duty. Well, he had. I had walked the perimeter a couple of times with him while drinking a concoction of blue Gatorade and vodka.

BT sat down with a heavy sigh. "Not really. I'd like to decompress for a minute then go get some sleep."

"Decompress? From what?"

"You realize on the three loops you did with me you talked the entire time, right? I've seen kindergarten classes after a Halloween party less bouncy than you. What gives?"

"I know you can never go home again, but man, I'll tell you, this is the closest I've felt in a good long while."

BT held his fist out, and I bumped it.

"Lay it on me." He made a come-hither motion with both his hands. "I know it's useless protesting, I could better spend that energy elsewhere, like with your sister."

"That's never not going to be an eww thing for me."

"Why do you think I say it? It's the only thing in my arsenal that appears to derail you. Before you inevitably start, this theory of yours, is it a conspiracy theory?"

"Why, do you want it to be?"

"No, I don't think I can take any more."

"Fair enough, although, I have a great one about Montana."

"Nope, too close. Go on with the one you were going to tell."

"You ever hear of the Toba eruption?"

"You're not the only one that had insomnia and stayed up all night watching documentaries. Considered a super volcano, it erupted seventy-four thousand years ago. Nearly wiped-out modern humans."

"That's the basic view of it, yes. And science was wavering back and forth on just how much effect it did have on humans. Gonna be a while before that debate is argued again. Around the same time, there was a homo-sapiens bottleneck."

"Allegedly," he said.

"Allegedly," I agreed. Scientists were having a hard time coming to a consensus on that one too. "If you do believe in this bottleneck, like I do, there was supposedly only a thousand to a hundred-thousand people left on the planet."

"Feels like that now sometimes," he said.

I couldn't disagree. We could go weeks without seeing people. I don't think our population was quite as low as that bottleneck, but we were moving closer rather than farther away from it. A lot of the problems we were having were the general level of distrust groups had for each other. We didn't comingle, familial units stayed tight and closed, making any significant procreation highly unlikely.

"Can you imagine, man? The entire planet, a thousand people? Boggles the mind. And if that was the number, how many mating pairs were there? Couldn't have been more than a couple hundred. Damn near as close to Adam and Eve as could be."

"Yeah, but it didn't sound like any idyllic garden though," he added, reclining back on his chair.

"Wasn't it, though? No fucking people."

"Hardcore, man, hardcore. Not wrong though." He tipped an imaginary beer my way.

"So, humanity has extinction in its sights, as close to a footnote in history as can be, another failed species to go alongside the millions before us. Then something happened to change that."

"If you say aliens I'm leaving." He opened one eye to peer at me.

"This isn't about aliens, but it could just as easily be them watching from the sidelines and stepping in at the last minute to make sure we survived."

"Should have picked a more deserving species, if that's the case. Dolphins, maybe."

"And I'm the hardcore one?" I responded.

"Tell me I'm wrong."

I did not tell him he was wrong. First off because not many people told BT he was wrong, and secondly, I more agreed with him than not.

"That's what I thought," he said after a few seconds of silence.

I continued on. "If this bottleneck happened, they think that the few homo sapiens left survived by developing sophisticated social, symbolic and economic strategies that enabled us to eventually repopulate the world some sixty thousand years ago."

"Those are some big words for you."

"Blow me. And I'm completely parroting what I saw."

"That would imply you remembered something."

"Are you going to bust my balls this entire story?"

"What. Can't take a little heckling? It's the only enjoyment I get when you regale me with your tales."

"I'm not sure what you think you're going to accomplish here. I won't give up, most likely I'll double down, making these things longer and more eccentric."

"Sounds like a nightmare. Fine, I'll be quiet."

I eyed him suspiciously, couldn't trust the man in this matter. He had closed his eyes again, a smile on his lips. I had to talk fast before he fell asleep. Although, I suppose it didn't matter if he did or not; I'd told him other stories with him snoozing away. "The question is why."

"What question? You never posed one."

"This super volcano pops its top, there's a cascade of ensuing issues that push man to the brink of extinction then boom—"

"Boom?"

"You're fucking up my reveal."

"Ah the plot twist. Keep going."

"Boom," I said with less oomph. "We're dying out, and then all of a sudden we have this major fundamental shift and develop all these refined societal structures that allow us to continue on—to not just survive, but thrive. Why?" I paused for dramatic effect. He fake snored or maybe it was real. "Mushrooms!" was my ta-da moment. He was unimpressed.

"Fungi was the answer?"

"Ah, you were listening. Not just your garden variety mushroom, I'm talking psilocybin. Magic mushrooms."

"Drugs. Yes, Mike, drugs saved us from annihilation. Trip would have loved this story, or maybe he was the one that related it to you."

"Turn off your inner cop for a minute and think about it. You have some nomad group desperate to survive, starving to the point where they're eating anything available, taking chances where they wouldn't have necessarily done so in the past. They literally stumble upon an outcropping of these bright red-topped growths in a dusty field."

"Red in nature is generally used as a warning."

"It wouldn't be out of the question for a reindeer or maybe a big horn ram to eat some."

"Sounds like you're reaching."

"No, hear me out." I was indeed free balling here. I had

no idea. "What if they watched another animal eat it, and deemed it somewhat safe?"

"You don't think the dancing sheep with the half-closed eyes swinging to early Grateful Dead music would have been enough to scare them off?"

"Listen, man, when you're starving, I've seen you wolf down my sister's cooking."

"We said we were never going to talk about that again, and besides, I don't have to do that anymore."

"Right, but the point I'm making is starving people aren't too discerning. So they come across a grove of those. Is it grove? Maybe a field? Or is it some other weird collective name like a dose of 'shrooms?"

"Now I know you're making this shit up. And just so you know, when you're trying to dupe someone in the future, it's a cluster or troop."

"Troop? I told you it would be something weird."

"Whatever. I'm trying to get some rest here."

I continued on undeterred. "These desperate people eat a batch of 'shrooms, I mean a lot of them. The mushrooms start creating neural pathways we may never have evolved on our own. Without the help of the psychedelic, I mean. They're seeing the world in a whole new way. It's tantamount to a religious experience, probably seeing gods in everything—the trees, the sky, the blowing grass...pebbles, for all I know."

"Maybe just the goddess of nature," he said.

Not sure if I'd set the hook, but he seemed mildly interested at this point. And then he retreated.

"I'm not sure how you can make the leap from a clan tripping nomads, to repopulating the earth."

"Speaking as one who has partaken a LOT of 'shrooms, you may reach a depth of understanding about life that cannot be achieved when you are merely trying to survive. They were taking the first steps to self-actualization, an improvement of the person to create a better civilization. I can't get into the particulars because I don't know what they are."

"Man cannot survive on psilocybin alone."

"There's a point here, and you're deliberately avoiding it."

"If this population bottleneck did happen, I'm not going to base the success of the human race on drugs."

"And why not? Look at what drugs have done for the medical field? Probably doubled our life expectancy! Better living through chemicals, I always say."

"How's that worked out for you?"

"I'm still here. We're still here."

He grunted, that was as close to agreement as I was going to get.

"Let it ruminate. What they were doing wasn't going to work, people were dying out. They were in the tunnel looking at the fast-approaching light, and then they weren't, they had a fundamental shift in their perception of the world. They were simultaneously closer to their mortality and could also look at it objectively from a distance. Problem solving in ways they'd never done before."

"All thanks to illegal mushrooms."

"You're getting it now, and I'm pretty sure they weren't illegal back then."

"There could be a hundred, a thousand other things that led to a rebound—"

"Of which mushrooms could be a part," I tossed in quickly.

"Fine. Because I know you won't let it go, and I'm exhausted, there's a chance, albeit a tiny one, that mushrooms played a part in humanity's comeback."

"I knew you'd see it my way." I boogied on out before he could find something to toss at me.

17

TALBOTSODE TWO

According to the calendar it was the middle of Fall, but up in the mountains, that's considered early winter. The harsh, bitter cold hadn't quite settled in, but a light snow was drifting down. BT was sitting in the lobby not five feet from the fire, an open book on his chest. His head was resting against the back of the oversized chair and his eyes were closed.

"Do you have a tracker on me?" he asked without looking at me.

"If you're trying to avoid me, maybe you shouldn't have parked your ass right outside the bar. We'd moved into the haunted Stanley Hotel. Why? I don't know if I can say exactly. Lord knows there were nicer and newer accommodations in Estes Park, then it hit me, and I knew exactly why. The enormous bar to the left of where BT snoozed hadn't been touched, I mean, not until I got there.

"What do you want?" he asked.

I walked across the lobby and went outside, grabbed the six pack I had nestled in a snowbank. Kirby waved as he made a circuit on his patrol. I nodded and headed back in.

"You know common courtesy would have you close the door when you go outside," BT said.

I ignored him. He was right of course, just never dawned on me. Not sure what that said about me. I popped the top off a beer and plopped down next to him.

"There are ten seats here and that's where you sit?"

"It was cold out, and you throw off waves of heat. In your other life you could have been a radiator...or perhaps a minor star."

He grunted. "I'm trying to finish this book."

"Looks like it. Did I ever tell you about the time I got PTSD?"

"If this has to do with you getting your dick stuck in places you shouldn't have stuck it, I'm out of here."

"What about improper lubes?"

"Vapo-rub? Because I'm down for some laughs. Super glue?"

I winced.

"Dish it." BT clapped his meaty hands together and rubbed furiously. "Man, this is going to be good."

"I mean, I don't really have one I would like to share."

"So you do have one? This day is shaping up. And you're going to erect boundaries now?" He smiled. "Heh. I said erect."

"Yeah, I caught that," not at all liking the direction of this conversation.

"Either start talking or start walking."

"Is my pain some kind of enjoyment for you?"

"Last I checked I didn't interrupt your solitude for storytime."

"There's that," I told him. "This isn't necessarily what I was going to talk to you about. It started off traumatic, but worked out in the end."

"Hmm, I like the stories better when they don't."

"Numbing cream," I blurted out.

"*Why?*"

I looked over my shoulder. "This was before I got married, and it had been a minute since…you know."

"I think I can infer what you mean."

"The woman I was with, we'd gone on a couple of dates, and apparently the third date was her number. She was…" I looked over my shoulder again, even peeked into the bar.

"Worried?"

"My wife is a damn ninja when it comes to these stories. So anyway, this woman, when I say she was hot, I am not embellishing."

"So you say. Nearest actress lookalike."

I didn't hesitate. "Marisa Tomei. Specifically *My cousin Vinnie*, Marisa. First time I saw her I was wondering what the hell she was doing in a bar in downtown Boston. Figured she must be on a shoot. Seeing my problem yet? Hot woman, fully loaded…cannon, hair trigger. I didn't want to blow it."

"Literally!" he exclaimed, laughing at his comment.

"Hardy har. I'm glad this discomfort is at least as entertaining as that book for you."

"If I had popcorn I would gladly be munching away."

"Oh to be young and dumb."

"And full of…" he didn't finish his sentence when he saw Porkchop head to the door. He was carrying two steaming mugs. My guess it was cocoa; he and Kirby seemed to have bonded since we'd stopped here, and every time Kirby was out on patrol the kid would bring him a hot drink.

"Crude."

"I love when you spontaneously get all moral. Like watching goats fly."

"Can I finish this story I had no intention of ever talking about?"

"It's all you, playah. Wait, I need to know why you had numbing cream in the first place."

"Wasn't mine. She had just got a tattoo. I'd gone to use her bathroom, and it was sitting on the vanity counter."

He shook his head. "George Germaphobe grabbed a random tube of what I would suppose is open and used, cream? How is that even possible?"

"First off, I had a few in me and secondly, my germ thing didn't kick into full gear until after I had kids. Those little bastards are disgusting. I'm talking about all little kids *and* germs."

BT nodded in appreciation of half that statement.

"I'm standing there feeling immense relief while I take the pressure off my bladder, sort of leaning against the counter. Looking over, I see the tube, read the label and then look down, and well, the rest as they say, is history." I took a swig of beer and sat back.

"Oh hell no. There is no way that's where you cut that off. I've read serialized novels with less of a cliffhanger."

"No, I've already been tempting the gods. I've been talking far too long about a sexual escapade and no Tracy sightings, I'm not pushing it."

"I have great lines of sight. She's not going to sneak up on us. You tell me now, or I'm going to talk to Tracy about having dinner tonight at our place. Your sister has decided to cook on occasion."

"I thought we were supposed to be friends."

"It's worse than that, we're family, and it's the ones closest to you that you can't trust."

"You suck. What's she trying to make?"

"You're actually considering this? Your story, or the fact that you might get caught retelling it is worth anything your sibling might concoct?"

"Fuck it, nope, nothing is worth a week's worth of gastrointestinal distress. I was in the final shakes, so to speak, and did I mention it had been a while?"

"Yeah, I was able to infer that."

"So finishing up, and I'm thinking about the beauty in the next room, and I'm already getting *tumescent*."

"Tumescent? Seriously? Did we just get dropped off in a historical romance?"

"I'm trying to be less crude."

"Go on with your dignified self."

"I was worried, man. I didn't want to be a one pump chump. I saw the label, and figured what's the worst that could happen? I smeared some on."

"Did it stink?"

"No."

"Did it sting?"

"Again no."

"What was the problem?"

"Dude, someone could have slammed it in the door I wouldn't have felt it."

"Nooooo!" BT put his hand up to his mouth and gasped. "Tell me it ain't so!"

"Oh, it was so."

"So you're there with Marisa…"

"Katelyn, actually."

"You're there with Katelyn and…"

"Nothing man. Between the booze and the cream, nothing. Zilch."

"You had FCS?" he asked.

"FCS?"

"Floppy cock syndrome."

"I hate you sometimes."

"Did you run out of there? Or did you *limp* out."

"I'm never telling you another story."

"Okay, okay...please continue."

"I fessed up."

"No way!" He stood. "You never know what you're going to get when a Talbot walks into a bar, but one way or the other, it's going to be entertaining. You fessed up?"

"Everything. I told her I hadn't been with anyone in a

while, and that I thought she was drop dead gorgeous, and I was afraid of letting go a little early."

"What did she say?"

"She laughed for a second, which, you know, given the fragility of the male ego and my inability to rise to the occasion, wasn't helping the situation. Then she got down to business."

"Down to business?"

"She was an overachiever, took it as a personal mission to overcome the obstacle in front of her."

"Or lack of one."

"Words hurt, man."

"Sorry," he said the word, but I didn't feel any sincerity behind it.

"The things she did that night…if I'd had a ring on me, I would have proposed right there and then."

"What happened? Did she sober up and see the error of her ways?"

"You're not going to believe this shit."

"Don't worry about it, I don't believe half the things you say."

"Good to know. Anyway, come to find out she was a doctor, and she was heading overseas the very next week to do a Doctors Without Borders tour."

"She went to some great lengths to get away from you."

"It's not healthy that you get most of your pleasure from the suffering of others."

"Just your suffering."

"That makes it better."

"So what happened to her?"

"Did I mention the part where I was young and dumb? She was going to be gone for year; what do you think happened? I got in trouble and went in the Corps."

"Is that where the PTSD story you wanted to relate came from?"

"Oh *now* you want to hear it?"

"Yeah. I was expecting more drama from the Katelyn story; that it worked out in your favor just didn't have enough oomph for me."

"I wish I could find another giant Black man to call my friend."

"As if any others would have you."

"I bet me and Terry Crews could be friends."

"We could take a road trip to Hollywood, see if he's still around. I wouldn't mind tagging out and handing you off. Nobody told me the chore it was going to be to have a white friend. You all are high maintenance."

I would have liked to deny the accusation, but to do so would have been hypocritical. "I don't even believe I'm going to now tell this story after that last one. We're going to need to find me a therapist."

"How many of those poor bastards have you made retire early?"

I popped the top on another beer. "Fuck it. This about a year after we got Henry. I had to take the dogs to the vet. George, our rescue bully, was getting up there in years. I miss that magnificent beast. Anyway, not that he ever had been much of a jumper, but as he got older, that completely changed. He would wait patiently at the back hatch while I stooped to pick him up, always making sure to lift with my legs and not my back. I grabbed him and put him in the back of my Jeep. Henry is sitting there watching, but I could tell he was nearly bursting with excitement to go for a ride. So I stoop down in the same manner to grab him, but he's got other ideas—he's jumping while I'm leaning." I stopped talking because this part was difficult for me.

"What the fuck happened? You turned white? Like whiter than your normal honky self. You're like Saltine cracker white right now."

"I grabbed his dick, man. THERE! You happy?! I grabbed his dick!"

BT flinched from the force of my words before laughing his ass off.

It was then I had the good fortune of seeing Porkchop's flushed and surprised face looking at me from the front doors and also my wife's as she was coming down the staircase.

"Perfect, just perfect." I grabbed my remaining beers and headed into the lounge. The even funnier thing about that day, I mean, if you weren't personally involved, was that Henry wouldn't look me in the eye for about three days afterward.

18

TALBOTSODE THREE

"Fuck my life, how do you keep finding me?" BT asked. He was on the roof of the hotel, wrapped up in a heavy blanket, sitting in a chair he must have dragged out onto the widow's walk. Snow was lazily drifting down.

"The ceiling was sagging down where you're sitting; I was coming to investigate, not look for you."

He slid his blanket down just far enough to display one sausage sized finger—yes, *that* sausage sized finger.

"I feel like I've told you this story before," I started.

"Oh, then by all means interrupt my alone time and regale me with it again. I cannot wait."

"Cool."

"For one who oozes sarcasm out of all of your North-eastern pores, it amazes me that you cannot detect when it is redirected back to you."

"Oh, I can tell, I just don't care."

"It's weird for me to think of a time before you. Sort of like a person living with chronic arthritis, they can't remember what it was like to live pain free. I miss those days."

"You going to share some of that blanket?" I pushed in

next to him on the oversized chair. "Fuck me, man, this thing is the size of a loveseat, and I can barely fit in."

"Just because we're in the mountains doesn't mean I want to broke back it."

"Nice." I gave him my fist for bumping while I wiggled my ass down onto the cushion. "Should have brought some oil to help me slide in. Hah. that's what he said."

"Great. Yes, by all means, let's give people more to talk about. Baby oil, cozying up under a blanket, alone in a spot away from prying eyes. The tabloids would love this shit."

"Whoa, whoa—who said anything about baby oil? We could be manly and use motor oil," I said as I yanked a sliver of blanket from him. "It's like you're part mummy," I grunted as I pulled. "I smell booze."

"How? I haven't even cracked it open yet."

"Ah I knew it. What is it?"

"Gin."

"Man, I'm not really a fan of gin. Hand it over."

"Mike, don't take this personally, but piss off."

"Ah, no worries. I know your words only come from a place of love."

"Love? Disgust, maybe."

He handed over the canteen. I spun the top off and took a sniff, definitely had the scent of Juniper going on and... "Is that grapefruit I smell?" I asked.

"It's called a Long Drink."

"Grapefruit juice and gin? Sounds fucking fabulously gross." I handed it back.

"That was my intention, find something you would absolutely detest so that I could drink it without having to share."

"What's next, you going to brew a chocolate stout? Maybe a ham-infused vodka? That's selfish, man."

I watched BT take a good long swig; he didn't grimace, which I found strange given the combination of ingredients.

"What else is in there?" I asked suspiciously.

"Nothing."

"You lie for shit."

"Sorry, I didn't practice the craft as well as you."

"Avoidance...ah. So you are learning. Spill it."

"Cranberry juice. It's just cranberry juice."

"Interesting. Got the tartness of both those juices, what would they do to the gin? Hand it over."

"You had your chance."

"That was before."

"Before what?" he asked.

"Before I thought I wanted to try it."

"There were a few times during my career I thought about just saying fuck it and heading up into the mountains and living as a hermit. It's the shots you don't take that you regret. I think that was a Michael Scott re-quote." He reluctantly handed the canteen over. We fist bumped again for his *Office* reference.

I sniffed again, still not liking what my nose was picking up. I shrugged and took a tentative swish and swallow. "Hey," I said, looking at BT. My eyes felt like they'd grown wide. I took a much bigger pull. "What did you call this?" I asked after I smacked my lips.

"A Long Drink." He pulled out another canteen.

"You have another?"

"I knew you'd find me."

"Then why did you drink half of the one you gave to me?"

"Consider that a pain in the ass payment fee."

"So, gin, grapefruit, and cranberry juice make this concoction?"

He nodded.

"It's delicious."

"I know. And just so you know, all roads for future ingredients go through me. I have scoured this town and have hoarded everything I could find."

"How very Capitalist of you."

He tipped his canteen at me.

"So, you ready for the story I may or may not have related to you at some time before?"

"Hold on." He glugged down half the contents of the canteen. "Getting closer," he said when he was done.

"I don't remember all the particulars. I was pretty shittied by the end of the night."

"Shocker. You ever think you may have a problem?"

"Oh, I know I do. That's how I cope with it, acknowledgment. Anyway, Paul and I had ended up at an off-campus party. I don't remember who invited us—"

"Probably crashed it."

"Are you going to let me finish?"

"I'm stalling, waiting for the alcohol to coat my frontal cortex."

"We were invited, or I guess the dude that brought us there was invited. Shit, I guess we did crash the party."

"Shocker." BT held up his canteen.

"Don't like having my actions analyzed. Whatever. So we're at this party at the neighboring college. It wasn't a state university, which meant tuition was absurd. The kids that went there weren't born with just silver spoons in their mouths, but apparently gold flake enemas were included or they should have been—never seen so many stuck-up individuals in one spot. Not sure how they could deal with it. Paul and I did our best to go through all their top-shelf liquor in record time so we could get out of there and salvage what remained of the night."

"You're saying the women at this party had standards that neither you nor Paul measured up to?"

"It was all about the money," I defended.

"Sure it was."

"We were good and buzzed and decided it was time to go, unfortunately, our ride was nowhere to be seen."

"So you're saying the guy that brought you, who was most likely in the same socio-economic sphere as yourselves, succeeded where you failed?"

"It was politics."

"Your argument is getting weaker."

"This part is only the buildup. I'm not delving deeper into it."

"Wise choice."

"We were about ten miles from our campus, it was cold, wasn't snowing, but there had been a major storm a few days prior. Plowed snowbanks lined the road."

"That relevant?" BT took another swig and tossed the empty canteen to his side, pulling out another that I figured was a full one.

"How many of those do you have?"

"Enough to get through the extended director's cut of whatever this is."

"I'm conflicted. I do appreciate the planning, though. Stage is set." I rubbed my hands together. "We leave the party and start walking—"

"Because that's what smart college kids do in the dead of winter," he finished.

"Hey, we started thumbing almost immediately."

"Even smarter. No one ever hears horror stories about getting picked up by strangers."

"Keep talking, funny man, I'll drag this out to the point you give me another canteen just to shut me up."

He clammed up quickly.

"Good. So there we are, thumbing down the road, Paul pulling up his pants to show some leg, when this station wagon from the 70s bounces off a snow bank and comes to a stop about twenty feet away. Big dude, like cupcake big, not gym big, sticks his head out the window and asks if we had any cash or grass. Pretty happy he didn't ask for ass, especially with Paul showing some leg. Told him we had some green. He told us to hop in."

"Couldn't get in the front passenger seat, dude, it was packed midway up the window with candy wrappers, fast food bags, empty bottles of every imaginable type of soda. The car stunk of old and moldy leftovers. He turned to look at us when we got in the back. I think he was more wrecked than we were, and we'd already shown how much we were by getting into a car that couldn't stay on the road. His eyes glowed like the cherry of a cigarette."

"You didn't get out, did you?"

"What do you think?"

"This sounds familiar."

"I feel like you're just saying that so I won't continue."

"Were cops involved?"

I was looking at him, trying to figure out if he was guessing or just knew. I didn't want to be the rube of a pretend psychic. and give him the answers he was fishing for.

"Maybe?"

"You don't remember?"

"I mean I do, but I don't know how I feel about relating a story a second time."

"Just do it. Most of the time I don't pay enough attention to what you have to say, so even if it's a repeat it'll be like I'm hearing it for the first time."

"I feel like I should be insulted, but I have this Long Drink to keep me company. The dude stared at us for an uncomfortable amount of time, like he was afraid we were going to rummage through his trash pile for some food. 'Gonna need that weed now,' he said as a car blared its horn at us as it passed. He smoked that entire bone as he stared at us—I mean the *entire* time. It was fucking weird."

"Did you get murder vibes from him?"

"Not really, but now that you mention it, I wonder if he was sizing us up, wondering if he could overpower Paul."

"Overpower Paul?"

"Oh yeah, I could run way faster than him."

"Good to know you were going to bail on your friend."

"Come on man, who wants to end up as a victim to the Cupcake Killer?"

"Good point."

"So he smoked that bone down to the point he was sucking more on his fingertips than the roach. Ate the piece that remained, then finally turned around. He clicked his blinker off but instead of pulling out into the road, he dragged the length of the car against the snowbank. I laughed then stopped when he whipped his head back around and glared at me, the whole time he did that the car was moving. He finally did get back onto the road. We'd gotten about halfway back to campus when his head dipped slightly and he was again using the snowbank like a kids' bumper on a bowling alley. This was the first time and maybe the only time I can honestly say I was happy to see the red and blues of a cop car. The dude popped his head up immediately and was then losing his shit, like raging. Never seen someone on weed act like that. He was slamming his fists down on his steering wheel and his dashboard, we could hear plastic cracking, no idea what he was breaking. The cop had to come up to the passenger side, because well, Cupcake had the thing shoved up against the snow and ice again. The cop shines his light in, the driver still going nuts like he's playing an invisible drum set, and me and Paul are sitting in the back looking like choir boys."

"I'm sure."

"The cop is tapping on the window for the driver to open it, wasn't happening. He finally taps on ours. Paul immediately rolled it down. What's the matter with your friend? The cop asked. He was about to tell him the guy wasn't our friend when the dude just starts slinging a verbal assault at the cop. Paul and I were like damn! Now this was back before they wore body cams and were way more likely to seek retribution, not taking any of that crap from a snot-nosed kid. Cop reached through our window, fiddled around with the passenger door, and finally yanked it open. Paul and I had pressed ourselves into the backseat, didn't need a textbook to realize this was going south in a fucking hurry, and we had no desire to be collateral damage. I had issues with cops, but not ever was I stupid enough to do what that guy was. The door creaked open, and I'm not sure exactly what spilled out onto the cop, but it made him angrier than the cussing he was getting. Bunch of empty booze bottles at the minimum, probably green fuzzy beer residue, too. If I thought that driver was already going spastic it had nothing on what he started to do when that cop shot him with his taser. The car rocked around on its springs like we were centered on the San Andreas fault during the big one.

"Garbage was flying all over the place as the guy shook around. Cop is yelling at him the entire time. 'Got nothing to say now, do you asshole! I'm going to tase you hard enough that your unborn kids are going to feel it!' Bud, that cop was losing it. He must have been having a bad week. He was turning red in the face, veins in his neck were bulging out, spittle flying from his mouth as he screamed. A part of me wondered if we hadn't been there would he have just shot the idiot then planted a gun on him. Then there was a second where I thought maybe he would take care of all of us. There was no way to sneak out my side, not pressed up against the snowbank like we were. It was when two more patrol cars pulled up that I felt a bit better. By this time the rampaging cop had yanked the driver out the door, and Cupcake was flopping around on the cold wet pavement. If the smell was any indication, he'd pissed and shit himself, and still that man kept his finger down on the plunger, sending waves of electricity through the bastard."

"Holy shit! I wonder if he faced any disciplinary action," BT said.

"I need you to focus here and remember that I was like, eighteen-ish and blitzed out of my mind."

"Okay..." BT said tentatively.

"Besides the little bit about worrying if we were going to get shot for being witnesses, everything else was fucking hilarious. Paul and I were laughing so hard we had tears streaming down our faces. There's like three cops, and they finally propped the noodle limp driver up against the car, mashing his face into the windshield. The faces they were forcing him to make, dude, you had to be there. It was fucking hilarious. We're pointing and laughing."

"You are such an asshole, altruistic to a fault."

"Hey man, Paul was there too."

"I'd call him one too if he was here."

"The cop that ended up frisking the guy starts yelling about how he had shit on his hands—at that point I couldn't even see straight I was laughing so hard. Cop is losing it, holding his hands as far from his body as he can, he's gagging, walking back and forth. He wasn't the fastest thinker on the planet; he had frozen water all around. He could have gotten most of it off. He finally ended up wiping it off on the newly minted perp's back. Perp ended up puking all over his hood, the shitty-handed cop ended up puking all over the perp's back. Dude, you can't make this shit up. It was like we had front-row seats for a slapstick comedy."

"You two are laughing while you're watching an individual get tortured?"

"*Have you not been listening?* First off, he got tased, um, extensively and second, he kind of deserved it."

BT was still looking at me disapprovingly.

"Fine, fine, Mr. Humanitarian. That's not the really funny part anyway."

"Do tell."

"It's the plot twist that brings it home."

"You don't warn your audience about the plot twist, you let it unfold organically. What kind of storyteller are you?"

"You're sucking the fun out of this."

"Makes us about even then."

"If I had a Taser," I mumbled.

"What's that?"

"I said I wish I'd brought my blazer."

"I'm sure. Could you maybe hurry this up?"

"Try to bring a little joy into people's lives and this is how they treat you."

"Mike."

"Fine, fine, driver's face smeared all over the windshield, he's cuffed and wrenched up, he's getting arrested for DUI and a bunch of other charges. The initial cop had finally got himself under control and he came up to our window. 'Ah, fellas, we're arresting your friend. I'm going to let you take his car home. I don't want it to sit out in this weather for two hours waiting for a tow truck. And I'm not taking you two home.' He walked away before we could tell him the guy wasn't our friend and neither of us were in any condition to drive."

"So what did you do?"

I said nothing.

"No." He stood to make it more dramatic.

I still said nothing. This was unexpected and fun.

"So you just watched a man get arrested for DUI, and then decided to hop in the very seat he was yanked from?"

"Of course not! I didn't just hop right in. We had to make sure the seat was somewhat clean."

"You are unbelievable."

"Dude, it was hilarious. Yes, of course, now I know it was incredibly stupid and I wouldn't ever advocate someone driving drunk, not unless it was a zombie apocalypse and you didn't have to worry about hurting people, other than that, drunk driving: bad."

He smiled. "It is kind of funny then." He was smiling as he sat back down. "What did you do with his car?"

"Didn't mean to, but I fucked that thing up. To be fair, he'd probably already totaled it out in damage, I just sent it over the edge. The more of this story I relate, the more I feel like I've already told you."

"Not in this timeline you haven't."

"Fair enough."

ABOUT THE AUTHOR

Visit Mark at **www.marktufo.com**

Zombie Fallout Book Trailer
   https://youtu.be/-u_pc7QI7eY

Zombie Fallout TV Trailer
   https://youtu.be/OvKPd80XRxg

For the most current updates join Mark's newsletter
   http://www.marktufo.com/contact.html
   I love hearing from readers, you can reach me at:

email

mark@marktufo.com

website
www.marktufo.com

Facebook
https://www.facebook.com/pages/Mark-Tufo/
133954330009843?ref=hl

Twitter
@zombiefallout

For information on upcoming releases please join my newsletter at:
newsletter sign up

All books are available in audio version at iTunes Audible and Barnes and Noble.

DevilDog Press LLC

If you enjoyed the story please take a moment to leave a review. Thank you.

❋ 𝕏 ⧇

ALSO BY MARK TUFO

Zombie Fallout Series

Lycan Fallout Series

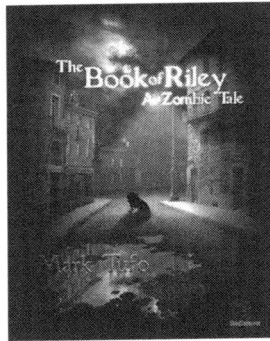

The Book Of Riley Series

Timothy Series

Indian Hill Series

Dystance Series

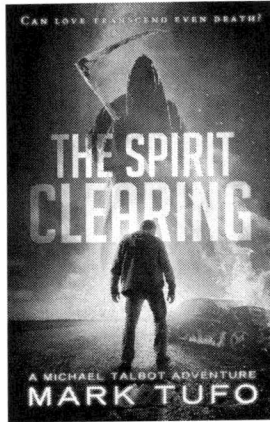

The Spirit Clearing

Callis Rose

Demon Fallout

Devils Desk

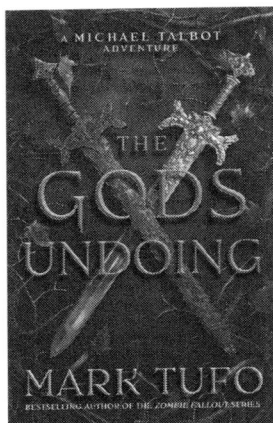

A MICHAEL TALBOT
ADVENTURE

THE
GODS
UNDOING

MARK TUFO

BESTSELLING AUTHOR OF THE ZOMBIE FALLOUT SERIES

ALSO FROM DEVILDOG PRESS

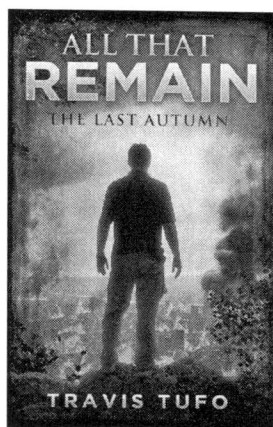

All That Remain *By Travis Tufo*

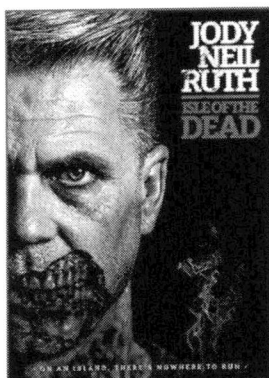

Isle of The Dead By Jody Neil Ruth

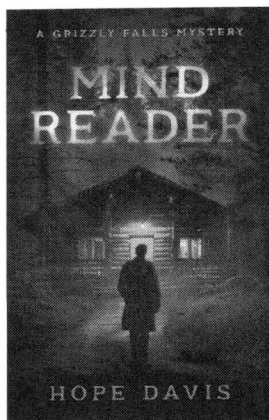

Mind Reader by Hope Davis

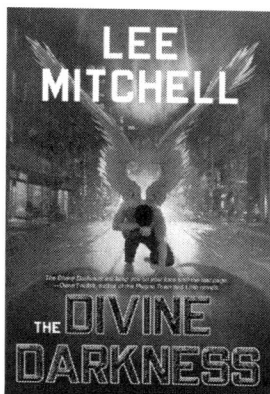

The Divine Darkness by Lee Mitchell

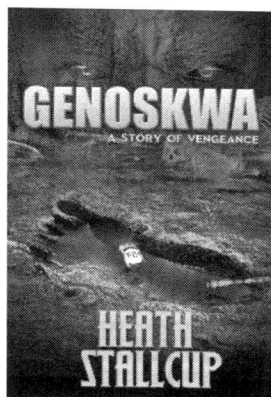

Genoskwa by Heath Stallcup

CUSTOMERS ALSO BOUGHT

CUSTOMERS ALSO PURCHASED:

SHAWN CHESSER
SURVIVING THE
ZOMBIE APOCALYPSE

WILLIAM MASSA
OCCULT ASSASSIN
SERIES

JOHN O'BRIEN
A NEW WORLD
SERIES

ERIC A. SHELMAN
DEAD HUNGER
SERIES

HEATH STALLCUP
MONSTER SQUAD
SERIES

MARK TUFO
ZOMBIE FALLOUT
SERIES

351

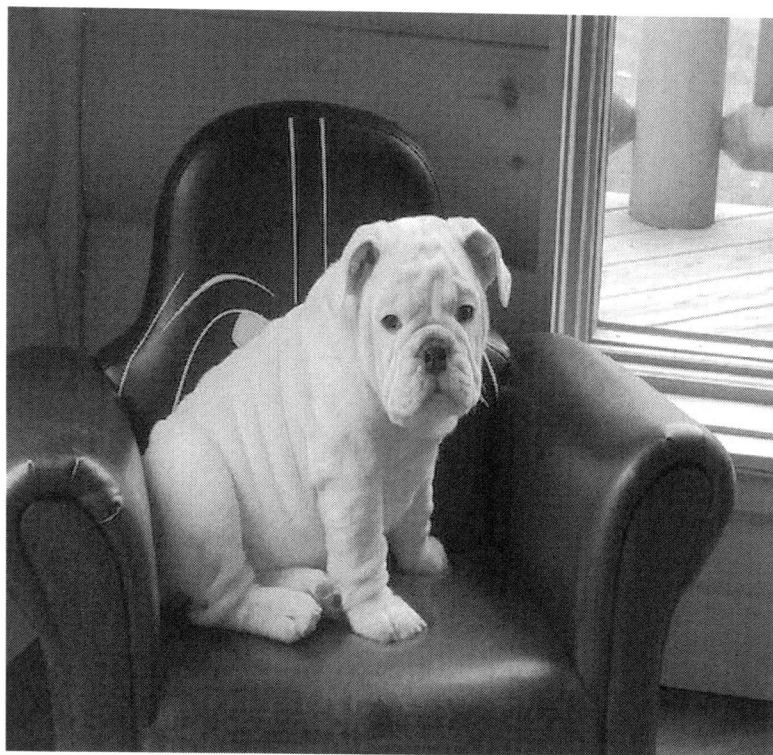

Made in the USA
Columbia, SC
20 April 2025

56857411R00196